"'I was drawn to this book by its breezy, pretty cover, but the story about love and what it means to be a family is what kept me engaged,' says Patty Bontekoe, *First* executive editor. Unbeknownst to her family, Harlow had a baby when she was eighteen and put him up for adoption. So eighteen years later, when he walks into the family bookstore she runs, her entire life (and that of his adoptive mother) is turned upside down. 'I loved this emotional story, which had me laughing, crying, and feeling for both moms,' says Patty. 'I really didn't want it to end!'"
—*First for Women*

PRAISE FOR
Out of the Clear Blue Sky

"The perfect beach read. *Out of the Clear Blue Sky* provides the kind of heartwarming tale of hard-fought growth, crazy family, and welcoming community that will linger with you long after the final page."
—#1 *New York Times* bestselling author Lisa Gardner

"Reading a Kristan Higgins novel is like spending time with a dear friend, one who understands your soul, captivates your senses . . . and every now and then makes you snort with laughter. Higgins never disappoints! If you're looking for a novel brimming with heart and humor, look no further than *Out of the Clear Blue Sky*. Each time I opened this book, it felt like reuniting with a dear friend. With her trademark wit, Higgins tackles tough issues, and does so with sensitivity and heart. *Out of the Clear Blue Sky* is everything I love in women's fiction—smart, hilarious, and brimming with heart and hope."
—Lori Nelson Spielman, *New York Times* bestselling author
of *The Star-Crossed Sisters of Tuscany*

"Your big summer read has arrived! Book after book, Kristan Higgins is a can't-miss author who always serves up stories that are fresh, relevant, and deeply involving."

—#1 *New York Times* bestselling author Susan Wiggs

"From the first page, I was deeply invested in Lillie's plight and desperate to keep turning pages. Kristan Higgins nails it with this laugh-oud-loud, pitch-perfect, heartfelt novel about a woman's life upended and the unexpected ways she finds her way forward. Full of hope, positive messages, and humor, *Out of the Clear Blue Sky* is the perfect book for summer, or anytime!"

—Elyssa Friedland, author of *Last Summer at the Golden Hotel*

"A fantastic journey with a brave, delightful, and mischievous heroine who will keep you laughing and rooting for her from page one. I did not want this book to end!"

—Jane L. Rosen, author of *Eliza Starts a Rumor*

"With a blend of humor and poignancy reminiscent of Nora Ephron's *Heartburn*. . . . [*Out of the Clear Blue Sky* is] a beautifully told blend of grief, hope, and humor that showcases Higgins at her best."

—*Kirkus Reviews* (starred review)

"Higgins has created an accomplished protagonist with strong values, a good heart, and an enviable network of friends. Everyone in the community is on her side; take that, ex-husband! This will be satisfying for readers who like to see a strong woman thrive during times of trial."

—*Library Journal*

"Higgins is known for her emotionally potent novels about characters whose lives are in transition. . . . A bighearted treat for relationship-fiction readers."

—*Booklist*

"An emotional, funny tale of second chances."

—*Woman's World*

"Higgins brings hope and humor to intensely personal dramas and makes them everyone's story."

—#1 *New York Times* bestselling author Robyn Carr

"Readers will be riveted as the well-drawn characters uncover one another's hidden depths and heal old wounds."

—*Publishers Weekly* (starred review)

PRAISE FOR
Good Luck with That

"Masterfully told, *Good Luck with That* is a story with which every woman will identify. We all deal with body image, self-esteem, and acceptance of love at one time or another. Bravo, Kristan Higgins, bravo!"   —#1 *New York Times* bestselling author Debbie Macomber

"Kristan Higgins is at the top of her game, stirring the emotions of every woman with the poignant reality of her characters."

—#1 *New York Times* bestselling author Robyn Carr

"Wholly original and heartfelt, written with grace and sensitivity, *Good Luck with That* is an irresistible tale of love, friendship, and self-acceptance—and the way body image can sabotage all three."

—Lori Nelson Spielman, *New York Times* bestselling author
of *The Life List*

"I LOVED *Good Luck with That*! It's hilarious, heartbreaking, surprising, and so true to life."

—Nancy Thayer, *New York Times* bestselling author
of *A Nantucket Wedding*

"Higgins writes with her trademark heart, humor, and emotion, addressing the serious and somber subject of body image. . . . Highly recommended."   —*Library Journal* (starred review)

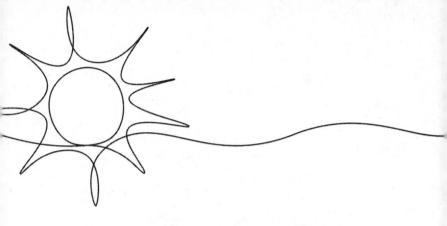

Look on the Bright Side

Kristan Higgins

Berkley
New York

BERKLEY
An imprint of Penguin Random House LLC
penguinrandomhouse.com

Copyright © 2024 by Kristan Higgins
Readers Guide copyright © 2024 by Kristan Higgins
Penguin Random House supports copyright. Copyright fuels creativity,
encourages diverse voices, promotes free speech, and creates a vibrant culture.
Thank you for buying an authorized edition of this book and for complying with
copyright laws by not reproducing, scanning, or distributing any part of it in
any form without permission. You are supporting writers and allowing
Penguin Random House to continue to publish books for every reader.

BERKLEY and the BERKLEY & B colophon
are registered trademarks of Penguin Random House LLC.

Library of Congress Cataloging-in-Publication Data

Names: Higgins, Kristan, author.
Title: Look on the bright side / Kristan Higgins.
Description: First Edition. | New York: Berkley, 2024.
Identifiers: LCCN 2023046608 (print) | LCCN 2023046609 (ebook) |
ISBN 9780593547656 (trade paperback) |
ISBN 9780593547649 (hardcover) | ISBN 9780593547663 (ebook)
Subjects: LCGFT: Humorous fiction. | Romance fiction. | Novels.
Classification: LCC PS3608.I3657 L66 2024 (print) |
LCC PS3608.I3657 (ebook) | DDC 813/.6—dc23/eng/20231005
LC record available at https://lccn.loc.gov/2023046608
LC ebook record available at https://lccn.loc.gov/2023046609

First Edition: May 2024

Printed in the United States of America
1st Printing

Book design by Elke Sigal

This is a work of fiction. Names, characters, places, and incidents
either are the product of the author's imagination or are used fictitiously,
and any resemblance to actual persons, living or dead, business
establishments, events, or locales is entirely coincidental.

This book is dedicated to Shaunee Cole and Joss Dey.

Thank you for the kindness, the boundless wisdom, the easy laughter and the ideas. And the wine. Let's not forget the wine.

Look on the Bright Side

ONE

LARK

The sobbing has to stop, Dr. Smith."

Larkby Christina Smith, MD (at least for now), gulped and looked at the head of Oncology at Hyannis Hospital. She wiped her eyes with one of the tissues he'd passed across the desk. Outside, the steady May rain beat against the windows.

"I know," Lark whispered, then cleared her throat. "I'm sorry." There. Her voice sounded *slightly* less pathetic.

Here in his office, Dr. Hanks (no relation) doled out bad news on a daily basis. Usually to his patients, but today, Lark suspected, to her. The good doctor's voice was firm but gentle, his eyes kind. "The thing is, Lark, it doesn't get easier. Not at all. Oncology isn't for everyone."

First name, not Dr. Smith. That didn't bode well.

"I know you felt close to the patient," Dr. Hanks added.

Lark tried to stifle a sob, failed, and put a hand over her eyes. "It's just . . . you're right. I did. Very close." She swallowed another sob, but traitorous tears still leaked out of her eyes.

Three hours earlier, Lark's favorite patient, Charles Engels, had died after an eight-month battle with pancreatic cancer. And yes, she may have (she had) let emotions get in the way. How could she not? Charlie, as he insisted she call him, had been so wonderful, so funny and kind and positive. He'd been only sixty-four . . . same age as her dad. His wife had been at his side the past three horrible days as Charlie faded in and out of conscious-ness. On the last day, Mrs. Engels (Patty) had climbed into bed with him, and even though he was barely alive, Charlie had put his arm around her. Their three sons had all been there, crying softly, and the grandkids had visited the day before. Lark had been present for Charlie's last, labored breath, and when Mrs. Engels let out a wail, well . . . so had Lark. She hadn't meant to. It just . . . slipped out.

"Dr. Smith. Get a grip." Dr. Hanks folded his hands in front of him and looked at her firmly.

"Sorry," she said, blowing her nose. God. At thirty-three, she should be in better control of her feelings.

"It's one thing to be sympathetic. It's another for the widow to be comforting *you*, Lark."

She winced at that. "They, um . . . they felt like family. Charlie . . . that is, the patient told me he wished I was his daugh-ter." She stifled another sob.

"But you're *not*." Dr. Hanks's voice was a little harder. "And while I commend the commitment you put into your work, it was *their* loss, not yours."

"Fair point." She'd miss Charlie. He was so sunny, even when he was in pain, someone she really looked forward to seeing every chance she got. Even after her long shifts, she'd stop by his room if he'd been admitted, chatting with him, holding his hand, even singing to him one night.

Dr. Hanks sighed. "We can't have you falling apart every time a patient dies. This is Oncology. We lose patients. We have to make friends with death, at least on some level."

Lark nodded and blew her nose.

"I'm going to transfer you to the ER," Dr. Hanks said, and Lark jolted.

"No! Please, Dr. Hanks! I'll get my shit together. I promise."

Dr. Hanks leaned back in his chair and squinted at her. "We're about to admit a thirty-nine-year-old woman for stage four breast cancer, metastatic to liver and brain, for palliative chemo." He looked at Lark, waiting.

Lark tried to hold her face still. Felt her lips wobbling, and tried not to blink so the tears wouldn't fall. Didn't even breathe. Nodded in what she hoped was a clinical yet compassionate and professional manner. "I see." Her voice was tight, but not choked. *Well done, Lark.*

"Three kids. Ten, six, and three. Found out she had cancer when she couldn't nurse the last baby."

"Oh, God! That's so unfair!" So much for restraint, Lark thought as she shook with sobs. Her *niece* was three. What if Imogen lost Addie? What if *Lark* lost Addie, her identical twin?

"Again, the sobbing," said Dr. Hanks. "I'll call the head of the Emergency Department and make this official. It'll be good for you. Fix 'em up and ship 'em out, no chance to get too attached."

"Wait. Wait. What if I, um, improve?" She took a breath and tried to sound more convincing. "I was meant for this field, Dr. Hanks. You know my history. Give me a chance to prove myself."

Dr. Hanks sighed in that *can we please end this conversation* way. "I won't rule it out. We can talk about it in a couple months, how's that? Take a couple days off, and best of luck."

Lark's fellow residents hugged her, told her she had a good heart, was a great doctor, all that. It helped, a little. But everyone was aware she was leaving because she couldn't hack it. And hacking cancer was supposed to have been her life's purpose.

The second she got outside of the hospital, she did what she always did in times of crisis—called her twin.

"What happened?" Addison asked before she said a word. This was typical for them, not always needing words to communicate.

"I got kicked out of Oncology and was transferred to the Emergency Department," she said.

"Ouch. Demoted."

Lark winced at the word, which was all too accurate. "Yeah." Not that emergency medicine was for stupid people, of course. But being an oncologist took years more training. You spent more time with patients, got to know them, helped them through the worst time of their lives, and hopefully cured them. Plus, the whole life's-calling part. Her plan had been to work here on the Cape as an oncologist, admitting patients to Dana-Farber Cancer Institute in Boston as needed, just ninety minutes away. She'd imagined being absolutely adored by her patients for her intelligence, her compassion and commitment. Her, um, grace under pressure.

Her eyes filled again.

"You were crying too much, weren't you?" Addie asked.

"Mm-hmm." Weeping had always kind of been her thing. Addie had gotten the tough genes when their egg had split thirty-three years ago. She'd had Imogen after twenty-seven hours of back labor and not a single drop of painkiller. Lark knew this, since she'd been on one side of the bed, Addie's wife, Nicole, on the other. It had been one of the best days of her life. Lots of tears then, too, but all so happy.

But if Addie had gotten the tough genes, Lark got the smart genes. Like their older sister, Harlow, Lark had been valedictorian at Nauset Regional High School. She'd gone to Boston University, then Tufts for med school, graduating in the top 2 percent of her class.

"Well," Addison said, "this doesn't mean anything." Lark heard her sister clicking on a keyboard. "You can go back to Oncology. I just checked."

"My chances just threw themselves off a cliff, though."

"Try not to overthink it, Larkby," she said, one of the few who used her full name. "The ER will toughen you up. You'll see all sorts of amputations and crushed limbs and gunshot wounds, right?"

"More like drug overdoses and tick bites."

"Well, it doesn't matter. You're amazing. You're already an MD. This will all work out in the end."

"Thanks, Addie." Lark smiled a little. Addie's confidence in her was always a boost.

"Gotta go. Esme's bus is due any second." Esme was her older daughter, the bio-baby of her wife. Same sperm donor, so the girls were half sisters.

"Send me a picture of the girls, okay? Love you." She ended the call, waited five seconds and smiled as the picture came through. Addie always had fresh photos of the girls, being one of those moms who posted on Instagram and TikTok at least three times a day. It was the only reason Lark still had social media accounts—to see her nieces. She couldn't remember the last time she'd posted herself. At least seven years ago, she knew that.

The photo from Addie was of three-year-old Imogen, dressed all in beige, her blond hair shining. She had the same green eyes as Lark and Addie, the same long blond lashes. Lark's heart gave a happy, hard squeeze. She could spend at least some of her enforced time off with her nieces, and that was never a bad thing.

Her phone buzzed again—the hospital, asking her to call in. She probably needed to do some paperwork, because what was medicine without paperwork? Obediently, she called the number.

"Hi, Vanessa, it's Lark Smith," she said to the receptionist, recognizing her voice. Saying Dr. Smith still felt weird. She'd been an official doctor for only two years.

"Hey, hon. You have an urgent message from Dr. Santini," Vanessa said. "He needs you to return his call as soon as possible."

"Dr. Santini? The surgeon Santini?" she asked, faintly alarmed. "Maybe you have the wrong number, Vanessa?"

"I'm just the messenger, honey. He was clear."

"Huh. Okay. He didn't say what it was about?"

"He just growled your name and said you needed to call him."

"And it was definitely Lark Smith? Not Odell Smith?" Please, God, let it be Odell.

"It was you, kid. Sorry." Vanessa recited the number, which Lark typed into her phone.

"Thanks, Vanessa. Tell your handsome hubby I said hello."

"I will, honey, I will." Lark could hear the smile in Vanessa's voice.

Dr. Santini. It was probably a mistake. The man was loathed, feared and admired, the last for his abilities in the OR. Outside of that, he was referred to as Dr. Satan. She couldn't imagine why he'd need a lowly (now somewhat disgraced) resident. She'd only met him during the painful weeks of her surgical rotation, during which she tried to blend in with the walls. Lark didn't even know his first name. Though he was probably only around forty, he was definitely old school, the kind of doctor who used terror, intimidation and ridicule to educate. As she well knew.

Happily, he worked only occasionally at Hyannis Hospital, swooping in from the great institutions of Mass General Brigham, Dana-Farber, Beth Israel. On top of being truly gifted, he had also invented a device that kept organs oxygenated during transport, making it much more likely for them to be successfully transplanted. According to rumor, it had made him fabulously wealthy. Lark had seen him getting out of a Maserati one day in the parking lot but had ducked down behind an SUV so as not to attract attention. No one wanted attention from Dr. Santini except his patients.

During her surgical rotation, she'd gotten some, unfortunately. The godlike Santini had agreed to do rounds with them, the lowly residents! It was terrifying and thrilling. "Santini! Educating *us*! Can you believe it?" Also: "Stay on your toes. Don't speak unless spoken to. Don't make an ass of yourself. He eats people like us for a bedtime snack."

Lark had been the snack. During rounds that unhappy day, he'd barked out, "What diagnosis should be considered for anal fissures that are *not* at six or twelve o'clock?" No reason. Just whimsy. Just a sort of gotcha pop quiz.

At the words *anal fissures*, one of her classmates snickered. Unfortunately, he'd been standing right next to Lark, who went red with terror as Dr. Santini turned toward them. His eyes settled on her, and she swallowed.

"You think this is *funny*?" he snarled. "You think someone's pain is *funny*, Dr. . . ." He looked at her jacket. "Smith?"

"No, sir," she said in a near whisper. She didn't do well with angry people, but neither was she about to rat on Tomas. "Not at all."

"Answer the question, then."

By then, she'd forgotten the question. To be fair, she'd been awake for thirty-two hours straight, and also fear tended to make her mind go blank. "Can you repeat it, please?" Her voice shook. Her fellow residents oozed away from her, including Tomas. No one made eye contact.

"No! Do you think I have time to repeat it? Someone else, answer."

"Crohn's disease," said Lacey, a Nigerian student with a photographic memory. She cut Lark an apologetic look.

"Crohn's disease, Dr. Smith! Anal fissures anywhere but twelve and six o'clock indicate Crohn's or another underlying disease. Dr. Smith, do us a favor and name at least three other diseases that could indicate anal fissures at anywhere but twelve and six o'clock!"

He sure liked saying *anal fissures*. "Ulcerative colitis and childbirth?" she said meekly.

He glared. "Two more, and try to speak like a doctor and not a scared sixth grader."

"Colon cancer and . . . um . . . HIV."

He turned and strode off to the next patient, the five residents following like a swarm of fearful bees. Blessedly, that had been the only time he'd spoken to her, since she was a peasant who didn't want to become a surgeon.

Why he would want her to call him now, she had no idea. She dialed the number, which went right to voice mail. "Dr. Santini. Leave a message."

"Um, hi. This is Lark Smith. Dr. Smith? Um . . . you asked me to call you, I think. So here I am. Okay. Well. Make it a great day!"

Shit. She should've planned what to say.

Maybe he was calling because he'd heard Charlie Engels had died. Two years ago, he'd done a Whipple procedure on Charlie Engels, in fact, which had certainly extended Charlie's life. It was one of the most complicated surgeries there was, removing the head of the pancreas, the bile duct, the gallbladder and part of the small intestine, then reconnecting everything. Postoperative complications were common. But Dr. Santini, despite having the personality of a feral boar, had done a beautiful job, and Charlie healed without incident.

But calling her because he thought she'd be sad? That didn't seem like him.

A second later, her phone buzzed with a text.

Meet me at 6:30 at the Naked Oyster on
Main Street.

She frowned. I think you have the wrong person, she typed.

I don't. Be on time. Obviously, I'll pay.

Gathering her nerve, she typed, Can I ask why you want to see me?

No answer. No three dots, either. God didn't have to answer a lowly resident.

It was quarter to six now. Wellfleet, where she lived, was forty-five minutes away, so going home to change wasn't an option. Today, she wore the typical, sensible-professional garb of a hospital resident—a knee-length black skirt, white oxford and Naturalizer flats Addie described as "shoes that would make a nun weep with boredom." But Addie didn't have to spend twelve hours a day or more on her feet. Hospital policy had her wear her hair up, keep her earrings small and cover the one tattoo she had.

In other words, she looked like she was about to knock on someone's door to talk about the Church of Jesus Christ of Latter-day Saints.

She'd never been to the Naked Oyster before. She googled it, saw it was very swanky. And expensive, so she was glad Dr. Santini had already cleared up who was paying. Her stomach growled, reminding her that the last food she'd had was an energy bar at five forty-five this morning. The Naked Oyster it was.

Lark drove carefully. The aging Honda hybrid she'd had since college had 267,493 miles on it, and didn't take well to potholes or sudden stops. She should buy a new car, but she loved it. It had been through a lot with her. She did need to get new wipers, though, because the windshield smeared with rain. Perfect weather for a nap and a long, hard think. She wished she was home right now, or at least headed home, so she could get into her cozy bed, maybe snag Connery, the Cairn terrier she and her landlady shared.

When she arrived she saw the restaurant was a tiny place right next to the London Brewing Company, a place she had been with her hospital friends. She found a parking place two blocks away, checked the car floor for an umbrella (nope), and then grabbed her purse and ran through the rain.

"Whoo! Rainy out there," she said to the maître d', who smiled. "It's been such a wet spring."

"Don't I know it. My tulip bulbs rotted, it's rained so much."

"Oh no! I love tulips. They're my favorite," Lark said. "I'm Lark, by the way."

"Chloe. Nice to meet you. Do you have a reservation?"

"Um . . . maybe? Under Santini? I'm early," Lark said, smoothing her hair, which she knew from experience looked limp and flat. Her oldest and youngest siblings had gorgeous curls; she, Addison and Winnie had the kind of hair that was completely straight no matter what.

"Oh . . . Dr. Santini?" asked Chloe, her smile slipping.

Lark tried not to grimace. "That's the one."

"Well. Good luck." Chloe picked up some menus and headed to a small table in the back of the bar. Lark's stomach growled again, triggered by the smell of bread.

"Do you want a drink before he joins you?" Chloe asked. It seemed like more of a firm suggestion than a question.

"Okay," Lark said. The memory of the anal fissure humiliation flared again. "What's the most expensive cocktail on the menu?"

Chloe smiled. "I'll tell the bartender to make you something special."

Lark's stomach growled again. "Can I have some bread? And maybe an appetizer?" She glanced at the menu. "How about the Oishi oysters? Are they good?"

"They're amazing."

"Sold." She beamed up at Chloe, who beamed back.

"You have such a pretty name, by the way."

"Thanks! You do, too." Her stomach growled audibly. "You didn't hear that, of course," she said.

"Of course I didn't," Chloe said with a grin. "But I'll put a rush on your order just the same." She smiled and headed for the bar.

Lark made a mental note to bring her some tulips. Joy, her landlady, wasn't the outdoorsy type, but had a beautiful garden, thanks to the previous owners. She always told Lark to help herself. Whenever she had time, Lark would pick Joy a bouquet, and a smaller one for the tiny guesthouse she rented on the property. If she could manage, she'd stop by with flowers for Chloe, just because she'd been so sweet.

Addie often told her she tried too hard to make people like her. It was true, but there wasn't anything wrong about that. Her twin would prefer that Lark had only her. But Lark couldn't help it. She smiled a lot. Too much, Addie said. As if on cue, she smiled at an older man at the bar, who was looking at her. Smiling never hurt anyone, after all. Smiling made people's days better.

Her phone was filling up with supportive texts from her family, since Addie was unable to keep news to herself. It was fine. She'd answer them later. Right now, Chloe returned, balancing a tray, and set down an absolutely beautiful cocktail containing a sprig of rosemary *and* a slice of dried orange.

"Oh, how pretty!" Lark said as her new friend put down the bread and oysters.

"Gotta go, Lark, but it was so nice talking to you. Good luck with Dr. Santini." She lowered her voice. "We call him Dr. Satan, by the way."

"So do we! At the hospital, I mean."

"Are you a doctor?"

"Yep. Um, emergency room." Her smile faltered a bit.

"If I ever need stitches, I'll ask for you." Chloe smiled again and was gone.

Lark took a long sip of the drink. Oh, yummy. Vodka, some kind of citrusy liqueur, maybe some lemon and egg white foam on top. She'd bet it cost twenty bucks. She took another sip. Worth it, especially on Dr. Santini's dime. Almost immediately, the drink relaxed her. She was a lightweight, and on an empty stomach, the alcohol might as well have been administered intravenously. One more sip.

And these oysters! So fresh, with a nice wasabi kick. She slurped one down, then took a warm roll and smeared it with butter. Heaven. She ate another oyster. It was such a cozy place, this restaurant. Comfy, too. Outside, it was dark and wet, and it felt wonderful to be here, resting, eating like an adult, rather than like a starving raccoon, which was how most residents ate.

She could get back into Oncology. She'd figure out a way to toughen up. How? Watch those documentaries about people with terminal disease? She winced. She'd ask Grandpop for some advice. After all, he'd watched Grammy die a slow and quiet death and had been a rock the entire time. Lark had been around, too, of course, but hadn't been much good at the end. She'd been fine handling the work of it—washing Grammy, giving her morphine, adjusting her nasal cannula—but when she had to think of losing her beloved grandmother, she ended up sobbing in the corner.

Hospice, maybe. Yes, hospice! Darlene, the director, was wonderful, and Charlie had been on hospice the last two weeks. Maybe she could ask for some help from Darlene. That would be a great first step.

She glanced at her watch (wearing one was required for all doctors): 6:16 p.m. Nervousness shot through her, and she took another gulp of liquid courage, finished the oysters and buttered another roll, the butter soft and creamy. One more sip of her drink, and Lark closed her burning eyes. God, that felt good. She'd just give them a little break before Dr. Satan—er, Santini—arrived. Mm. Cozy indeed. Lovely, in fact.

"Dr. Smith!"

Lark jerked at the sound of her name. "Yes! I'm awake! I'm here! What do you need?" Ah. Right. Not at the hospital. She brought her napkin to her mouth. Positive for drooling. Crap.

Dr. Santini sat across from her, arms folded, face grim.

"Hi." She tried to smile.

He said nothing. Just shifted his eyes to her martini glass and the half-eaten roll in her hand, the empty oyster shells sitting on a platter of ice.

"I ordered an appetizer," she said.

"So I see." He glanced at the menu, then raised his hand and beckoned a waiter. "Artisanal salad, hold the gouda, grilled salmon, steamed asparagus, garbanzo beans, no butter on anything." He didn't deign to make eye contact with the kid, who couldn't have been older than eighteen.

"Um . . . none of that is on the menu," the poor lad said.

"Just write it down and hand it to the chef. I'm known here."
I'm known here.

"Do you want anything to drink?" the kid asked. "Our wine list—"

"Water."

"Dieting?" Lark asked. She probably had chugged that drink too fast.

Dr. Satan stared at her with dead shark eyes. "Dr. Smith? Did you wish to have more food, or did you eat enough before I got here?"

He wasn't universally despised for nothing. Lark sat up straighter. "You know, I would *love* some more food." She turned to the terrified waiter. "What's your favorite thing on the menu?"

Dr. Santini sighed.

"Um . . . the burger?" the kid said.

"Hm. That does look good." Not expensive enough, however. "I think I'll have the rib eye, please. Medium rare. Oh, and the smoked burrata. That sounds *amazing*. And a lovely big glass of cabernet, okay? And you know what? Bring me a Caesar salad, too, what the heck." The boy scribbled furiously. "What's your name?" she asked.

"Brian."

"Thank you, Brian." She beamed at him, and his face reddened.

"Hurry up, *Brian*," Dr. Santini said. "This is a business meeting."

"Yes, sir. Um, Doctor, sir." Brian scurried away.

"So," Lark said. "A business meeting. Um . . . are you looking for help on something?"

"Please," he said. "I wouldn't ask a *resident* to get me a napkin, let alone help me with something medical."

Lark blinked. *You're not at work. And he's not your boss*, Addie's voice said in her head. *He doesn't get to push you around.* "Why am I here, Dr. Santini? Other than to eat?"

"I'll get to that."

All right, then. At least she'd be fed, and fed very well. Brian, the sweetheart, slid her the glass of wine to her and melted away. She took a sip and stared at her dinner companion.

If he never opened his mouth and you were unaware of his personality, Dr. Santini would be considered very good looking. Indeed, almost every blissfully ignorant nurse or doctor got a jolt of appreciation when they first saw him, right before he crushed their souls. He had thick, wavy dark blond hair and blue eyes. Strong jaw, Cumberbatch-style cheekbones, not an ounce of fat on him (and after hearing him order, Lark could understand why). He had the unforgiving build of a Tour de France bicyclist—tall, thin and steely, like . . . like a scalpel. Yes. Great comparison. She bet he ran six miles a day. At least.

"I heard you were dropped by Oncology today," he said.

She jerked a little, felt her face flush. "Technically, yes. But I'm hoping to get back in."

"Reports were that you couldn't take it. Too soft."

Hospital grapevine, ever reliable, faster than the speediest internet connection on earth. He'd probably heard before she called Addie. But why did he care? "Dr. Santini, you asked me . . . well, ordered me here tonight. I'm your guest. Please don't insult me."

"I was told you have issues with people dying. Oncology is a strange choice in that case. I'm not sure how much better the ER will be."

"Thanks for your opinion."

Their salads arrived, his nutritious looking, hers smothered in delicious garlicky dressing and buttery croutons. She took a bite and groaned a little. "So good," she said around the romaine. "Is that why I'm here?" Was there some sort of hospital requirement for senior doctors to mentor residents? "Did you want to advise me on my career?"

He scoffed. "Hardly. I imagine you'll be churning out babies in three years, not practicing medicine at all."

"Wow. Okay. I think you need to talk to an obstetrician. Babies aren't exactly churned." The buzz was really . . . helpful. "What's your first name, by the way? Since we're enjoying this lovely meal together?"

Dr. Satan considered the question, as if wondering if she was worthy. "Lorenzo," he said after a minute.

"Oh, nice. Tell your mom she did a good job." He said nothing, just chewed his greens. "My name is Lark," she added. "Larkby, but everyone calls me Lark, except for my twin sister. We're identical." People loved twins. He didn't comment. "Do you have siblings, Lorenzo?"

His eye twitched. Didn't like being called anything but God, she guessed. "Yes. I have a brother and two sisters," he said after too long.

"I have a brother and *three* sisters," she said. "Harlow's the oldest; then Addie, or Addison; then four minutes later, me; then Winnie, whose real name is Windsor; and then our baby brother, Robbie. Robert. Named after our grandfather. And Addie is married to Nicole, and they have two daughters, Esme and Imogen. Oh, and Harlow . . . well, never mind. That's a story for another day."

"Did I indicate interest in your family?"

"No, but someone has to fill the silence."

"Why?"

Fair point. She took another sip of wine and continued eating her *excellent* Caesar salad. The burrata came, and she dug into that, too. So creamy, so delicious. "Want a bite?" she offered.

Lorenzo Santini's answer was in the disdain in his eyes. He drank his water. Drummed his fingers against the table.

It was only after his healthy meal and her cholesterol fest were set down in front of them and Brian had once again scuttled away that Dr. Satan spoke.

"I'm looking for someone to do a job for me. Unrelated to medicine."

"I see. What is it?"

He took a bite of salmon and chewed thoroughly, not looking at her. If this is what dating was like, Lark was glad she didn't waste her time.

"Dr. Santini? Do you need a new roof? A driver? A housekeeper?"

Still no answer.

"Do I have to guess?" She took a bite of steak. "Oh, my God! This is the best steak I've ever had."

Her dinner companion took another couple of tidy, joyless bites of his fish. Then he set his fork and knife down.

"How is everything?" asked Brian, coming over to check.

"Go away," Dr. Santini said.

"It's wonderful," Lark said. "Thank you, Brian."

The boy widened his eyes at Lark in sympathy and obeyed Dr. Santini. More silence ensued. Lark found she didn't mind, because the food was so good. And the wine! Like velvet.

Finally, after an interminable amount of time had passed, Dr. Satan—Lorenzo—took a breath, paused, then exhaled. "It's a delicate situation," he said. "It involves my family."

She waited for more. More did not come.

"Does someone need an organ?" she asked suddenly. "A bone marrow transplant, maybe?" She leaned forward, concerned. "Did you run my blood type at the hospital?" Now, *that* made sense. She was a match for something, so he took her out for dinner to ask. And she'd do it. She'd give her bone marrow, no questions asked. Saving lives was her life's mission, after all. "I'm in. You don't have to ask twice."

"Calm yourself, Dr. Smith. It's not that." He looked at a spot over her head. "My sister is getting married on Labor Day. Our grandmother is ninety-nine and is in poor health."

"I hope she makes it until then." He didn't say anything else. "And how does this involve me?"

Dr. Santini took another yoga breath in order to tolerate her questions, then let it out slowly. "My grandmother and I are close. She recently told me she . . ." He paused. "Never mind."

"Just spit it out," Lark said. "Rip off the Band-Aid." She was realizing the wine was so good, she might need to Uber home. Also, she could cut this rib eye with a spoon, it was so tender. Philosophically, she wanted to be a vegetarian, but the kind who ate steak once in a while. And cheeseburgers. And bacon. But otherwise, no meat. Better for the planet.

"She's worried about me never getting married or having children."

"Sure. Grandparents are like that. My grandfather wants to fix me up with his girlfriend's grandson."

He stared at her. "I . . . I'd like to reassure her that I'm fine. Not lonely. Not . . . unattached."

"*Are* you lonely and unattached?" she asked.

"No, and yes," he said, irritated. "That's why you're here. The unattached part."

Lark stopped chewing. "Say again?"

"I would like you to be my companion at family functions this summer and my guest at my sister's wedding."

Ah ha. He wanted her to pretend to be his girlfriend, bless his heart. Based on this interaction, however, she'd actually rather give her bone marrow. "Um, I'm sorry, I doubt I'm the person for the job."

"I'll pay you for your time, of course." His voice was flat.

Lark choked on her wine, recovered, and wiped her lips with her napkin. "Um, isn't that illegal?"

"No, Dr. Smith, paying for *sex* is illegal. Paying for your company is not."

"Right. So I'd be an escort? An amateur escort."

"I suppose." He shifted in his seat, the only sign of his discomfort.

"Why not just *get* a girlfriend? You're not ugly, and you make a great living."

"I don't know any women I'd want to date, and I don't have the time to find one. You're attractive and not entirely stupid, so you'll do."

"Not entirely stupid. I blush." She set down her fork and blinked. "So you want to rent me? For the summer?"

"Yes."

Dr. Satan needed a girlfriend. That was a good one. "What's in it for me?" she asked.

"The money, for one." He glanced at her torso. "I'd buy you some decent clothes."

"So I'm Julia Roberts now?"

"Sorry?"

"You haven't seen *Pretty Woman*?"

"No."

God. He hadn't seen *Pretty Woman*. "Get on Tinder or something. I bet you'd find someone pretty fast, Dr. Santini. Why lie to your grandmother? Just do it for real. I'm sure *someone* would like you." Whoops.

"I have yet to find a woman whose company I enjoy more than solitude."

"I'm guessing that last sentence is why you're trying to rent a human, Dr. Sat—Santini."

"Look. I'd rather pay you than lead someone on. I'm sure you're well aware I wouldn't date you in real life, so there will be no hurt feelings."

Lark threw her head back and laughed, and honestly, after the day she'd had, it felt great. "Aren't you *delightful*," she said. "Well, this is a very special offer, but I have to say no. Brian? Could we have dessert menus, please?"

Brian was holding the dessert menus, conveniently.

"I can't believe you want dessert after that enormous meal," Dr. Satan said. "I can *hear* your arteries hardening."

"I just want to run up the bill. Thanks, Brian." She glanced at the menu. "I'll have the chocolate torte. And a cappuccino, too."

"Of course. Sir?"

"Nothing for me," he said, still staring at Lark.

"Be right back, then," Brian said.

Lark looked at him, tilting her head. Plenty of women dated assholes, especially wealthy assholes. She knew (again, through the hospital grapevine) that Dr. Santini had a place here on the Cape and one in Boston. This indicated that he was loaded, given the real estate market. Surely women would be interested in him, and a man had needs, right? But maybe he was more the sex-doll type. Or asexual. That seemed more likely.

The thought that he wanted to make his grandma happy, though . . . that was kind of sweet.

Brian returned with her torte and coffee. "Thanks, Brian. Everything was delicious."

"You're welcome," he said, blushing again.

"Bring the check in ten minutes," said Dr. Satan. "Not before, not after."

"Yes, sir."

"Sorry he's so rude," Lark called as Brian practically ran away.

"You haven't asked how much I'll pay you," Dr. Santini said.

"It doesn't matter. I'm not interested."

"I'm sure you have a lot of student debt."

"I'm a doctor. Of course I do. But I generally don't whore myself out to make payments." She smiled as she sipped her coffee. "Just as a general practice."

"There'd be no whoring. Just attendance at a few events and the wedding itself. All at very nice venues with good food. My family has high culinary standards, and you obviously love to eat."

Maybe it was the alcohol, but this was getting fun. "Okay. What's your opening offer?"

"Ten thousand dollars."

She choked. "*American* dollars?"

"Yes. But you couldn't tell anyone about the arrangement."

"Oh. Why?" That would be much harder than just going to a few parties.

"Because it's a small world. My sister's a nurse at South Shore Medical Center. Nurses gossip."

"Doctors gossip, too, Lorenzo. A lot more than nurses, in my limited experience."

His left eyelid twitched. She took a bite of the creamy chocolate torte. She was going to ask Addison to take her here for their birthday, since Addie was loaded. "And ten grand, while a lovely number, isn't enough to role-play all summer, especially at work. My debt is a quarter of a million dollars. But I'm sure you could find someone else to take you up on your offer."

He sighed. "Twenty-five, then."

Her fork clattered against her plate. "Holy crap. Are you serious?" Ten percent of her student debt wiped out just like that?

"Yes."

Wow. A *lot* of money. But that wasn't how she wanted to pay off her loans. It wasn't honorable. She *wanted* to be an oncologist, beloved, devoted and, sure, well paid.

"I'm sorry, Dr. Santini. It's, um, very nice of you to consider me, but no. It's not really my style."

He paused, looking at that fascinating spot over her head. "I could get you back into the oncology program. In Hyannis or somewhere in Boston."

Lark blinked a few times. "How . . . how could you do that?"

He shrugged. "I carry a lot of influence. I went to Johns Hopkins with the president of Dana-Farber. You're not stupid, just embarrassingly emotional, from what I hear." He glanced at his watch. "Twenty-five grand, and I introduce you to the right people, and the rest is up to you."

"What if you think I'm an idiot? It would be unethical to recommend me to a profession you think I can't hack."

"I said I'd introduce you, not recommend you."

Still, it would be like Bill Gates saying, *There's a young programmer I want you to meet.* Obviously, she'd have to carry the ball into the end zone on her own merit. But she could do that. She *would* do that. "You don't think that would be unethical?"

"No. I would never do something that would breach my ethical standards."

"Like ask a younger doctor who works at a hospital where you're a god to pose as your girlfriend?"

He glared at her. "You know what? The offer is off the table. I thought, given today's professional humiliation, you might be interested in what is a completely unromantic business arrangement. Forget I asked."

"Wait. Hold on." She took a bite of cake, staring at him while she chewed. "What aren't you telling me?" Because there was something, she was sure. Being single wasn't so awful that a person would rent a date. In fact, she had the impression Lorenzo Santini *liked* being single. Jesus never dated, after all.

He shifted. Folded his napkin very precisely. "My grandmother was put on hospice a few weeks ago. I don't want her to die concerned about me being too . . . alone."

Oh no. Those were two powerful words right there. *Hospice* . . . and *alone*. She herself knew the feeling all too well.

Dr. Satan had an Achilles' heel, and it was a sick old lady. Her eyes stung with tears. If Grandpop was dying—please, God, never—and told Lark all he wanted was for her to be with someone, wouldn't she do the same thing Lorenzo was? Just to soothe his soul for a month or two?

And let's be honest. That introduction wouldn't hurt. If she didn't get back into the oncology program here on the Cape, she'd at least have a chance to try again in Boston. There was a damn good reason she'd chosen that field in the first place.

Besides, a few parties this summer in pretty places with pretty clothes . . . she didn't have much of a life outside the hospital and family stuff. Maybe this would distract her from the yawning hole in her life.

"I'll do it. No money. Maybe the introduction. We'll see. But I'm a softie where grandparents are concerned."

His shoulders loosened a centimeter or two.

"This is where you say thank you," she said.

"Thank you."

"So a few family parties, the wedding, and then we break up."

"Yes. And if my grandmother dies before that, your services will no longer be required."

She almost wondered if he'd prefer that. She stuck out her hand. "You have yourself a girlfriend, Dr. Satan."

He didn't blink. Guess he knew his nickname. "I don't *want* a girlfriend. Just show up and be pleasant." He glanced at her hand, took out his wallet and pulled out an Amex Black card. "Can we be done now?"

TWO

LARK

No! It's not possible! You cannot be dating Dr. Satan," barked Luis Gonzalez, her friend and a nurse at Hyannis Hospital. "When did this happen? How? My whole worldview has been shot to hell. I feel like I did when my parents got divorced. Betrayed. Stunned. Unsafe in the world. It's like Snow White hooking up with Voldemort."

"Okay, let's use our inside voices," Lark said. "And yes, he's . . . unexpected. I get that." Oh, this was a wee bit uncomfortable. She was lying. But Luis loved gossip and rotated throughout the floors—emergency room, maternity, oncology, medical/surgical—and had a face that invited people to share their deepest troubles, even knowing his inability to keep a secret. He wasn't mean about it . . . just wanted everyone to be up to date. He was probably the one who let everyone know she'd been kicked out of Oncology. But in telling him about supposedly dating Dr. Santini, Lark wouldn't have to tell anyone herself.

Today was her first day in the ER, where Luis was currently working. Her shift hadn't started; she and Luis were having breakfast in the cafeteria so she could begin the lying process.

"It's still new," she said. "But he has some nice qualities."

"Name two." Luis took a hostile bite of his blueberry muffin.

"He's smart, of course." She forced a smile. "And . . ." Shit. Did Lorenzo Santini have another quality? "He's very family oriented."

"He has a family?" Luis asked. "I assumed he was hatched in a dark underwater cave."

"Well, he has his parents, of course." Did he? Had he said they were both alive? "A brother, two sisters. He's really close to his grandmother." She swallowed, not making eye contact. "It's really sweet."

Luis gave her a look. "Think about what you just said."

Yeah, *sweet* and *Santini* didn't belong in the same sentence. "It's hard to believe, I know." She smiled.

"Is he great in bed? Is that it? Are you dickmatized?"

"Sorry?"

"In love with his junk?"

"Oh, God, no! I mean, we're not . . . there just yet." There was Ellen, one of the cafeteria workers, thank God. "Hi, Ellen! How's Raymond's arm?"

"It's great," Ellen called. "Thank you for the cookies. He devoured them." Lark had been grabbing lunch here when Ellen got the call that her son had broken his wrist sliding into second base at Little League.

"So glad he's better," Lark said. "Give him a hug from me."

Luis waved to Ellen, then turned back to her. "Has he kissed you? How did he even approach you? Did he actually know your name? Seriously, Lark, give me context."

Lark fake laughed. It sounded like little Connery coughing up some grass. Addie would have to give her some advice . . . she'd gotten the lies-with-ease part of their DNA. "Well," she said to Luis, "I think we can all agree he's *very* attractive."

"Aside from his black and tarry soul."

"Oh, look at the time. We should go, right? Don't want to be late on my first day."

"We're not done here. I want all the details. If he frenches you, don't be surprised if his tongue is forked."

Another fake laugh. "I'll see you in there, I guess," she said.

"Okay, sweetie. I'm gonna grab another coffee. You good?" Luis asked.

"All set." She smiled her thanks, but it faded the second his back was turned.

She needed Dr. Satan's schedule and more information. Without some basic facts of his life, it would be harder to pretend to be dating him, even a little. She hadn't heard from him since their meeting three nights ago, but she had googled him late the other night. Mostly scholarly articles and his bio (Harvard, Johns Hopkins, fellowships at the Mayo Clinic and Mass General). More about his organ transplant device and significant net worth.

But she needed to know where he lived, the names of his siblings, that kind of thing. Aside from joyless, survival-only eating, she had no idea what he did in his spare time. She was meeting his family for the first time this weekend.

She took out her phone and texted him as she walked toward the ER.

> It occurs to me that we should exchange some information if we're going to sell this. I don't know anything about you.

Already, she knew better than to wait for an immediate response. She put her phone in the pocket of her white doctor's coat, took a deep breath and went into the emergency room.

"Dr. Smith! So nice to have you join us!" came a loud voice. A balding, fiftysomething man with glasses and a bow tie twinkled at her.

"Hi," she said. "I'm Lark Smith, your new resident."

"Oh, we know all about you," he said, "and listen, don't feel bad because Oncology doesn't want you. You're more than welcome here as long as you keep the sobbing to a minimum."

There was a ripple of laughter from the small cluster of people behind him. Her reputation preceded her, apparently.

"No promises," she said, feeling her cheeks warm.

"I'm Howard Unger," he said. "Medical director of the Emergency Department here. King, really. These are my subjects—Lalita Williams, MD; Miriam Fishbein, APRN; Daniel Newton, DO; and Mara Goshal, MD." Three women and a guy nodded or waved or smiled. Cheery group. "Rena is the unit secretary," Dr. Unger continued. "Our dark overlord and commander."

"That's my actual title," said a middle-aged woman sitting behind a series of monitors. She smiled, too.

"Hi, Rena. Hi, everyone," Lark said. "Great meeting you."

"How do you feel about fecal impaction, Dr. Smith?" Dr. Unger asked, donning a serious expression.

She felt her mouth tug. "I'm passionate about fecal impaction."

"That's the attitude! She'll fit right in. Okay, let's go, team. Lark, you're technically a second year, but since you're new to us, you're gonna get the crap jobs for a couple of weeks. Literally. Hello, Mrs. Hendricks! Rumor has it you haven't pooped in more than a week. How are you feeling?"

Lark listened as Dr. Unger asked Mrs. Hendricks, a sour-faced woman in her seventies, about her medical history, pain, food consumption, bowel habits.

"What other questions should we ask, Dr. Smith?" he asked, turning to her.

"Uh, what was the consistency of the last stool you passed?"

"It was ropy and hard," Mrs. Hendricks said.

"Was it dark or tarry?" Lark asked. Same words Luis had asked about Dr. Satan's soul.

"Tarry? No. It was beige."

"No blood?"

"No! Just ropy and beige! God! Do we have to talk about this, or can you people just give me something for the pain? My stomach is killing me."

But emergencies required that the right questions be asked and answered, and the interrogation continued. Mrs. Hendricks snarled her answers about rectal discomfort, abdominal pain, anorexia, vomiting and a whole host of other questions.

"Okay," Dr. Unger said. "Give us a minute, and we'll be back soon." Lark and the others trailed as Dr. Unger went to a computer station, logged in, flew through some screens and ordered an x-ray.

"We'll have to wait a little while till you can scoop the poop, Dr. Smith, so let's keep busy, shall we? Come, my little ducklings." Dr. Unger led the way to the next bay. On the bed lay a teenager who'd cut his head while skateboarding. His dark hair was matted with blood, and the entire side of his face and neck were stained red. His mother sat beside him, looking both stressed and irritated.

Dr. Unger introduced himself and asked what happened. "Took a fall on my skateboard," the kid said.

"Were you wearing a helmet?" Dr. Unger asked, pulling on some gloves to examine the wound.

"Nope."

"No helmet," Dr. Unger chided. "I'm inclined to let you bleed for another hour or two, just to teach you a lesson."

"Cool," said the kid, taking a selfie. "Bro, don't even stitch me up. I'm a total badass."

"Stop being such an idiot," his mother told him, snatching his phone out of his hand. "This phone is mine now, and I'm burning that stupid board when we get home." She looked at Dr. Unger. "He was videoing himself, skated right into a signpost, and now he's making jokes."

"Cause of injury: idiocy," Dr. Unger intoned. "But, Jackson, seriously, thank you, because we *love* stapling heads. Mara, you're up, I believe."

"Thank you, Jackson," Mara said. "This will truly be a highlight of my day." The cheeky attitude was sure different from Oncology.

"I don't even want you to numb his head," the mom said. "Maybe this way, he'll learn a lesson."

"I'm sorry I can't accommodate you there," Dr. Unger said. "That pesky Hippocratic oath. But Lark here could kick him really hard in the shin, right, Dr. Smith?"

She smiled at the kid, who abruptly noticed her. His cheeks flushed. "I won't kick you *this* time," she said. "We all do dumb things when we're kids. But you don't want to end up with a traumatic brain injury. Or worse."

Her eyes stung abruptly. Because of course, he could've *died* from one stupid moment. An image of another mother, staring into the middle distance, flashed through her brain, and the sting became a burn.

"Go on, Dr. Smith. Safety lectures are part of our job here."

She cleared her throat. "Imagine living the rest of your life in a nursing facility, unable to talk, walk, feed yourself, understand simple sentences. Or worse, imagine your mom having to hear you didn't make it, just because you didn't wear a helmet. Her life would be ruined." Her voice cracked.

"She's crying," Danny whispered. "The rumors were true."

A tear slid down Lark's cheek, and she wiped it away.

"I'm sorry, Mom," Jackson said, his voice considerably more somber. "I really am."

The mother wiped her eyes. "You should be. She's right. I adore you, dummy."

Mara got the staple kit; irrigated the wound, which was a good four-inch laceration; shot the area up with lidocaine and put in thirteen staples. It touched Lark to see that Jackson reached for his mom's hand while Mara worked on him.

They moved from patient to patient, stopping to log in to the computer, order meds, ask Rena to get a consult, schedule follow-up visits, admissions. Most of their clients today were upwards of seventy-five. A sweet old man having chest pain who reminded Lark of Grandpop. A woman with dementia who had fallen out of bed at a nursing home. A diabetic man with a festering wound on his foot, noncompliant with medication and lifestyle changes. A woman who'd stumbled in the parking lot resulting in a very swollen, tender ankle.

After two hours of racing around from bay to bay, they circled back to Mrs. Hendricks. Dr. Unger asked Lark to palpate the patient's abdomen, which she did. "What does Radiology think, Dr. Smith, and do you concur?"

She looked at the films. "The rectosigmoid looks full of a malleable substance," Lark said, "which would confirm fecal impaction. No signs of obstruction or dilated small bowel. Physical exam negative for perforation."

"Well done," Dr. Unger said. "Treatment?"

"Manual disimpaction, since laxatives haven't worked."

"Correct. Please inform the patient."

Lark looked at Mrs. Hendricks. "Mrs. Hendricks, what we'll try first is—"

"Yeah, yeah. This isn't my first rodeo. Just get going, okay?"

Lark gloved up, put on protective glasses and a mask, lubed her finger, got the bedpan and did the job, narrating as she did so. The rule was that the patient was told what was happening before and during the procedure. And once, er, things got moving with Mrs. Hendricks, they definitely moved. The poor woman. No wonder she was so sour.

Lalita gagged, then excused herself.

"Remember the Vicks next time," Dr. Unger called after her. "Not that your poop doesn't smell like roses," he added to the patient. "Lark, if you don't have one already, get a little container of Vicks VapoRub for under your nose. Cases like this, or gangrene, maggots, necrosis, you'll really need it."

"Fun," she said, and Dr. Unger smiled at her.

The thing was, it *was* actually fun. By the end of the shift, there hadn't been a single scary moment. No one's life had been in imminent danger, except the little old man with chest pain. (He'd been admitted to rule out a heart attack.) Hyannis was a small city, and sure, there'd be the inevitable horrible car accidents, especially as traffic beefed up over the summer. Drownings, gunshot wounds and stabbings, acute and serious illnesses, but today . . . well, today had been good. No one had been told their loved one had died. No one had been giving a terminal diagnosis.

You might like it here," Dr. Unger said as they both sat at the computer station at the end of the day. "I try not to overwork my residents, because the whole work-life balance thing turns out to be true. And you do have to work nights. You'll learn something in every field of medicine here . . . we all have kind of a professional attention deficit disorder, by necessity."

"Yeah, I was picking up on that."

"It can be really fun. We have the best team anywhere, the best nurses and CNAs, orderlies, everything. But when it's bad, it's horrible. We lost a twelve-year-old last week from anaphylaxis. Same age as my nephew. In April, a woman came in with her skull, jaw and arm broken because her husband beat the shit out of her. In the winter, a tree fell on a car full of college students during that ice storm. One of them died, two almost did."

Lark had read about that and cried (obviously), thinking about the families.

"But mostly," Dr. Unger said, "we don't lose patients. We send them up—" He pointed to the ceiling, indicating the five other floors of Hyannis Hospital. "Or we send them out." He pointed to the exit. "We don't get as close to them or their families as you would in Oncology, which has its upsides." He paused. "I should tell you, Heather and Theo Dean are friends of mine."

Lark's heart jerked, and her eyes abruptly blurred with tears. "They're wonderful people," she said, looking away from him.

He put a hand on her shoulder. "Have a good night, Lark. You did well today."

She finished up, said goodbye to the nurses and techs, made a note to bring in cookies so everyone would like her. Then she swung up to Hospice. Darlene, the director, wasn't there, so Lark left her a note about hoping to volunteer, even informally, over the summer, wherever they might be able to use her.

On her way to the parking lot, she checked her phone.

Ah. Lorenzo Santini had deigned to answer her.

Check your email.

She did. No note. Just his CV.

Taking the chance that he might answer, she called him. It went straight to voice mail. "Hello, this is your fake girlfriend calling," she said. "Since Memorial Day is five days from now, I'm going to need something other than your GPA and list of fellowships. Did you play sports in high school? What was the name of your dog growing up? Your middle name? Favorite food? Books you like to read. Things you do for fun, if you have fun, that is. Names and ages of your siblings. Your address, maybe."

Then she got into her car and headed for her sister's house. She'd lie to her coworkers. Not her family. Dr. Satan would have to deal.

Esme and Imogen tackled her as she walked into Addie and Nicole's house. "Auntie, I'm your favorite, right? Right?" Esme said.

"No, I favorite!" three-year-old Imogen declared.

"No you're not. I'm much older," Esme said.

"You're both my favorites," Lark said, grabbing a niece in each arm and smooching their beautiful cheeks, inhaling the smell of sun and shampoo in their hair.

"Oh, it's you," Nicole said. "Addie didn't tell me you were coming for dinner. Addie, why didn't you tell me Lark was coming? I thought she was at work! Now I have to reset the table."

"I don't have to stay, Nicole," Lark said. "You're having company?"

"Of course it's okay," Addie said, bursting into the room, her voice loud and hard. "It's always okay, and you can always stay

for dinner. Or breakfast. Or lunch. Or brunch. You can sleep in
bed with us if you want to. Back off, Nicole. It's my *sister*."

"Like I could forget," Nicole said. But she gave Lark a be-
grudging smile.

"It sucks to be married to a twin," Lark said, smiling back.
After all, Addie's wife had a clone whose bond had begun at the
moment of conception. It was hard to compete, and Nicole liked
to win, even if no one else was playing.

"Got a second?" she asked Addison, setting the girls down.

"Not really. Family dinner. I texted you to see if you were
free, but you didn't answer."

"Sorry. My first day in the ER."

"Right! How was it?"

"Kind of good, actually," she said. Not that she'd stay there,
of course. "Who's coming tonight?"

"Everyone. Except Frances," Addie said, naming Grandpop's significant other. "Her daughter's visiting or something.
Can you watch the girls while I finish up in the kitchen?"

"Sure. My favorite thing to do."

The girls were parked in front of their dollhouse in the vast
playroom. "No, *you* make dinner!" Esme said, sounding very
much like Nicole in tone. "I'm very busy and important!"

"No, I important!" Imogen's dollhouse person attacked Esme's,
and the girls snarled and laughed. Perhaps a teeny bit concerning,
their eerily accurate reflection of their mothers' dynamic, but they
were kids. She watched for a moment, smiling, remembering similar
times with her own sisters. Esme looked just like Addie (and there-
fore Lark, a thrill that could not be understated). Someday, she'd
have her own kids, maybe. Hopefully. For now, she had her nieces.

Her phone buzzed . . . another email from Lorenzo. (She was

working on not thinking of him as Dr. Satan.) He'd typed out her questions and answered them.

> Did you play sports in high school? **Baseball**
> What was the name of your dog growing up? **Remy**

Lark put those two facts together and guessed the dog was named after Jerry Remy, the great Sox player turned announcer. Not that original, not in Massachusetts. At least the dog hadn't been named Fenway.

> Your middle name? **Carmine**
> Favorite food? **Sardines**

Whose favorite food was sardines? Really?

> Books you like to read. **Medical journals, an occasional biography. I do not read novels.**

Of course he didn't.

> Things you do for fun, if you have fun, that is. **I run 6 miles a day.**

"Nailed it," she murmured.

> Names and ages of your siblings. **Dante, 35; Sofia, 32; Isabella, 28**

Lark would have to compliment his parents on their excellent name choices.

Your address. **35 Beacon St., Boston; 93 Monomoy Road, Chatham**

Lark glanced at the girls, who were now making the dollhouse people pick out pets—a giraffe for Imogen, a Dalmatian for Esme—and googled the first address. Zillow showed a gorgeous apartment with a paneled library, marble countertops, a soaking tub in the bathroom, a vast living room and dining room. That condo wasn't his, necessarily—the building had six units—but she imagined his would be similar. Last sold three years ago for $3.5 million. Rooftop access to a common area. (She bet he never went up there, not if the great unwashed could enjoy it, too.)

The second property, though, made her briefly consider marrying Dr. Satan. Holy guacamole! Zillow showed a property on Morris Island in Chatham, no longer on the market. Morris Island was an exclusive neighborhood in the most exclusive town on the Cape. Whereas the rest of the Cape, even Provincetown, still had neighborhoods where regular folks lived, Chatham was fast becoming a billionaire's playground. Lorenzo's house was mid-century modern and on a full acre, right on the water. Private beach (that sounded more like him), fireplaces, deck, a lush green lawn that probably used a separate well for watering.

Damn. Lark knew he was wealthy, but damn.

"Gran's here!" Imogen announced, charging from the room. Esme scrambled to catch up. Mom was indeed a rock star with her granddaughters.

And Mom would not approve of her arrangement with Lorenzo Santini, Lark knew. She was a brutally honest person. Dad, though . . . he'd probably get a kick out of it. Grandpop definitely would.

Could she get through the summer without having Heather

and Theo Dean hear about this, though? She sure would try. She still saw them. Why make them think she had a new boyfriend when it was just a pretense? The Deans lived here in Wellfleet, but if her family didn't tell anyone, she'd be safe. She left the playroom and went downstairs, where her family was streaming in, hugging, insulting, laughing.

She had always been so glad to be one of the Smith kids. Her siblings were her armor. Harlow's little sister, Addie's twin, Robbie's big sister. Winnie, well, she was a little different, a little standoffish compared to the rest of them, but she was rock solid. Mom was holding Imogen; Dad was letting Esme climb onto his back. Her parents beamed at each other for a minute, their special look of *my God, our love made all these people, aren't we amazing.* Sure enough, her parents kissed. Not a peck, either.

"Please stop torturing us with physical affection," Robbie said, covering his face with his hands.

"Seconded," Winnie said. Their parents laughed, delighted at once again horrifying their kids with their chemistry.

"Be glad your parents still find each other smoking hot," Dad said, getting a chorus of groans in response.

"Larkby Christina, you beautiful girl!" Grandpop called, his blue eyes twinkling.

"Hi, Grandpop," she said, leaning into him for a hug. The comforting smell of Old Spice and Bengay enveloped her.

"I heard you're switching specialties," he said. "And I'm glad! Did you know, I nearly fell off the roof the other day? And if I had, you could've patched me right up and set my old bones."

"Why were you on the roof, Grandpop?" she asked.

"There was the prettiest bird out there! It was blue, but it wasn't a bluebird. I think it was an indigo bunting!"

"That's exciting," she said. "But maybe use those binoculars we got you for Christmas instead, hey?"

"Now that I nearly lost my balance and almost fractured my skull, I think I will!" he said. "Hello, Nicole, aren't you wonderful for having us over for dinner. Thank you, sweetheart!"

Even Nicole's stony heart couldn't resist Grandpop.

Eventually, everyone found their place around the giant dining room table. When they were growing up, Addie and Lark had talked about their adult lives, the way all kids did. They both wanted to stay on the Cape, both wanted to be married and have kids, both wanted a big beautiful house so they could have family dinners and show off their domestic skills—cooking, hospitality, flower arranging.

Addie had made that dream a reality. Lark had been on track, but God had intervened. Or not intervened, as the case had been.

"This is gorgeous," Lark said. "Is that bread homemade?"

"It is," said Addie, smiling, "and you're welcome. It's true, I'm amazing, but you're a doctor, Larkby. Many people would see that as an accomplishment."

Lark sat down next to her. Grandpop was on her other side, Mom across from her.

"Did everyone know that Cynthia and Bertie are in Paris?" Grandpop asked. "Paris! Mon Dieu!" Cynthia was his niece (or something; no one really knew, but she called him Uncle Robert). "They're having a splendid time! They FaceTimed me from the Arc de Triomphe! I felt almost like I was there."

"Aw," Harlow said. "That was very sweet of them."

Addie and Nicole brought out vegetable lasagna and salad, Dad poured wine for those who wanted it, and the Smith family fell on their food like hyenas on a limping baby zebra. For a few minutes, it was silent aside from the sounds of eating, and Lark figured it was time to seize the moment.

"I have some interesting news," she said.

"Heard you got kicked out of Oncology," Robbie said. "Probably for the best, don't you think?"

"No, Robbie, she *doesn't* think," Addie snapped. "She wants to cure cancer. Or at least, treat it. Because she's an angel, not like you, loser."

"Or you, you snobby, materialistic Instagrammer," Robbie answered.

"Shit! I forgot to take a picture of the lasagna," Addie said.

"I got a few in the kitchen with the tulips in the background," Nicole said. "And don't swear in front of the girls."

"Anyway," Lark said, "that *is* true, Robbie. I'm now working in the ER, but it's temporary. Um, but that's not the news. It's something else." She glanced at Addie apologetically. Addie hated not knowing things first. "It's a little complicated." Yes. Addie was scowling.

"I love complicated!" Grandpop said. "Complicated makes life interesting."

"What is it, honey?" Dad asked.

"Um . . . well, it's kind of sweet, actually. This doctor who works at the hospital wants me to be his sort of date for the summer. His sister's getting married, and he doesn't want to be the bachelor brother, so he asked me to . . . hang out."

Robbie gasped dramatically. "Oh, my God, I love that. Fake boyfriend turns real. *The Proposal. The Wedding Date. Single All the Way. To All the Boys I've Loved Before. Pretty Woman.* I'm here for it."

"Since when do you watch rom-coms?" Winnie asked. "I thought you were straight."

"Since forever, and stop forcing all that heteronormativity on me, Winfrida," Robbie said.

"My name is Windsor, and okay, fair point."

"How charming this is!" Grandpop exclaimed. "Maybe Robbie's right and it *will* blossom into something real! I think this family is overdue for a wedding, don't you, Harlow?"

"No comment," Harlow said, smiling. She *was* pretty serious with her guy.

"I take it you're friends with him already?" Dad asked.

"We know each other a little," Lark said. Her face felt hot.

"What aren't you telling us?" Addie demanded. This was the punishment for not telling her first.

"Um . . . nothing! He's a surgeon. Uh . . . successful. Handsome."

"I hate supper, Mommy," Esme said. "Can I have macaroni and cheese instead? This is yucky."

"I hope he's paying you," Robbie said. "Tell me he's paying you. It just makes the falling in love part better. *The Wedding Date* and *Pretty Woman* have set a strong precedent in the love-for-money arena."

"Of course he's not paying her, Robbie," Mom snapped. "She's not a sex worker."

He offered to pay me, Mom. Quite a bit, in fact. "He's not paying me, Mom. Well. Not in money."

"She *is* a sex worker!" Robbie crowed. "I knew you were too good to be true, Lark!"

"Can you not say 'sex worker' in front of the girls?" Nicole asked.

"What's a sex worker?" Imogen asked. "I want a sex worker!"

With a sharp sigh, Nicole rose from the table and took the girls by the hand into the kitchen, accusation trailing like fog behind her.

"Obviously, I'm not a sex worker," Lark said. "It's just . . . he . . . well, he's going to maybe help me with some introductions at Dana-Farber, that's all. As a favor."

"Why does he need you to pretend to be his girlfriend?" Mom asked. "That sounds unethical."

"Not exactly his girlfriend," Lark said. Crap. "More like someone he might be dating."

"And what is the difference?"

"Uh . . . we're not serious yet."

"Why does he need anyone at all?" Winnie asked. "Being single isn't the worst thing in the world."

"Agreed," Lark said. "But his grandmother is really old, and he wants her to think he's . . . settling down. For her peace of mind, before she dies."

"Rom-com city!" Robbie said. He raised his hand for a high five, and Grandpop obliged.

"So you're lying to an old woman," said Mom.

"It sounds so bad when you put it that way," Harlow murmured. "I liked the way Lark said it better."

"Thanks," Lark said. "I seriously doubt we'll fall in love, because he's"—*horrible*—"not my type."

"Someone has to be your type again, honey," Dad said. "You never know."

"I do know. Thanks, Dad. I think."

"No one could take Justin's place, Lark," Dad said. "We know that. Doesn't mean you can't fall in love again."

There was a moment of silence at the mention of Justin's name. Winnie reached past Grandpop and patted her shoulder awkwardly.

"Right," Lark said. "Thanks. Yes, well, anyway, I'd love to

keep this a secret from Justin's parents, okay? No need for them to know. It's basically me going to a few pre-wedding events, meeting his family, the wedding itself, and that's it."

"Why would we tell the Deans?" Winnie asked. "We won't say a word."

"What's his name?" Addie asked.

Lark looked at her. "Uh . . . Lorenzo Santini."

Her twin raised an eyebrow. "The anal fissure guy?"

This was the problem with telling a sibling everything. Especially a sibling with a wicked good memory.

"This just gets better and better," Robbie said. "The anal fissure guy! What a title! I can't *wait* to meet him."

"You won't meet him," Lark said. "But yes." She looked at her parents. "He grilled me about . . . well, about anal fissures on my surgical rotation."

"Lorenzo Santini," Dad said. "The one everyone called Dr. Satan?"

Addie got her memory from Dad, apparently.

"Mm-hmm. He doesn't have time for a girlfriend, and he asked me, and I said yes."

"In exchange for a *job*? Don't you want that to happen because of your own merit, Lark?" Mom asked, sliding the knife in with expert precision.

"He's just going to put me in touch, Mom. The rest will be up to me."

"I don't like it," Mom said. "Pretending to be in a relationship with a prestigious surgeon way above your pay grade . . . it sounds like sexual harassment to me. You could report him."

"Nope. Not gonna. He's just kind of socially awkward, and I'm helping him out."

"He once made a whole team of radiologists cry," Dad said almost fondly. "We nurses knew to run when we saw him coming down the hall. I was at the head of the pack."

"Good thing you're in such good shape," Mom murmured, squeezing Dad's bicep.

"I'd love to show you more later," he murmured back.

"And here we go," said Winnie. "Would anyone like to ask *me* something?"

"Is there something you're trying to tell us, Winnie?" Dad asked.

"Nope. Just making a point. Completely meaning to change the subject, does anyone want to go out for ice cream later? Nicole said she made kale cake for dessert."

"Why would someone be that cruel?" Robbie asked. "Why?"

This was the best thing about being part of a big family, Lark thought. No one could have the attention all the time.

And thank God for that.

THREE

LARK

On Sunday of Memorial Day weekend, Lark put on a blue-and-white sleeveless dress, braided her hair into a side ponytail, put on sunscreen, a little mascara and some tinted lip gloss, and stepped into her red espadrille sandals for that patriotic touch.

With Joy's blessing, she'd raided the garden and made several bouquets, including one for Joy herself. For the past ten months, Lark had rented a tiny guesthouse from Joy Deveaux at a ridiculously low price. Situated on a protected inlet on Wellfleet's raggedy bay side, the main house was utterly splendid—a gray-shingled, three-story charmer with five bedrooms, a chef's kitchen (largely unused, since Joy didn't cook much), a vast living room and sliding glass doors showcasing the view of the water. The yard featured lush beds of flowers, which Lark tended whenever she had the time.

Lark's little house, to the south of the main residence, was no more than six hundred square feet, but it had everything she needed. Tiny kitchen, living room, bedroom and a little deck that gave her her own view of the sunset . . . not that she was often here to enjoy it, but still. It had been her lucky day when Joy offered her the place. The fact that she and Joy had become friends was even luckier. Joy was older—in her sixties—and treated Lark like a favorite niece, a role Lark was happy to fill, especially since Joy didn't have family of her own. As part of the rental agreement, Lark dutifully injected Joy with Botox and filler every few months, saving the older woman a trip to the dermatologist in Hyannis.

It was an odd friendship, but it was refreshing, too. So many people knew Lark's story; Joy had not. She was easy to talk to, completely without judgment, having lived a somewhat unusual life herself. Already, Lark had told her about her arrangement with Dr. Santini, knowing Joy herself had had unconventional relationships, too.

Right now, the smell of lilacs and peonies filled the car. One bouquet for Lorenzo's grandmother, one for his mom, and one for each of his sisters, all wrapped in turquoise blue tissue paper and sitting pretty in the back seat of the Honda. Hopefully, they wouldn't wilt on the ride. And hopefully, Connery wouldn't eat them.

Joy had asked if she would take the dog today so she could run some errands, and Lark had texted Lorenzo to see if she could bring Connery with her. He hadn't answered, so she took that as a yes. Connery would help ease the awkwardness, she figured. Who didn't love a dog, especially one who knew myriad ridiculous tricks, such as "hiding," where he'd put both paws over his eyes; fainting when Lark put the back of her hand to her forehead and said "Oh no!"; and dancing on his hind legs? A person had to have a hobby, and Connery spent most nights with her, since Joy slept late, and Conn's little bladder couldn't wait till 11:00 a.m.

Now the wee mutt sat happily next to her on the car seat, his silky fur ruffling in the breeze as he snuffled the wind. She was glad he was here. She was nervous. For one, she hadn't met someone's parents since . . . ever, really. She'd always known Justin's parents, the way kids do.

"We're not nervous, though, are we, Conn?" she asked her dog. He wagged in response, and she let her hand settle on his little square head, petting his soft fur. "Thanks, buddy." A car passed on her right. (It was Massachusetts, and traffic laws were quaint suggestions from a gentler time, not something that anyone enforced.) The driver slowed when she saw Connery, then blew him a kiss and sped ahead. She had curly blond and gray hair, like Mom.

And speaking of Mom . . . Lark's own did have a point. Being Lorenzo's summertime honey was an uncomfortable exchange for an introduction to the gods of oncology. But it was, what? Five events, maybe? Pretending to date a guy for a couple of months so his ancient grandmother wouldn't worry about his single state (or tarry soul) wasn't the worst thing. Besides, she understood Lorenzo's desire not to be solo during a summer full of wedding stuff. She'd endured that when Addie and Nicole got married, and having to explain why she wasn't with someone every time someone asked had been agony.

This would be worth it. She'd make a fantastic oncologist. Her soft heart . . . that wasn't a negative, no way. She'd never wanted to do anything else. This adjustment time, working in the ER, *would* help her toughen up. Darlene had said yes to doing a little hospice volunteering, and Lark could start by visiting patients. That was it. Just visiting and talking. No medical stuff, no bathing or feeding or administering drugs. Just being there.

In a few months, she'd go back to the oncology program and live out her destiny. Lorenzo's introduction might not even be necessary. But even in the world of medicine, where everything should be based on merit and skill, there was an invisible club that helped you get ahead. Your father was head of surgery at that Ivy League hospital? Of *course* you got into their residency program. Your mother donated $40 million to a world-famous clinic in the heartland? What a coincidence! They just offered you a fellowship. Say again? Your uncle is the surgeon general of the United States? Your mom is the CEO of a big pharmaceutical company? Your brother is a full professor at NYU Langone? Well, well, well. Just pass organic chemistry and come right this way.

Lark didn't have those connections. A dad who'd been an ER nurse was not medical royalty. Medicine still struggled with gender discrimination; while women made up almost 50 percent of doctors, most were in fields dealing with women or children. In neurosurgery, cardiology, urology and, yes, oncology, female doctors were a lot more rare. She wasn't selling out. Hell, no. She'd endured four years of medical school and aced the MCAT, done almost two years of residency. Getting a possible introduction from Lorenzo was *not* selling out.

Nevertheless, she was strangling the steering wheel hard. She turned on the radio for distraction, and God was listening, because "Purple Rain" had just started. She cranked up the volume and sang along until the Chatham exit. And even better, the DJ had decided to run a Prince marathon, so happy thoughts kept her company until she pulled into Lorenzo's driveway.

Showtime. She checked herself in the mirror, smiled, clipped on Connery's leash and gathered up the bouquets of flowers, then made her way to the house. Connery stopped to pee on the emerald lawn. She hoped Lorenzo wasn't looking.

God, the place was even more impressive in person. The smell of freshly cut grass, barbecue and salt air made her feel a little drunk as she approached the front door. There were several cars and a red pickup truck in the driveway, all sporting the usual

Massachusetts bumper stickers—the Sox, Cape Cod, a shark, Tunnel Permit and, on the pickup, a Boston Fire insignia. Connery sniffed each vehicle before letting her proceed.

"Lorenzo!" came a female voice before she had a chance to knock. "She's here! Open the door, hurry."

Lark took another fortifying breath and smiled.

Lorenzo opened the door. "You're late," he said, glancing at a complicated-looking watch with many dials. "You were due eleven minutes ago. And what is that?" He looked down at her dog like he'd never seen one before.

"Hi. Nice to see you, too." She widened her eyes at him. "Be nice," she whispered. "You're supposed to like me. And this is my dog, Connery. He's a great judge of character, so be careful around him." From behind him came the murmur of his family, and her nerves flashed again.

"Come in," he said. "Everyone else is already here."

He led the way through the spacious front hall and into the kitchen, where a small mob awaited, silent. Lark dimly noted that the décor was stark modern and the smells were incredible. A small ocean of smiling faces greeted her.

"Hello," she said when Lorenzo said nothing. "I'm Lark. This is my dog, Connery."

"He's so cute!" said one of the sisters, and Connery tugged free and went over to her to prove it, standing on his stumpy little legs and wagging.

"Hello!" said a short, dark-haired woman. "I'm Anita, Lorenzo's mother, and I'm very happy to meet you. You're so pretty!" She gave Lark and her four bouquets a hug.

"It's wonderful to meet you," Lark said. "These are for you," she added, handing her a bouquet.

Behind Anita, Lark spotted a tiny lady in a wheelchair under a blanket, bent with age like a tree worn down by the wind. "You must be Lorenzo's grandmother," she said. "He's told me so much about you."

"She's might be asleep," said Anita. "She doesn't close her eyes all the time. Right, Noni?"

Not that being stared at from those faded blue eyes was creepy, not at all. "I hate dogs," Noni whispered in a voice as dry as old paper. So, not asleep. "Why you bring a dog?"

Her Italian accent made the words sound threatening. *That* scene from *The Godfather* flashed through Lark's mind, and she glanced back at Connery to make sure his head was still attached. Both sisters were currently fawning over him, so it looked like he was safe for now.

"Sorry," she said. "I . . . well, I brought flowers, too. I hope you like flowers," she said, extending them. Noni didn't respond, just narrowed her eyes. She didn't take the bouquet.

"Hi! I'm Izzy. This is our grandmother, Noni," said one of the sisters. "She's a little grumpy when she's hungry." Izzy held up a piece of bread, and without looking away from Lark, Noni opened her mouth. Anodontia, Lark noted. Not a tooth to be seen. The sister popped in the chunk of bread. "I'm the single sister. Nice to meet you."

"Great meeting you, too," Lark said, handing her a bouquet.

"These are gorgeous! From your garden?"

"My landlady's."

"Well, thank you. I'll get a few vases." She began opening cupboards.

While Noni chewed and Lorenzo stood silently glaring, Lark was hugged and greeted by Silvio, Lorenzo's father; Sofia, his sister (and the bride); and her fiancé, Henry.

"Congratulations, you two," Lark said. "I can't wait to hear about the wedding."

"Oh, you've opened a can of worms with that sentence," said Izzy. "The wedding of the century. Look out, Priyanka and Nick. You ain't seen nothing yet."

"We promise to bore you with color schemes later," Sofia said. "These are lovely, Lark. Thank you." She gave Lark a beautiful smile.

"Which one of you is the nurse?" Lark asked.

"I am," Izzy answered.

"I bow to you, as every doctor should," Lark said.

"Lorenzo!" Izzy exclaimed. "She's wicked nice and also brilliant. How did you trick her into dating you?"

Lorenzo stood there, brick-like, and didn't answer.

Lark forced a laugh. "He's not that bad," she said. "If you squint, he's kind of cute, even."

"*Finally* he found someone," said Anita. "We'd all given up, but here you are, Lark. Poor Noni wants to see him settled before she dies."

"Don't say that out loud, Mom," Lorenzo said sharply. "Noni, you're in great shape."

"We're just hoping she makes it till Sofia's wedding," Silvio murmured. "But she's ninety-nine."

"So," Anita said, "you're dating my son. This is so exciting. I can't wait to get to know you."

"No pressure, Lark," Silvio said. "Hon, maybe we feed her first before we call a priest?"

"Oh, Silvio, stop. I didn't say a thing about weddings." She sparkled at Lark. "But sure, weddings are on my mind."

Silvio pressed a cold glass of something pink into Lark's

hand. "Cranberry and club soda, but I can add vodka if you want."

"This is perfect, thank you, Mr. Santini."

"Silvio, dear, call him Silvio. Tell us how you and Lorenzo met."

All eyes were on her. *We met over anal fissures.* "At the hospital," she said. "Here on the Cape, that is. I know Lorenzo practices all over Boston, too."

"Are you a surgeon, too?" Henry asked.

Lorenzo snorted, and Lark cut him a look.

"Or even better, a nurse?" Izzy asked.

"Right now, I'm doing my residency in the Emergency Department," she said.

Then someone came in the back door. "Dad, you said you wanted to grill the steaks, so I—oh. Hi."

Lark looked up, and there was someone who could only be Lorenzo's brother, staring at her, tongs in one hand. Connery ran up to him, twining through his legs, tail wagging furiously.

An odd, dark warning flashed through Lark. The Santinis were still talking, but it suddenly felt very quiet. Dante Santini did not look away.

He wasn't quite as perfectly handsome as Lorenzo, but he was much, *much* more attractive. Around six feet tall, more bulk on him than his runner brother, broad shoulders. Brown hair lightened by the sun, dark, smiling eyes. His navy blue T-shirt had a logo over his heart that read *Boston F.D. Rescue 2.*

Hence the decal on the truck outside. Lorenzo's brother was a firefighter. Suddenly, her entire body flushed.

"Hi," Dante said, the corner of his mouth lifting. "I'm the brother."

"Hi. I'm the girlfriend." They looked at each other, and then, to cover the awkwardness, Lark reached for Lorenzo's hand. Almost to her surprise, he took it.

"Now that the meet and greet is done," Lorenzo said, "why don't we go outside and have some food?" He dropped Lark's hand, grabbed the handles of Noni's wheelchair and pushed her outside, maneuvering her expertly through the French doors onto the deck.

Everyone else grabbed a tray or platter and followed. The smooth wooden deck was sheltered by an arbor dripping with purple wisteria. A hundred yards away was the Atlantic, tucked against the curve of Chatham and its ever-changing shoreline. They sat around a large table, Noni unblinking and silent at one end, Lorenzo next to her, the rest of them sitting and moving and pouring and passing, questions about traffic, food, how people wanted their steaks and burgers. Lark knew the drill. She was from a big family, too. She passed and dished and smiled and said "Not too bad, just a little slow at the rotary" when Silvio asked about traffic. Connery, like the good boy he was, curled up on a chaise longue and went to sleep.

"That dog, he on the furniture," Noni whispered.

"That's okay," Anita said. "He's adorable, Lark. And very clean, Noni. His fur is so silky."

"People sit on furniture. Not animals." Noni glared at her. One of her eyes was deviated about twenty degrees off center— exotropia—but the one-eyed glare was enough to do the trick.

"I'll get him a blanket from the car." She smiled and stood up, but Dante was already folding a beach towel for the same purpose. He picked up Connery, who licked his hand, and put him down on the towel.

"Thank you," Lark said.

"No problem." He cut her a quick look, then petted Connery's head. "What's his name?"

"Connery. He's Scottish."

"Like Sean. Got it." He smiled and sat back down, and that dark, unpleasant jolt, like cold electricity, zapped her again.

There was green salad, burrata with beefsteak tomatoes, potato salad, pasta salad, a charcuterie board full of cured meats and cheeses, grapes and crackers. That was just to start. Then came a huge casserole dish of eggplant parm, a platter of burgers, pulled pork, hot dogs and steak, three loaves of crusty bread. A quartet of olive oils, two pitchers of water with lemon slices, and bottles of wine crowded the table. In a giant copper tub filled with ice, there were more bottles of wine, and beer and soda. Silvio filled up her glass with rosé, and Lark thanked him.

"What if we go hungry?" Izzy asked, tilting her head.

"We can always hit Kream 'n Kone after," Sofia said, smiling at Lark. "You're from the Cape, right?"

"Yes. Wellfleet," she said. "I'm happily familiar with Kream 'n Kone."

"Did you grow up here, Lark?" Silvio asked.

"I did, and my parents and siblings are all still around. I have three sisters, including an identical twin, and a brother. My mom owns an art gallery. My dad retired from nursing last fall—maybe you know him, Isabella? Gerald Smith? He worked in the ER."

"Can't say the name is familiar," she said. "I'm mostly at South Shore."

"Got it. And let's see . . . my oldest sister and grandpa own the bookstore in town. Open Book. Have you ever been?"

"I don't think so," said Anita, "but we'll have to take a drive. I love Wellfleet. Haven't been for ages."

"Where do all of you live?" Lark asked. "Is everyone on the Cape?"

Cape Cod was somewhat oddly divided into quarters—since the peninsula was shaped like an arm flexing a bicep, the towns closest to the mainland were considered the upper Cape—the upper arm, as it were. The next chunk moving eastward was the mid-Cape, where the hospital, big-box stores and mall were. Then came where they were now—Chatham was the elbow, considered part of the lower Cape, along with Brewster, Harwich and Orleans. Then came the most romantic and beautiful part (to Lark, anyway) . . . the Outer Cape, where she had grown up, where the national seashore began, where the best beaches were and fiercest storms hit.

The Santinis all lived in the upper Cape area. Silvio and Anita had recently moved from the house where they'd raised their kids in Sandwich to a bigger house near the water. "Lots of bedrooms for the grands, if we're so blessed, please, God," Anita explained. "That was our thinking, anyway." She sparkled at Lark, potential provider of said grands.

Sofia and Henry were renting in Falmouth but hoped to find a starter home soon. Izzy shared a house with two other nurses and lived in pretty Barnstable. Lorenzo, of course, had the house here in Chatham and the apartment in Beacon Hill.

Only Dante was no longer a Cape Codder. "I live in Boston," he said.

"Quincy," Lorenzo corrected. "You live in Quincy. *I* live in Boston."

"Sorry, Lark," Dante said easily. "I should've been more specific. He's right, I live in Quincy."

"In a two-family house," Lorenzo said, not looking at his brother.

"He's on a roll. Correct again," Dante said, unperturbed. "I think Lorenzo is trying to point out that he lives in a much nicer area because he's a doctor, and I'm a lowly public servant."

"Boston's bravest," Sofia said, smiling at Dante.

"That *wasn't* what I was trying to say, but you're not wrong," Lorenzo said. "And I don't apologize for having money. You'll be glad I do, if you ever need a loan."

Okay, then. Lorenzo obviously had something to prove. Dante sighed. Izzy rolled her eyes.

"Henry, do you have siblings?" she asked, and Henry told her he had a half sister thanks to his dad's second marriage, fifteen years younger than he was. The conversation drifted to the wedding, which Lorenzo was funding. He made that clear by saying, "Just send all the bills to me." On the one hand, so nice. On the other, so obnoxious, too. Noni seemed to be asleep. Or dead. But no, no, a little snore escaped her.

The sun was hot and lovely, and Lark took off her sweater.

"Oh, you have a tattoo," said Isabella, tilting her head as she stared at Lark's arm. "I'm thinking of getting one."

"Over my dead body," said Mr. Santini with a smile. "You might be twenty-eight, but you're still my baby. No offense, Lark. Yours is quite pretty."

"'We loved with a love that was more than love,'" Izzy read.

"Guess it's not about Lorenzo," Sofia quipped, grinning at her brother. He almost smiled back. They were closer, Lark realized. Lorenzo seemed to like her more than Izzy or Dante. Interesting family dynamics.

"What's it from?" Izzy asked.

"It's from my favorite poem," Lark said. The words were stacked in two lines on the outer side of her bicep. She ran her hand over the tattoo, which was discreet as tattoos went, just two lines of black cursive handwriting.

"'I was a child and she was a child,'" Lorenzo said, "'in this kingdom by the sea, but we loved with a love that was more than love, I and my Annabel Lee.'"

Silence fell over the table. Lark stared at Lorenzo, stunned.

"Edgar Allan Poe," Lorenzo said. "Everyone knows that one."

"Not everyone," Dante said. "Not me."

"Big surprise," Lorenzo said.

"Our brother memorized her favorite poem," Sofia mock whispered to Izzy. "Somebody, get him to a doctor."

"He's smart, my boy," hissed Noni, making Lark jump. "He know everything."

"We call him God," Dante said. "Everyone needs a nickname."

"He goes by Dr. Satan at the hospital," Lark said, and everyone laughed (except Lorenzo and Noni). "What does your tattoo say, Dante?" She had seen it flirting with the edge of his sleeve.

He pulled the sleeve up so she could see, but she was momentarily blinded by the perfection of his upper arm. Tan, chiseled, muscled, a badass tat showing words against a fireman's cross, flames behind that.

"'Be not afraid, for the Lord thy God goes with thee; he will not fail thee, nor forsake thee,'" Anita recited. "I actually made him get that when he became a firefighter. It made me feel better, with my little boy running into burning buildings."

Dante lifted an eyebrow at Lark, then kissed his mother's temple. "Still works," he said, rapping the table with his knuckles, which caused his grandmother to stir. "Noni, do you want a burger?" he asked. "Cheddar? Provolone?"

"Too much fat," Lorenzo said.

Dante sighed.

Lorenzo put a piece of grilled fish on her plate with some wilted greens and bread. Noni groped in her sweater pocket, pulled out some dentures and popped them in, then scarfed down the food. But Lark wasn't thinking about Noni's teeth (not much, anyway).

We loved with a love that was more than love— / I and my Annabel Lee.

Lark took a long pull of her wine. Dr. Satan knew her favorite poem by heart. That he had *any* poem memorized was shocking, let alone one so romantic and haunting. It didn't match up with any other information she'd gotten so far.

Dinner progressed, and Lark ate and talked, charmed by and charming the Santinis (most of them). Lorenzo pretty much ignored her, but that was maybe because his mother was doing all the talking, asking about her parents and siblings. It was impossible not to like Sofia, who seemed a little shy but so sweet—she was a kindergarten teacher, Henry an accountant. They'd met online, as people usually did these days, and fell for each other right away.

"Love at first smile," Henry said, gazing softly at his fiancée.

Isabella was spicier, funny and irreverent, sharing stories from her career, laughing easily with Lark, asking questions about medicine, where she went to school.

Silvio and Anita were sort of like Lark's own parents—devoted to each other, but maybe a little more . . . normal than hers. Not quite as in your face with their love.

She insisted on helping clear the table, almost having to wrestle Anita to pitch in. Lorenzo remained seated at the table, talking quietly with his grandmother. Silvio asked if he could take Connery down to the beach, and of course Lark said yes. Women doing the work, Lark noted, though Dante helped by taking out the trash and recycling (without being asked, unlike her own brother, who needed a poke or a smack to motivate him).

Anita and her daughters got dessert ready—a platter of homemade Italian cookies, soft and frosted, sprinkled with red, white and blue jimmies. Lorenzo came in to make espresso from a very complicated-looking machine, and made a cappuccino for his grandmother. He did not ask anyone else if they wanted one.

Lark was learning quite a bit today.

"Lorenzo, what was it about Lark that made you ask her out?" Izzy said as they were nibbing on cookies, once again around the table. "Since you hate most humans, I mean."

"Yes, Lorenzo," Lark said, setting her wineglass on the table. "What was it exactly?"

He looked at her a minute, not answering; probably hadn't expected that he'd have to say something nice about her. "I don't hate humans," he said.

"Maybe ninety-five percent of humans," Sofia said, smiling at him.

"Ninety-eight," Izzy said.

Lorenzo was not amused. "To answer your question, Lark is pretty. As you can see."

"Boring!" Izzy said. "There are millions of pretty women in the world."

Not entirely stupid was the phrase he'd used when pitching this idea to her. She waited, enjoying his discomfort.

"She's uncomplicated," he said. "You get what you see. She's a nice, kind person. Very caring."

For the second time that day, Lark was a little gobsmacked. "Thank you," she said. Almost added *honey* but couldn't quite manage it. "That's very sweet."

"Okay, we'll accept that answer," Sofia said. "Lark, how about you? What drew you to my brother?"

"His desperation?" she said, and everyone laughed. (Except Lorenzo. And Noni.) She caught Dante looking at her.

"Seriously, though," said Anita. "We'd all but given up on him finding someone. He's forty already, and he can be a little . . ."

"Rude? Obnoxious? Cocky? Arrogant? Humorless? One-dimensional?" Izzy suggested.

"Shush! That's your brother you're talking about," Anita said. "The one who paid off your student loans. And bought his parents a beautiful home, which—thank you, honey, as always."

"He's also generous," Izzy added. "You're not *all* horrible, Lorenzo."

"Gosh, thanks," he said.

"I think that underneath that hardened exterior, he's a puppy dog," Lark said. "He's got a Mr. Darcy kind of thing going on. But we're still getting to know each other. I may be wrong." She smiled at Lorenzo. He, in turn, knelt down to say something to Noni in Italian, leaving her hanging. Dante, on the other hand, narrowed his eyes at her slightly, as if he already didn't buy it. That was fine. What had Lorenzo said? Five family events. Dante didn't have to buy it for long.

All in all, the afternoon was less awkward than Lark had expected. She'd always had an easy time talking with people, and the Santinis (minus the firstborn son and slightly scary grandmother) were lovely. Connery had been a hit, chasing a tennis ball, lying on Izzy's lap for his nap, sneezing on command, his latest trick. Silvio and Anita were warm and kind, asking about her family, admiring pictures of Esme and Imogen and, like most people, fascinated by the resemblance between her and Addie.

People did love identical twins. Sofia and Henry cuddled up against each other, and Sofia and Izzy told Lark about the wedding, showed her pictures of the dresses and asked for her opinion on bouquets.

But Noni, the reason Lark was here, was a tougher nut to crack. She stared at Lark with her off-kilter gaze, her toothless mouth frowning. Lark smiled, asked if she could get her anything. No answer. Okay, then. She'd take a little more work. But the poor old lady was on hospice, and so old, and quite possibly uncomfortable for a plethora of reasons. Lark was not going to judge her.

There was also the palpable tension between the brothers. Dante seemed far more comfortable than Lorenzo with his family, teasing his sisters, talking about the Sox with his dad, making sure his mom's wineglass never got empty. The sense of competition was thick, and every time Dante made his sisters or parents laugh, she felt Lorenzo's irritation mushroom. When Noni asked to be taken in for a nap, Dante stood up to wheel her away, but Lorenzo cut him off and did the job himself.

Otherwise, Dante was polite, but he didn't talk to Lark much. Whatever weird, uncomfortable sensation had flashed was no longer present, and Lark made sure not to pay him too much attention. But Dante Santini . . . there was something about him. She'd *felt* something, a tectonic shift, just for a second.

She'd ignore that. Her job was to be Lorenzo's new girlfriend. She'd be done with that after Sofia's wedding, but there was no reason that she couldn't enjoy and get to know his family until then.

When the sky began to darken, Dante stood up. "I gotta get going," he said. "I'm on tomorrow. Noni, I can take you back to your place, if you want."

"Sure, kid," she said. Her voice sounded like dry leaves rustling in the wind. This triggered the exodus, but not before Tupperware was packed and Lark had given her number to Lorenzo's sisters and Anita said it was wonderful to meet her and she couldn't wait to see her again.

Lark stood in line to hug Noni. "It was so lovely to meet you," she said to the old lady, who sat there like a statue, not bothering to lift her arms to fake a hug back.

"I watching you," Noni whispered so only Lark could hear. "I no trust you yet."

Lark stepped back and smiled, as she often did in times of stress. "I'm looking forward to seeing you again."

"Nice meeting you, Lark," Dante said casually as he lifted Noni out of her wheelchair and placed her carefully into the passenger seat of his truck. She didn't clear the dashboard.

"Same here," she said.

Lorenzo moved in to check that Noni was secure. Then the rest of the family piled into their vehicles, beeped horns and left as Lark and Lorenzo stood there, Connery tucked under her arm so he wouldn't leave with Izzy.

"What a lovely family," she said at the same time Lorenzo said, "Thank God that's over."

They looked at each other a minute. "Come back inside for a few minutes," Lorenzo said.

"Sure. This house is really gorgeous, by the way. I wasn't sure if this was supposed to have been my first time here, or if your family thought I'd visited before."

"It hardly matters."

"Mm. Well, it's very nice, Lorenzo."

"I had an interior designer deal with it." He glanced around as if unfamiliar with the place. "Nice enough, I suppose. Kind of a stupid career, though, isn't it? Furnishing other people's houses."

So condescending. "It's not stupid to make someone feel comfortable and at home, Lorenzo."

"Well, anyone could do it. Just order things from a catalog. It's not exactly hard."

Rather than argue the merits of that particular career, she said, "How do you think today went?" She sat down on the couch, Connery jumping neatly into her lap.

Lorenzo took a sip of water, the only thing he'd had to drink. No weekend beers for him. "Fine."

"Did I sense some tension between you and your brother?" she asked.

"Probably. He's always been jealous of me. He's not exactly setting the world on fire."

"No, he's keeping it from burning down, isn't he?" Lorenzo gave her a semi-irritated, semi-quizzical look. "Because he's a firefighter, Lorenzo."

"Whatever. It's actually a cushy job most of the time. They sit around and play cards a lot more than you'd expect."

Which brother is jealous, now? "Did you know that firefighter is the most respected career in America? Nurses come in second, and we lowly doctors rank fifth."

"Did you just make that up?"

"No. It was from a study somewhere."

"A study somewhere. *That* sounds reliable."

"Hey. The poem, 'Annabel Lee' . . . you have it memorized?"

"I have a photographic memory. I have a lot of things memorized."

That killed any rom-com notion that their mutual love of the tragic poem hinted at a deeper connection.

"Anyway," he said, "I imagine you have somewhere to go, so . . ."

She was dismissed. "Right. Thanks for inviting me." She stood up and smoothed out the skirt of her dress.

"The next event is an engagement party," he said. "In Boston at the Copley Square Plaza. Black tie. I don't expect you to buy a dress out of the pittance you make, so I'll pick out something decent and pay for it so you don't look so . . ." He scanned her critically. "Pedestrian."

"Wow. Rude, Dr. Satan."

"Just stating a fact. I'd like you to look nice. You're welcome."

So many little paper cuts, so fast. She did have Addie's vast wardrobe to choose from, and black tie would not be a problem, given the number of fundraisers and galas her sister attended with Nicole. But he wasn't wrong about the pittance. And why borrow her sister's dress when he wanted to buy her something new?

"Thanks. Anything else?"

"Get your nails done next time. Pale pink, nothing trashy. Maybe consider doing something with your hair so it's not so . . ." He waved his hand in front of her. "So like that."

"This is why you're single," she said.

"I'm very happy being single," he answered.

"The entire *world* is very happy with you being single."

"Do you have anything substantive to say, or can you just get going?" he asked, opening the door.

"Your grandmother isn't quite sold on me yet," she said.

"She's not stupid. Try harder next time. To win her over, I mean. You don't have to bother with my sisters or parents."

"I really liked them."

"Whatever. But it's my grandmother who matters here."

"Got it. Have a nice evening, Lorenzo." She picked up Connery and her bag and went to the front door.

He did not walk her to the car. He didn't say "take care" or "thanks." In fact, he closed the door before she was even in her car.

"I can see why you had to rent me," she called, waving to the house, though she was sure by now Lorenzo Santini had dismissed her from his mind entirely.

Once, with Justin, it had seemed so easy, the idea of a happy marriage. Love had been effortless. Even in high school, her siblings had called her and Justin Mom and Dad 2.0. She couldn't remember her parents ever fighting. That was how she and Justin had planned on being. Had been, in fact. Happily ever after. A modern-day fairy tale.

It seemed so long ago.

FOUR

ELLIE

The day Elsbeth Smith's life veered off the road was completely, charmingly normal right up to the moment of impact.

First order of the day: Kiss husband. Intentionally, not just a peck. Second, text the kids in birth order—Harlow, Addison, Lark, Winnie and Robbie—and tell them to have a wonderful and meaningful day. Sure, they made fun of her for this, but she didn't care. She was used to it.

Third, get to work. Bills to pay and all that.

She'd driven down to Long Pond Arts, her gallery down by the marsh with its picturesque view of Uncle Tim's Bridge and Hamblen Island, before eight. Turned on the lights, opened the back door, since it was a sparkling day and the smell of the salt water was irresistible. She spent an hour and a half working up-stairs on her latest—the third in a series of autumn on the cran-berry bog. Each painting showed the same view, but at different times of day—dawn, with a golden and lavender sunrise, mist clinging to the trees at the edge; full afternoon, with the berries glowing red, the sky's vivid blue contrasting with the bright white clouds; and number three here, the bog in late evening, a sliver of a moon rising, reflecting in the water.

She'd changed the gallery's hours to be from nine thirty to

six last year, worried that waiting till ten meant losing foot traffic that could translate to more sales. No one was here yet, though, so she wrapped up a painting for a lovely young couple who'd ordered something via the website, jotted them a note of thanks and left it for Meeko, her beautiful and lazy Lithuanian assistant, to address and ship.

"Good morning, and you're late, Meeko, honey," she said as he slouched in.

"Traffic very bad today," he lied.

"Leave earlier next time." She smiled firmly until he nodded, then went into the office. Inventory, orders, banking, emails, sales, updating the website, while Meeko, seemingly exhausted, dragged a feather duster along the shelves, phone in one hand.

People came and went, and whenever possible, Ellie popped out to welcome them. "Hi! Thanks for stopping in! Where are you from? Beautiful day, isn't it?" She rang up smaller purchases—handmade ceramic mugs, limited edition prints, charming cards, mobiles, coasters . . . the type of merchandise that filled in the gaps between sales of actual paintings and sculptures. Texted Gerald a note that said she couldn't wait to sit on the deck this evening, and received a martini emoji and heart as a response.

She smiled at her phone. God, she was lucky. They both were. Thirty-eight years of marriage, and they still flirted. Still loved each other. Still had a more than healthy sex life. Just this past September, the last of the kids had finally flown the nest when Lark got that sweet little guesthouse—and she and Gerald had adjusted to the slower rhythm at home, eating later, talking more.

At first, sure, it had been an adjustment. A natural one, she read, but a little surprising nonetheless. Without the kids as a cushion, they'd bumped and scraped more than they ever had.

Had it always taken Gerald so long to finish a project? Could he ever completely clean up the kitchen, or was he marking his territory by leaving crumbs on the counter? And how about the garage? It had been built for housing a car, not the myriad tools he still wasn't quite sure how to use. Their house had always been in a state of charming disrepair, but things were getting a little more shabby these days. Since Gerald had retired fully, she had hoped the glacial pace of getting things done would have picked up a bit. It had not.

Ellie loved home projects, but just didn't have the time. If their positions had been reversed, she would've done repairs systematically, finishing what she started before tackling something new, as was her way. Without Robbie there, kicking off his shoes and leaving them in the middle of the floor, without Lark coming home from the hospital needing to eat and talk about her day, every little flaw of home and husband seemed magnified. It had felt weird. Just the two of them. Not bad, but weird.

Gerald had felt it, too. He'd even snapped at her one day—"Do you ever hear something I said the first time I say it?" It was so unlike him—unlike them. Yes, she'd been tuning him out, because the truth was, she wasn't actually fascinated by the story of his trip to Ace Hardware in Eastham. But point taken. She had apologized and feigned interest in his adventures in screen door repair, though a hummingbird could fit through the hole that was still there. A little less talk, a little more action, Gerald, please?

Another fight came in October after she asked if he could be more aware of leaving knives in the sink after he used them. The man loved his knives. God forbid they had the kind that could go in the dishwasher. And God forbid Gerald wash them within an hour of using them. Nope. Apparently, there was a man-rule that if you used a knife, you waited for your wife to come home to wash it and put it back, then inform her you were going to do that, so she didn't have to.

But whatever little bumps and scrapes they'd encountered had smoothed out by winter, and she once again felt like they were the happiest couple on the Cape, which was what everyone considered them. Sure, more time off, more time away would've been nice, but it wasn't in the cards at the moment. Her career—her paintings, the gallery—was as demanding as ever. More so, really. Gerald took care of the house and yard (more or less) and did errands for his dad and their kids. She earned. It wasn't how she'd expected it to be, but it wasn't so bad, either.

Just too busy.

Around lunchtime, Ellie took her salad into the little courtyard behind the gallery. A family of geese paddled past, placid and calm, reminding her of herself when the kids were little. Happy times. She missed that. These days, family dinners were always at Addison and Nicole's, since they had such a big and splendid house and did things like iron napkins and make place cards. Lots of times, Ellie would stop by the bookstore to find two or three of her other children hanging around, chatting with Harlow or Robert, her father-in-law. All the kids revered Grandpop. Sometimes, they took him out en masse or went over to make him dinner. They didn't do that with her and Gerald. It made Ellie feel a little left out.

Those days when her little goslings had followed her, confident that she would keep them safe and make their lives fun . . . she missed those days.

Through the window, she could see Meeko standing mournfully by the window, taking selfies as he practiced his *hello, I am an Eastern European model* poses in front of some of the larger canvases.

She put the lid back on her salad container and went inside. "Meeko? Did you update the website?" she asked.

"No. Tomorrow I do it."

"Today you do it. Or you can clock out." The man-child had seemed like a good idea at the time of his hiring, but what he had in good looks and a decent knowledge of art, he lacked in work ethic.

"Fine. I clock out. We are slow today besides." He gave an existential-crisis sigh and slouched off.

He had a point. They *were* slow. It was Tuesday, and hopefully this weekend would bring in more customers. Around three, a couple pulled into the parking lot in a big Porsche SUV. The woman held a Chanel purse and wore diamond studs; the man was dressed in Tom Ford. Wellfleet was a posh little town when the summer folk came in, and Ellie had gotten good at spotting designer labels.

"Welcome," she said. "Thanks for coming in. Is there anything special you're looking for?"

"We have a spot in our house here that just cries out for something dramatic," the husband said, and for the next hour, Ellie discussed the light in their dining room, their style, the other artwork they owned. (They clearly wanted to show her what great taste they had.)

"What mood are you trying to express in the space?" Ellie asked.

"Interesting, bright, nothing too depressing." He indicated one of her own oil paintings, *Oyster Beds at Dusk*. "And nothing too banal."

Ouch. "How about something like this?" she asked, guiding them to a corner where one of her baby artists' work was hung. Miles was a talented kid who did post-neo-expressionism (or graffiti, as her daughter Winnie described it). It was important to feature a range of styles. Only a few Cape artists featured their work exclusively in their galleries. Most of them, Ellie included, needed to hedge their bets.

"I love this," the wife murmured. "So impactful."

The landline rang. "Excuse me one second," she said, since Meeko was gone. "Long Pond Arts," she said, picking up the phone.

"Hello! I'd like to talk to you about refinancing your house!" said a humanlike voice. She hung up and returned to the corner where she'd left the couple. They were gone. She glanced out the door and saw them wandering farther down the street to her friend Jo's gallery. Dang. She'd really thought they might buy Miles's painting. But even if they didn't, they could've said goodbye, at least. *Thanks for your time. You have a lovely gallery. Nice talking to you!*

Rude.

The wind chimes out back clanged gently. She checked the cranberry painting, added a bit more color to the scrubby bushes at the edge of the bog, poked her head out again. No one else in the gallery.

"That's okay," Ellie said out loud. "It'll be a great season."

She needed it to be. She always needed a great season. The familiar thread of fear tightened around her stomach.

Being an artist on Cape Cod was not exactly an unusual occupation. After all, anyone who got their hands on paints could call themselves an artist. Ellie had put herself through art school—Massachusetts College of Art and Design, one of the best. She'd been a standout student, gone to Europe to take some extra classes and had every intention of supporting herself on her art.

She'd gotten married instead. Had five children and painted

only sporadically for twelve years. But since she'd opened the gallery . . . gosh, twenty-three years ago? . . . she'd put the pedal to the metal. Already educated, she'd been diligent about honing her craft to reach the level of accomplishment she had now. Workshops from other painters, online tutorials, poring over other people's work and thousands and thousands of hours painting had made her a proficient and talented artist. She knew that.

But popular opinion was nothing if not fickle. She'd started this gallery as a way to create and sell her work, sure, but also to bring some money into the family. And she had. She'd ended up bringing *most* of the money into the family. She still did. And she still needed a good season. A really good season. Again. Financial security, that wispy, elusive creature, was always just around the next corner.

So now, with no one in the gallery but her, looking critically at her cranberry bog painting (was it banal?), it was easy to feel like she was running to stand still. What if she hadn't chosen well with the young artists she was featuring? What if her very slight increase on prices backfired? What if her work wasn't current . . . again?

Because that was a thing, too. What did the customer want *this* season? Hopefully, her lovely landscapes and charming Cape scenes, so carefully crafted over the winter, would sell, but it depended. What were the interior decorators pushing? Whose work had been featured in *Cape Cod and the Islands* or *Cape Cod Life* or *Yankee* magazine? Sunset paintings? That was so two years ago. Now alleyways bursting with flowers were all the rage. Nope, scratch that, do you have any still lifes with fruit? Actually, we're so over fruit. Still lifes with flowers? No, wait, hyperrealistic waves, please. The beach in the snow. Provincetown in the snow. Provincetown in the rain. Make that *Paris* in the rain, please. Got anything whimsical, like a mouse stealing a raspberry? Oh, sorry, we'd prefer kids swimming. Or no, young men swimming. Do you have any nudes? How about some oyster shells? Didn't you use to sell paintings of those cottages with the flower names? I wish you had some Jackson Pollock kind of stuff. Hey, what about sunset paintings?

A gallerist needed to be psychic. What would be hot this year? How much to charge? You didn't want people leaving because they could get a painting of oyster shells for a thousand bucks less at a craft fair. But maybe you should be charging *more*, implying that your art was elite and rare. But then you'd have to compete with the Provincetown art scene, where galleries were in every third building, and paintings could sell for tens of thousands of dollars.

Young talent was becoming more and more important. The art world was ageist these days. Ellie had just said to Gerald that Monet would've been put in a nursing home and tied in his wheelchair if he were alive today. No one cared if you'd had a good, solid career with a technique forged by years of experience. Customers wanted to *discover* art, as pretentious as that was. *We have an early Deborah Constantine*, they wanted to say (once Debbie got huge, of course). "Only paid four thousand dollars for that baby there." Reviewers, too, fawned over young artists. *Bursting onto the art scene* was a phrase Ellie was heartily sick of (and a phrase that had been used to describe her, once upon a time). These young artists didn't have to be great, or even innovative. They just had to be *new*.

A few years ago, a young oil painter made a splash getting $20,000 a canvas for scenes of Coast Guard rescues back in the early part of the twentieth century. They looked almost *exactly* like Ellie's own vintage rescue scenes from a decade ago, which had sold for a quarter of the price. Same black-and-white under-painting, same alla prima method in which wet paint was applied to still-wet paint, same scumbling texture effect. Brushstrokes the same thickness and size. One of Ellie's paintings had shown four men on the beach, waving to the listing boat offshore. One of this painter's—same thing.

Ellie didn't know the artist, and wasn't naïve enough to think that the guy had copied her, but come on. It would've been nice if just one reviewer mentioned her work. *In the same school as the Elsbeth Smith series* would've been nice. Instead, it was as if Ellie's paintings had never existed.

Twenty grand a piece.

Raise your hand if you, too, burst onto the scene or were praised for your fresh perspective of old Cape Cod, Ellie wanted to say. After all, she had burst. She'd been fresh. She'd been named a young artist to watch. Over the years, she'd seen at least twenty young artists burn out after a few years. The reviews of their early works had been *too* fawning, maybe. The expectations were too great. Too much pressure to remain the it girl or guy. You couldn't develop a style, produce for years and still be new. It was one or the other, and if you made your name too early on, chances were high that you'd be packing your canvases or chopping your prices.

Ellie knew this. She didn't need those titles or accolades—*Ten Young Artists to Watch* or *Artists Redefining Cape Art.* In fact, it was only *after* she'd burst, after she'd been watched, after she'd been new that she produced some of her best, most elevated work. Back then, she didn't worry too much. She had a voice, and her work was strong and beautiful, and surely people would relate to it, no matter what her age, or how long Long Pond Arts had been open.

That had been true . . . until four years ago. The gallery had been in the black for the eleventh year running, and Ellie felt confident. Since she'd opened Long Pond, she had painted what the people wanted—seascapes, pretty Cape houses, children frolicking on the beach, sunsets and sunrises galore. Then she decided to do something different for the simple reason that she felt inspired. Wasn't that what art was all about? Wasn't her career solid enough for her to reach a little? It was, she thought. She never wanted to be that painter who did the same thing over and over and over.

All that autumn and winter, she worked on a series of huge canvases . . . stormy skies and dark oceans with incredible layers and detail, rich with the intricacies, the sense of foreboding and power of the weather, the atmosphere so thick you could almost smell the rain. The work was moody, striking and yes, *fresh*, and she couldn't wait to unveil it come spring. She planned a big, splashy opening—caterers, bar, musicians. This series would get back some of that early attention, she was certain. Maybe even a review in the *Globe* or the *Times* or *Yankee*. Sales would spike. This work was her best ever. She was so thrilled that in her late fifties, she could be so innovative and energized, her skills sharper than they'd ever been in her life.

Confident and excited, Ellie sent out three *hundred* invitations to the opening of *The Fury of the Storm* in early March. Yes, said the *Globe* reviewer, she'd love to come. Wow, said the editor at *Cape Cod Life*. Incredible. Count him in.

A week later, and eighteen days before the planned opening, a huge nor'easter named Mathilda ripped out great chunks of the Cape, taking down giant trees, swallowing houses on the ocean side, vomiting up the destruction on the formerly pristine beaches. The Outer Cape was without power for upwards of a week. Families were displaced, beaches destroyed. Marinas were littered with broken boats. A federal emergency was declared, and two people were killed during an attempted rescue of an overturned boat, including a coastguardsman.

Nineteen people came to the opening, and a third of them were related to her. Ellie had already dropped the prices, sensing the impending doom of her show. It was worse than she'd imagined. She didn't sell a single painting. The only "reviewer" who came was a high school student from Truro who was writing an article for the school newspaper.

Out of the twenty-two formidable, breathtaking paintings she'd created over the winter, painting till her hands cramped, loving her craft once again, confident, excited and happy, only one painting sold all season long. At a 75 percent discount. It was a disaster.

Down the street, Tim's Bridge Gallery held a huge show for a new artist who had just burst onto the scene—angular houses painted in vivid, nearly neon colors, all sharp angles and weird proportions. Every painting sold at the opening. The owner had looked at Ellie with apologetic eyes as she talked with the thrilled consumers.

It was frustrating, how the worst times seemed to have so much more power than the good times. Those good seasons, that sense of pride and accomplishment, shriveled compared with the year of Mathilda. Even today, as she did at least once a week, Ellie wondered if she'd ever feel truly confident again, business-wise. The days of painting for love, and not just for sale, seemed like a dream from long ago.

Which did not mean Long Pond Arts wasn't about to have a great year. "Keep on the sunny side," Gerald liked to sing to her when they took a shower together. It always made her smile. No matter what, she had led a very lucky life. Money worries were never fun, but most people had them. In times of financial crunch, like they'd had the year of Mathilda, Gerald took extra shifts at the hospital. But now, at last, he was retired, even though he'd kept his certification. For more than forty years, he'd worked full-time, and while he'd loved his job, it was draining—the many healthcare crises, chronic understaffing, the physical labor of his work, some horrible coworkers, an ever-changing administration with batches of new rules every time someone was replaced or quit, not to mention the many grim situations he faced close up.

It wasn't that she resented his retirement. She just wished she could retire, too. She loved the gallery, but if she hit the lottery (tough, since she didn't play), she'd sell it. Sell it and spend her mornings reading *Atlas Obscura* and the *New York Times* the way Gerald did. Go to the places they talked about visiting. Garden again, because she loved gardening. When the kids were little, she started seeds in March, and by July, they could make an entire meal out of what they had grown in the now crumbling raised beds she'd built back then. She could spend more time with Esme and Imogen; visit their oldest grandchild, Matthew, at Georgetown; read and take long walks and set up her easel somewhere, painting just because she wanted to. She and Gerald could lie under the big tree in the backyard with their books, holding hands, drinking iced tea, reading passages aloud to each other. Because yeah, they were that couple. The poster kids for marriage done right.

As if on cue, her phone rang. "Hi, babe," she said.

"Hello, gorgeous," he answered. "Wondering what you want for dinner. And also wanted to brag that I got *Wordle* in two."

"Wow," she said, smiling. "Smart *and* sexy." She'd tried the game a few times and liked it—plus, word games were good for the brain—but never remembered to play it daily, the way Harlow and Gerald did. Didn't really have the time.

"Any food preferences?" he asked. "I'm going to Stop & Shop in Orleans, so the sky's the limit."

"My hero. Um . . . how about roast chicken?"

"It's a little hot for that. You know, running the oven for hours."

Her old recipe, back in the days when she was the one who cooked, had required only an hour for roasting, but she didn't want to micromanage. "Okay. Something vegetarian, maybe?"

"How about steak?"

"Steak would be fine, hon," she said, rolling her eyes. Why call for her opinion when he obviously didn't need it?

"What about a vegetable?"

"Whatever looks good. Hon, I have to run. I have a Zoom call with the arts council. Love you!"

"Love you more. I have plans to demonstrate that later, too."

She smiled as she hung up and clicked on the link for her meeting. Part of being a business owner was being active in the community, and the council's annual appeal was coming up.

For an hour, she talked about donors and listened to the impact of a handwritten note versus a mass email. "Ellie, you do that beautiful calligraphy," Janet said. "Can you handwrite the letters?"

"To five hundred people?" she said. "No. Sorry. I can do one, and we can print them up, though. No one will be able to tell."

"But that's so impersonal!"

"I just don't have the time, Janet." No one else volunteered to help, or reminded Janet there was an easier way to reach people—this new thing called email.

"Well, can you at least handwrite in each of their names so it looks more organic?"

"I . . ." Would it take more time to just agree than it would to field seventeen or thirty calls from Janet? "Sure."

The thought of a home-cooked meal, a martini and sex at the end of the day eased her irritation.

She and Gerald had met backpacking in Europe in their early twenties. Ellie and her friend had gone to a beach in Spain, and there he was, coming out of the water like Neptune's hottest son—tall, black-haired, tanned and ripped with muscle. He saw her and smiled, and Ellie's whole body flushed and tightened. Before they'd exchanged a word, she already wanted to sleep with him. At twenty-three, she'd been in love before, had had two serious boyfriends (if a person could say anything was serious at twenty-three). But with Gerald Robert Smith, things felt momentous from that very first second. Ellie *knew* he'd be important to her. She felt it in her bones before he even said a word. Then he did say a word—"Hi"— and they were pretty much a done deal from then on.

After a week, they felt like they'd known the other for centuries but also couldn't wait to share more new things together, hear each other's stories, see each other in different situations, introduce their friends and get their take. She and Gerald—never Gerry—spent the next six weeks traveling around Europe, drinking cheap wine, making love and inhaling each other's souls.

People predicted it would fade. "You're not going to feel this way forever, you know," her mother had said. "Marital bliss is a lie." Ellie ignored her. Dad didn't seem to care that much, saying only that hopefully Gerald could support her, since Ellie was *an artist*. Dad always used air quotes and dropped his voice to a whisper when he said those words. "She thinks she's"—pause for effect—"*an artist*." He had hoped she'd become an actuary. Grace, Ellie's sister, was the only one who was enthusiastic. Sweet Grace. They'd always been close.

Gerald believed in her talent and was in awe of her work. He loved her passion for art, admired her, listened to her. They eloped five months after they'd met. Grace was their only witness and only guest, because they didn't care about a wedding. They cared about *marriage.* Harlow was born a year and a half later, and parenthood only made Ellie and Gerald love each other more. She stayed home while he worked his long days—twelve-hour shifts, sometimes longer. Ellie made sure he knew how much she appreciated that. When he came home, the house was tidy, a meal was in the works, and there were fresh flowers in a jar to welcome him back. Her heart tripled as he got out of the car and ran—yes, ran—up the steps to her and Harlow. "My girls," he'd say. "I'm so happy to be back with my girls."

And Ellie was in heaven with her little look-alike daughter, all blond curly hair and big eyes. Harlow was a lovely, curious baby and toddler, so happy and full of life, noticing everything and tucking it away, very smart, Ellie was sure. As a mother, she was awash in love, dazed by luck and joy. She'd never known she could be as happy as she was . . . and made the mistake of telling her own mother this.

"You do think she's smart?" Mom asked, frowning. "Seems average to me."

The twins came next, their most beautiful children, like ethereal fairies from another realm. It wasn't easy, nursing two babies while trying to play Candy Land with your toddler, and it was *so* much more expensive . . . two of everything at once. Larkby seemed to only smile or sleep, but Addison was fussy almost around the clock. Harlow was so cute and invested as a big sister. She'd called the twins the Littles, and the name stuck for all the younger kids.

She and Gerald bought their fixer-upper, wincing at the cost of even the lowest end of the real estate market on the Cape. It had potential, though. It would be a lovely home because it was *their* home.

Then came Winnie, a bit of a surprise baby, since three daughters had seemed like plenty of children. It was Gerald the nurse who'd been confident that the rhythm method was just as effective as condoms, and it was Ellie the ovulator who believed him.

Not a problem. What was one more girl? She was a gift, their Windsor, so independent and solemn and focused (rather like Elizabeth Windsor, for whom Ellie had named her, having always admired the queen). Four daughters! How lucky! The house projects remained, but the family was healthy and happy, busy and noisy. Gerald's parents, Robert and Louisa, were thrilled and helpful, just around the corner, which made up for Ellie's parents. They weren't the babysitting type. Too tired, too worried, too nitpicking. "She's still not toilet trained? But she's two!" Or "Do they always bicker like that?" It was just as well. Her parents were the pee in the swimming pool of life. The opposite of her and Gerald.

Then Gerald decided he wanted a boy.

"One more time, babe," he said. "Wouldn't you love to have a son? A grimy little boy digging in the sand, giving the girls a run for their money? Plus, it'd be nice to know someone could carry on the family name."

"Is that really still a thing?" she asked. Winnie was three and a half, and the past six months had been a little easier, no diapers, the high chair relegated to the basement.

"It is. Maybe," he said, grinning at her. He pulled her onto his lap, kissed her neck, making those reproductive organs of hers squeeze and sigh.

Nine months later, Robert Harrington Smith was born, he of

the sparkling brown eyes and black curly hair. He was worth it, a smiling, gurgling baby adored by his four sisters. Their family was complete, and Gerald had been right. She hadn't known how much she wanted a son until she had one.

When Robbie was five months old, though, he uncharacteristically started screaming in the middle of the night. Gerald was at work (always seemed to be the way when one of the kids was sick). Ellie rushed into his room. Robbie was in agony . . . then, just like that, stopped crying. The screaming started again fifteen minutes later. When she went to change his diaper, Ellie saw that his poop looked like cranberry sauce.

"Call Grammy," she told Harlow, then eleven. "Stay with the Littles until she gets here."

She put Robbie in his car seat, not wanting to wait for the ambulance, and flew to Hyannis Hospital. It was intussusception, a condition where Robbie's intestine folded back onto itself, "like a telescope," the surgeon explained. He was transferred to Boston Children's Hospital for emergency surgery, followed by a three-day stay, where Robbie's status as young prince was reaffirmed by the adoration of everyone who crossed his path. He was fine. He'd be fine.

Ellie was the one who was wrecked. He could have died. Her baby could have *died*.

Their meager savings account was depleted. The copay from the hospital was staggering, even though Gerald was a union nurse.

"I'll take more shifts," Gerald said. "Don't worry, honey."

She worried anyway. It was impossible, even if Gerald did six shifts a week—seventy-two hours—to make ends meet, let alone pay off their seemingly insurmountable debt.

She went into the attic and looked at some of her old paintings. She hadn't had much time since she'd had Harlow, so most were from her pre-motherhood days, with—she winced—only seven completed paintings in the past eleven years. But they were good, she thought. At least, they weren't bad.

She used her third credit card to rent space at the Eastham Outdoor Arts Show down by the Visitor Center, and asked Louisa to watch Robbie. Then she put the five paintings in the back of the minivan and loaded the girls into the car, the twins in their booster seats, Winnie in a car seat and Harlow in front with her. In Eastham, she parked the Littles outside the tent and told them to listen to Harlow. By the end of three hours, the girls had sunburn—she'd forgotten sunscreen—but she had made $2,300 in a single afternoon.

People had bought her paintings. Every single one.

"Why aren't you showing in a gallery?" asked one woman, her face alight as she paid Ellie for two oil paintings. "These are breathtaking."

The girls were so proud of her. "You were the best one there, Mommy!" Harlow said in the car.

Gerald had been dazzled (oh, the sex that night had been amazing). "We can make this work," he said. "This is what you were meant to do. I'm not surprised, but, my God, honey! Great job!"

But with the glow of accomplishment came a disquieting whisper of truth. If they were ever going to pay down their mortgage, get out of credit card debt, improve the house or essentially ever have anything extra, it was going to have to come from her.

Gerald encouraged her, stopped taking overtime shifts so she could paint more (a terrifying risk) and believed in her. He thought she was the best artist on the Cape. "Go big or go home," he said, so after a year of those little art shows and selling at the flea market, Robert and Louisa cosigned a loan for them to buy the building for Long Pond Arts. It was water damaged and needed a new roof, new bathroom and windows, but they did the work themselves, and Ellie vowed she'd never miss a payment and make her in-laws regret their generosity.

And through the chaos and exhaustion and laughter and noise and worry, she and Gerald remained in love. They did. They had promised to make an island of peace for each other in the crashing oceans of parenthood, and it wasn't even hard. The Littles would go to bed, Harlow would go up a half hour later, and in the quiet of their ramshackle house, they'd hold hands, make a drink or a cup of coffee, talk and listen. All the marriage advice said never take each other for granted. Be affectionate. Show your gratitude. Have each other's backs. Be your children's role models for a good relationship.

They did. They definitely did.

Obviously, they argued from time to time. Did Gerald *have* to tell her how toxic her mother was? Ellie already knew she was difficult. Did he have to bring it up every time the woman called or visited? Could he do a little more for the kids instead of acting like one of them? On her side, Ellie knew she got wrapped up in the issues of the gallery, which could be utterly consuming—washing windows, fixing the roof, hanging art, choosing vendors, advertising, social media . . . not to mention *creating*. She did not slap out paintings. She wished she could, but she was unable to do anything but her best, and that took mental energy and focus and time.

Her marriage was golden. Her career was helping the family financially and gave her another role in addition to Mommy. She was doing it. She was rising to the occasion, making a living through art. She was . . . dare she think it? . . . a success.

I don't know how you do it, friends would say. *The kids, the art, the*

*business! Well, you have Gerald. You're so lucky! I wish Ted/Jim/Leah/
Spencer was like him. You two found the golden ticket, that's for sure.*

She wondered if men were told their success was due to a supportive spouse. As the kids got older, she painted more, arranging a list of chores so the kids could pitch in, overseen by Harlow, whom she and Gerald called the General. One by one, the kids graduated from high school, went to college, groped around, found their way. Poor Lark went through all that stuff with Justin. Addie moved to Boston for a few years, then got married and started a family. Harlow dropped out of law school and came back home while Winnie went from job to job, not finding anything that really grabbed her. Robbie finally managed to pass his certification and become a marine mechanic.

Life happened, of course. When Louisa died, it was crushing. She'd been more of a mother to Ellie than her own mother had been, in terms of unconditional love and role modeling. Ellie worried that Harlow had made a huge mistake, leaving law school with just a few weeks to go. Would Winnie ever find something that really suited her? What about Addie and her fixation on money? Or Robbie still acting like a teenager? Her sister Grace's marriage was always stressful, so unlike hers—Larry was such a blowhard, so full of himself and, Ellie suspected, a cheater.

And then, last fall, the autumn of life began. The kids were grown and settled. Gerald was still fit and vibrant, finally done with the hard work of being a nurse. Lark moved out for good this time, she'd assured them. Welcome, empty-nest years! Welcome, Time, that most precious of all commodities. The time her friends and acquaintances talked about when they finally could do all those things they'd been waiting for. Travel. Grandkids. Reading. Just . . . being.

But Ellie's life was just as busy as ever. The gallery had stalled in recent years . . . the pandemic, the economy, competition from new galleries. After Mathilda, it was hard to trust her own vision, and there was more temptation to phone it in. "Just give the people what they want, hon," Gerald said, and it hurt, the idea that she was able to slap out a few paintings a month and be happy with it. That had never been her.

But the inspiration and joy had been leaching away for years now. Since Mathilda. Since Louisa's death. Since her days stopped revolving around the kids, when painting had been the release and reward, not the job.

Speaking of her parents, she saw that she had six missed calls from her mother. Shit. She really shouldn't put her phone on silent, but she hated being interrupted at work. She hit her mother's number.

"Hi, Mom, is everything okay?"

"Oh, Ellie, it's you. Hello."

"You called me six times. Is Dad okay?"

"What?"

"Is Dad okay?" she repeated, raising and slowing her voice. Mom never wore her hearing aids.

"You don't have to yell at me. Yes, he's fine. Why did you call, Ellie?"

"You called me, Mom. Six times."

"I did?"

"Yep. But if everything's good, I'll catch up with you later, okay? I'm just closing the gallery."

"Oh, the gallery." Mom's tone was accusatory. "You're so busy all the time."

Tell me about it. "Okay, Mom, talk to you soon."

"Well, your aunt isn't doing too well. Her knee is really bothering her."

Aunt Sharon's knee had been bothering her since Ellie was a teenager. "I'm sorry to hear that. Listen, I have to run, Mom. Love you."

"Fine. You called me. Apparently, I shouldn't have answered." Mom hung up.

Deep breath. Unclench the jaw. Keep on the sunny side. Call Grace later to vent.

Mom was increasingly needy, especially with technology. "The link didn't work for me" or "How do I look at these pictures Addie sent me?" Dad, meanwhile, started subscribing to conspiracy theories. "You really think someone could survive in *space*? That people have walked on the *moon*? The gravity alone would crush you. Stop drinking the Kool-Aid."

She hoped with all her heart that her kids wouldn't ever think of her as an aggravation. Or if they did, that Gerald would have her back and not agree that the other was a pain in the ass, the way her parents did.

One last round in the gallery, making sure the back door was secure (she needed to replace the whole slider, but that would have to wait for fall). If the gallery had a good season, that was.

It'll be okay, she told herself. The kids were healthy, the grandkids were doing great. Gerald was waiting for her, would be delighted to see her. Her rock and her comfort. Her love. She slung her bag over her shoulder, locked the gallery door and went home, breathing deeply, her shoulders loosening, enjoying the wind in her hair. Her husband adored her.

She was so lucky. She felt that with all her heart.

Which was why finding his iPad was like a sledgehammer to the head.

FIVE

LARK

It was her third week in the ER, and Lark was a little surprised at how *competent* she felt. In Oncology, the cases were so complex and fraught and challenging, and she had loved that part of it. In the ER, though, things were a bit more straightforward. If a patient was complicated, you did your best to narrow down the reasons, ordered tests and worked the problem. But the problem lasted for only your shift. Either you had the patient admitted, or someone else took over. Granted, she spent the drive home wondering if she'd done the right things, but Dr. Unger was a great supervisor, so she had that reassurance.

She'd worked overnight, and the vibe was different, for sure. Some standard emergencies—a seven-year-old boy with a broken arm, courtesy of a tumble out of his bunk bed, where he'd been wrestling with his brother. A patient who'd overdosed on fentanyl, treated in the field with Narcan, brought in for evaluation. A chef who'd sliced the webbing between his thumb and forefinger and needed a referral to a hand surgeon. A young man who said he was coughing up blood, but really wasn't . . . he just had a bad cough, and his throat was irritated, causing a speck or two of blood.

There'd been a toddler with a diaper full of black poop that had his parents thinking he was either bleeding internally or possessed by the devil. Turned out the little guy had just eaten half a quart of blueberries, and that's how blueberries looked on the other end. The mom had burst into tears of relief.

"You have NPS, I'm afraid," Lark had said with a smile. "New parent syndrome. My sister brought her daughter to the ER four times in the first year. It's normal to worry." She bent down to look at the beautiful little boy. "You are the cutest little guy in the whole world, mister," she said. He sparkled up at her, all dark gray eyes and drooly smile.

Babies. God, she loved babies. She hoped Addie and Nicole would have another. It was the closest thing to her own she could imagine right now. Would she ever have a family of her own? Her own baby? The kind of love her parents shared? It had once seemed so close, and now was a million miles away, a shimmering city so foreign and far it felt like a barely remembered dream.

Well. Anyway. The ER had also hosted a woman who thought she had a spider in her ear (she didn't), a young man with a nasty cut on his foot that Lark got to stitch up (so much fun!) while he flirted with her. There'd been a boyfriend patient, as Luis called them . . . Horace, a sweet little old man who was a repeat customer, in from his assisted living facility with another UTI. Lark knew she spent too much time with him, but she didn't care.

Emergency room medicine was a microcosm for all that was right and wrong in American healthcare. A couple of true emergencies (the sliced hand, the cut foot, the broken arm); a couple of "it was good that you came" cases, like the blueberry baby. The guy with the cough just needed some antibiotics and cough medicine, but he didn't have a primary care doctor. The specks of blood had scared him, so rather than a routine visit to the doctor, or a trip to urgent care, he'd ended up in the ER at 10:00 p.m. on a Tuesday, which would cost him a lot more than necessary.

Assisted living facilities tended to be revolving doors—the patients lived there, were cared for, but if anything was even slightly off, they were shuttled to the ER, treated and often admitted, returning to their facility to repeat the cycle.

And the computer work! She probably went through twenty-five screens per patient, clicking, dictating notes, checking boxes, logging in, logging out. She was getting better at dictation, and she and Lalita would look at each other and smile, seeing who could murmur their notes in faster. No one was as fast as Howard Unger, though, who sounded like a New Yorker on speed when it came to that.

But in most cases, the patients were happy or relieved to see her (or any one of the doctors, PAs or APRNs). Usually, the staff could either treat the problem or reassure the patient. That's what she'd wanted in Oncology. Still wanted.

To that end, she'd started volunteering with the hospice program here at the hospital, and had seen her first patient last week—Alice Fontaine, late-stage Alzheimer's, admitted to the hospital so her daughter, herself in her seventies, could have a little break from caregiving.

"Hello," Lark had said upon entering. She kept her voice low, since Mrs. Fontaine appeared to be sleeping. "I'm Lark, your hospice volunteer."

Mrs. Fontaine opened her eyes. "Mama?" she asked. "Will you take me home?"

Immediately, Lark felt tears surge. But no. She was not going to *cry* in front of this woman. Her job was to provide comfort, a peaceful presence, companionship. Not to make the patient feel worse.

"I'm Lark," she said, clearing her throat. "I don't think I know your mother. What's she like?"

"She's pretty. She loves me."

"I bet she does," Lark said, swallowing. "What do you like doing best with her?"

"I like baking. She makes the best pies. Is she here?"

Was it okay to lie? That hadn't really been covered in the training sessions. "She'll be here soon," Lark said. It seemed kinder. "Is it okay if I call you Alice?"

"That's my name. Alice." The old lady reached out for Lark's hand, her skin so thin and dry and speckled.

"Can I put some lotion on your hands, Alice?" Lark asked.

The patient didn't answer, so Lark decided it was okay. She always carried some, since she washed her hands so often at work. Now she took out the tube and gently rubbed it into Alice's little bony hands. She'd done this for Grammy, too.

"That feels nice, Mama," Alice said.

Lark swallowed again. "I'm glad." After the lotion, Lark just sat there for a while, watching Mrs. Fontaine sleep. The poor woman had barely eaten in eleven days, according to the notes, and had been refusing water. Her breathing had a catch in it, but wasn't exactly Cheyne-Stokes just yet, that pattern of erratic breathing that was a harbinger of death. But Mrs. Fontaine *looked* dead, that was for sure. Her skin was pale, her mouth open, and she was so still. Lark waited, watching her chest. There. Another breath. Another minute.

Lark wished she could stay till the end. Hold Mrs. Fontaine's hand until the last breath. Whisper something comforting that would help. As it was, she could only sit here and . . . well . . . just be. It was hard to wrap her brain around that. She couldn't do anything as a volunteer, and of course, with the patient's age and condition, there wasn't anything to be done. Just bear witness. Just be there.

She sang a lullaby, the same one she sang to Esme and Imogen, an old-fashioned song about flowers falling asleep and mouse babies curling up in their beds. She'd learned it, gosh, in second grade? A memory of a springtime school recital, Justin standing in the row behind her, flashed from the depths of her memory, and she held it gently, its realism and power dissipating even as she tried to keep it close.

The song had stayed in her head all week. Not just the sweet words, but that memory of Justin standing right behind her. It felt possible, though, for someone to be part of your DNA. Your cells. Imprinting so early and so deeply that you would never be apart.

"You going home, sweetie?" Luis patted her shoulder as he walked past her in the locker room.

"Yes."

"How was your shift?"

"Good! Actually really good."

He smiled. "Yeah, I like it here, too. What are you up to for the rest of the day, chica?"

"Dinner with friends."

"Nice. Have fun, honey. I gotta get in there."

It would not be fun. As if on cue, her phone dinged. She had a slew of texts she hadn't yet looked at, but this one was from Justin's mom.

Are you still free for dinner tonight? Heather asked.

Yes, of course. What time?

Five o'clock at the cemetery?

See you then. Love you, Heather.

She looked at her other texts, which always poured in on this date.

There were six photos from Addie of Esme and Imogen eating breakfast. Try to be happy just for a few minutes today, the text read. Love you.

A picture from Harlow, too—her dog, Ollie, looking at a seagull, being adorable.

Thinking of you today, sweetheart. Love you.

Winnie, Robbie and Dad had also texted. Last night, just before she'd left for the hospital, she saw that Mom had left a mason jar of peonies and a loaf of rhubarb bread on her steps with the simple note *I love you*.

She listened to a voice mail from Grandpop. "Hello there, young Lark, it's your grandfather speaking. I know this is a sad day, my dear. I think Justin would be very proud of you. I know I am."

Tears rushed to her eyes. Grandpop always knew what to say. He was perfect. She texted back and said she was doing okay and reminded him that she was cooking him dinner on Saturday. What did she have to do until five? Nap, hopefully. Shower. Pick some flowers.

One more text . . . Lorenzo. It was a link. Nothing else. She clicked, and there was a stunning halter dress in a deep, luscious pink. Silk with a low back, crisscross rhinestone straps, slit on one side . . . super sexy, but also really sophisticated. From the front, it was just a lovely dress, not formfitting, but from the back, it was a fuck-me dress in the best possible way. She scrolled lower to see the cost. Sweet baby Jesus, $2,000!

Three dots showed that Lorenzo was typing something.

Another link, this time to shoes in same shade of pink, but metallic. Three-inch heels. Eight hundred fifty dollars. And one more link . . . a beaded clutch bag. Frickin' gorgeous.

I see you have a great interest in women's fashion, she typed.

I don't want you to look poor and out of place was his response.

"What a kind thought," she grumbled, then typed, It's your money.

I'm well aware.

She sighed. Can we meet? I have questions and we should get to know each other a little more.

There was a long pause. No waving dots. With a sigh, she walked out of the locker room, slinging her bag over her shoulder.

"Lark?" Luis said, standing up at the nurses' station. "Good, you're still here. We have a code, two minutes out. Patient is elderly, no advance directives, so it's all hands on deck."

"Okay. Thanks, Luis."

Tonight, Naked Oyster, 7:30 p.m.

Apparently, the Naked Oyster was going to be their place. I have plans tonight. Sorry.

Then why didn't you say so? Tomorrow, same
time. Don't be late.

Rather than an answer, she just gave a thumbs-up, then ran down the hall, her fatigue melting in the rush of adrenaline. The patient was being wheeled in, barely visible on the gurney, a paramedic straddling her, doing compressions, and a panicky-looking man following close behind.

Dr. Unger was running the scene, getting the history from Anton, the paramedic alongside the patient. "This is Mrs. Almeida, age ninety-four. She collapsed at her rehab center forty minutes ago," Anton said. "History of dementia, atherosclerosis, stroke, breast cancer. Two milligrams of epi in the field with no response."

Ah. The patient was gone, then, but Lark knew they'd keep working on her. You didn't just pronounce someone without even trying, especially with a family member present. It was a commandment in Dr. Unger's ER.

"Mom! Mom, don't leave me!" said her son, who had to be close to seventy. "Please, Mom!"

"Dr. Smith," said Dr. Unger, "take over compressions, and Danny, work the bag."

"Bagging," Danny said.

"Taking over compressions," Lark said.

Shit. Compressions on a very old lady were akin to beating her with a baseball bat. It wasn't a request, though. Lark went to Mrs. Almeida and started, the Bee Gees' song "Stayin' Alive" immediately playing in her head, keeping her compressions fast and hard. She heard a rib crack and winced.

On TV or in the movies, CPR looked like nothing more than a brisk massage. In real life, to make blood flow through a still heart, you had to push so hard the whole rib cage compressed and expanded, and ribs often cracked under the pressure. It was brutish and dreadful for the patient, with about a hundred compressions a minute. Only occasionally did someone come back fully after CPR, and most of those people weren't ninety-four.

Lark herself had a DNR already in place. Most doctors and nurses she knew did.

"Give her another milligram of epi," Dr. Unger said.

"One milligram of epi going in," said Mara. It was habit, Lark had learned, for people to echo the order to avoid any mistakes.

A bead of sweat fell off Lark's forehead and onto the patient's chest. She could hear Dr. Unger giving the talk. "Your mom is very sick . . . we're doing everything we can . . . do you think she'd want this level of intervention?"

"Give her everything!" the son yelled, an edge of hysteria in his voice. "Save her! I don't care what it takes!"

"I understand, and we're doing everything we can," Dr. Unger said, his voice low and kind. "The problem is, I'm not sure we're helping at this point."

"Don't give up, Mom! Please, Mom!"

Another rib cracked under Lark's hands. *I'm so sorry*, Lark thought. The patient was so thin . . . if she had severe dementia, like Mrs. Fontaine, she might not have been eating much.

"Amiodarone, three hundred mil," Dr. Unger said. "Charging to one twenty."

"IV amiodarone, three hundred mil," Luis said.

"Stop compressions and clear."

Lark stood back, and for a second, silence fell over the room. Dr. Unger put the paddles on Mrs. Almeida's naked chest, which was bony and thin, her small, shriveled breasts barely visible. The charge made her body jump, but no pulse showed on the monitor.

"Again," said Dr. Unger. Another jolt. No response. "Continue compressions. Lalita, take over for Lark."

"Taking over, Lark. Good job." Lalita took her place, and Lark wiped her brow with her arm.

Dr. Unger looked at her. "Dr. Smith, would you mind speaking to the patient's son?"

She nodded, still breathing hard, and went over to the man. His face was stained with tears, and his eyes were too wide. Oh, God. This shouldn't be his last memory of his mother alive . . . not that she was. But research showed that it was better for a loved one to see that the staff was doing their best, to witness the process themselves, rather than be shoved into a room to wait.

"I'm so sorry about this, sir," she began.

"You have to get her back," he said. "Try everything. I'm not ready to lose her."

"We're trying, but her condition is grave," Lark said, putting her hand on the man's sleeve. "We're doing everything we can." She knew—everyone in the room knew, except the son—that the woman was not going to make it. The patient had been down for almost an hour now, and she had earned the right to die. But without advance directives, and with the son standing right there, CPR continued. "I'm afraid she's not responding, even though we're doing our best."

"I don't care about your best! I want her back! Mom, please!" There was a primal anguish in his voice, unguarded and raw.

Oh, it was wrenching, and on today of all days . . . Lark's eyes filled with tears. "I'm so sorry," she said, swallowing a sob. "There's nothing more we can do."

"Please don't give up," he wept. "Please."

On impulse, Lark put her arms around him and hugged him close. Was that against protocol? She didn't know. Didn't care that much, either. "I bet she was an amazing mom for you to love her so much," she whispered.

He clutched her hard, a desperately sad man on a terrible day, and she felt his whole body shake.

"Be a good son now," she said, "and let her go."

His grip tightened, and she felt him sob. Then he straightened and looked at her, and she gave a little nod.

"Okay," he whispered, wiping his eyes. "Okay. They can stop." His mouth worked, and then his face was suddenly calmer and so, so sad.

"Stop compressions," Lark said, taking his hand.

They all looked at the monitor, which showed a flatline. Mrs. Almeida's face was gray underneath the mask.

"Call it, Dr. Smith," Dr. Unger said.

"Time of death, seven thirty-four a.m." She squeezed the son's hand. "Why don't we go down the hall for a minute?" she suggested. "They'll tidy her up and you can see her again. Okay?"

"Okay," he said, his voice shaking, and she took his hand and led him to the family quiet room and sat with him as he wept.

Yes, his mother had been old and frail and her mind and personality had been eaten away by dementia. But she was his *mother*, and he'd never spent a day of his life without her in this world. That was absolutely worth crying about.

When Dr. Unger came in, the son was talking to someone on his phone, crying softly as he detailed what had just happened. Howard squeezed Lark's arm. "Nice work in there," Dr. Unger said quietly. "The kindness, I mean."

Lark wiped her eyes. "Well. Thank you."

"You're a human golden retriever, Dr. Smith. You make people feel calm and special."

She huffed a laugh. "That may be the nicest thing anyone's said to me."

"There's generally a moment when you kids go from being residents to being doctors," he said. "Was that today for you?"

She tilted her head. "Um . . . I don't think so. I think today was just my golden retriever moment."

"Well, it'll come. You won't have to ask yourself when it does." He smiled. "Hey. Give Heather and Theo my best, okay? Heather, um . . . posted about today."

Her throat clamped shut, and an awful thought came to her.

The Big Lie of her and Lorenzo had already spread through the hospital. What if . . .

"Dr. Unger," she said, swallowing, "you might have heard something about . . . um, my personal life recently."

"That you're dating Lorenzo Santini?"

Crap. "Yeah. It's very, um, casual and new and I'd rather not tell Theo and Heather anything until there's actually something to tell."

He looked away from his screen. "Got it." He paused. "Can't say I'd put you and Santini together, but maybe it's a beauty and the beast thing. Good luck all around." He smiled and turned back to his computer.

Napping had proved elusive. She thought about going to Addie's or stopping by the bookstore to see Harlow and Grandpop, but she wanted to be alone, too. So she got her bike from beneath the deck where she kept it and rang the little bell on the handlebars. Joy would still be sleeping, but Connery had a doggy door. Sure enough, he came flying through the yard and jumped up against her legs. "Want to take a spin, handsome?" she asked, scooping him up and putting him in the basket.

A nice long ride on the bike trail, a cute dog for company. She headed west, needing to fill the hours of the day. Down past Blue Willow Bakery, past Maurice's Campground, already full of RVs and tents, past the spot in Eastham that smelled like roasting coffee, courtesy of Beanstock Roasters. The sun was warm, and the bike path was filled with other bicyclists, walkers, runners and rollerbladers. On autopilot, Lark smiled and said hello to every single one.

She was grateful for the life she had, for her family, for her health. But she was sad, too. Seven years ago, Justin had died, the only boy she'd ever loved, and for seven years, she hadn't been able to shake this feeling that she was a ghost, too. Not really here. On the days when reality broke through, it felt like she was walking across a partially frozen pond, and every step had to be careful and deliberate, because if she thought too much about the icy water below, she'd fall straight in and drown.

She got off the bike path near Bridge Road and pedaled her way past the lovely old homes and bursting gardens to Boat Meadow, the prettiest bayside beach in Eastham. She had never come here with Justin. It was one of the best things about the place. No memories of the two of them here, nope. She sat on the warm sand and watched her little dog snuffle and run for the next hour or so. "Cute dog," someone would say, and she'd answer "Thanks!" That was about all she had room for today.

But she had to get back, of course. Took a shower, changed, kissed Connery's little head and then said "Go home!" and watched as he streaked over to the big house. Texted Joy that he was on his way.

The evening was painfully beautiful . . . June, just before the tourist season began in earnest. Already, Wellfleet was cheerfully busy. The Ice House and Winslow's had people sitting on their patios, sipping and eating. Tourists and locals alike walked down to the water, past her mom's gallery, to stare at or walk over Uncle Tim's Bridge. Lark drove carefully, throat locked, heart flopping in her chest.

Justin had been cremated, and Heather and Theo (and Lark) had buried some of his ashes in the Deans' backyard, where his old swing set had been. Some they'd taken out to sea to scatter in the bay, and some were buried here, at Pleasant Hill Cemetery, where there was a small stone marking his spot. Lark knew the way without looking; she visited at least twice a month. Cemeteries were beautiful in general, and this one was especially so. Sometimes, she'd bring a picnic, which felt maudlin but also appropriate.

After all, they'd loved picnics. For their engagement, the Deans had given them a splendid, high-end picnic basket, the kind where the forks and knives tucked into leather straps, and the plates were blue-and-white porcelain, the wineglasses sturdy. The Yorkshire Breakfast Hamper, such a ridiculous, over-the-top name. When she and Justin would plan a picnic, they'd ask each other at least five or six times, "Darling, do you have the Yorkshire Breakfast Hamper?" or "My love, would you like me to carry the Yorkshire Breakfast Hamper?" The last time she'd brought a picnic here, she said, "I hope you're noticing the Yorkshire Breakfast Hamper, honey," then surprised herself by the fury of the tears that followed.

She got to Justin's spot. Cape Cod rambling roses spilled neatly around the headstone, the daffodils and tulips now past.

JUSTIN EDWARD DEAN
A beautiful and courageous soul loved by all.

These words, while true, did nothing to capture Justin. What about his sense of humor? How good he was at listening, that intent expression on his face, the pause before answering? Where was the stuff about how dazed and befuddled he was every morning, like a chick who'd just pecked through its shell and blinked at this new thing called daylight? What about his intelligence? How about the way he'd cook and pretend to be on a cooking show, talking in a goofy voice as he narrated the steps? What about his beautiful hands and unexpectedly loud laugh? The way he'd narrow his eyes just before kissing her, as if he wanted to get it just right. Where was that, huh? Beautiful and courageous, loved by all . . . meh.

Heather and Theo were approaching, and Lark fixed her face. "Hey," she said, and her voice shook.

"Sweetheart," Theo said, hugging her. There were tears in his blue eyes, the same dark blue as Justin's had been. She swallowed hard and smiled (she hoped), then moved on to Heather, who grabbed her so hard.

"Oh, Heather," Lark whispered, hugging back.

"Hello, sweetheart," she wept. "You're so good to be with us."

"I wouldn't be anywhere else."

The three of them stood there, looking at the ground. It felt awkward and sad and ridiculous and forced. Seven years. No Yorkshire Breakfast Hamper today.

She had known Justin Dean for twenty-one years. Twenty-one. Someday, he would be gone for twenty-five years, and her life would tip into a new sphere, in which she'd be without him longer than she'd been with him.

"It doesn't get easier, does it?" Heather whispered.

"It gets harder," Theo said, reaching for his wife's hand.

"We miss you so much, Justin," Lark said, her voice breaking, and they all cried then, no toughing it out, no being brave.

Then, as they had for the past seven years, they went back to the Deans' house for a dinner of Justin's favorite foods—barbecued ribs, street corn, guacamole, hot dogs. A strawberry-rhubarb pie sat on the counter.

Once, when Justin was still alive, she'd made almost this same meal and packed it into the Yorkshire Breakfast Hamper. It was when they were in college, and they'd eaten till they were stuffed there on the Common, lying back on the blanket afterward. They'd held hands. At least, she thought they'd held hands, looking up at the sky. They probably had. Maybe they'd talked about baby names.

Or she was just making that up, false memories to soothe her broken soul.

We loved with a love that was more than love.

Damn straight, Mr. Poe. The man had known what he was talking about.

"How's the ER treating you?" Theo asked, and Lark stepped up with some funny stories. "Last week, we had someone come in during active labor," she said. "She didn't know she was pregnant. I mean, the baby's head was crowning, and she said, 'This can't be possible, I just went through menopause. I haven't had my period in, like, nine months.' And the kicker is, she was twenty-six."

"Oh, no!" Theo laughed.

"So lucky," Heather said, and Lark instantly regretted the story. A surprise baby for them—or for Lark herself—would've been very welcomed. As if in response, her abdomen cramped. She'd never have Justin's baby, and because Justin was an only child, his DNA would be gone when Heather and Theo died.

"But you'll go back to Oncology, right?" Theo asked.

"Oh, yeah. Definitely. This is just a temporary switch. It's so I can work on some . . . skills. Mostly in giving out information." Without sobbing. "In the ER, you have to be fast and clear, and my adviser thought it would be really helpful. But back to Oncology, yes, once this is done. I'm actually doing some hospice volunteering, too."

"Oh, God, you're an angel," Theo said.

"Lark, really," Heather said. "I've never met someone who knew so young what they wanted to do."

"That was all because of Justin," Lark said. "He was so . . ." Shit. Here came the tears. Again. "You two raised the best person I've ever known. He's the foundation of my entire life, even now."

"That means so much to us," Theo said, reaching for her hand. "You're part of his legacy, Lark. People in his shoes will be better off because of you."

"Are you, um, seeing anyone, Lark?" Theo asked, and Lark flinched a little. Heather was giving her an apologetic look, but it was part of the tradition of this day. The Deans would ask, assure her they'd be fine with that, and then sag in relief as she said no.

"No, of course not. I mean, it's just . . . I haven't met anyone I want to . . . get to know." Heather was nodding. How could anyone compare to Justin? No one could, and Heather knew it as well as Lark. Certainly, Lorenzo Santini wasn't a contender. "But guess what? I got the sweetest text from Grady Byrne yesterday. He wants to know what Addie, Winnie and I think about a ring for Harlow."

"Oh, how wonderful!" Heather said. "I just love your sister. And that store! Did I tell you I joined their Mystery Lovers Book Club?"

"Really? What are you reading?" she asked, and for the rest of the evening, she and the Deans sat and talked and tried not to look at the space where Justin should have been.

SIX

LARK, MANY AND MANY A YEAR AGO

Lark had always loved the term *puppy love*.

For one, was there anything cuter than puppies playing together? Of course not! And two, the thought of two puppies growing up together, best friends for life, having cute puppies of their own . . . perfection. She was repeating a family tradition—Grandpop had moved to Grammy's street when she was ten years old, and Grammy said to her sisters, "I'm going to marry that boy someday." And twelve years later, she did! They were married for more than sixty years, and they had loved each other so much.

Yes. People were too quick to dismiss puppy love. To say that it wouldn't last, it was just a crush, to chalk it up to adolescent hormones. *Who marries their first boyfriend, after all?* people said.

Lark had loved the idea.

Being an identical twin was the best thing ever . . . except when it wasn't. Addison was the outgoing twin, the star, the one who was funnier, faster, louder. She was the kind of five-year-old who simply sat next to someone and said, "I like your hair band. Let's be friends." By the second week of school, she was the queen of kindergarten. And Lark was proud, not jealous. Because they were twins, Addie's triumphs were hers, too . . . just not on the outside. Being Addie's sister made her interesting to her class-mates, but that was where Lark's popularity ended. Unlike Ad-die, Lark was shy, hesitant to intrude, worried that people might not like her or, worse, think she was Addison and then be disap-pointed to find she was not.

So, like any good lady-in-waiting, she attended to Addison, obeying her without question at lunch and recess, always near her, loving her and not minding a bit that she was in her sister's shadow. Except academically. Lark was more like their big sister, Harlow—bookish and a good listener, as her mother often told her. Addie was not. Addie had to protest, object, resist the small-est things so she could make her mark. If Mommy said to brush their teeth, Addie would say no, not yet. Or she'd pretend to brush her teeth, going so far as to wet the brush, spatter water, even eat a little toothpaste to have minty breath.

"Why don't you just brush?" Lark asked. "It's easier than fake brushing."

"Because I don't *want* to brush my teeth," Addie said.

The same was true in school. It wouldn't have even *occurred* to Lark to not sit down in story circle or do all the math problems (they were so easy, after all, and fun). Addie would sigh dramati-cally and say, "Mrs. Rogers, this is boring. Can't we do art in-stead?" or "I'm just too *exhausted* for gym, Mr. Carvalho. I'll be taking a nap in the nurse's office instead." Her classmates would laugh at her outrageousness, her boldness, her confidence. Lark would smile, full of admiration for her strong-willed sister, but she'd never follow her naughty example. She loved school, and was immediately put in an advanced reading and math program, which irked Addie. Sometimes, though she felt guilty thinking it, Lark was glad for the separation. It made her feel a bit more . . . free. Here, she could just do the work and be herself without Addie needing her, just for a little while. And she could have a friend or two who wasn't Addie's friend first, a new experience for her.

Justin Dean was one such friend. One of two, really, the other being Jordyn Rae, a girl who was cheerful and smart *and* had a golden retriever puppy she let everyone pet at pickup. Jordyn was friends with everyone, though, and when neither Jordyn nor Addie was available, Lark felt a little tremulous.

Justin Dean was one of the nice boys. The nicest, in fact. He always said hello and never chased or yelled or shoved. Then, in October of her kindergarten year, Lark sat at her desk as Ms. Ryan explained how all the clouds were made of water, and she felt her stomach roll and squish. Addie was home with a stomach virus, and Lark knew this was a bad sign. There was a bitter taste in the back of her mouth, and suddenly, she vomited all over her desk.

"Gross!" cried her classmates, leaping away from her. Brooklynne, the mean girl, laughed. Shame and bile burned in Lark's throat, and tears spurted out of her eyes as she kept her face down.

Ms. Ryan got paper towels to mop up the mess, and put her hand on Lark's head. "It's okay, sweetie. Justin, would you walk Lark to the nurse, please?"

Justin took her arm gently, and she stood up.

"Feel better, Lark," said Jordyn.

"Don't puke on me, you pukey puke-face!" crowed Brooklynne.

"Leave her alone," Justin said, and his voice was firm but not mean. He opened the door and guided her out. "It's okay," he said. "I always feel better after I throw up. Plus, you get to go home early."

Lark nodded but didn't look at him. At the nurse's office,

since her throat was too tight to speak, Justin said, "Lark threw up. You should call her mom." Then he looked at Lark, and she saw that his eyes were dark blue, like the sky just after the sun set. "I hope you feel better, Lark." He gave her a pat on the shoulder and left.

She felt her cheeks flush. Justin Dean had just transformed, right in front of her eyes, from a nice boy in her class, to . . . to someone she loved.

Daddy picked her up, which was better than Mommy, because Daddy was a nurse. Addie was already well enough to be at Grammy's bookstore for the day, and Lark hoped she, too, could have a day there. Daddy felt her forehead, then tucked her into bed and lined up all her stuffed animals at the foot of her bed.

"They're very worried about the patient," he said. "They're going to stay and keep an eye on her while she sleeps."

He gave her a sip of ginger ale and some Ritz crackers, and for a little while, Lark felt very special. Winnie peeked in at her with solemn eyes, and Daddy brought Robbie to the doorway so he could wave his chubby little arm at her before she fell asleep.

"I *knew* you were sick!" Addie declared when she got home. "I was reading with Grammy, and I felt sick, too, but in you, not in me. Are you better yet? We can stay home again tomorrow and play all day."

Lark didn't tell her family—even Addie—about Justin Dean walking her to the nurse. It was a secret glow in her chest, but she went over the memory of his hand on her arm, the way he held the door for her just like Daddy held the door for Mommy, the pat on her shoulder, the assurance that she would feel better. She had believed him.

When she went to school two days later, there was a card in

her locker. Flowers and a smiling sun drawn in crayon. She unfolded the paper and read the card. *I hope you fell beter. Ervyone feels sick somtimes. From Justin.*

When she lifted her head, he was looking at her, and she smiled. He smiled back, and there was that glow in her chest again. She hoped that if *he* got sick or hurt, she could walk *him* to the nurse and be just as nice to him as he'd been to her.

Justin had no siblings, which Lark found fascinating and exotic. She asked her mother if he could come play at their house, and he did. He was nice to Addie even though she was bossy. He played peekaboo with Robbie and made him smile, asked Winnie what her favorite color was and blushed when Harlow told him he had nice manners. Over Christmas break, his mother called her mother and asked if Lark would like to see the latest Pixar movie with them. Lark had never seen a movie without Addie and her parents present, and it was strange and thrilling to sit in the dark, sharing popcorn with someone not related to her.

In first grade, they weren't in the same class, but they talked at recess and lunch, Addie allowing him to sit at her table (at the end, but next to Lark). In second grade, they both had Ms. Murray, who had long red hair and was the nicest and funnest teacher in school. Addie and Jordyn were in Mrs. Harrington's class, so when it was time to pick a partner, she and Justin always picked each other.

In third grade, when the school had a talent show and she played Bach's Prelude in C Major, Justin wrote her a note saying he couldn't believe how good she was and that he bet she'd be famous someday.

In fourth grade, when Addison started sitting with Kaylee Doane on the school bus, Justin saved a place for her, and they'd talk quietly, shoulders bumping, sometimes sharing a snack. In fifth grade, they were buddies on the field trip to the New England Aquarium in Boston. As they stood in front of the coral reef tank in its mysterious blue glow, their eyes met for a long moment, and something passed between them, a kind of shared wonder, not just at the teeming life inside the tank, but at the feelings between them.

In sixth grade, Justin stopped coming to school.

One cold February day, he was absent. And the day after that, and the day after that, and then Monday and Tuesday and Wednesday. Every day that week when Lark got on the bus, his spot was empty. She sat on the aisle, as if he *was* there. If his family had taken a vacation, he would have told her, because they talked about everything. Mr. Dean's car was gone from their driveway, and Lark felt a hollow ache. Something was wrong. She knew it. No one in their class seemed to know where he was.

On the seventh day of Justin's absence, she asked Mr. Michalski, the science teacher, if he knew why Justin was out. His eyes were kind . . . and sad. "I'm afraid I can't tell you that, Lark," he said. "But maybe one of your parents can call Mr. or Mrs. Dean."

She told Harlow she'd be getting off the school bus at the gallery and would walk home later. Harlow said okay—she knew Lark was worried, and also that she was responsible enough to walk home alone. She was twelve, after all. The second Lark ran into Long Pond Arts, she said, "Mommy, you have to call Mrs. Dean. Something's wrong."

Mom did call. "Hello, Heather!" she said in her chipper phone voice. "It's Elsbeth Smith. How are you?" There was a pause. A *long* pause. Then Mom's face changed, the smile sliding off like ice cream melting in the sun. She looked at Lark, then took the phone into the office and shut the door, leaving Lark alone with her mother's paintings and the sharp smell of oil paint.

When she came out, Lark could see tears in her mother's eyes. "I'm sorry to tell you this, honey, but Justin has leukemia. He's at the hospital in Boston, and his parents are with him."

Her insides clenched like a fist. Lark often curled up with one of her father's medical books, since she liked science and thought she'd be a doctor someday, probably the kind that delivered babies so she could help her sisters when the day came. She knew what leukemia was. It was bad. "Will he be okay?" she whispered.

"Yes," Mom said firmly. "It's the kind with a really good cure rate. ALL, I think. And Dana-Farber is probably the best place in the entire world for someone with leukemia to be." She smoothed Lark's hair back, since her hair was slippery and always fell out of braids. "Maybe you could write to him. I bet that would cheer him up."

Instead, Lark ran home, asked Winnie to get off the computer and googled *ALL leukemia, 12 years old*. Mom was right; it was the "good" leukemia to get, with a 90 percent survival rate. Justin had had a nosebleed in January. At the class holiday party, he'd fallen asleep at his desk, and she'd gently shaken his shoulder to wake him up.

She wrote to him without even taking off her coat. A seven-page handwritten letter telling him how much she missed him; what was going on at school; how her little brother, Robbie, had stolen her favorite pen, so she'd gone out and bought him three of the same type, so he wouldn't have to steal anymore. She told him how much she'd loved babysitting little Isolde from down the street, and even though she was only twelve, Mrs. Schultz had asked if she'd come again. How was Boston? Did he have a nice room? Was he bored? Could she visit? She'd bring him brownies, the kind they shared at lunch sometimes. Then she went outside to the sunny side of the house, where the snowdrops had just peeked up. She picked one, pressed it between the pages of a fat medical book, and slipped it into the envelope.

After he got that letter, he emailed her. He was okay, sometimes pretty sick, but okay. He missed school and being home. She rode her bike to his house and took a picture with Harlow's phone, then to Marconi Beach, even though it was so windy, and took more pictures there. When she got home, Harlow showed her how to send the photos.

After that, they emailed every day. She continued to hand-write him letters so he'd get something when the volunteer came with the mail cart. They talked on the phone a couple of times a week, when he wasn't too tired or sick. He told her about the bone marrow biopsy and how much it had hurt, the spinal tap, the vomiting from his chemo, and she tried to hide the shakiness in her voice so he wouldn't know she was crying.

"I wish I could visit you," she said, three weeks after she'd sent the first letter.

"Me too," he said. "But I can't see anyone right now, except my parents. The chemo basically erased my immune system." He paused. "You could send me a picture, though. You know. Of yourself."

Addie chose which outfits Lark should wear, braided her hair, told her to smile and took a dozen pictures of her. Lark sent two, as well as other small gifts—shells from the beach, a sprig of pitch pine for him to smell, a bag of sand. She read about chemotherapy, stem cells and side effects, and peppered her father with questions.

When Justin's parents brought him home three months after

he'd first left, she visited him with the promised brownies and cried with relief at the sight of him, and he'd reached out and held her hand. He was taller, and thinner, and bald, the lack of eyelashes and brows making him look like a baby bird.

"I missed you, Lark," he said, and his smile was the same, so sweet, a little dimple just below the left corner. "Come visit again, okay?"

She did, every day, except for the week she'd had the sniffles and was afraid she'd give him something. For the rest of the school year and into the summer, she became a fixture at the Deans' house. Sometimes, Justin would be asleep, so she'd sit at the kitchen table, drinking tea with Mrs. Dean, or helping her make dinner. Her own parents were proud of her for being such a good friend and keeping up her grades.

The truth was, Lark loved it at the Deans'. The big, elegant house; the quiet; the ability to talk without interruption from her sisters or brother; the way Mrs. Dean asked her questions and looked at her as she answered, really listening.

It was different (Lark couldn't bring herself to say *better*) from the happy chaos of her own home, where Robbie was always torturing Winnie, and Addie was practicing makeup and hair, and Harlow was always trying to organize them to do their chores or homework, and Mom and Dad were scattered and busy and always coming and going. That was home, but this . . . this was wonderful, too.

"I can't tell you how much it meant to him, your letters, all the little gifts you sent," Mrs. Dean said. "If he didn't have a crush on you before, he sure does now."

Lark felt her face grow pink. "He's always been the nicest boy in school."

"And you're the nicest girl, Lark. You're a jewel."

Mrs. Dean ("Call me Heather") was so easy to talk to. She didn't work—Mom had used the words *trust fund* at one point. Their house was filled with beautiful things—a chandelier from Venice, a statue from Greece, a pure white couch that never got dirty. They didn't have pets, and their whole house smelled like oranges.

Justin was still getting treatment, and still weak and tired. Sometimes she'd sit by his bed or on the couch, reading to him as he dozed. She tutored him when he had the energy so he could catch up on all the school he missed. Mr. Dean had taken a leave from his job as an attorney, so if he drove Justin to his chemo appointment in Hyannis or a doctor visit in Boston, Lark would help Mrs. Dean—Heather—arrange flowers cut from their garden, or hang sheets on the clothesline, because line-dried sheets smelled like love, Heather said. At Lark's house, there wasn't enough time to hang out clothes, since there was a minimum of three loads of laundry to be done every day.

When Lark stayed for supper, she'd set the table with the cloth place mats and napkins the Deans used every night. After dinner, they'd all play Scrabble or Scattergories or Boggle, since the Deans loved word games.

To Lark, it was the kind of family she might want to have someday. Orderly, peaceful, friendly, thoughtful. They talked about serious subjects—politics, war, other cultures—and Heather and Theo listened to both Justin and her, nodding or suggesting an article they might read if they were interested. Lark learned that not only was Justin nice, he was eloquent and a deep thinker. Alone in his room or on a walk along the Cape Cod Rail Trail, which was flat and paved and not too much for him in his still-weakened state, they talked about what they hoped to do in the future, the friends they thought they'd keep when they started high school, their families.

By late July, the bulk of Justin's chemo was done, thank God, though he'd have to have "touch-ups" for the next few years to keep the leukemia from coming back. He had a 90 percent chance that he'd be just fine. Ninety percent was an A, Lark reminded herself, worrying over the remaining 10 percent. An A–, but still.

Then, one hot August day as they walked through the gentle trails of the Audubon center, where the Deans were lifetime members, Lark got up the courage to ask the question she had not dared ask yet. The sky was a stunning shade of pure blue, and birds warbled in the trees. The breeze off the bay was warm— thunderstorms were predicted for later with an ensuing temperature drop, and the smell of pine and salt marsh was strong and comforting.

"Did you ever think you were going to die, Justin?"

He stopped walking, frowning thoughtfully, looking out at the bay. His hair was just starting to grow back, and his eyes no longer looked so unprotected, since his lashes and brows had come in. He was achingly beautiful.

"I did, yeah," he said. "The first round of chemo was so hard, I almost wanted to. Everything hurt so much, even my bones. Maybe especially my bones, because, you know, my bone marrow had cancer. Even lying down hurt, and then I'd have to puke. Sometimes I couldn't even lift my head. I'd just throw up on my own pillow." He grimaced. "I had sores in my mouth all the way down my throat, and it hurt so bad to puke like that."

"Throwing up is how we first started being friends," she said, putting her hand on his skinny arm to let him know it was okay.

He smiled at that, and her heart swooped up like an osprey on a current of wind. "That's true." His face grew serious again. "The thing I kept thinking was, I couldn't do that to my parents. I couldn't die, because it would wreck them. But it hurt so much to be alive." He gave her a sideways glance. "That's when my mom would read me your letters."

Her eyes filled with tears, and she looked away, fast. "That's . . . that's good. I'm glad I wrote them."

"Me too." He leaned in and kissed her, a soft, sweet kiss, short enough that she didn't have to feel uncomfortable, long enough that it was utterly perfect. Her first kiss, age thirteen. Her first love with this gentle, quiet, kindhearted boy.

"Will you be my girlfriend, Lark?" he asked.

She smiled and bit her lip. "I thought I already was."

"You are. I just wanted to make it official." He grinned, then took her hand, and they kept walking, their conversation returning to their last year of middle school and what lay beyond.

When Mrs. Dean dropped her off later that afternoon, Lark ran into the house and pounded up to the room she shared with Addison.

"We're going out," she announced breathlessly.

"Did he kiss you?" Addie demanded.

Lark nodded. "It was . . . it was perfect."

Addie didn't smile. "Well. Okay, then. If it has to be someone, I'm glad it's Justin. Just don't forget about me. Twins first, everyone else, take a number."

Lark laughed and flopped on the bed next to her sister. She could feel her sister's jealousy as much as she felt her own happiness. She squeezed Addie's hand, reassuring her without words.

"Twins first," she echoed, though she knew that someday

soon, it wouldn't be true anymore. It *shouldn't* be true forever, after all. Someday, Addison would find the love of her own life.

Lark knew she herself already had.

Once they got to high school, the puppy love didn't fade. Instead, like a puppy, it grew in leaps and bounds. Everyone knew they were together—Lark and Justin, Justin and Lark. Larstin, Addie had dubbed them, still jealous but trying to keep it hidden, which Lark appreciated. It wasn't that Addie resented her for having someone; it was that she'd figured she'd have someone first. But she was gracious in her way, and Lark made sure to include her often, which served both of them well. Addie didn't feel left out, and Lark had a chaperone.

Despite their mother's frank and embarrassingly frequent talks about human anatomy and how babies were made, Lark still felt shy on that front. So far, she and Justin had just kissed. Justin hadn't tried anything else, and she was glad, because as flushed and taut as kissing him made her feel, she didn't want to rush anything. Their love was in its earliest springtime—snowdrops and crocuses just blooming. Giving in to impulse might have the same effect as a hard freeze, and something this beautiful, this new and fragile, should not be tampered with.

Their love was *perfect*. They could talk about serious things, and they could laugh together. He knew she cried easily for happy and sad reasons . . . when Grammy was diagnosed with cancer, he had simply held her and stroked her hair and let her sob, something she couldn't do at home, since *everyone* was sad there, and she didn't want to add to their burden. But Justin had plenty of room for her and all her feelings, which could overwhelm her sometimes.

When she was happy and proud—learning she was the top student of their freshman class, for example—he knew that after she blushed and smiled and accepted her classmates' congratulations, she'd need to cry to get out all that pride and embarrassment. She'd need to cry if Addie was mad at her, and she needed to cry when Harlow told the family she was going to college in Colorado, even though she was happy for her big sister. Sometimes, she cried just because she felt such intense love—for him, for Grandpop, for Justin's mother, for Amos, their creaky old cat who wouldn't be around forever.

Everyone else in her life hated when she cried. There was often a stampede to console her—Daddy, Harlow, Mom, Addison, and Robbie, who would cry along with her. Winnie would avoid her, because Winnie hated tears from anyone. Justin was the only one who understood that without crying, her feelings would make her pop like a bubble.

She was aware that most fourteen-year-old boys were not quite as remarkable as Justin Edward Dean. Oh, he wasn't perfect (though he kind of was). He got moody. He didn't vocalize his feelings until he was in control of them, which made him private and glum sometimes. He resented not being able to do sports (his parents forbade it), and he was a bit spoiled, not understanding that she *had* to babysit most weekend nights, and later work waiting tables, because she was saving money for college. Her parents supported them, and Grammy and Grandpop had put away a little nest egg for each grandchild, but college (and medical school) would be expensive. Smith family vacations were to Aunt Grace and Uncle Larry's house in Maine for one week of the summer. The two Smith cars were old and worn. The Deans went to Europe and Canada and Norway for their summer vacations. Heather drove an enormous SUV with heated leather seats, and Theo had more shoes than anyone Lark knew.

Justin preferred it to be just the two of them, though he accepted that Addison was going to be a significant part of their nonschool hours. Lark's circle was bigger than his—she had her siblings, Addie's group of friends, and Jordyn Rae, whose family continued to own the most beautiful golden retrievers, and who hosted the best sleepovers. Lark didn't want to be one of those girls whose entire social life was only with her boyfriend. At school, knowing from Harlow that she'd have to be more than just a good student to get into the best schools, Lark joined the Gay-Straight Alliance to support Addie and other LGBTQ kids, and the Green Club to make the school campus as ecologically harmless as possible, and kept up with her piano lessons, though Addie had since quit.

But, gosh, it was so wonderful, having Justin. She loved the dinners at the Deans' house, loved when her parents would invite Justin to go to the Land Ho! with all of them for dinner—the seven of them plus Grammy and Grandpop. Over the cheerful noise of the restaurant, Grandpop pointed out that he and Grammy had met young, as well.

"I never even *looked* at another girl," he said, and Grammy gave him a sweet smile. "Why would I? She's perfect! Keep this one close, young man," he said to Justin, putting a hand on Lark's head. "She'll never let you down."

She and Justin had looked at each other and smiled, even as Winnie said, "Stop trying to marry them off, Grandpop! They're fourteen!" Ever wise, Winnie. Ever cynical, even at eleven.

And of course, underneath their blooming, gentle love was the terror—that Justin's leukemia would recur. If he made it five years without incident, he'd be officially cancer-free at eighteen. Cured. For now, every bruise, every yawn put Lark (and his parents) on high alert. After the initial year of chemo finished, Justin went to Dana-Farber every three months, then every six, and each time nothing was detected, it was like God invented a new level of happiness. To celebrate, Heather and Theo always took Justin and Lark to the Mews, that beautiful, elegant restaurant in Provincetown, all of them giddy with relief. The staff got to know their reason for coming, and always saved a great table for them overlooking the water.

One year post-leukemia. Then two. Three. During the second half of the fourth year, Justin grew a little withdrawn and somber, waiting for each week to pass. As the five-year mark crept closer, each day was an eternity.

It was the only time they weren't in harmony, and it hurt her heart, seeing him shut down, staring at the floor, not telling her what she already knew. She wrote him little notes and tucked them around his room or put them in his locker. *I love you. You are my favorite person. Stay hopeful. The finish line is getting closer. I'm with you no matter what.* He didn't mention them, and even dinners with his parents were stiff and forced.

At night, she'd cry silently into her pillow until Addie snapped. "Stop planning his funeral already! At least wait till he's sick again, for God's sake!" Then her sister climbed down from her top bunk and got into bed with her, spooning against her. "Just go to sleep," she whispered, and Lark did.

Lark and Justin decided not to go to junior prom . . . well, he decided, which was fine. Except what if the cancer *did* come back? What if they never made it to senior prom? What if he died? What would she *do*?

And then, finally, in January of their senior year, Justin was cleared. He was officially in the 90 percent of kids with ALL who made it out just fine.

The next morning, the school held a secret assembly. All the teachers and staff and the entire senior class came to school early and gathered in the gym with balloons, the pep band in uniform, instruments ready. They sat in nervous silence on the bleachers until Mrs. Arrow, the school secretary, spotted Mrs. Dean's car. Justin was detained in the office briefly over some pretense so Heather and Theo could scurry around to join them. Then, over the PA came a voice. "Justin Dean, please report to the gym. Justin Dean to the gym, please."

A second later, the door opened, and there he was. The band burst into the theme from *Rocky*, confetti cascaded from the ceiling, and everyone cheered. Justin jumped; his mouth fell open. Then, realizing this was for him, he covered his eyes with his hand for a few seconds. Shook his head. Then he held up his arms to the class, as if in a prayer of gratitude.

Everyone went wild. He was *done*. He had beat it. He was finally unfettered from that insidious fear. Then Addie pushed Lark out from the front row, and she ran over to him, tears of joy streaming down her face. With those dark blue eyes laughing, he kissed her, right in front of everyone. Another huge cheer. "Justin! Jus-tin! Jus-tin!" their classmates chanted, and Heather was crying, Theo had his arm around the principal, and it was the happiest moment of Lark's life.

There were donuts from Hole in One and coffee from Dunkin', and everyone swarmed off the bleachers to hug Justin or clap him on the shoulder.

"You two make me believe in love," said Jordyn, grinning. "Seriously. The rest of us are like, ugh, so ordinary."

It was *glorious* to be ordinary. To have a boyfriend who no longer had to get chemo or check his lymph nodes or wait with grim patience to see if he would die or not.

"I'm really sorry I've been so . . . withdrawn," Justin said that night as they sat in his bedroom (door open, a house rule). "It's just . . . I kept picturing you without me, and it made me so sad, I couldn't bear talking to you."

"I understand," she whispered.

"I love you, little bird." It wasn't the first time he'd said it, but it felt different tonight. More adult, more mature, more meaningful . . . more *true* than ever before.

"I love you, too," she said. She kissed him with all her heart then, not the sweet, chaste kisses they'd had before now, but full-on passionate, long, deliciously wet kisses, and wrapped her arms around his waist. He got up and closed his door silently, and second base was achieved, his hands hot on her bra, slipping underneath the lace, her body limp and aching with lust, him on top of her, and it was all the hotter, knowing they wouldn't go any further. Not with his parents downstairs.

The rest of their senior year lit up like a Cape Cod sunset, dazzling with color and possibility. Freed from the fear of dying, Justin seemed to burst from his cocoon into everything Lark always knew he was—funny, smart, so kind, so good. And my God, so handsome. That sweet boy with the blue eyes had become a man who shaved every day and was suddenly three inches taller than he'd been the year before. The smell of him gave her a contact pheromone high, and home was wherever he was. He made his parents laugh till they cried, threw the baseball to Robbie, brought her mom flowers whenever he came over for dinner and told Addie she was his second favorite girl in the world. Even Winnie liked him.

They were prom king and queen. No one was surprised. On

Awards Night, Lark was named the second Smith child to become valedictorian and nabbed seven extra scholarships, courtesy of local businesses and organizations. She felt simultaneously stunned and embarrassed and sorry for the other students who didn't win, but Justin stood up and whistled each time Larkby Smith was announced by the speaker. By the end of the night, she had $13,400 more for college than she'd had that morning, just shy of the record set by Harlow three years before.

Lark and Justin had both decided to go to college in Boston. After all they'd been through these past five years, there was no way they were going to be apart. Half their class would be going to school in Boston, more or less. Why not? It was a great city, full of colleges and universities. It had the Common and Fenway Park, water views and history, the North End and the Freedom Trail, the Boston Pops and the Head of the Charles.

The plan to become a doctor had been cementing itself since Lark was little. Science and math were her strongest subjects, and she slayed the AP exams and the SAT. (Addison didn't bother taking them; she wanted to be an interior decorator.) Boston University gave Lark a solid work-study package, and between that, her scholarships and savings, the nest egg from Grammy and Grandpop and a modest student loan, she could swing it.

Justin would be at Boston College, where his dad had gone, with the plan of becoming a mechanical engineer. No need for him to get any scholarships, the lucky guy. Addison would be studying interior design online and was doing some modeling here and there. Being Addison, she had also landed a job as an assistant to a prestigious Boston interior designer, who offered Addie the use of a tiny, adorable apartment as part of the package. It was only a fifteen-minute walk from BU.

Home was just an hour and forty minutes without traffic

(which was silly, because it was Boston, and there was always traffic). Still, not that bad, and between Mom and Dad and the Deans splitting chauffeur duty, all three were able to go home pretty much whenever they wanted to.

Boston was big enough, small enough, far enough and close enough. It was a cozy city where you'd bump into someone you knew every day. Harlow had gone to college in Colorado, which Lark couldn't even imagine. Why live anywhere but Massachusetts? Aside from the long, gray winters, gritty and biting winds, wicked bad nor'easters and more and more frequent scorching temperatures each summer; despite the Massholes who did ninety on the Pike and never used their signals; despite the traffic in the tunnel, where you prayed chunks of the ceiling wouldn't fall on your car; despite the fanatical and sometimes violent devotion to the Sox/Bruins/Celtics/Pats; despite the Irish Mafia and rampaging drug problems, Boston was paradise.

The entire state was, she, Addie and Justin all agreed. They'd never leave the Bay State. The beaches, the fresh seafood, the beautiful small towns outside Boston, the gentle hills of the Berkshires, the bustling North Shore, the quieter South Shore and the magical Cape . . . it had everything.

That first year, Lark and Justin met up two or three (or five or seven) days each week, getting together for dinner or a walk, or one of them going to the other's campus to study as their feet entangled under the library tables, or lying in some ridiculously pretty spot outside, watching the leaves turn yellow and gold. Lark loved being able to touch him just for no reason, lean against him, hold hands. She'd known his hands since they were small, guiding her down the hallway to the nurse's office that singular day. Sometimes, they just looked at each other, no need to talk, their eyes shining with love, still a little stunned that after all these years, after all the changes of childhood and adolescence, after five years of cancer treatment, after the mini-dramas and changes of high school, they were still so right.

At the end of their first semester, Lark and Justin decided they were both old and responsible enough to sleep together. Justin booked a room at the Copley Square Plaza. And though they'd been friends since kindergarten, it was strange, stepping into that room. It seemed so . . . adult. So committed. Her heart nearly thumped out of her chest, and her fingers shook as she unbuttoned her blouse.

But when they got into bed, they just lay on their sides, facing each other, smiling. This wasn't a simple hookup. This was love, soft as velvet, strong and enduring as granite. How many people could say they'd met the One in kindergarten? Love and happiness—no, joy—bubbled inside her. They were both virgins, and still, it was exactly right. They'd been waiting years for this moment, and it was tender and thrilling and a little awkward, but awkward was fine, because it was the two of them.

"Sorry," he said as he leaned on her hair, making her yelp. "I'm new to this."

"You better be," she said back, and for some reason, that set them off into unstoppable giggles, which turned into sighs, which turned into hums and moans and whispers of love. It was perfect. Meant to be.

Afterward, they ordered room service, ate turkey club sandwiches and drank root beer, since they weren't yet twenty-one, and made love again.

"I think we're figuring this sex thing out," Lark whispered afterward, and there it was, that laughter, that abundant love.

College was wonderful. The classes were challenging and fun, and Lark made friends, though Addie and Jordyn Rae maintained their top-notch rank. Jordyn was at Suffolk University, so theirs was a happy triangle. It also took some of the twin pressure off Lark, knowing Addie had Jordyn and not just her. Lark's grades were stellar, the professors liked her (but told her to speak up more) and her roommates were nice people.

Sophomore year, Justin got an apartment, telling his parents the truth—he could study better without dorm life, and he wanted to be able to spend time with her. Already, he was declaring his commitment, and the Deans lectured them both about safe sex and committing too early, but they didn't protest, either. Justin had an inheritance from his maternal grandfather, so money wasn't an issue, something Lark couldn't quite imagine. She didn't move in with him, but gosh, it was so nice, those nights when they made dinner together, when she could study at his kitchen table or read in his bed, highlighting text and taking notes. It was, she thought, the way things would be forever.

During her junior year, Lark went to Rome for a semester. She missed Justin horribly, despite the beautiful architecture, appreciative men and confident women, the amazing food and abundant wine. But she was determined to have these adventures and not be joined at the hip, as her mother often worried. Addie came to visit, and they laughed and finished each other's sentences and analyzed Addie's latest girlfriend, then cried at the airport, both reassured that nothing had changed between them and sad that they had to part. Once again, she took to writing to Justin almost every day, signing the letters *Love from your little bird.* When he came to visit for spring break, she fell into his arms and sobbed with relief and joy.

It was fair to say she was no longer a puppy. She was twenty-one and had been with Justin Dean for most of her life. She'd never even had a crush on anyone but him. Some people were made for each other, like her parents and grandparents . . . and now, continuing that family tradition of perfect, drama-free love that grew with each passing year, Justin and Lark.

During that visit, they rented a tiny car and drove to see some more of the country. Florence was glorious, Milan sophisticated, but Venice . . . Venice took her breath away. They booked a gondola ride to go under the Bridge of Sighs at sunset, because legend had it that if you kissed at that time under that bridge, your love would last forever.

As the gondolier paddled along past the pastel-colored houses that lined the canals, singing, Lark looked at Justin. This beautiful man, his hair now thick and short, had filled out in the past few years. His smile still made her heart melt; she knew their love *would* last forever. At the exact moment they went under the bridge, they kissed, and the gondolier said, "Bravo, bravo, bellissimi amanti! Il primo amore non si scorda mai!"

First love is never forgotten. Lark smiled against Justin's lips and pulled back. The sunset lit up the sky, and when she pulled back, she wasn't surprised to see that he was holding a small velvet box. Sure enough, he dropped to one knee.

"I love you more than I can ever say, Larkby," he said. "We grew up together. Let's grow old together, too. Marry me."

She couldn't speak, her throat was so tight with joy, and tears spilled down her cheeks.

"Say yes, signorina!" said the gondolier.

Lark wiped her eyes, held Justin's face in her hands and kissed him. "Yes," she said. "Yes. Yes. Yes."

"You didn't even see the ring," Justin said.

"I don't need to."

"Well, since you're gonna wear it every day between now and a hundred, take a look and make sure you like it."

Of course she liked it. It was an art deco ring, the diamond set in white gold with sapphires on each side. Delicate scrollwork held the stones in place, and it was the prettiest piece of jewelry she'd ever seen.

Sure, they were young. No, they didn't have a single doubt. Not one.

Her mother was worried they were rushing, her dad cried and said he didn't want his little girl to grow up too fast. Heather hugged her and wept with joy, and Theo said he'd raised a smart son, and he was thrilled that Lark would be his daughter-in-law.

The wedding would be . . . someday-ish. They were in no hurry. Babies would come after she was done with residency. They were barely adults, and planning a wedding was a whole endeavor neither of them wanted at the moment. They were still in college, after all. A wedding could wait.

"We could just sneak off and get married at city hall," Lark suggested, but Justin said she deserved a beautiful dress and Addie as her maid of honor, Winnie and Harlow as her bridesmaids.

"Your parents would kill me if they didn't get to walk you down the aisle," he said. "I'd never do that to them."

After graduation, Lark got a job as a certified nurse's assistant—direct patient interaction was required for med school—and loved the work (if not the degrading pay). Being old-fashioned, she didn't want to live with Justin before the wedding, so she moved into Addie's adorable little place, wanting this last bit of unmarried life to be spent with her twin, even though she was with Justin at least a few nights a week. In her off time, she studied for the MCAT. She wanted to get into medical school somewhere local—Harvard, Tufts or Boston University so they wouldn't have to move—and they put off the wedding until she could know for sure.

Justin had a job at an architectural firm in the South End and would be starting off designing ventilation systems for large-capacity buildings. His parents bought a condo in Chelsea—"We're not trying to smother you, we just don't want to deal with the traffic!"—and had dinner with them two or three times a month. Lark went home to the Cape to keep tabs on Robbie and check in with Winnie, who was studying at Cape Cod Community College, not sure what she wanted to do for a living just yet.

While home, Lark would practice her nursing skills on Grammy, who was getting over some cancer treatments of her own (and doing very well). In the evenings, the Smith family would play rowdy games of Scattergories or try to beat each other at *Jeopardy!*, yelling answers at the screen. Harlow had just moved back from Colorado and was helping Grammy renovate the bookstore, and it was all just wonderful.

When she and Justin were at the Deans', it was quieter but just as fun. The four of them would have dinner and talk about the future—Heather was so excited to help plan the wedding, hinting that they should pick a date. She offered to contribute (by which she meant pay for everything). Lark envisioned a simple, family-only wedding in Wellfleet with dinner at the Ice House or Winslow's afterward, but she sensed she'd be having a pretty big bash. Justin was an only child, and the Deans wanted to go all out and would fund just about anything.

"After all," Heather had kindly said to Lark's mom, "you two were blessed with five kids. We only have Justin."

It was *very* generous, and it made Heather happy to take the reins. Mom made a few noises, but she didn't have the same interest in all things wedding that Heather did. Honestly, Lark didn't care what the wedding looked like. It would be beautiful, she had no doubt. For now, she just wanted to be in the moment.

Getting through college with a 3.98 had taken a lot of mental energy, and a lot of stress and exhaustion were waiting for her in med school. These early adult days, the "flower of her youth," as Grandpop said, felt so new and precious, and she didn't want to rush them. She and Justin had decided to work and save for her medical school for two solid years before marriage, then start a family later, unless a happy accident occurred. She knew one woman, a couple of years ahead of her at BU, who was currently pregnant and in med school, so it could work.

Not one of their former classmates was surprised to hear they were engaged. Lark heard many times that she and Justin were the fairy tale, that they gave those on dating apps hope, that they were what love looked like in real life.

"It's true," Justin would say. "The first time I kissed her, I knew. Then I had to wait seven more *years* to propose. It was hell."

"It wasn't exactly *hell*," Lark said. "But yeah, I was naming our kids in geometry." And they'd look at each other and smile, dazzled at their luck, brimming with happiness in the moment and hope for the future.

The months slid by in a happy rhythm. It was nice not to be in school, lovely to be able to go grocery shopping and plan dinners and study for the MCAT. The second year after graduation, they finally set a wedding date—December tenth, more than a year away. Heather hit the ground running, as promised, and first things first—wedding dress shopping. She made an appointment at a posh bridal salon in Boston, rented a limo to bring the female members of the family to Boston. The store was fabulously fancy, and it was just like one of those TV shows. Champagne was passed, and the consultant wanted to hear all about Justin and how they met.

"Kindergarten? Oh, my gosh, how romantic! We have to find you something to match that beautiful love story."

"I'll only wear it for a few hours," Lark said. "No need to break the bank."

"But it's special," Grammy said, smiling. She and Grandpop were picking up the tab on the dress, as she had promised to do for all their granddaughters, and Robbie's partner, if he ever got one.

Lark would've been fine with anything—just a nice dress, really, bought from a department store—but she didn't fight it, either. This was the first dress her *husband* would see her in. She would say her vows in this dress, and yes, it should be special.

And so she talked to the consultant about her preferences (simple, comfortable, not too intricate). Addie pawed through racks. Heather, Mom, Grammy and Harlow commiserated over how fast Lark and Justin had grown up, and Winnie stared into the middle distance, trying not to let her boredom show.

"Why don't we try some of these on?" the consultant said.

"Let's go, Addie," Lark said, because of course her twin would be in the dressing room with her.

The consultant had four dresses, plus two that Addison had liked. Addie unzipped the first dress bag, one that she'd picked out.

"Can I help her put it on?" Addie asked the consultant. "We're twins. This is special for us."

"Of course, of course. Let me know if you need me." The consultant smiled and left the two of them alone.

"I just want to say something," Addie said, her eyes filling with tears. Lark's, too, immediately welled. They reached for each other's hands simultaneously, gripping hard. "You're the best sister, the best person, in the whole world, Larkby. I love you with my whole heart, and . . ." Her voice thickened. "And if anyone deserves you, it's Justin. You'll always be my best friend. We're two halves of a whole. No one will ever change that."

"Of course not," Lark said. "Just because I'll be someone's wife doesn't mean I stop being your twin."

"I was here first, after all," Addie said with a watery smile.

"You were. And you were so *nice* in Mom's uterus. You always made sure I had enough room."

"And you always made sure I got enough placenta," Addie said, and they giggled and hugged and cried a little more. "Now stop crying, you sentimental idiot, and try this dress on."

Lark took off her flowery dress and stepped into the puddle of fabric. Addie gently guided it up, and Lark slipped her arms through the sleeves. Addie fastened the buttons on the back and fluffed the skirt.

"Oh," they said in unison, staring into the mirror. For a moment, neither moved. They didn't even breathe.

"This is the one," Lark whispered. "This is it. Great job, Addie." She hugged her sister, and it was hard not to sob with joy, with nostalgia, with love. The wedding wasn't for sixteen months, but suddenly, she could taste it—the simple, joyful constancy that married life would hold. Just like Grammy and Grandpop. Just like Mom and Dad.

The dress was a classic—pure silk with a wide neckline, three-quarter sleeves, a tiny bow at the waist, princess skirt. Grace Kelly would have looked quite at home in it. Lark had never seen herself look so . . . adult. So gorgeous, so much herself, and yet so much more.

"Well done," the consultant said, a little misty herself. "Let's go show the crowd."

Everyone gasped as she came in, and Mom burst into tears.

"Oh, Lark! My little girl! You're so beautiful!" They hugged, Lark's eyes streaming again.

"Well, that was easy," Harlow said. "I'm guessing this is one of Addie's choices."

"It is," Addie said proudly. "I know my sister."

A veil edged with satin ribbon, and that was that. Lunch followed, with lots of champagne and laughter and love.

There was a moment at the restaurant where Lark just looked at everyone—Mom, her sisters, her grandmother, Heather, all so full of support and love for her and Justin, their happiness, their future children, their entire lives. She was so *lucky*. So loved. If this was what the future held, her life would be incredible.

But the future, the hateful bastard, had other plans.

SEVEN

ELLIE

Babe? Everything good up there?"

Ellie jumped at her husband's words, as if *she* were the guilty one. "What?" Her voice was strangled.

"Did you find the lamp?"

"I . . . I . . . I did. Be down in a sec."

The air of the attic was stifling and dead, and for a second, Ellie felt faint. What was she supposed to do now? She sat frozen, then slid the iPad under a nearby box, picked up the lamp that had caused her to go into the attic in the first place, and came down the rickety, pull-down ladder.

"Got you, hon." Gerald's hands were at her waist, and he took the lamp from her. For a second, she wondered if she'd just hallucinated that whole thing.

"So this is the lamp your mom's got her panties in a twist about?" he asked.

"Yeah. I know. Um . . . hey, I have a wicked headache. I think I need to go to bed."

"Yeah, you sound a little off," he said. "Want some Motrin? A cold cloth?"

"No, no, I'm . . . I'll just sleep in Harlow's room."

"Want me to rub your shoulders or anything?"

"No. Thanks, though. Good night." She paused. "Um . . . sorry." Then she hated herself for apologizing. Without further thought, she went into Harlow's room and closed the door.

"I'll let you sleep in."

"Okay," she called through the closed door.

"Love you."

Another pause. "Love you, too."

Three hours earlier, she'd come home to their ramshackle house, not minding the disemboweled lawn mower in her parking space. Barely noting the broken parts of the fence. Idly thinking she'd like to weed the flower beds. As she opened the door, Gerald was pouring her a glass of wine, bless him, her thoughtful, handsome husband.

They had indeed sat on the deck, as promised, and talked about their days. Gerald had cut down a branch that overhung their property line, and was quite proud of himself, detailing the exchange he'd had with their backyard neighbor. She told him about the wealthy couple who'd sneaked out of the gallery when she'd gotten a call. He grilled chicken, she made a salad. They talked about the kids . . . Robbie wanted to go deep-sea fishing on Sunday, and Gerald thought he might tag along.

"That sounds very manly," she said, smiling. "Go ahead. Have some father-son time."

It was only after she'd cleaned up the kitchen and was about to sit down and add a few things to the gallery's Instagram that she remembered the lamp. Her sister had texted her over the weekend, asking if Ellie knew about an old lamp from their grandparents' house that their mother suddenly *had* to have. Ellie did have it; Mémé had given it to her when Ellie had moved into her first apartment after college. It had a carved wooden base with a creamy porcelain shade painted with violets. She'd put it up in the attic when Robbie was about six, since the child seemed to break everything. Aside from smiling every time she saw it up there, Ellie didn't use it, though she'd been meaning to put it in one of the empty bedrooms. But if it would make Mom happy to have it again (and if that meant Mom would stop torturing Grace), fine.

Their attic was the kind with the pull-down stairs, which screeched as she extended them. Up the narrow ladder she went, the air hot and stuffy. Someday, they were going to put in central air-conditioning, which would mean using this space, and probably reinsulating up here, which would then require a new roof. It seemed like a big project, and Gerald was not exactly a strong closer. Case in point: the lawn mower in the driveway was celebrating its second month in that spot.

She pulled the string for the light, and there was the lamp in a cardboard box in the corner, next to the old rattan rocking chair with the tattered back. She picked it up now and sat on the chair, the painted porcelain shade smooth and warm under her hands. Ellie felt a fond pang for her grandmother, a plump, white-haired woman who'd always smelled like lemons. That lamp had been a little hint of gentility in Ellie's otherwise grungy first apartment.

Then something caught her eye. There, almost under the chair runner, was Gerald's iPad. He'd been searching for that thing for *months*. Why on earth had he been using it up here? The attic was freezing in the winter, unbearably hot in the summer. The only light up here was from the bare bulb. She smiled as she reached for the device. It always made her feel triumphant, finding something that was lost. It was a mother's superpower, after all.

As she picked it up, the screen lit up. Battery hadn't run down yet, then. Without thinking, she typed in the password—their anniversary. They both used it on all their devices. Not exactly original or safe from hackers, but really, who'd want to hack them?

The screen showed Facebook messages, which was odd, because Gerald didn't have a Facebook page. So whose messages were these? She set the lamp down for a better look.

A blue balloon read, I do miss you, but I have to stop. I love my wife and I don't want to make a huge mistake. I'm sorry.

The gray balloon below it said, I can't believe you're just going to throw this all away. Please, please reconsider. There were no further messages.

That was from Camille Dupont. Weird. Ellie didn't know anyone by that name. She didn't think Gerald did, either. Could these be someone else's messages?

Her legs suddenly felt weak and wobbly. *Don't look*, said a distant voice in her head. But no, already her eyes were roaming around the screen. She wasn't terribly familiar with personal pages on Facebook, since she didn't use hers much. But there, in the upper-right-hand corner, was a picture of Gerald.

It was a nice picture. A picture that, if you expanded it, would show Ellie standing right next to him, both of them smiling. It had been taken at the family picnic last summer. But in this image, Ellie had been cropped out.

So her husband *did* have a Facebook page. *Gerald R. Smith, member since last year.* He'd posted three times, all shots of the water—sunset over Mayo Beach, the autumn colors over by the kettle ponds and a storm rolling in on the ocean side. That was it. No photos of the kids or grandkids . . . or her. The biographical information listed him as a graduate of Nauset High School and Boston University. He was married. Was friends with twelve people. No one she knew. Wait. Jack Farraday, that name was familiar. He'd been a high school buddy who used to live in Orleans. She and Gerald had met Jack and his wife (Karen? Caroline?) a few times way back when. But the Farradays had divorced years and years ago, and they hadn't stayed in touch. Luis Gonzalez, right. A fellow nurse from Gerald's hospital days. Otherwise, no one she knew. None of their kids. Not his cousin, Cynthia. Not his own father, who had quite an active social media presence.

Ellie had a page for the gallery, of course, but that was all. She *was* on Instagram for work, and also so she could see what the kids were up to from time to time . . . mostly Addison posting pictures of the girls, which made that platform worthwhile. Otherwise, she generally posted and left.

Back to Gerald's messages. Jack Farraday had said, Hi, Gerald, how's the fam? I live in Florida now! You should visit. Great fishing!

Gerald had replied, Everyone's great. I've got three grands now, can you believe it? Glad you're doing well. No further chatting.

Otherwise, just messages from this Camille Dupont person. There were so many balloons. This didn't . . . this didn't make sense. Hands shaking, she clicked on Camille Dupont's picture and came to the woman's page.

Camille was attractive. Long, straight brown hair, artfully highlighted; a big smile. Good makeup, probable Botox or just excellent genes. She was *pretty*. Here she was in Times Square with a female friend. On horseback in Wyoming. She had gone to Bali. She did yoga. Gerald missed and cared about her.

Ellie stood up fast and took a step back, as if she could walk away from the knowledge, and hit her head on a beam. She barely noticed.

On September twenty-fourth of last year, Camille had reached out to Gerald. OMG, I can't believe you're finally on social media! How ARE you, Gerry?

Gerry. The very first time she'd met him, he'd introduced himself as Gerald, and she'd called him just that. A week later, he told her he hated being called Gerry, and appreciated that she used his full name. She had never, ever thought of him as Gerry. His parents never called him Gerry. His coworkers didn't, either.

But *Gerry* had reached right back. The words blurred, and between the stifling air up there and the vise that seemed to be crushing her chest, Ellie thought she might faint.

Then he called out, and she stuffed the iPad under the box and went down the stairs.

Was she dreaming? She was happily married, right? But the iPad . . .

All night long, as Ellie lay in Harlow's old bedroom, her brain bounced away from what she had found—those messages she had read, the ones she hadn't yet. *I must have misinterpreted something. There has to be a mistake.* It felt as if millions of tiny bees had made a home under her skin. She couldn't hold a single thought, since too many were banging at the door of her brain. Then something mundane and irrelevant would appear. Had she asked Meeko to repaint the back wall? She had, right? Was she supposed to babysit Esme and Imogen this Saturday, or next? Wait. Hold on. Had Gerald *slept* with that woman?

This couldn't be real, could it? It was almost like waking up from a dream . . . a dream that had lasted her entire adult life . . . only to find that she wasn't a wife, a mother, an artist. To find that she was washing dishes in a Waffle House on a bleak secondary highway in Tennessee or Kentucky, and all that happiness, all that love and security, was as ephemeral as fog.

Obviously, she didn't sleep.

The next morning, Gerald went for his usual five-mile run. The second she heard the front door close, she yanked down the attic stairs and retrieved the iPad. She'd take it to work, where she could read everything, then make a decision about what to do. Her mind was blurry from fatigue, and her whole body felt the sick buzz of adrenaline.

He would be gone for only about forty minutes. She threw on some clean clothes, grabbed her bag, stuffed the iPad deep inside it and headed for her car, tears of rage and anguish blurring her vision. Got behind the wheel, slammed the door and tore out of the driveway so fast, she nearly took out the mailbox.

Not an hour later, she had learned a lot.

At 8:43 a.m., Gerald texted to ask how her headache was.

Better, she replied.

Want me to bring you lunch today?

All set, thanks.

When Meeko got to the gallery at 10:12 a.m., she was already locked in her office. "I have a lot to do today," she said rudely. "Earn your keep and don't interrupt me unless there's a fire or a tsunami." She closed the door in his face, relocked it and grabbed her thermos of coffee.

Before today, she had loved her office, which had a skylight and a view of the courtyard. After today, it would be the place where she'd learned about her husband's betrayal.

She read and reread the messages till her tired eyes burned.

What was she going to do now? Confront him? She had to. And then what? Kick him out? She certainly wasn't going to live in the same house. He'd go to his father's. No, he wouldn't be able to stand that for more than a day or two, because he'd actually have to *do* things with Robert if he was living there. No. He'd go to Addie's, sleep in that beautiful guest suite and have more access than ever to their granddaughters.

That didn't seem fair.

No. Let him stay in their derelict house. *She* would go somewhere better with fewer responsibilities. Maybe he'd fix the fucking lawn mower with his extra time.

She could go to her sister's, but Grace's husband was a pompous ass. Her parents? Hell, no. The kids? Addie's guest room *was* truly beautiful.

Even if the kids would have her, it wasn't practical. Or fair to them, because they all loved their father. But she didn't have to tell them, did she? Even so, Nicole and Addie liked things a certain way, and that didn't involve a mother-in-law staying with them. Winnie shared a tiny house with a roommate; Robbie lived in squalor; Harlow was seeing Grady and would probably be getting engaged soon. Lark lived in that teeny little guesthouse, so there was no room even if Ellie asked.

Hold on. Lark's landlady, Joy . . . she had a *huge* house. And Joy was lonely, without family or many friends, if any. Ellie had noticed it, of course, the four or five times she'd met Joy. The woman adored Lark (everyone did, it was practically the law). That house . . . that sprawling, waterfront house, so beautiful only an out-of-towner could afford it.

Ellie grabbed her phone. She had Joy's number somewhere in here, from a time when she'd invited Joy to Christmas, yes, that was it.

"Hello, Joy," she said, her voice shaking. "I have a huge favor to ask, and you are absolutely free to say no."

Joy did not say no.

EIGHT

JOY

Joy Deveaux was getting a *housemate*. Well, a guest. She did not have the words to say how happy that made her.

For nearly a year, she had lived in this vast, beautiful house on the water—a stranger's house that technically, she owned—and for a year, she'd been so, so lonely. She had Lark out in the little guesthouse, and her tenant was amazing and beautiful and magical, like a unicorn that had wandered into the yard. But even Joy knew that, like a unicorn, Lark was a little unreachable, like if you looked directly at her, she'd disappear. What was that word, that fancy word that was so pretty but sort of magical? Something you couldn't pin down? *Ephemeral*? Yes. That was it. Lark was ephemeral.

But her mother was quite real. Joy hadn't really bonded with Ellie, though Lark had made sure Joy was invited to various holidays since they'd met. Ellie was so *accomplished*. Pretty and confident and fit, filled with busyness and security as a wife, mother, grandmother.

The idea that she needed Joy was bananas.

"You want to move in *here*?" Joy had asked when Ellie called just a little while ago, half a Hostess cupcake in one hand, the phone in the other.

"Yes. I know it's unexpected, but—"

"Yes! Of course! I would love that, Elsbeth! You can come right now! Which bedroom do you want? You can have your pick!"

"Oh, gosh, Joy, thank you. Thank you. I'll explain later." There was a pause. "Actually, if you're free tonight, I could come over around seven."

"Yes! Sure! Whatever works for you. See you tonight! I'll have wine." She hung up, stuffed the rest of the cupcake in her mouth and practically ran to the kitchen. She had plenty of wine, of course she did, she had a wine fridge, after all. Ellie Smith, coming here to stay! It was so exciting. There was some cheese, too. Ice cream. Pasta. Eggs. Aging lettuce for a salad Joy hadn't yet made. That was about it. Maybe she should order some food to be delivered. Did she have time to run down to Wellfleet Marketplace? She did. She'd go.

The Smiths were all so normal and healthy and fond of each other. The sweet old grandfather, the happily married parents, the healthy and employed children, the attractive, spoiled little girls. It was like watching zoo animals or something. Joy knew the invitations to Thanksgiving and Christmas Eve dinner were pity invitations, but she didn't care. It beat spending those wrenching firsts all by her lonesome.

And now Ellie wanted to stay with her. Gosh! It was like having Joanna Gaines ask if she could hang out for a while. Ellie was Wellfleet famous . . . she was an artist, of course, and a good one (well, *Joy* liked her stuff because you could tell what the picture was, not like those smear-and-splatter or white-on-white types of things her brother, Paulie, had loved). She was naturally attractive like . . . like . . . like, well, Michelle Pfeiffer, maybe. Then there was her husband. Those two had the kind of love that was in the *movies*. The kind that didn't look like Joy's three and a half marriages one single bit. (The half marriage was to Carl, who'd proposed, set her up in an apartment, supported and slept with her, but had a wife and family the whole time. Live and learn.)

Joy didn't even care why Ellie was coming. Maybe their house needed work and she was allergic to the smell of paint. Or no, that wouldn't be right, because she was a painter. Maybe dust? At any rate, Joy had four hours to get ready. Her housekeeper had just been in, so there were clean sheets and towels.

This was just so exciting.

She'd never had a true girlfriend. Only her brother, Paulie, and his gang. In a lot of ways, Joy had always been Paulie's costar, and that had been fine with her. Since he died, though, she wasn't sure who she was supposed to be.

As she reapplied blush and bronzer, adjusted her left eyelash and grabbed her giant Chanel sunglasses, Joy's heart was soaring. Someone needed her. Well, her house, to be specific, but still.

Joy had always been expected to follow in her mother's footsteps. Marry an overbearing, abusive little man; give up all your rights and freedom; have a few babies; steep in bitterness and fear but never call a divorce attorney because Jesus would hate that; and take all that misery out on your own kids. You'd think Mama would've wanted better for her own daughter. Not the case.

Joy—and Paulie—had wanted a better life even so. Not that Joy had ever been able to picture it. Her only plan was to be someone other than Gianna-Marie Moretti, the name she'd been born with. The truth was, she still wasn't sure what her life was supposed to be about.

She'd moved to Cape Cod on impulse, six weeks after she lost her brother so suddenly, unable to bear the familiarity of life without him. He had been her best friend, her only sibling, the other survivor from their awful childhood. When she did have a job, it had been in his salon. When she was with friends, they were his friends. She'd married his lover, for heaven's sake. Sweet Abdul, or Abe, as he asked to be called. Her favorite ex-husband.

Joy had bought this house on impulse without even seeing it first. Misery-scrolling through Zillow one night, she'd typed in *Cape Cod*. Seen this house, called the listing agent, offered a couple hundred grand over asking price. She had plenty of money. The house had come furnished and decorated. The only other things that were new were the bed linens and towels. One day, she was in their brownstone in New York; the next day, she was here, like Dorothy dropped into Oz.

It was awful. In her grief and befuddlement, she couldn't remember how to talk to people. She was fifty-eight, and without the most important person in her life. The first week had been murder, Joy crying almost nonstop, drinking wine at ten in the morning, ordering crap online for no reason. The second week, she went to the local pet shelter, adopted a puppy—a Cairn terrier mutt already named Connery—and then almost immediately regretted it. What did she know about dogs? Nothing. He ran around the house, barking, then peed on the kitchen floor, ate with such gusto that kibble flew, and wrestled with the curtains in the living room, tearing the bottoms to shreds. But that night, he slept in her bed, curled against her chin, his fur soaking up her tears of loneliness.

On Monday of Labor Day weekend, as the summer people left to return to their regular lives, Joy sat on the deck and looked out over the beach, so empty inside her heart felt like it was made of the thinnest, sharpest glass. Just two months ago, she'd had her brother. And not that long ago, she'd had Paulie *and* Abe and their beautiful life to share, their friends, their stories, their gossip and lives to enjoy, a delicious buffet that filled her up. Now there was nothing.

She was on her third martini (Smirnoff vodka poured into a glass, if that counted as a martini) when she heard yapping coming from the beach. Oh, goddamn it, the dog! She'd forgotten about him! What if he ran into the ocean and drowned or was eaten by a shark? Or a coyote? Or a bear? Were there bears on Cape Cod? She wasn't sure. You know what? If she got him back, she'd return him. All she did was clutch him and cry, anyway. The shelter had suggested puppy training, but Joy could barely make it to the little market in town, let alone focus on teaching a puppy anything.

She ran crookedly down the long wooden boardwalk that connected her property to the beach, twisted her ankle, kept going. "Connery! Connery, honey! Come to Mommy! Oh, damn it all to hell, Connery, please!"

There he was, racing into the surf, then yapping at the waves. "Honey! You'll get sucked out! Come back here!" Was there a ripped tide? Why did they call it that, anyway? Because it ripped you in half? Joy didn't swim. She didn't know these things. "Connery!"

Then she saw someone, a young woman with long blond hair, throwing a stick, which Connery chased and pounced on. "Hi," the young woman called. "Is this your dog?" She bent over and scooped Connery into her arms.

"Yes! Oh, God, thank you!" Joy said, teetering on her kitten heels in the sand. "Connery, I was so worried!"

"What a sweetheart he is," the woman said. She looked about twenty. "And he's so good at fetch. You love this stick, don't you, honey? Connery, you said his name was? That's so cute. You're a smart boy, Connery."

"He is?"

"Oh, definitely. I've been playing with him for about half an hour. I was going to start knocking on doors to see whose he was, but we were having a lot of fun." She smiled and handed the dog to Joy. "I'm Lark Smith," she said. "One of the Smith kids? My mom owns Long Pond Arts, and my sister owns Open Book." At Joy's blank stare, she added, "The bookstore?"

"Oh. Right." She was the prettiest person Joy had seen in real life.

Connery whined and leaned back toward the woman. Lark. Even her name was beautiful.

"I'm Joy Deveaux," Joy blurted. "My brother died two months ago, and I just moved here and I don't know anyone. I just bought this dog for company, but . . ." Tears rushed to her eyes, and she was horrified. "I'm still adjusting. My brother was my best friend." Mama would be disgusted at her, spilling her guts to a stranger.

"Oh no!" said Lark. "I'm so sorry."

"Would you come up to the house with me? I'm a little"— drunk—"unsteady. The fear, right? Are there sharks out here? I was so afraid Connery would run in the water and get eaten. Like in *Jaws*? The movie?"

The rest, as they said, was history. Lark came back to the house, accepted a glass of wine and sat in the living room with Joy, as Connery, now exhausted, curled on her lap. She was an intern, in her thirties (what skin-care line did she use?), still living with her parents. "Kind of hard to find a place on my own, and I don't have a lot of time to look."

"I have a guesthouse," Joy said immediately. It had come with the property, though the main house had five bedrooms. Joy had only looked into the tiny cottage once. "You could have it. For free."

"Oh, no, that's crazy. You could get a bundle, renting that." Lark smiled and petted the sleeping dog.

"But would they be nice? Would they like dogs? You could pay me something if you wanted." *Please say yes.* "Connery already loves you, and you could help me train him. I don't know anything about dogs."

"We had a dog growing up," Lark said. "I did love teaching him tricks. Mostly dumb stuff, like balancing a cookie on his nose and then flipping it into the air and catching it."

"We can share Connery, then," Joy said. "Joint custody. Please?" She looked at Lark, her pretty eyes and smooth hair. "Please say yes. I'll give you a break on rent if you can give me some Botox once in a while. And some filler, since you're a doctor and all that."

"That's way too generous of you," Lark said.

"You'd be doing me a favor. I'm . . ." *I'm not sure I can go on living this way.* "My brother was all I had. We were so close, and I'm . . . I'm lost without him. I'll leave you alone, I promise, but I'd be right here if you wanted company. Or food. Or to use the house or anything."

Lark looked at her then, and Joy saw something she recognized. Sadness. For all her smiles and prettiness, Joy had the sudden feeling that Lark was, possibly, a little lost herself.

She moved in the next weekend. Some nights, Lark would come in after a hospital shift and tell Joy about her patients, why she wanted to become an oncologist. She told Joy about Justin, and tears had streamed down both women's cheeks. "I'm okay," Lark said. "I mean . . . I'm not, but I am."

"I get it," Joy said. "I totally do. Come on, let's go get something to eat. My treat."

Besides her sweetness (and excellence at dog training), Lark was . . . how to think this without sounding creepy? . . . Lark was like a Pinterest board come to life. The smooth waterfall of naturally blond hair. Green eyes with a golden starburst around the irises. (Joy's eyes were brown, and there wasn't a lot you could do to romanticize brown eyes.) Lark was tall and slim and had a hearty appetite, and when she and Joy ate together, Joy watched, fascinated, as Lark scarfed down a cheeseburger without bemoaning the fat or calories.

But there was also a sense of fragility about Lark. Joy recognized that glued-back-together look. But on Lark, even grief looked beautiful. She was everything Joy had once wanted to be. Had been obsessed with being.

Joy had fought her physical self since the age of eight onward, both self-obsessed and horribly insecure. Joy didn't go to the mailbox or the operating room without a full face of makeup. She got her hair colored every four weeks, a manicure every ten days, a pedicure once a month, a spray tan every six weeks. She wore a peignoir around the house and didn't own a pair of yoga pants or sweats, thanks to her brother being the kind of gay man who thought women were gorgeous, glam and mysterious and should dress the part at all times. She had spent a fortune on plastic surgery and upkeep over the years, from her first nose job at age seventeen, forging her mother's signature on the consent form, Paulie driving her to the hospital and letting her spend the weekend at his apartment. Since then, Joy had lost count of the number of times she'd been under the knife. Boob jobs, lipo, butt lift, chin implants, eyelids, lip fillers, more lipo. The unfortunate result was that she now looked neither younger nor well rested . . . just like a woman who'd had a shit-ton of plastic surgery.

She bet Ellie Smith had never had a single procedure done in her life. As Joy hustled to and from Wellfleet Marketplace and flew through the house, trying to see it through Ellie's eyes, she couldn't help comparing herself with Ellie. They were about the same age, but Ellie . . . she knew who she was. Joy never had.

Joy remembered with great clarity the day her quest to change herself had started. It had been the summer before fourth grade. Her parents were in the bedroom, Mama crying, Daddy yelling. There were some thuds, which caused a sick, weak feeling in Joy's knees. She knew what caused those sounds, and no matter how often she heard them, it wasn't something a person could get used to.

She'd been on her way to sneak down to the cellar but stopped to grab some Oreos, since Mama hadn't made lunch. Unfortunately, she'd underestimated the length of her parents' fight, and her hand was in the package when her father was suddenly storming through the kitchen. She froze.

If only Paulie had been there that day to scoop her into his room or take her to the park or to the corner store. But he hadn't been. Joy's eight-year-old self felt her soul curl into itself like the injured dragonfly she'd tried to save last week. Whatever happened next would be bad. She knew that with her whole heart.

"Whaddaya standin' there for, huh?" Daddy barked, striding across the kitchen and grabbing her by the shirt. "You stupid or somethin'? And you're eating junk, of course. You're fat and ugly, just like your mother. Too bad you weren't a boy. Maybe I coulda had a *real* son if you had been. Don't just sit there, frog! Clean up the kitchen and do something useful for once." He shoved her aside as he left, slamming the door so hard a pane cracked, and it would remain cracked until the house was sold forty years later.

Gianna-Marie did not clean up the kitchen. Instead, she stood there, Oreos still clutched in her hand, as her father's words burned themselves on her soul. She knew to slip and slide around

Daddy, to try to be invisible and away and quiet. She knew that he was always angry at Paulie, though why, she had no idea, since Paulie was perfect. But until he'd said those awful words—*stupid, fat, ugly, frog*—she hadn't thought much about how *she* was. It wasn't like anyone told her she was pretty, of course. They weren't that kind of family. Until that moment, she hadn't thought too much about herself at all, really.

There wasn't a lot of room for anyone's feelings but Daddy's in the Moretti household—Gianna-Marie knew that before she could put it into words. Mama told Paulie and her to be quiet, to listen to Daddy, to understand how hard he worked, how smart he was. When Daddy was home, she'd coo and fuss and serve him, which kept him calm . . . until it didn't.

She and Paulie didn't talk about their parents. Daddy's parents, who lived on the third floor, didn't, either. When the fighting started, Nonna would turn up the TV, and Papa would leave the house. Her other grandparents lived in Brooklyn, and when they visited, they only talked in rapid-fire Italian. Kids were not invited into the conversation. Mama wore long sleeves even on the hottest days. If the bruises were on her face, the priest would ask how she was doing, and she'd glare at him. "Fine, Father. Just *fine*," Mama would say, and she'd sound almost proud. "It's nobody's business, that's what it is," she'd add to Paulie and Gianna. "We're a family. What happens at home is our business, and you two keep it to yourselves, you hear me?"

That day in the kitchen, Gianna-Marie became suddenly aware of how *disgusting* she was. She went into Paulie's room, since he had a full-length mirror on the door of his closet. She ignored Mama's quiet sobs from the bedroom. Experience had taught her not to knock on the door, because Mama would just yell at her.

What she saw was dark hair on her legs. Bulging calf muscles, fat upper arms that jiggled, like Nonna's. Her neck was stubby and fat, and her stomach bulged like there was a baby in there. Daddy was mean, but he was also right. She did look like a frog. So what if she was the best kickball player in third grade? So what if Sister Noreen praised her for getting a B+ on her math test?

Why couldn't she look like Paulie, who took after their grandfather? Paulie was *beautiful*. He was skinny. His black hair was thick and curly, not frizzy, his brown eyes coppery and clear with long lashes that every woman loved. Women fawned over Paulie, and he flirted right back.

Moments after her father crushed her soul, Gianna-Marie went on her first diet, one of the hundreds she would undertake during her life. That weekend, she asked Paulie to walk her to the pharmacy, where she stared at shampoo and conditioner.

"Don't get that stuff," Paulie said when she reached for a bottle of Breck shampoo, handing her a bottle of Lustre-Crème instead. "This is way better for your hair. And get the cream rinse, too. Also, Gia . . ." He dropped his voice. "You should probably start shaving your legs." He made a kind face, and Gia felt weak with relief that he was so *nice*. "And your arms."

By puberty, Gia, or Joy, as she called herself outside the house, was religiously saving for a nose job. Paulie gave her skin- and hair-care products for her birthday and Christmas (on the sly, of course, because Daddy would have a fit that his son knew so much about feminine beauty). The two siblings had an unspoken agreement that Paulie's advice and expertise would be kept from their parents, and in exchange, she'd cover for him on the nights he told his parents he was on a date with a nice girl from New Brighton (or Livingston or Great Kills . . . these imaginary relationships tended not to last). When Paulie joined the NYPD, Daddy said, "Finally I got something to be proud of with my kids. About fuckin' time."

"Yes, I'm a police officer now. And I don't know if you know this, Dad, but domestic violence is a crime. Mom doesn't have to press charges for you to get arrested."

There was a stunned silence at the table. For a second, the world trembled, and hope bloomed like a million white flowers in Joy's chest. Finally, *finally* someone would put their horrible father in his place.

"You ever say *anything* like that again, you can kiss your mother goodbye," Daddy hissed. "You think she wants to see her faggot son making a scene? Right, Anna?" He turned and glared at their mother.

"You watch your mouth, Paulie," Mama said. "You don't know nothin' about anything."

Those white flowers shriveled and turned brown. Paulie looked at Joy, and his eyes were so, so sad.

So nothing changed on the home front, except Paulie wasn't around. Her father continued to beat up her mother, and everyone ignored the violence and bruises. Joy sequestered herself with a fictional world—TV movies, magazine covers, where the citizens were blond girls with blue eyes, straight noses and pink cheeks, or Black girls with flawless skin and perfectly straight teeth. Thin arms, tiny waists, flat stomachs, trim thighs . . . things Joy had never experienced. At night, she pinched the flab around her abdomen mercilessly, wishing she could just cut it off with a knife. Mama's cooking and Moretti genetics eradicated any weight loss she achieved by drinking cabbage juice or eating only iceberg lettuce for five days straight.

Stupid. Fat. Ugly. Too bad you weren't a boy.

Paulie was the only one she could talk to. Though he'd never said the words out loud, the fact that he was gay was like the sky being blue. He lived in the West Village, never invited his parents to his apartment, visiting them on Staten Island only on major holidays. But he did invite *her* to the Village. All his friends were men, and they *loved* Joy, told her how fun she was, admired things about her that she'd never have thought were attractive.

"You have such a kind soul," said one of the friends, and Joy was in shock. Did she? Well, *that* was a nice surprise!

"Honey, I could stare into your eyes all day," said another, sighing. "If I was straight, I'd marry you so fast."

The nose job made her look more like Mama, especially with the bruises under her eyes. Her grandmother told her she was a vain whore, her father said, "For fuck's sake, Gianna! Why you wasting your money?" and her mother, always backing him up, said, "If you think that makes you pretty, you're wrong."

Finally, high school ended. First order of business—get out of her parents' house. Getting a job that could cover rent and everything else she wanted . . . she wasn't that naïve. Instead, she went to LaGuardia Community College and looked for a boy who'd marry her.

Husband number one: Frankie O'Dell, a nice Irish Catholic boy who couldn't take his eyes off her 42E breasts. His family owned an auto parts store—they were well off, in other words. She let him kiss her, let his hands wander, told him they should wait to get married. When he protested and seemed like he might be losing interest, she let him rid her of her virginity. Afterward, she mentioned that her father might be connected to the Mafia (he wasn't) and would kill Frankie if he found out.

The next day, Frankie bought her a sizable diamond ring,

dropped out of college and went to work at his dad's store in sales. Joy started working at the register. College had served its purpose. The wedding night was not awful, though she had to let Frankie see her naked, something she'd been able to avoid in the back seat of his car.

"Hon, you're beautiful," he said, making her roll her eyes. At least sex didn't hurt this time. Frankie wanted kids right away, but Joy said no. Not until she had some work done. O'Dell's Auto Parts was a good business, and Frankie made enough money for plastic surgery if they didn't buy a house and lived in his parents' basement. Besides, she'd probably like sex more if she liked her own body, she argued. If he loved her, he'd understand. He was no match for her single-minded determination. She was going to change herself with or without him.

First surgery—tummy tuck with liposuction on her thighs and arms. The pain was staggering and lasted for weeks, and the bruising was hard to look at, but she *was* smaller. Not thin, not svelte, not yet, but better.

"Oh, my God, you look amazing," Paulie had said when she hobbled up the stairs to his apartment. "Joy, you're beautiful!"

But now her breasts looked even more ridiculous, so six months later, she had a reduction, bringing her down to a 38C, as well as more liposuction on her thighs and ass since it was before the days of Sir Mix-a-Lot praising big butts. Her parents said nothing, if they even noticed. Her mother-in-law, a stern Irish woman, had correctly guessed Joy was using her son, and barely spoke to her.

Oh, well. Joy wasn't done. Oh, no. Not by far. Early tech laser hair removal on her upper lip, cheeks, hands and forehead. It hurt like a son of a bitch and left her face red for days, but it was worth it. She took makeup lessons from one of Paulie's friends, who was a drag performer. It was the age of "more is more" in plastic surgery, and boy, did Joy want more.

When she told Frankie, three years after their marriage, that she wanted cheek and chin implants, he put his foot down and said no, it was time for kids. If she didn't agree, maybe they should get a divorce.

Divorce it was. She'd been flirting with a client at O'Dell's—Carl, who owned a used car dealership, one of O'Dell's biggest clients. She had a feeling he'd be happy to pay for plastic surgery for a sweet young thing such as herself. She was only twenty-two, after all. Carl's wife didn't put out, and his kids were spoiled and disrespectful, "like their mother," he told her. He gave Joy a diamond ring (a carat, not bad), told her he was filing for divorce and rented her a nice apartment near the ferry, so she could pop across to Manhattan to see Paulie and his crowd whenever she wanted. And yes, he gave her a generous allowance, which Joy had no problem spending on more procedures.

When Carl inevitably dumped her to stay with his wife, Joy quickly found another man, an actual husband this time. George was twenty-seven years older than she was; they dated for two months before she became his fourth wife. He owned a construction company on Long Island. Immediately after the honeymoon, she got two more plastic surgeries (butt lift and another breast reduction with implants this time, to make them "perkier," by which the plastic surgeon apparently meant "like two cannonballs lodged under your collarbone"). George was pleased, anyway.

Then came the night when he came home all coked up, told her she was a whore and punched her in the face. Unlike her mother, it was one and done. She called Paulie, who came over, beat the ever-living crap out of George and promised him a very short life span if he ever came near her again. Paulie took her to his apartment for a month. George put fifty grand in a Swiss bank account for her . . . something he and Paulie worked out. As a cop, her brother knew pressing charges would probably result in nothing substantial, not back then.

When Paulie was about forty, he retired from the NYPD and opened a salon, which had always been his dream. Joy was so proud of him. He put her to work as a makeup artist, which she enjoyed, and between what she got from her two divorces, she had plenty. She had a second tummy tuck, an eyelid lift and surgery to give her dimples. Her lips were plumped with the first fillers on the market.

Still, she saw that eight-year-old girl when she looked in the mirror. Fat. Frog. Ugly. Stupid.

But she had Paulie. His friends, his clients, a job in his salon, an automatic invitation to any party he was hosting or attending. She didn't seem to be able to make female friends, though. Her own mother and both her grandmothers operated in some Italian cone of silence, and it had rubbed off. It was okay, she guessed. She only needed her brother, and with him, she was her best self—funny without trying, sometimes without even knowing; pretty, accepted, kind.

She changed her name legally—she'd changed it both times she was married, but now chose her own name—Joy Eloise Deveaux. It was very glamorous, she thought, and far, far away from that sad little girl she couldn't seem to shake. Paulie approved.

Then one summer day, a limo was rear-ended by a cab in front of the salon. Paulie invited the driver and his passenger into the air-conditioned salon as they waited for limo number two. The passenger's name was Abdul. Joy had been working that day, and it was just like the movies—the meeting of the eyes, a charge in the air, a sense of wonder and potential. That second limo took the driver away, but Abdul and Paulie went around the corner for dinner.

Abdul—Abe, he immediately asked to be called—was handsome, well educated, funny and surprisingly down to earth for a man whose wealth literally could not be measured. He was . . . oh, what was that word? When you can't stop thinking about someone because they're so great? *Captivated.* That was it. Yes, he'd been captivated by Paulie, the gay former cop turned salon owner and hairstylist with so many friends. He loved talking to Joy, asking questions about Paulie and her as if they were aliens from a very charming planet he'd only read about.

Paulie had always dated, but he'd never been in love. Not until now. The two men couldn't keep their eyes off each other. Abe had an apartment in the super-luxe St. Urban, where his family occupied several floors when they were in town. Every time he was in New York—at least once a month—he took Paulie, and sometimes Joy, out for dinner, sometimes buying out the entire restaurant, sometimes picking up a few pizzas from around the corner, a novel experience for him.

"I can't believe how much I love him," Paulie said one night when the three of them were out for dinner at Jean-Georges, reputedly the most expensive restaurant in Manhattan. Abe had gone to take a phone call, and Paulie's eyes got shiny as he spoke. "I have never, *ever* felt like this before. I didn't even know I could. I mean, you're basically the only other person I've ever loved, Joy."

"Aw, honey," she said, tearing up herself. "Well, you know, he's lucky, too, because you're amazing, Paulie." She didn't even feel jealous.

The problem was, Abe was deeply closeted, way more than Paulie had ever been. Paulie had simply not discussed his sexuality with their parents. Abe—Abdul Hamza Mohammed al-Fayez—was from Saudi Arabia, a culture where being gay could be punishable by death. The pressure for him to marry a woman was mounting from his conservative parents—Abdul was thirty-nine and had been ducking and dodging marriage for years. They were getting suspicious. His family business, whatever it was, did plenty of work in New York, and his mother had started tagging along on Abdul's trips, not letting her son off the leash of family obligations . . . and cutting into his free time.

The three of them were sitting in Paulie's apartment in the Village when Abe admitted this, wiping his eyes. "It's getting harder to get away," he said. "I hate to lead you on, Paulie. I just don't know how much time I can realistically spend with you. Last night, my parents introduced me to a girl they want me to marry. She's nineteen! It was horrifying." Paulie put his arm around his lover, both their faces awash in misery.

"What if *I* married you?" Joy suggested, looking at her nail polish. The neon pink had been a mistake. Should've gone with red. She glanced up at the two men. "Would that work? I mean, I'm forty-four, so probably no kids, plus I can't say I really want any. But would that get your parents off your back?"

Paulie and Abe looked at each other, eyes wide with hope.

Within a month, it was done. Abe set up a trust for her, bought a four-story town house right on Washington Square Park—"I am nothing if not rich"—and had the first-floor apartment completely redone for Joy. He and Paulie would live on the top two floors, with one for guests in between them, for privacy.

It was with glee that she and Paulie visited their parents with the news. Dad, who was unabashedly racist, was furious. "You think I'm gonna watch my daughter marry some—"

"You're actually not invited to the wedding," Joy said. "Neither are you, Ma. Just figured you should know my new last name is gonna be al-Fayez. Oh. And I'm really, really rich now." She and Paulie laughed all the way home.

Their wedding was the only time Joy would meet her in-laws, who didn't speak to her, only glared. The ceremony was at city hall, to cover the shame of their son marrying a white, twice-married, older woman. Joy smiled back. Let them fume. Abdul loved her brother, and if Joy was a prop, who cared?

It was the happiest time of her life. She had plenty of money to keep on chipping and melting and slicing away at herself, and both men thought she was wonderful no matter what. They avoided Staten Island as much as possible, opting not even to go to their father's funeral when he died from a stroke, which infuriated their mother. Oh, well.

The years slid past in a luxurious, happy blur. Joy still did makeup a few times a month, usually for a bride or a C-list actor. Paulie and Abe included her in nearly everything. When Abe traveled, it was just her and Paulie, and that was great, too.

Sometimes, though . . . sometimes Joy wondered if there was more to life. She didn't have a lot of ambition to do anything, really. She tried various things over the years . . . Abe bought her a luxury apartment so she could flirt with interior design, but once she'd bought sequined throw pillows and an orange range that cost $100,000, she lost interest. Besides, there were an awful lot of wealthy women in Manhattan who considered themselves interior decorators. Getting a client was harder than she'd thought. She tried a lifestyle blog in the days before Instagram, but didn't get much traction, and she often forgot to post.

It was fine. She was very lucky in so many ways. She shouldn't want more than what she had, even if she did feel like a costar in her own life.

But then, horribly, Abe sat them both down one night, more than a decade into their marriage, and announced that he was leaving them. He'd been traveling more and more the past two years, and the pressure to marry a Muslim woman and become a father finally broke him. The cost of secrecy was too high. He missed his parents and sisters, and yes, maybe he did want children after all. He was sorry, but he couldn't do this anymore.

Paulie was broken. Furious. He screamed and threw things, their father's temper finally showing itself, then fell to the floor, sobbing.

Of course, Abe gave Joy a generous settlement, including the town house, but it wasn't the same. A devastated Paulie moved to the second floor because it was too painful to stay in the home he'd shared with the man he loved. Within a month of their divorce, the *New York Times* Vows section informed them that Abdul married a Muslim girl twenty years his junior. A year later, they had a son.

"Guess he got what he wanted," Paulie said bitterly.

His light dimmed without Abe. He tried, going on mindfulness kicks, talking about purpose and gratitude, but Joy could see the truth. He was a whisper of the man he'd once been. That was what love did to you. It ruined you. Once upon a time, she'd loved her parents, and all they'd given back was anger, resentment and disappointment. She'd used Frankie O'Dell without a thought to his feelings, breaking his heart, maybe. She'd loved Abdul as a cherished friend, but he blocked her number the day he made his announcement. Paulie's, too.

Love was . . . what was the word? When something eats away and destroys something? Corrosive. That's what it was.

The only person she was sure she loved was her brother.

Then, one summer day, Joy was walking home with a pair of shoes she'd probably never wear, and a strange number came up on her phone. She answered, her hands tingling with premonition.

"Hello, I'm looking for Joy Deveaux," said a deep voice.

"Speaking," she said.

"My name is Ralph Colchek, Ms. Deveaux. I'm a chaplain at Mount Sinai Hospital. I'm afraid I have some very bad news."

Suddenly, Joy was sitting on the gritty sidewalk, tearing her hair, extensions coming out by the fistful, rocking back and forth as she wailed. Just like that, the deep voice at the end of the phone shattered her life.

Paulie had been riding in a cab on his way uptown. A crane toppled off a building and crushed the car he was in. The driver was unharmed; Paulie died instantly, and with him went Joy's whole world.

She gave him the send-off he deserved with a Michelin-starred chef making all his favorite foods, a live band, disco ball, a fog machine, huge flower arrangements and balloons. There were eleven speeches that she counted—she wasn't able to talk herself, since her throat was locked tight. More than four hundred people came (though not Mama). Even Abe came, sobbing as he hugged her. He had five children now. Paulie was toasted repeatedly, and Joy drank and drank and ate and cried. Paulie's friends were wonderful, said how much Paulie had loved her, reassured her that they were here for her.

But they weren't. Or they tried, maybe, but it didn't touch her gaping fear and aching loneliness. Hence the house on the Cape. It would be different, at least. It wouldn't be soaked with reminders that she had once been Paulie's sister, and without that title, she wasn't anything anymore.

Maybe Paulie had sent her Lark. He would have loved Connery. And now Ellie was due in just fifteen more minutes.

Judging by Ellie's shaky voice, Joy had the feeling that once again, she was needed.

NINE

LARK

"Hi, Lark!" said Chloe as she and Lorenzo went into the Naked Oyster. "It's so nice to see you again."

"Hi, Chloe! How are you? How's your garden doing?"

"Great. Loving this sunshine. Thanks again for stopping by with those tulips a few weeks ago. That was the nicest."

Behind her, Lorenzo growled.

"Do you have a reservation for Dr. Satan?" Lark asked innocently.

"Come this way, please, Dr. Santini, Lark." Chloe grabbed the plethora of menus and led them to the same table they'd sat at the first time.

"I guess this is our place now, huh?" Lark said as she sat down.

"Brian will be right over," Chloe said. "Enjoy your dinner."

"Send Brian over now," Lorenzo said. "I don't have time to waste."

"Tell Brian I'll protect him," Lark added. "Lorenzo, you seriously have the worst manners. Didn't your mother or Noni teach you better than that?"

"They did not."

"Well, allow me. We say please, and thank you, and excuse me. It shows people you respect them."

"Why would I respect a waiter or some twit who passes out menus?"

Lark stiffened. "Because they're humans with brains and hearts and feelings and histories and friends and families. You might be surprised at how interesting people can be if you'd stop trying to prove how superior you are."

"I don't need to prove anything."

"My God. You're horrible." She almost smiled. "So smart, so gifted with a scalpel, so unpleasant with fellow humans."

Brian appeared. "I'll just have club soda with lime," Lark said.

"Tap water, no interruptions," Lorenzo said.

Brian started to leave, but Lark grabbed his arm. "Hold on, Brian, I think Dr. Santini forgot to say something."

Lorenzo glared. "No, I didn't."

"Yes, you did." She glared back and didn't let go of Brian's arm.

Lorenzo rolled his eyes. "Tap water, *please*, and *please*, no interruptions. Thanks."

Lark gasped with feigned delight. "See? Wasn't that easy, Lorenzo? Brian, I'll have . . . oh, the Kobe burger, please. Medium rare. Thanks. And, Lorenzo? What would you like?"

"Nothing. You had questions, this is a convenient spot, let's get this over with."

Lark looked at the menu. "He'll also have a burger."

"No, I won't. I'll have six oysters, the roasted chicken and asparagus."

"Don't forget to say please," Lark said.

He stared at her, unamused. "Please," he said after a beat.

"You got it, you two," Brian said. "And I'll be totally cool about not interrupting."

"Thank you," Lorenzo growled.

"You get an A for effort," Lark said. "An F for sincerity, but it's a start."

"Why did we have to meet again?"

"Because we're dating, Lorenzo," she said.

"No, we're not."

"We're coconspirators, then, making you feel less alone at your family events and giving your sweet grandmother the impression you've found happiness."

"Accurate. And after the wedding, we never have to speak again."

"Which I'm really looking forward to," she said. "The never-speaking part. By the way, you said Noni was on hospice, right?"

"Correct."

"How is she?"

"Fine."

She waited, but he said nothing more. "I just got approved to be a hospice volunteer. In case you need anything."

"Why would I need anything from a volunteer? I'm a doctor."

"As am I. But neither of us works in hospice, do we? I'm volunteering there, so let me know if you need me to do anything for your grandmother." He failed to acknowledge her words. "Anyway, Lorenzo," she went on, "about this fake relationship. Your sisters both texted me separately, then started a group text, and we're all having drinks on Sunday."

"Oh, for God's sake, why?" he asked. "That's not necessary."

"Right. But they're nice, and I'm nice, and when nice people meet, they often want to spend more time together, enjoying each other's company. It's called friendship."

"They're not your friends."

"Friends in the making," she said. "Anyway, I thought maybe

we could change tactics here. I feel bad lying to your siblings. Can we tell them? They're so nice, and—"

"No. I'd look ridiculous."

"Wouldn't they understand, though? You're doing it to make Noni happy?"

Another eye roll. He was going to detach a retina if he kept this up. "They *wouldn't* understand, and it would become fuel for mockery, gossip and speculation, which is what I was hoping to avoid by asking you to be my . . . whatever you are. Besides, confidentiality is part of our agreement, Dr. Smith."

"Yeah, about that. My whole family knows." He sighed with immense irritation. "I told you I wouldn't lie to them. For what it's worth, my grandfather and brother are totally into it."

"This is an arrangement between colleagues, Dr. Smith. Your benefit is professional. Mine is personal. Although I think it's fair to say you'll also benefit personally, if people think you're dating me."

She managed not to snort. "Yeah, okay. But if Sofia asks me to be a bridesmaid—"

"You'll decline."

"I was kidding." She took a sip of water. "But don't be surprised if I'm asked. I've been in ten wedding parties so far."

"Why would you *want* to be friends with my sisters? Don't you have enough of your own? How many friends do you need? Are you trying to prove something by the sheer number of them? Do they fill some empty hole inside you?" Irritation flew off him the way water flew off a dog after a bath.

"That's very insightful. Yes, friends do fill an empty hole in me," she said calmly. "The only difference between you and me is that I know there's something missing. You don't."

"Possibly because nothing is."

"Oh, there is, believe me, Dr. Satan. It's not normal to be so . . . aggravated all the time. Especially with your family."

"Family is the *best* place to be aggravated."

"Why? What's wrong with yours?"

He spared her a glance. "My brother is about as deep as a puddle," he began. "His hobbies include eating tacos and watching baseball."

Nothing wrong with that. They lived in Red Sox Nation, and who didn't love tacos? "He volunteers with Big Brothers Big Sisters, too."

Lorenzo's head snapped up. "Is that true? How do you know that?"

"How do you *not* know that?" She sipped her club soda; Brian had slipped them their drinks like a ninja. "Your mom told me."

"When?"

"At your *house.* That's what happens when people talk." Especially when women were clearing up after dinner. Anita had seemed very intent on listing the qualities of each of her children, which was awfully sweet. For Lorenzo, she'd said, "The hardest-working, smartest guy on the East Coast," to which Sofia had retorted, "Don't let him hear you say that, Mom! You have to say North America!" and they had all laughed, but not unkindly.

"Anyway," Lark said, "I get it. You don't have a lot in common with your brother, that's clear. But your sisters—"

"Sofia is marrying a man with limited earning potential and will probably have a baby within the year. She has no goals outside of that. Isabella *could've* been a doctor, and took the easy way out by becoming a nurse."

"I should tell every nurse in New England you just said that, then stand back and watch them come for you."

"She's smart enough. Just too lazy."

"You're the first person on earth to have called a nurse lazy. Maybe she wanted to actually take care of patients, not just stick her head in the door, read the nurse's notes and make decisions from there."

"At least she should get her APRN." He paused as Brian returned with their dinners, and looked up and said "Thank you" so sharply that Brian nearly dropped her burger. Thankfully, he did not. The lad shot her a sympathetic look and melted back into the restaurant.

She took a bite of the incredibly delicious, perfect burger and closed her eyes. Had she had lunch today? No. Half a granola bar in between patients. "So your relationship with your family isn't great. Why is that? I need to know if you want them to think we actually spend time together."

He took a joyless bite of his chicken and chewed. "I wasn't raised at home," he said. "My parents, who like to think of themselves as devoted and adoring, shipped me off to school when I was seven. I stayed with my grandmother. Alone. She did the bulk of raising me."

Okay, that was grounds for being on edge, even if Lark thought he should maybe be over it by now. "Why did they do that?"

"There was a school for gifted boys. Noni lived in Brookline, the same town where the school is, so my parents had me live there."

"St. George's?" she asked.

"Yes. How did you know?"

"I used to go running there. Beautiful campus." It was an institution, St. George's, all the boys wearing uniforms—blazers with insignias and shorts, knee socks, British-style. The school had produced at least two Nobel Prize winners, a dozen members of Congress, a surgeon general and probably a member of SCOTUS. "Did you like it there?"

"The school was fine."

"And you're obviously close to your grandmother. It doesn't sound like a Dickens novel. More like Hogwarts."

"Yes. But at the time, it felt a lot like . . . abandonment."

Lark's heart lurched. She pictured a little blond boy staring at the family car as it drove away. Sleeping in a room by himself, no chatter or company from his siblings, just the quiet. The pressure and strangeness of a new school. Coming home to one person and one person only after having had two parents, a brother and a sister or two.

She reached across the table and put her hand over his. "I'm sorry," she said. "That must've been really hard. And confusing."

He withdrew his hand. "It sent a message. The expectations were different for me. I was being groomed, almost, to be the success I am today."

"Groomed?"

"Yes."

"Maybe 'given special opportunities' is a better way to think of that." She ate a french fry. "Do you feel like a success?"

"Would you like to see my W-2?" he returned.

"I'm not talking about money, Lorenzo. Your dad, for example, is also successful. He has a loving wife and four children and seems like a very happy man. You don't have to see an income statement to know that."

"Easy to be happy when your son buys you a house, pays for vacations, covers the tuition of your daughters, pays for your mother's care and can, at any moment, give whatever else is needed. Of course he's happy. Wouldn't anyone be happy in those circumstances?"

Wow. A *lot* of bitterness there. "There's a saying my mom brings out once in a while. 'You're only as happy as your least happy child.' Maybe your father wishes things were different between the two of you."

"Maybe he should've thought about that before he sent me off, then."

She nodded. Patted his reluctant hand. "I get it," she said. "They gave you advantages, but there was a price. It makes sense that you're hurt."

"I'm not *hurt*, Lark," he said. "It's just how things are."

"You ever talk to him about this stuff?"

"No. Of course not. I've never talked to anyone about it." He glanced sharply at her, a little startled.

"Until today," she said with a small smile.

He started to speak, stopped, then said, "You won't tell anyone about that, will you?"

For the first time, a little humanity sat like a baby bird between them, fragile and afraid. "Of course not."

"Thank you."

"You're welcome." She smiled again. "Well, I guess I just wanted to let you know that I really like your family, and your mom wants the Santinis to meet all the Smiths. She wants to throw a picnic."

"Never going to happen."

She laughed. "Okay, Dr. Satan. Do you want dessert?"

He narrowed his eyes a little, and then, somewhat miraculously, allowed a small smile. "No. But you go ahead. I don't want to deprive you of the pleasure of running up the tab as much as possible." He looked at his phone. "And I like watching you eat."

Okay, then. That . . . that might've been a compliment. At least, it was an admission that his time with her wasn't all agony.

"Molten lava cake," she told Brian. "Two spoons, okay? Just in case Satan here changes his mind."

She was starting to understand why Lorenzo Santini was so emotionally strangled. That poor little boy. No matter how smart he'd been, how glamorous the school, she bet it had hurt, being sent away from his parents and little brother, infant sister. Then to have Izzy born while he was in school . . . well. It was hard to imagine. When Robbie had come home from the hospital, they'd all been obsessed with him. She and Addie had been six at the time, and Lark used to sneak out of bed and stand beside his crib, reaching through the slats to touch his little hand.

Getting to know people was one of Lark's favorite things to do. And eating out in a nice restaurant with a handsome guy . . . that wasn't awful, either. It had been a really, really long time.

She pulled into Joy's driveway, a little surprised to see her mother's car there. She saw the lights were on, so she ran up the steps to Joy's door, knocked and went in. "Hello?"

"We're in here!" Joy called. "Your mom and me!"

Lark went in and saw her mother curled up on the white couch, Connery in her lap, a bottle of wine on the table.

"Hi, honey, how was your day?"

"Good! Is everything okay?" She looked at both women, who seemed quite relaxed, but there was a box of Kleenex next to Mom, a few wadded tissues next to her that Connery was eyeing for a snack. "Have you been crying, Mom?"

"Just feeling emotional today," Mom said, taking a sip of wine.

"Everything is great," Joy said. "Your mom's going to be staying here for a little while. Isn't that fun?"

"Why? Is something wrong?" Lark asked. Mom and Dad were *never* apart, not willingly. Mom would occasionally go stay with Aunt Grace for a night, but that was only twice a year or so. Less, even. "Where's Dad?"

"Dad's home," Mom said. She didn't look at Lark.

"And . . . um, why aren't you with him?"

"There's some work that needs to be done there," Mom said. She took a sip of wine. "There may be something wrong with the septic system, and . . ." Her voice squeaked, and she coughed.

"And who wants to be around all that shit, right?" Joy supplied, squeezing her mom's hand. "Have a drink, honey," Joy said. "How are you?"

"I'm good, thanks." Lark got a glass, poured a little wine and sat down. She'd never thought Mom and Joy had hit it off, and while a staycation at Joy's was unexpected, it was also a little . . . sweet. On the surface, the two women had nothing in common. Joy was still fully made up, though it was after nine, and wore a green and blue caftan, five or six rings, two necklaces, bracelets, little kitten-heeled slippers with poufs on the toe. Meanwhile Mom's hair was in need of a brush, and she wore faded blue cotton pajamas.

"Were you on a date with your fake doctor?" Mom asked.

"Real doctor, fake boyfriend," Lark said. "And yes. Dinner."

"Lark says he's very handsome," Joy said to Ellie.

"That is true," Lark said. "And it was actually a little fun. Not him. Just . . . this. Doing something different." Mom looked at her intently.

"Being in a couple, even if you're not really in a couple," Joy said. "Ellie, did you know I was in a fake marriage? Well, the marriage was real. And we did love each other. But not *that* way. He was my brother's lover. This was my third husband."

"Oh! Wow. There's a story," Mom said. "You'll have to tell me sometime."

Lark waited for Mom to pick apart her arrangement with Lorenzo, but instead, Mom just stared into her wine.

Joy reached across and patted Mom's shoulder. "I'm so glad you're here, Ellie. We'll have so much fun."

Something wasn't right with this picture. She waited a beat, but neither Joy nor Mom said anything else.

"Well," said Lark. "I have to get to bed. My shift starts at seven." She stood up, kissed her mom, then gave Joy a hug. "Connery? My place or yours tonight?" The little dog leaped into her arms. "Guess I have custody till the morning, then. Good night, ladies."

Maybe it was a trick of the light, but she thought she saw tears on her mother's cheeks. "You okay, Mommy?" she asked from the doorway.

"Just fine, honey. Just fine."

TEN

ELLIE

O kay, she's inside," Joy said, peering out at the guesthouse. "So you found the iPad, saw that he was messaging her, and then what?"

Joy had been nothing but wonderful from the second Ellie had walked through the door four hours ago. To her horror, Ellie had burst into tears. She never cried! All the suppressed rage and fear and shock and hurt erupted out of her the minute Joy said "I'm so glad you're here!" and Ellie found herself leaning on the counter, sobbing.

Joy hugged her against her substantial chest, made sympathetic noises and showed her to her room. "I figured something had happened when you called," she said. "I'm sorry, hon."

Hon. From a woman she barely knew. Joy was an oddity—this flamboyantly dressed woman with huge false eyelashes and heels who rarely was seen anywhere but the market. She'd been included at the holidays—Lark had told them she didn't have family—but she and Ellie had only exchanged pleasantries.

Ellie managed to get out a strangled "Thank you, Joy," but Joy waved it off.

"Take a bath, get in your jammies and I'll make us a charcuterie board. I can't cook much, but I can slice, and I loaded up on cheese and stuff at the Wellfleet Marketplace. I also got chocolate, just in case. Take your time, honey. If you want to talk, sometimes it's easier to tell a stranger, and if you want to keep it to yourself, no hard feelings."

It felt like she was in a dream . . . . a horrible dream set in the prettiest room she'd ever seen. Hydrangea blue walls, a giant white bed, a view of the sunset, a floral-printed chair and ottoman. The bathroom had a soaking tub and a blue-tiled shower with myriad controls and bottles of expensive soap, shampoo, conditioner, moisturizer.

When was the last time she'd taken a bath? The old claw-foot tub in the kids' bathroom at home was scarred and chipped—but oh, the happy times the kids had had in there, like otters splashing and playing when they were little. The tub in the primary bath was plastic and not as deep. They'd been meaning to replace it for twenty years now.

What was she doing here? And how could she ever go back, knowing what she knew? She missed Gerald. She hated Gerald. She wanted to go back in time.

Instead, she turned on the faucets of the giant tub and did what Joy had told her to do. And when she came downstairs and saw the wine and the food and Joy sitting there like a peacock version of the Buddha in her bright clothes, all sympathy and kindness, the story had poured out.

Nutshell version, Gerald had once maybe dated this woman in high school, this Camille Dupont person. In the first few messages, they'd revisited their Nauset High School days. Camille had had a crush on him. He'd had one on her. They'd gone to a football game. There'd been some unspoken misunderstanding regarding someone named Lonnie. Too bad. They'd never gone out again.

Then came the *what have you been up to since then?* conversation. Camille had gone to college at the University of Alabama and become a geochemist. Got her PhD and worked in the oil and gas field. Lucrative? It was, LOL. Recently retired. Married once, long divorced. One grown son who lived in Seattle and worked for Amazon. No grandchildren. Had lived in Houston, Nashville, Santa Fe and now had a house on the coast of Maine. Couldn't resist the lure of New England.

That was as far as they got before Lark had come in. It felt so good to tell someone. Reading the messages in her office all day, the door locked, had been a surreal sort of hell. She'd barked at Meeko not to interrupt her and turned on some music so he wouldn't hear her crying. Sitting here on Joy's giant L-shaped couch, Ellie felt both comforted and furious at the same time.

"She sent him the link to her house," Ellie said, passing the iPad to Joy. "Four thousand square feet. Who lives alone in a house like that?"

"I do," Joy said mildly, clicking through the pictures. "But no offense taken. Wow. That's really pretty."

"I know. It's pretty much my dream house. Which I hate her even more for. It sold for one point eight million dollars. Is that what she wants Gerald to know? That she's loaded? I guess raping the earth for a giant gas and oil company paid well."

"My last husband was in oil, too," Joy said. "Literally more money than he could count." She passed the iPad back to Ellie, then poured them both more wine. "What else did they talk about?"

"Me. Apparently, my heroic nurse husband is ignored by his workaholic wife." Her voice choked off.

"You? Come on! Lark always talks about how happy you two are."

"I thought we were. Stupid of me, I guess."

Yes. The DMs told a very different story than the life Ellie thought she and Gerald had. As for Gerald, well. Ellie learned quite a bit about him, let's just say that. Gerald had had a very rich and rewarding career as a nurse. Heroic? Well, if Camille said so, that was very sweet. (She gagged when she first read that.) All nurses were heroes, Gerald replied. Yes, he'd wanted to become a nurse practitioner. But because of his wife's career, there hadn't been the time.

"I'm the one who wanted him to go back to school," she told Joy, dashing rage tears out of her eyes. "He told me he didn't want to be away from me and the kids more than he already was. It wasn't because of my career!"

"Men lie a lot," Joy said, taking another piece of cheese and nibbling on it.

"So I'm very talented, he said. Just consumed with my work. I have no time for him."

Joy rolled her eyes. "What an ass."

Yes, this woman Gerald was married to was a workaholic. Long days, very prestigious in the community, always trying to improve and move up. She gave her all to being successful, not leaving much left over for time together.

It was a punch in the stomach. No time together? They did everything together! Every dinner, every weekend, every family event . . . together. The only time she went away was a sleepover at Grace's house when she was visiting their parents. Not much time together. Bullshit.

"He told Camille how much he wanted to travel, especially to South America so he could do some mountain climbing. Joy, he has never once said anything like that to me! He's *in love with the Andes*," she said, making air quotes. "News to me! And how could we afford that kind of a vacation?"

Joy shook her head. "Okay, cut to the chase. Did they have sex?"

Ellie looked out the window. "I . . . I don't think so. Not

according to this." She handed the iPad back over to Joy, not able to look at it anymore. "But I think he . . . well. You read it." She practically had it memorized by now, anyway.

Camille and Gerald had met for lunch in Boston's North End at the end of October. I just wish they hadn't kicked us out! Camille said. I could've listened to you for days. Can't remember the last time I laughed so hard.

Me too. So great seeing you. You haven't changed one bit.

You're too sweet. The years look great on you!! I always knew you'd get more handsome as you got older. We have to get together again soon.

Definitely! I'll check my schedule.

Lunch with an old high school crush would've been . . . well, not great. But not the worst thing, either. It was the way he talked about *her*. His wife of thirty-eight years. How he painted her as tense and preoccupied. He admired her, he said, but it was hard, being married to an artist. Always in her head, being creative and thinking about what's next. Doesn't have much time for boring old me. Can't blame her.

The obvious fishing for compliments worked like a charm on stupid Camille.

Boring??? The opposite, I think! Seriously, I LOVE talking to you. You have the best sense of humor, Gerry! And I don't know, I feel closer to you than I do with most people. Probably

because we go back so far. Anyway, have a
sparkling day! Xox

A sparkling day. Gack.
Gerald had replied, You too! And . . .

Yes?

I really like talking to you, too. I feel like
my old self again.

A day or two later, he was telling Camille about how excited
he was, because his (not "their") grandson would be visiting for a
long weekend over Christmas.

More cute little exchanges, more flirting, more personal
things about their family. He missed his mom. She'd been a saint,
an "old-fashioned wife." Ellie felt those words like a knife in her
chest. Louisa had been a substitute teacher once Gerald started
first grade, then later opened the bookstore Harlow now ran. But
back then, it had been more of a hobby. Louisa hadn't needed to
make money to pay off their debt, because they didn't have debt.
Robert made a very healthy salary as an attorney.

A lot of Wellfleet families were wealthy, even before the Cape
had become quite so expensive. Ellie had never yearned to open a
gallery, not with five school-age children. She'd had to. And Gerald
had been so supportive of it. Only now, talking to this slutty, wealthy
Camille, suddenly he carried the burden of raising the kids.

"'Since Elsbeth is so caught up with work, I do most of the
grandparenting myself,'" Joy read. "That's not true, is it? I mean,
it doesn't seem to be, from what I've seen."

"No! It's not true! Not at all. God, Joy! I want to stab him. I loved him yesterday, and I hate him today."

"'Same with the house and property,'" Joy read. "'All on my shoulders, but I'm pretty handy and enjoy the work.'"

"I *wish* he took care of the house and property!" Ellie said. "He's been promising to paint the downstairs bathroom for twenty years!"

"'She sounds high maintenance. Do you have any time just to do your things?' Oh, wow. That's nervy."

"Tell me about it."

That line had made her screech when she'd read it this morning, rage-sipping coffee in her office. "He has *all* day, Camille!" she'd yelped. "All fucking day. He has no *things*. He putters. He moves shit from one place to another. He starts things and doesn't finish them, and he texts women he knew fifty years ago."

"Everything good, Boss?" came Meeko's voice.

"I'm on the phone!" she barked. "Don't disturb me, please." Then she felt guilty, so she stood up and opened the door. "I appreciate you holding down the fort today, Meeko."

"Is nothing."

It's your job, she thought, closing the door again. Back to the iPad to learn about this neglected, noble, underappreciated man named Gerry. Then . . .

Camille: I hope you liked the sweater . . .

Gerald: I LOVE the sweater! My favorite color.
You really didn't have to.

Camille: Oh, please. It was your birthday. 💜

Yes. He'd worn a beautiful green cashmere sweater sometime around Thanksgiving. Ellie had complimented him on it, caressed the fabric, asked him where he got it.

"A wicked good find at Marine Specialties," he'd said, naming the quirky, iconic shop in Provincetown. She hadn't disbelieved him for one second. Then, before Christmas . . .

Gerald: Did you get the clock?

> Camille: I was just writing you a note to thank you! I LOVE this clock! It's so me! Where on earth did you find it?

Gerald: Just saw it when I was out and about and thought of you. It's elegant and cool, just like you are.

Camille had attached a picture of the clock on her nightstand, her artfully unmade bed in the background. (Subtle, Camille. Subtle.) The clock was from Long Pond Arts. "He bought her a Christmas present from my gallery," Ellie told Joy, grabbing another tissue.

"Are you serious? What a jerk." Joy refilled both their glasses, the most Ellie had had to drink in years. The buzz helped, though. Made this feel like a shitty dream. "But did they ever have sex? You don't have to tell me everything, of course. But . . ."

Ellie blew her nose. "Well . . . I don't think so. She amped things up in January. Told him how hot he was and asked if he wondered what it would've been like if they ever hooked up. Made a pretty strong play for an affair. Here. You read it." She passed the iPad back. The words were already burned into her brain.

> Did you ever wonder what would've happened if we'd hooked up? I always thought you were incredibly hot.

LOL. Thanks. You're still so beautiful. You must have men after you like a dog chases beef.

> I'm extremely picky. I like them tall, funny and salt-and-pepper. (Hint: look in the mirror).

🙂 Thanks. You're too sweet.

> I'm gonna be honest here, Gerry. I love talking to you. I loved seeing you. I want to see you again. Let's get it right this time and not live in regret. You only live once, right?

I'm flattered.

> Life is too short for me not to put it on the line. I want to see you again. I want us to be involved. I'm falling in love with you, Gerry.

"Oh, ouch," Joy said, grimacing as she continued to read. "'I'd be lying if I said I didn't feel a little bit the same.' What a bastard." She read a little bit more. "Can I just say I hate this Camille person? What a whore."

Ellie's eyes were streaming. Her husband had fallen in love—a little bit, if there was such a thing—with another woman. He put it in writing.

"Okay, but then he just stops," Joy said. "She keeps asking him if he's there, he ghosts her for two weeks, and then he puts an end to it. "'I do miss you, but I have to stop. I love my wife and I don't want to make a huge mistake. I'm sorry.' Good! He didn't want to make a huge mistake. Not 'I made a huge mistake.' I'm taking that as they never hooked up. That's the end of it, right? Nothing more?"

"I guess," Ellie said. "Unless he sent her a letter. I looked at his email, but he didn't send her anything."

"He could've sent her something, then deleted it," Joy said.

"True. I don't think he's that tech savvy, though."

"Do *you* think that was the end of it? Did he act different after . . . what was it . . . January?"

Ellie sighed. "I . . . I mean, the holidays were over, we'd gotten used to being empty nesters, and we were back to being more like we were. We had a little . . . adjustment period last fall. No kids in the house, our oldest grandson living in town for a little while, so we were going to soccer games and that kind of thing. But we didn't fight, Joy. We didn't—" She hesitated, then figured what the hell. "We didn't stop having sex. Ever. We've always been pretty constant in that area. And yeah, I guess I felt like we just settled back into place. Nothing was ever wrong, really. Just a couple months of . . ."

"Being off," Joy supplied.

"Right. Meanwhile, he was dipping his toe in the infidelity pool. Maybe an entire foot. He drove to Boston to meet her. It doesn't sound like they had sex, but it was cheating just the same."

"My second fiancé?" Joy said. "He was married. Had another

entire family the whole time we were together. I mean, he did tell me. But only after we were engaged." She shook her head, then popped a mozzarella ball in her mouth. "What do *you* think, El-lie? Did he sleep with her or not?"

"I don't . . . I don't think so. Gerald has always been so . . . good. Decent, I mean. He has integrity. Well, he used to. I can't really picture him crossing that line. And I think it would be in the messages, don't you? I think Camille would say so. She wants to sleep with him. She doesn't say anything like 'Last night was so magical.' So no, I don't think he did anything physical."

The wind had picked up, and rain slapped against the many glass doors that faced the ocean. The two women were quiet a minute.

"Well," Joy said, "you can stay here as long as you want, El-lie. And I won't say a word to anyone, hand to God, okay? You're my friend now, and your secrets are safe with me."

Fresh tears flooded Ellie's eyes. "Thank you, Joy," she whispered. "I can't tell you how much that means."

When she woke up, it took Ellie a minute to remember where she was.

It was such a pretty room, even lovelier in the natural light. Deep blue walls, white furnishings and that view! A swath of beach plums delineated the land before the violet-colored ocean, and the sky was pale and clear, a swipe of coral pink at the horizon. She could paint that. She would paint that.

Then panic flashed over her in a bristling wave. Gerald. Her husband had fallen in love with another woman, all via Facebook. Sure, it had ended, but that it had happened at all . . . it was still a betrayal. To her. For thirty-eight years, they'd been damn near perfect. Happy. Solid. Best friends. And then, five minutes after he retired, he was flirting with a high school crush. Such a goddamn cliché.

She had texted Gerald yesterday from the gallery, saying she was driving down to spend a night with Grace, the only excuse she could think that wouldn't have him asking too many questions. Coming to Joy's house . . . that had been an unwitting genius-level move. Ellie had not predicted crying all over her daughter's landlady, but the second she'd seen the kindness in Joy's eyes, something had burst.

She got out of bed and stood for a second, looking out at the ocean. What a privilege, seeing that every day. Then she pulled on her clothes, messaged Meeko to say she'd be late and went downstairs, stopping to admire some of the paintings on the wall, recognizing some of the artists. Oh, here was one of hers! She hadn't seen it last night. Her heart swelled a little. Joy had bought one of her paintings . . . or the previous owners had. Joy had mentioned she bought it fully furnished. But someone had thought her art belonged in a house like this, and today, that was an ego boost she needed.

Joy wasn't up yet, but Lark's car was gone. Connery, however, was very happy to see her.

"Hello, puppy," she said, petting his funny little head. She was more of a cat person, but who could resist that face? Ellie made some coffee, then took a cup out to the deck, Connery dancing along beside her.

This was some house. If a woman was going to have her heart smashed, she deserved to stay in a house like this. But how long would she stay? Joy had said as long as she needed, but . . . shit. Should she talk . . . She swallowed. Talk to a lawyer?

There was only one way to figure it out. She brought Connery inside so he wouldn't be eaten by a coyote or fox, left Joy a note saying she'd check in later and thanks again, then got in her car and went home.

The house looked different now. Suddenly, everything seemed to be a message, a snotty snub from Gerald to her. The lawn mower still in her parking space. The rotting fence that she'd asked him at least twice to prioritize. The branch from the kids' climbing tree, lying in the backyard, yet another job that would remain unfinished. Why had he caved to their backyard neighbor, who was an entitled prick? Why hadn't he said, "Leonard, it's a tree. Deal with it." The kids had *loved* climbing that tree, and now it looked mutilated. Her granddaughters wouldn't be able to climb it.

The rambling roses had become choked off with weeds and seedlings. Half of the lilac tree was dead because they hadn't pruned it properly for years. Gerald hadn't weed-whacked along the road. The front door needed painting, something Ellie kept meaning to do when she had time. The living room windowpane was cracked. Gerald had promised to get that fixed before Christmas four years ago. No, five.

Was *this* why she was working so damn hard, painting, running a business, being wife of the year? For these weeds and this rot and a cheating husband?

"Hey," he said, opening the front door. "How was Grace's?"

"Who the hell is Camille Dupont?"

His face went gray so fast she thought he might faint. He gripped the door frame and bent over. "Oh, Ellie," he said.

She shoved past him into the house. "Don't just stand there like a weakling, Gerald. Get your ass inside." The kids used to say they were more scared of her when she was angry than they'd ever been of Dad. She had never been a yeller, or someone who got mad when a kid broke a glass or because the dry cleaner ruined a sweater. She didn't even yell at idiot drivers, a rare trait in Massachusetts. No. Her anger was always reserved for the times when it was richly deserved.

She sat down at the kitchen table, which, you guessed it, hadn't been properly wiped down after Gerald's dinner last night.

Gerald approached warily.

"Sit the fuck down," she said. Dug the iPad out of her bag and tossed it on the table. "Go ahead. Tell me all about your affair."

"It wasn't an affair. I did *not* cheat on you," he said, but his hands were shaking. "We never had sex."

What a shitty excuse. *I did not have sex with that woman.* Did men really think it was that simple?

"You mean, you didn't put your penis in her vagina. Or mouth, one hopes. Otherwise, yes, you absolutely did cheat on me, you stupid, ungrateful idiot."

He sat down, head hanging, and she could've punched him in the face, she was so furious. Gerald took a couple of breaths, his complexion still sickly. "Okay. Okay. Let me start by saying, Ellie, you are the love of my life."

"Absolutely meaningless right now."

"I had a . . . flirtation going on. You're right. But it was the typical midlife crisis stupidity and nothing more."

"It was a *lot* more, Gerald!" she yelled. "You were having an emotional affair. You cared about her. You missed her. You loved talking to her. It's all right there, and I read every damn word."

"Okay, honey, okay. You're right. It got . . . I just kind of got caught up in it and forgot who I was, I guess."

"You *forgot*? You forgot you were a husband for almost forty years? You forgot your wife loves you? At least, she used to. I mean, God, Gerald, what the hell was missing from our marriage that made you do this? Almost four months of pretending you were in high school again? Four months of leading some woman on? Four months of thinking about someone other than me?" Her voice broke on that.

"Ellie, no. I was just . . . you know. Just all the stupid clichés. I was bored. Robbie had moved out in the spring, then Lark in the fall, Matthew went back to California. Then Camille reached out, and I just . . . remembered."

"First you forgot, now you remembered. Remembered what?"

"Those . . . those dopey high school feelings, that's all. Like when your life is ahead of you and you have no idea what you'll be or do or where you'll end up. And . . ." He rubbed his hands over his face. "For a very short amount of time, I felt a little disappointed in where I ended up. Not with you, not that, not at all."

"Bullshit. I read what you said about me, Gerald. How consumed I am with work. How I'm too busy to be a good grandmother. How I don't have enough time for you, which is complete and utter bullshit. You didn't mention that I'm working seventy hours a week because we can't *both* retire. That we've been just getting by for the past forty years, and unless your father dies and doesn't skip over us and give everything to the kids or a dog shelter or his girlfriend, I'll have to run this fucking gallery until I'm eighty. Did you mention that? *You* got to retire, and this is how you show up for us? By fantasizing about Camille Dupont? Which totally sounds like a fake name, by the way."

He let out a bark of laughter, and for a second, she felt a rush of satisfaction. He always did laugh at her jokes, which a lot of people didn't appreciate. But he did. He had.

He stood up, dropped a hand on her shoulder, which she twisted away from. He did not get to touch her, no way. Gerald went to the sink, where he filled two glasses with water. As a nurse, he'd always been ahead of the curve on hydrating, long before everyone carried a Yeti.

When he sat back down, his color was better. Too bad. "What do you want me to say?" he asked. "I ended this back in January. If you read everything, you know that. I was stupid, I was bored, I was a little jealous and I flirted with a girl I knew in high school. I met her once for lunch. But that was it. I'm not defending it. I'm just defining it more clearly."

"You gave her a clock from my gallery," Ellie hissed. "Don't boil this down to some trivial little flirtation, Gerald. You have damaged our marriage. I can't trust you. That's what I've learned. You pretend to be a loving husband, holding my hand all the time, but then creep up to the attic to DM some woman you haven't spoken to in half a century."

He grimaced. "Look, I made a mistake. I . . . I dipped my toe, but I didn't jump in."

They'd been married so long that they even used the same metaphors. He covered her hand with both of his. She pulled away.

"Ellie, I stopped with her as soon as I realized the damage I could do. I chose *you*, honey. I didn't stop because I got caught. I stopped because I realized I was being an idiot. I am so sorry you found out, because it was never going to happen again. It was a blip on the radar, nothing more. Please forgive me."

Shit. It was a good apology. He said everything the advice columnists instructed cheaters to say. He had stopped it of his own volition. He hadn't let it go too far. He hadn't told her about it to get it off his own chest.

"Well, if you think you're getting a medal, think again. I've moved in with Joy. I've been at her house, not Grace's."

"Who's Joy?" he asked, his brows drawing together.

"Lark's landlady. She invited me to stay with her as long as I want."

"You told her?"

"Yes, I told her. I had to tell *someone*. You want me to tell the kids about this?"

His face grayed again. "No, but . . . I . . . Honey, this is your home. This is where you belong."

"You know what? I reject that, Gerald. This is where I live. It *used* to be my home, but I haven't had the time or energy to enjoy it or work on it in years. You get to putter around here, doing whatever you want to. You ignore my list of things to be done and spend your day cutting down the branch that didn't need cutting instead of fixing the lawn mower or the fence or moving your shit out of the garage or painting that hideous orange bathroom. I just go to the gallery, work, come home, work more and, if I'm lucky, get invited to Addie's for dinner and maybe get to babysit the girls when they deign to ask us."

"Honey, that's not—"

She slammed her hand against the table. "Shut it, Gerald! You are not in a position to contradict me." She pulled out her phone. "In fact, I'm calling a family dinner. Here. Tonight. Mandatory. And that's when we'll tell the kids Mommy won't be living at home for a while."

"Wait, wait, Ellie, hang on. Take a breath, honey." She glared at him. "What are we going to tell them? Are you . . . do you think . . ."

"Are you scared they won't love Daddy as much if they knew he was sexting someone?"

"I never sexted anyone."

"Semantics." But yeah, the kids would be furious.

At least, she *thought* they would be. What if they sided with him, though? *Yeah, Mom, you're so busy, you never, you always, Dad deserves, you should* . . . Fear stabbed her in the heart. What if they alienated her? Thought dear old Dad was justified in looking elsewhere?

"For now, no, I'm not going to out you, Gerald. Yet. Just make sure all the kids are here tonight. No excuses. Now I'm going to pack. And by the way, I'll be taking a lot of time off this summer, so you might want to get your ass back to the hospital and start working again."

An hour later, she was sitting in the gallery office, door once again closed. Meeko clearly knew something was up, because he brought her a chai latte from Blue Willow—"On me, Boss"—an unprecedented event. She should get furious more often.

She wasn't working. She was thinking.

She didn't *want* a different life. She didn't want a different man, or a divorce, or anything, really. But this wasn't nothing. This wasn't a blip. This had been more than three months of her husband engaging with another woman. Flirting, complimenting . . . talking about *her*, the grim workaholic artist, self-consumed. Every time he'd read or written a message, he'd been cheating on her.

If anyone had the right to complain about her, Ellie thought, it was her children. She and Gerald had bucked convention in having a big family. But they'd never been those parents who thought each kid was a superstar waiting to happen, or a fragile little hothouse flower who needed to be protected and explained and have special dispensations. They were *kids*. Let them bicker, make mistakes, get a mediocre grade (though Harlow and Lark never had). Let them figure it out. Free-range kids who could entertain themselves, do their own homework and help around the house while their parents were . . . well, the adults. Not the kids' friends, not only Mommy and Daddy, but people and, most importantly, a couple.

After all, they had always known there'd come a day when the kids would leave and they'd be together, alone, for the rest of their lives. They wanted that day to come. That *was* the goal— raise the kids, not keep them like pets for their own entertainment, or have them stuck in perpetual adolescence, playing video games in the cellar, forever unemployed.

Gerald? Gerald had no right to complain about her. Or their marriage. It was ridiculous.

He'd said something that had flashed in her brain . . . and faded. Thanks, menopause. What had it been? She'd been too angry to hear it clearly, her own brain shouting the entire time. Right. The . . . interactions . . . had begun after Lark moved out, the last child to leave. He'd said he was bored, but seriously? He'd *yearned* to retire. But what was that other thing he'd said? Her angry, fizzing brain couldn't grab on to it. She should've recorded the whole conversation.

Ellie thought of the divorced couples she knew. That pretentious idiot Brad Fairchild had cheated on Lillie Silva, and Brad had married someone else within the year (and ended up divorced from her, too). Grace suspected that Larry had cheated on her, but she was of the "don't ask, don't tell" school. Would she feel a sense of triumph to learn it wasn't all sunshine and daisies for her and Gerald?

Enough ruminating. Time to paint. Ellie went to the stuffy little studio upstairs, where *Cranberry Bog in Autumn #3* sat waiting. It was very pretty so far and would probably sell at a good price. Her plan had been to hang the bog paintings in August, when the summer people would be awash in melancholy about having to go home and would want to feel some fall, Capey vibes. Fishermen and cranberry farmers were popular subjects.

Instead of working on that now, though, she took out a fresh canvas—she stretched her own linen and always had a few primed and ready—and set it on the easel. Looked at her paints and chose a few colors for the palette. Navy, black, vermillion and gray. Then she attacked that poor, innocent canvas with slashes of color. She wasn't going for anything in particular, not a house, not a landscape, not a person. Just paint on canvas, applied with palette knife and stiff brushes, with her fingers, with steel wool. As she worked, she thought it resembled a murder scene more than anything, and you know what? That was okay with her. She painted until six thirty, cleaned up and then headed for home.

The message had gone out, apparently. Her children's various vehicles took up what room there was in the driveway. The lawn mower was still there, cutting off two spaces with its innards strewn about. It seemed symbolic that there wasn't any room for her here. Then again, she was mighty touchy today.

"Hi, Mom!" came a chorus, and her hardened heart softened as her kids greeted her with hugs and smiles. Imogen, who looked so much like Addie and Lark, held up her arms, and Ellie obliged, scooping up the little girl for a nuzzle. "How's my sweetie pie?" she asked.

"Gran, Gran, look at me! Do you like my dress?" Esme asked, twirling.

"I love it, honey. Such a pretty color. Did you know, purple's my favorite?" She bent and kissed Esme's head.

"Ah, the beautiful Elsbeth," said Robert. "How are you, my dear?"

"Fine, Robert, just fine," she lied.

"You're taking good care of yourself, I hope?" Those faded blue eyes saw a lot.

She looked away. "I'm trying, Robert. How are you?"

She didn't talk to Gerald until he served dinner. He'd gone all out—spaghetti with clams and garlic, fresh parsley, a green salad. There was even a cake sitting on the counter. Kissing up to the kids, she thought. Reminding them how great dear old Dad was.

"Hi, everyone, sorry I'm late," Lark said, coming through the door. "Just in time, though, I see." She dropped a kiss on Addie's head, smooched each girl and sat down. "I'm starving, Dad. This smells like heaven."

"How's the fake boyfriend?" Robbie asked, and Ellie sat and listened as her children joked and talked, teasing each other, referencing things that went over her own head. Nicole buttered bread for the little girls, who were picky eaters, and Grandpop held forth, telling them about a walk he and Frances had taken, in which they'd come upon a lemonade stand. He'd given the two five-year-olds all the money in his wallet. "The best eighty-seven dollars I've ever spent!" he said. "I think it made a *very* good impression on Frances."

"Or she thinks you're senile, Grandpop," Winnie said. "That's a lot for lemonade."

"She did offer to count the money out for me, now that you mention it," Grandpop said. "But I wanted to help the little girls. They were very adorable. Not quite as adorable as you two, though!"

"I very adorable," Imogen said.

"You gonna marry Frances, Grandpop?" Robbie asked.

"She says we have to date for two years first," he answered. "By which time, I may well be dead and buried! I suppose we have to trust the universe. That's what she says, anyway."

"Okay," Gerald said suddenly, his voice loud. Ellie knew his father's dotty wisdom and rambling stories could irritate him. "So, kids, Dad . . . um, Ellie, did you want to say anything?"

"I'll be living with Joy Deveaux for a while," Ellie said, twirling some pasta. She kept her tone light.

"Oh, my God, that house," Harlow said. "Can I come, too?"

"Why?" asked Winnie.

"I mean, I'd live there, too, if she let me," Robbie said. "Nicest house in Wellfleet."

"She'd probably say yes," Lark said.

"I think *ours* is the nicest house in Wellfleet, Robbie," Addison said sharply.

"Or Melissa Spencer's," Winnie said. "If you like modern, that is. But again, why, Mom?"

Ellie didn't answer for a minute. *Because your father has broken my heart, kids, and drastic measures are called for. Because I want to kill him and also sob for days. Because I can't believe he'd do something like this, after all the time and love and effort we've put into the past four decades, and I'm in shock, and I'm scared and I'm lost.*

"Are you getting divorce, Gran?" Imogen asked.

"Where did you hear that word?" Nicole asked, her eyes wide with horror.

"She's six, Nic," Robbie said. "She probably knows what 'divorce' means. And no, squirt, they're not getting divorced."

Gerald was looking at her. She could feel it.

She cleared her throat. "Grampy has some things to clean up around here, honey. I want to be away while he does it." For the first time that night, she looked directly at her husband. "Since it's not my mess to deal with."

ELEVEN

LARK

"Clearly, I won't be attending," Lorenzo said to Lark the night before the engagement party.

"Well, I'm not going to your sister's engagement party without you, Lorenzo." Actually, that might be more fun. "Why aren't you coming? By the way, I love the dress. You have excellent taste in women's clothes."

"I'll be at the *party*," Lorenzo said tightly. They were talking on the phone, a first, since he preferred to keep communication brief and impersonal. "I'm just not going to . . . that."

"The Renaissance fair?" she asked. Connery barked happily at the phrase, and she scooped him up for a cuddle. "It'll be fun."

"It will not be fun. It will be stupid."

Lark dropped a kiss on Connery's head, then set him down to better peruse her wardrobe options. What *did* a person wear to a Ren fair? Ah. Here was a white, off-the-shoulder blouse with puffy sleeves. Add a long skirt, and good enough. "Your whole family will be there. Even Noni."

"I'm a surgeon. I have more important things to do than watch a joust." It was almost funny, except that he was dead serious.

"You're allowed to have fun, Dr. Santini."

"My idea of fun doesn't include watching adults play dress-up."

"What is your idea of fun, then?"

There was a long pause, and Lark had to smile. "Reading," he finally said. "Eating a nice meal."

"I've eaten with you three times now. I think we know that's a lie. So you don't have fun. I get it."

"Can we end this conversation? I'll be seeing the family at the party—the party *I'm* paying for—and that's more than enough."

Lark pulled out the necklace Addie had given her on their thirtieth birthday, a simple pearl on a rose gold chain. She'd given Addie simple pearl earrings set in rose gold for that same birthday. "Here's a hint, Lorenzo. Stop reminding people that you pay for things."

"Why?"

"It's rude and it makes you look classless."

"And yet I *am* paying. It's merely a fact." He paused. "How is wanting to give my sister a nice wedding 'classless'?"

"That part's not. It's lovely. The classless part is making sure everyone knows you're paying for it. Your parents aren't, and maybe can't, and every time you mention your own generosity, you probably make them feel a little ashamed."

"Of me?"

"No, dummy. They're incredibly proud of you. But your dad was, what, a welder? Your mom worked at a school. Not the kind of incomes that let you save thirty or fifty grand for a big wedding."

"This wedding costs a lot more than fifty grand. A *lot* more."

"And there you go again. You're being wonderful, paying for this—"

"I can easily afford it."

"Yes, Lorenzo, we've covered that. But every time you remind people, you take away from that wonderfulness. Let someone else talk about how generous and successful you are. When it comes from you, it's bragging."

There was a silence as he processed her words. Then: "I'll meet you at the Copley Square Plaza at seven o'clock. Don't be late."

"Can I come to your place to change first? Then we can go together, like an actual couple."

"Fine. You have the address."

"Thanks. I think you're missing out with the fair, but—" He'd already hung up. She looked at Connery, who was watching her with rapt interest. "Can you believe this guy?" Connery whined. "You're a hundred percent right, puppy."

Lark had been Dr. Satan's pretend girlfriend for a month now. The two dinner dates at the Naked Oyster, the family picnic, and very little other communication. A small curveball had been thrown yesterday, when Sofia had texted Lark, inviting her to a Renaissance fair in Norwell, about half an hour south of Boston. Henry's mother was a falconer—so cool!—and was giving a demonstration. Lark had the entire day off, the first in six days, so she said yes, assuming Lorenzo would be there, too.

She texted Sofia now, sensing Lorenzo would fail to do so. Lorenzo can't make the fair but I can still come, if that's okay.

Of course! I figured Dr. Workaholic wouldn't make it, Sofia texted back immediately. Just find the falconing area around 2:00. The demonstration starts at 2:30. Xoxox!

Lorenzo had a point about the Renaissance fair. It was kind of . . . well, he'd used the word *stupid,* and that was too harsh. Dorky? Silly? Over the top?

Wicked fun, in other words.

People really got into these things, she thought as she admired a woman in a purple gown with wide bell sleeves, a leather corset and two pointy cone things on her head. There was a guy dressed all in leather, his long beard braided, leading a donkey. A teenager dressed up like a fairy, her face painted in exquisite detail to look half human, half insect.

Lark made her way through the crowd, following the hand-painted signs to the birds of prey demonstration. A man on stilts teetered toward her, blowing her kisses, and she laughed and dodged around him. Another guy, dressed as a knight, but spray-painted entirely silver to make him look like a statue, stood very still as people posed next to him. In general, there was lots of cleavage, lots of chain mail. A corral off to the left was filled with horses for actual jousting sessions, and there were signs advertising demonstrations on leather crafting, belly dancing, sword fighting. Vendors in colorful tents sold jewelry, witch hats, tiaras, circlets of flowers and, er, elf ears. Attempted accents of all kinds—Irish, Scottish, English—filled the air, with shouts of "m'lady," "prithee," "good morrow" and "fare thee well" punctuating the air.

It also smelled fantastic around here. Roasting meat on spits, turkey legs and donuts seemed to be the most popular foods, and her stomach growled. People drank out of enormous steins, and everyone seemed so happy. Imogen and Esme would love this, she thought. Little kids had butterflies painted on their faces, some folks wore horns, and heck, when was the last time she'd done something so weird and fun?

There was the birds of prey ring, and Lark immediately saw the cluster of Santinis—Silvio and Anita, Sofia and Henry, the delightful Izzy, Dante, and Noni in her wheelchair. A jangle of nerves shivered up her legs . . . without Lorenzo here, she felt even more guilty about pretending to be his girlfriend.

"Lark!" Sofia called, and welcomed her with a hug. "Your timing is perfect. They're just getting started."

"Hi, everyone," she said. Izzy hugged her, too.

"Hey, Lark," Dante said.

"Hey." Her cheeks warmed, so she turned away quickly. On the stage, there was Henry, dressed in . . . well, in tights and a puffy shirt, God bless. He saw her and gave a nod, and Lark waved.

"Good to see you," Lark said to Silvio and Anita.

"We're going to sit up front and be supportive," Anita said, blowing Lark a kiss. Such nice people. Silvio gave her a wink and a smile as he was led away by his wife.

Out of respect, she went over to Noni, who may or may not have been asleep, her pale blue eyes slits, and crouched down to be at eye level. Today, Noni wore a wig of thick, curly white hair, which was slightly askew and low on her forehead. Should she fix it? Nah. Best not to assume that much familiarity. The old lady didn't flick an eye or move, but in case she was awake, Lark whispered, "Hello, Mrs. Santini."

"You," she rasped, making Lark jump a little. "Whatta *you* doin' here?"

Awake, then. "Um . . . just here to see the falcons, I guess."

The old woman glared. "Where my food at?" she asked, not looking away. "Lorenzo, my food."

"It's Dante, Noni, and here you go." He lowered a massive turkey leg to Noni's mouth, and she took an impressive bite without using her hands. Dentures were in, then.

"How's it going, Doc?" Dante said. His dark eyes met hers, and there it was again, that weird, unpleasantly electric jolt and residual, slightly sick feeling. What was *that* about?

"Hi, Dante." She had already said hi, hadn't she? "How are you?"

"Doing great." He smiled, and Lark felt her knees tingle. He was perfectly nice and appropriate, so why the ominous feeling? He held the turkey leg to his grandmother's mouth, and again, Noni took a shockingly large bite. She seemed pretty hale for someone on hospice. Then again, you really couldn't predict how long a person had. That was one of the first lessons Darlene had taught her.

"Looks like she's eating a baby's leg, doesn't it?" he murmured. "She's got the personality for it."

Lark sputtered out a laugh.

"Lorenzo, gimme drink." Dante raised an eyebrow at Lark, then held a paper cup for Noni and adjusted the straw.

"My grandfather always messes up our names, too," Lark said.

"Noni here pretty much only remembers Lorenzo," he returned easily. "If he's not around, we just step in and hope she doesn't smack us." Another smile, another flood of warmth and that ominous warning buzz in her joints.

She didn't have time to dwell on Dante, fortunately, because Izzy grabbed her arm and led her closer to the stage. "This is actually supercool, so you don't want to miss it," she said. "By the way, no need to win Noni over. I've been trying my whole life. She's only interested in Lorenzo."

"How's her health these days?" Lark asked.

"Oh, she's circling the drain," Izzy answered. "Sleeps for, like, twenty hours a day, can't do any activities of daily living anymore, isn't eating that much. Aside from turkey legs, apparently. I'll be seeing *that* on the flip side." She pulled a face. "Being the nurse, I get to do all the fun stuff."

"I can help," Lark said. "I used to be a CNA. Worked in a nursing home for a couple of years before med school."

"Seriously, you're so nice, I have no idea what you're doing with Lorenzo."

"Shh," Sofia said, turning with a smile to her sister. "They're getting started."

Indeed, Henry's mother was just coming out, dressed in a flowing red gown with gold trim. Lark glanced at the sign on the stage—*Mistress Jocelyn, Master Falconer.* Now, *that* was a cool title.

"Do you want to meet a falcon?" Jocelyn asked.

"Yes!" chorused the crowd of about fifty. Henry opened a large cage and brought out a beautiful white and gray bird, who gripped Jocelyn's arm with its bright yellow talons. "This is Otto, a gyrfalcon," Jocelyn said. "He was injured by another bird as a baby, and since he recovered and grew up in captivity, he's not suited to life in the wild just yet. At our home, he flies freely, but every night, he comes home for dinner."

Jocelyn ran a raptor recovery center, she told the crowd, and was against keeping raptors as pets, but said that humans and raptors had a long history together. She educated the crowd on how the birds were revered in medieval times for their ability to hunt and acted in partnership with their keepers, catching rabbits and smaller birds for their humans to eat. Their eyesight was so good they could see a rabbit a mile away, and they could fly at speeds up to seventy miles per hour when chasing prey.

"As I said, Otto is a gyrfalcon, the largest species. He looks pretty big, don't you think?" she asked the crowd. "How much do you think he weighs?"

"Eight pounds?" someone suggested.

"Ten?"

"Fourteen?"

"He weighs two pounds, nine ounces," Jocelyn said, and Lark said, "Wow!" along with the rest of the crowd. "But he can bring down prey that weighs up to eight pounds, because he strikes so fast. So everyone here with a purse dog, you have been warned!"

Everyone laughed, and a couple of dogs were scooped up into their owners' arms, making Lark glad Connery was home.

"I'm so excited for this, I might pass out," Dante said, appearing next to his sisters. "If I do, you're in charge of Noni, Isabella."

"Absolutely not. It's your turn today. Where is she, by the way? Still alive?"

"Over there, and maybe," Dante said. "I thought the heat might be too much for her, so I parked her under that tree. Don't worry, I'm checking every thirty seconds to make sure she's not kidnapped. She ate that turkey leg like a starving wolf, and the tryptophan did its job. She's snoring away. Or at the gates of paradise. Hard to say."

"We should be so lucky," Sofia murmured, and Izzy snorted.

"Lark, we're not really this awful," Sofia said. "We do love Noni, more or less."

"It's just that she's a hundred and forty-two years old, and she made our parents' life a living hell until Lorenzo moved her into the care facility," Dante said. "She just recently stopped calling Mom a whore."

"Oh, my gosh!" Lark said. "And Anita's so nice to her."

"Exactly," Izzy said. "Now, let's watch this falcon show."

"Okay," said Jocelyn, Otto still on her arm. "In my pouch, I have pieces of chicken for Otto. I'll toss a piece as high as I can, and we'll see if he can catch it."

"He always catches it," Sofia said. "He's amazing."

"Maybe you can use him at your wedding," Dante said. "Ring bearer. Otto swoops in, drops the rings, flies off. Hopefully he doesn't poop on your dress, but I'm willing to take that chance."

Sofia punched him fondly on the arm. *See?* Lark told herself. *A nice guy. Nothing to be concerned about.*

On the stage, Jocelyn was done with her lecture. "Now, of course, you all want to see him fly, am I right? And hunt?"

"Yes!" chorused the crowd.

"Who else has goose bumps?" Dante asked, and Izzy shoved him fondly, then looped her arm through his.

"You ready, folks?" Jocelyn said, raising her arm. The crowd cheered, Lark included.

"Free, Otto!" She flung her arm up, and Otto soared straight up, his huge wings unfolding with stunning speed and grace. He was so beautiful, and Lark felt her heart lift. The bird circled over the stage and crowd, garnering gasps of awe, and Jocelyn threw a small piece of food high in the air. Otto turned, shortened his wings, and dove straight for it. Caught it like a boss and returned to Jocelyn's arm, a study in fierce grace and agility.

"Pretty amazing, right?" Jocelyn asked the applauding crowd. "Want to see that again?"

She repeated the action, tossing the snack farther out this time. Again, Otto took to the air, heading like a bullet toward its target.

But suddenly, he pivoted midair, shortened his wings and *whump.* Lark heard the soft collision before she located it by the abrupt shower of feathers. Shrieks rose from the crowd, and Otto circled again. A pigeon hung limp in his talons.

"Holy shit! That was an assassination," Izzy said.

"Whoa!" cried Jocelyn. "Nature at its finest, folks. He is a bird of prey, after all, and pigeons are definitely prey. Why have a little piece of chicken when you can have a buffet?" The crowd laughed uncertainly. "Come on back, Otto!"

Otto continued to circle. Laden with the weight of the pigeon, he was slower and less graceful, giving everyone quite a view of the dead bird. Kind of gruesome, Lark thought, but also wicked cool.

"The circle of life," Dante sang softly, and Lark bit down on a laugh.

"At least it was a pigeon and not, I don't know, a hummingbird or cardinal. Something we like, in other words," Izzy said. "You could say Otto is doing a public service."

"I'm actually afraid of pigeons," Sofia said.

"I think Otto sensed that," Dante said.

"The rats of the sky," said Izzy.

"They're not so bad," Lark said, feeling someone had to defend the poor birds. "I kind of like them."

"Come on back, Otto," Jocelyn called again.

But Otto did not fly back. No. Otto's wings drew back as he prepared to land and eat his meal, and that place was . . . that place was . . .

"Oh, shit," Dante said, bolting through the crowd.

That place was Noni's head.

"Where's my phone?" Izzy said.

Because yes, the falcon had landed right on Noni's little head and was tearing into the pigeon. Noni remained fast asleep. Thank God for the wig! People shrieked and backed away, as if Otto were Godzilla and not a two-and-a-half-pound bird, but yeah, those talons were sharp. Lark and Izzy followed Dante through the crowd. A mom covered her kid's eyes as Otto tore a chunk out of the pigeon and swallowed it. Noni's wig began to turn pink.

Lark felt a wonderful, horrible bubble of inappropriate laughter welling up in her. Robbie would love this story. Otto looked around, regal and pleased, then shifted, causing Noni's wig to slide a little farther. He ripped off another piece of pigeon and gobbled it up.

"Gross!" cried a teenager, stepping in closer with her phone. Plenty of people had their phones out. After all, how often did you get to see a falcon eating a pigeon, and on an old lady's head, no less?

Lark crept up behind Dante, not wanting to scare the bird and have it, oh, take out Noni's eye or something.

"Off you go, buddy," Dante said, approaching.

Otto considered the request and ignored it. Another chunk of pigeon, another "Ew!" from the crowd.

"That's my grandma, pal. Off you go," Dante said.

"Let's just remember *you* abandoned her under this tree," Izzy said, grabbing Lark's hand, tears of laughter bright in her eyes. Lark bit her lip shut to stifle her own laughter. "I'm so telling Lorenzo."

"You're not helping, Izzy," Dante said.

"It's *killing* the old lady!" said a little kid.

"From your lips to God's ears, kid," Dante muttered, and Izzy bent double. "Come on, bird."

Otto fluttered his wings, swallowing another chunk of his lunch.

Then Dante offered his arm—that was a good arm, all tanned and muscled, blond hair gleaming against his skin. Otto regarded it, looked at Dante and then, apparently full, dropped the pigeon into Noni's lap—more shrieks, more pictures—and stepped delicately from her head to Dante's outstretched arm.

"Check on Noni?" Dante asked, looking at Lark. She nodded, trying not to notice how smokin' hot he looked, completely at ease with the falcon.

"I'll take care of this, Lark," Izzy said, reaching toward her grandmother's head. "She's my relative, after all."

"No, no, I've got gloves and stuff in my bag."

"Excellent point, and since I'm so grossed out, I'll be happy to let you do it. Does anyone have a plastic bag? Oh, thanks, sir."

Noni's bloodstained wig slanted down almost to her eyes, but the old lady was still snoring. The crowd shifted, some going off to watch Otto up front, some staying for the cleanup. Lark could hear Jocelyn talking, welcoming Otto back.

Lark always carried alcohol wipes and latex gloves, just in case. Since starting in the ER, she had upped her game to include butterfly closures, a rawhide shoelace for an emergency tourniquet, an inhaler, an EpiPen, baby aspirin and a window-breaker with seat belt cutting tool. Always prepared, just like the Scouts. She pulled on the gloves and took Noni's wig off. A nearby toddler burst into screams, which made the giggles wriggle and leap again. Izzy wasn't even trying not to laugh now.

Lark put the wig in the plastic bag, then the dead bird, trying not to look at it, the suppressed laughter making tears stream from her eyes. *Predator and prey,* she could almost hear Sir David Attenborough saying. *One must lose the eternal game.*

Noni's head was free from scrapes or cuts. Seemed like the only casualty was the pigeon. And the wig.

Lark ran an alcohol wipe over Noni's scalp and ears, and Izzy pulled out a comb and fluffed her grandmother's thinning hair, then shook Noni's skirt to rid it of leftover feathers. Behind them, Jocelyn continued to discuss the wildness of raptors, their unpredictability, the reason they had bells on their talons. The show must go on, after all.

Then the old woman jerked awake, causing Lark to leap back a little. "You!" she rasped, glaring. "What you do to me, hey? You, stranger? Step back, eh?"

"Noni," Izzy said, tears of laughter bright in her brown eyes, "this is Lark, remember? Lorenzo's girlfriend? We're just, um, checking on you. Do you want a drink?"

"Where Lorenzo?"

"He's not here. But the rest of us are."

"Eh."

Izzy looked at Lark. "Isn't she delightful?"

"Lorenzo, he's a good boy," Noni rasped.

"Debatable," Izzy said. She looked at Lark. "You're awesome, by the way. Thank you."

There was clapping from the audience—the show had wrapped up—and a second later, Sofia, Dante and their parents joined Izzy and Lark.

"Oh, my God, I thought I was going to wet myself laughing," Anita whispered to the girls. "Noni, are you okay?" she said in a louder voice.

"Why wouldn't I be? I wanna go now. Take me home, boy."

"That would be me," Silvio said. "Okay, Ma. You're doing all right, though?"

"She's, um, unaware of the excitement," Izzy said. "Let's keep it that way. Me, though, I can't wait to find this on social media." She dissolved into giggles again and clutched Sofia's hand.

"I've got some pictures," said a young woman. "Want me to airdrop them to you?"

"Yes! Thank you," said Izzy.

Henry and his mother joined them. "Is she okay?" Jocelyn asked. "I am so sorry! That's never happened before."

"Who you? Your dress, not so nice," Noni said. "You look like a whore."

"Stop, Noni," Sofia said. "This is Henry's mother. My future mother-in-law."

"Eh. Cover yourself next time."

"I'm so sorry, Jocelyn," Anita said. "It's the dementia talking. She's very unfiltered."

"And mean," Izzy added. "Can't forget mean."

"No offense taken," Jocelyn said. "And again, I apologize for Otto."

"I don't know, Mom," Henry said. "I think you should change the show to include pigeons. YouTube will love this." Indeed, people were eager to share their videos and pictures with Izzy. The falcon show was deemed far more exciting than any other falcon show in the history of Renaissance fairs.

"We should get going," Anita said, smiling at her brood. "See you at the party, kids."

"We need to get back to the hotel and change, too, honey," Sofia said, sliding her arm through Henry's. "I'm getting my hair done and all that. Trial run for the wedding."

"You'll be so beautiful," Henry said. "You are right now."

"Ick," Isabella said. "Please, stop."

"I should go, too," Jocelyn said. "I have to take Otto home and clean up myself before dinner."

"Henry and I are having dinner with our parents before the big party, Lark," Sofia explained. "But we'll see you at the hotel, okay?" She gave her a hug, thanked her for tending to Noni and floated off, holding hands with Henry. He kissed her on the temple, and Sofia beamed up at him, eyes shining.

They reminded her of . . . well. Of her and Justin.

"You guys want to wander around?" Izzy asked.

"Sure," Dante said. "After you, fair maidens."

"Nope. Just shut that down, big bro. You don't get to use Ren fair lingo and have us still respect you." Izzy took Lark's arm and headed for a booth. "Come on, let's check this stuff out." Izzy bought a pair of horns attached to a hair band and put it on immediately.

"Devil horns. They suit you," Dante said.

Lark bought circlets of sparkly flowers for her nieces. They got lemonade and hot dogs and ambled through the fair, watching the jousts, avoiding the clowns, like any sane person.

"Oh, look, Noni's gonna be Instagram famous," said Izzy, checking her phone. "Shit! Look at this!" Someone had posted a shaky video of Otto calmly eating pigeon on Noni's tipped-back head, her mouth slack, those half-open eyes . . .

"Oh no," Lark said, and there it was again, that irrepressible laughter. Izzy was squeaking, and Dante's laugh was sooty and delicious.

"Good thing Lorenzo doesn't have social media. And don't show this to him, or he'll kill us all," Dante said, wiping the tears of laughter from his eyes. He glanced at Lark. "Well, not you, of course."

That warm flush engulfed her again. "I don't know," she said, looking at another photo on Instagram under the hashtags #massrenfaire #falconshow. It was a close-up of Noni's wrinkled hands next to the discarded pigeon. "This one has Christmas card written all over it."

His grin widened. "I like you, Dr. Smith," he said. "You're okay. Anyone who can handle a dead pigeon is pretty damn awesome."

Oh, shit. She liked him. She *liked* him. The knowledge hit her hard enough that she stumbled, and Dante grabbed her arm. Then came that warning flash again. There was something . . . off. Something bleak. A faint alarm that wouldn't stop ringing. She pulled her arm free. "Thanks."

"You good?"

"Just fine."

"I still don't understand why you're dating our brother," Izzy said. "Unless it's for his money, in which case we get it and promise not to tell. But for our sake, I'm glad, right, Dante? Oh, I want a turkey leg. Noni's looked so good. You guys want one?"

"I'm off poultry for a while," Dante said. "For obvious reasons." He grinned at Lark. "Izzy here is always hungry. I'm surprised she didn't finish off the pigeon. You want something, Lark?"

He was funny. Kind. Brave. A devoted brother. Wicked handsome. Had she mentioned that? Crap.

Developing a crush was not part of the plan.

"What?" she said, abruptly aware that she hadn't answered. "No, thanks, sorry. I'm actually gonna head for Lorenzo's and get ready, maybe take a nap," she said. "I'll see you guys tonight, though. Have fun!"

Once in the car, Lark took a few deep breaths. Her mind was both in hyperdrive and blurry at the same time.

Never once since the age of five had Lark ever felt so much as a tremor for anyone other than Justin. Why would she? She'd *had* love. She'd had the One. She'd felt all the purring, the delicious hot and liquid feelings of lust, all in the safe embrace of love and friendship, laughter and fun. One and done, she and Justin liked to say. One and done.

In the past seven years, aside from pure appreciation of, say,

Michael B. Jordan or Miles Teller, she had never felt any kind of romantic or lustful feelings for anyone.

Until now.

Awkward for several reasons. One, she was allegedly dating his brother. Two, he probably had women lined up from Boston to California to choose from. Good-looking firefighter with nice family? Maybe he was already in a serious relationship. She hoped he was. She hoped he'd bring a date tonight, a lovely, smart, beautiful woman. That would kill any little seed of interest poking through the barren soil of the past seven years. Please let him be seeing someone wonderful and funny and nice. Or let him be a man-whore, Tindering his way through the greater Boston area. She'd lose respect that way. Wouldn't want to kiss a man-whore. Not that she wanted to kiss Dante Santini. Not exactly. Not yet.

No, not ever. The third reason was that flash of . . . darkness or warning or whatever that was. Something in her was scared of something in Dante.

And four, Justin. No one would ever measure up, obviously. You couldn't replace a perfect love story. Besides, Lark wasn't even sure how to date. She'd never kissed anyone but Justin. Never held hands with someone other than him. Ever. Even if she *wanted* to be in a relationship—and she didn't, she was a medical resident, for heaven's sake—she had no idea how things worked these days. It made her feel old and out of touch just thinking about it.

But the image of Dante sparkling down at her, laughing . . .

"Shit," she whispered. Not convenient.

Well, she'd just have to chill, wouldn't she? She had a job to do. A role to play. There was tonight's party, possibly another family gathering, then the wedding weekend itself and its associated events—rehearsal dinner, day-after brunch, whatever else. After that, she'd be done with the Santini family.

The thought gave her a pang. She really liked the Santini family.

With a sigh, she started her car, pulled up a podcast on oncology treatment and headed to Boston.

She found a miraculously available parking spot two blocks away from Lorenzo's apartment, got out of her battered little Honda, lugged her dress bag and suitcase to 35 Beacon Street. She pushed the buzzer next to a nameplate that read *Santini*, and a minute later, Dr. Satan appeared.

He really was gorgeous, despite his neutral expression at seeing her. He looked like a Scandinavian model—the blue eyes, the fierce cheekbones—too cool and sophisticated for a mere American to comprehend.

"Hi," she chirped, abruptly uncomfortable. "How are you?"

"Come in."

"Nice to see you."

"You too." That was a lie, she was sure. But he took her suitcase and led the way through the foyer and opened the door for her. The apartment was 1A. Of course it was.

"Wow," Lark said as she stood in the foyer. "This is . . . wow, Lorenzo."

"Thanks."

She walked into the living room and laid her dress bag across the back of a chair. The place was tasteful, posh and elegant. White furniture, Persian rugs, dark wood trim, a brick fireplace. The art on the walls was modern and mostly black on white. She should take pictures and send them to her mom for an assessment. Bet they cost a fortune. His bookcases were filled with medical tomes and hefty biographies (many about dictators, she noted with a grin, but one of Gandhi, too). Lots of stuff that had no purpose but looked pretty . . . a tray holding decorative rope balls. A glass orb. A twisted bronze sculpture. Some shell-like thing that wasn't actually a shell. (Faux shells? In coastal Massachusetts?)

Tall windows overlooked a courtyard lined with neat inkberry bushes, and sunlight spilled in from the west. The apartment was stunning, she thought. And barren.

There was one family photo—Lorenzo in a gold cap and gown, his arm around Noni, who had been quite cute back in the day.

"Med school graduation?" she guessed.

"Yes. Johns Hopkins."

She had a similar photo of her own med school graduation from Boston University, except everyone was in it. Mom, Dad, Grandpop, Mom's parents, her four siblings, Esme and Imogen, who'd been an infant. And the Deans. Of course the Deans. It was one of at least a dozen family photos she had on display, and her place was a fraction of the size of this place. "You have a beautiful home, Lorenzo. Did you use the same interior decorator as the one who did your Cape house?"

"Yes. You can have the guest room. Third door on the right. I'm working right now, so if you're hungry or thirsty, help yourself. Just don't get drunk."

"I wouldn't get drunk, Lorenzo."

He stared at a point over her head. "Questions?"

"Uh . . . no."

"Good. Be ready by six thirty. Don't be late." He started to turn away.

"Wait, Lorenzo."

He sighed.

"Ask me how my day was."

"See, I asked you to be a . . ." His voice trailed off as he searched for the right word.

"An escort?"

"A *companion*, so we don't have to do this . . . talking thing."

"How was your day, Dr. Satan?" she asked, folding her arms across her chest. "Did you get outside and enjoy this beautiful weather?"

He sighed and rubbed his eyes. "Yes. I went for a run at six a.m. I also ate lunch in the courtyard." He nodded toward the window.

"What did you have?"

"Chickpea and avocado salad."

"Sounds yummy. Now ask how my day was. Come on. You can do it."

A huge sigh. "How was your day, Dr. Smith?"

"Wicked fun," she said. "I loved hanging out with your family. Henry's mother seems lovely, and her falcon is—" She bit down on a laugh. "Breathtaking. We had a great time."

"How wonderful for everyone involved."

She laughed. She couldn't help it. It may have been her imagination, but he almost smiled.

She went into the kitchen—white cabinetry, black stone countertops—and opened the refrigerator. It was like an ad for Marie Kondo—neat little rows of San Pellegrino, same-sized glass containers full of cut-up fruits and vegetables, glass bottles of orange juice and milk. Cartons would be so pedestrian. There was a bowl full of lemons and limes, another of reddish gold apples. Fresh dill in a vase. Pricey condiments lined the door, all in same-sized jars. No butter, no cheese. She took out some milk, and he got a glass from the cupboard and handed it to her. "Got any Oreos to go with this?"

"No." He didn't smile.

"That was a joke," she said as she poured. "Hey, I have to warn you that your grandmother still doesn't seem to like me. I haven't been able to make any inroads there."

The milk was amazingly good, creamy and rich. Whole milk? Was this a sign that he was indeed human and subject to indulgence now and then?

"That's fine," he said. "Noni's very particular. She doesn't have to like you."

"I thought you wanted to reassure her that you'd end up with a lovely partner, and weren't a bitter, dried-up husk, alone except for his work."

"That *is* the point, but she doesn't have to like you."

"Does she actually worry about you finding someone?"

He sighed. "She said it would be a shame if I didn't have children. That I should find a woman who . . ."

"Go on." This would be good.

"Who appreciates my gifts and would be a traditional wife."

"Oh! A traditional wife? In other words, worship you and do all the work of marriage, home and child raising herself while asking nothing from you."

"She'd have financial security, beautiful surroundings and every comfort, so yes."

"Sounds like a housekeeper-slash-nanny. Is that what *you* want?"

He sighed. "I suppose, yes."

"Have you ever been in love, Lorenzo?"

"I'm in the middle of reviewing notes for a very complicated surgery, Dr. Smith. Can we not . . . talk?"

"Sure. I just thought it'd be more convincing if I knew—"

"Lark, you're just an . . . obstruction, okay? A human barrier preventing my family from trying to set me up, or wring their hands over my lack of attachment. My parents still feel guilty over sending me away to school. If they think I have someone, they feel better. My grandmother knows I'm not close to many people and worries that I'll be bereft without her. Even if we're not really together, even when we break up, you give them a reason to . . ."

"Hope?"

He cut her a look. "To back off."

Had he smiled, it would've been . . . but he didn't, so . . . "At least you're honest," she said. "Okay, the interrogation is over. Which is my room again?"

"Third door on the right. Six thirty. Don't be late." He turned his back to go into his office.

"I'm never late," she said.

"You were eleven minutes late for the family picnic."

"That was intentional. It's called fashionably late."

"It's called eleven minutes late," he said, then closed the door.

She couldn't help a smile as she went down the hall. The guest room was similarly well appointed and sterile. White bed, white decorative pillows, sumptuous gray throw blanket, beautiful maple dresser. She unpacked, hanging her pink dress carefully, then peeked in the guest bathroom. Okay, she'd definitely be taking a bath in that giant tub. But first, a nap.

The conversation with Lorenzo had left her soul feeling a little unsettled. She hadn't anticipated liking his family quite so much . . . or having Noni be such a tough nut to crack. When Lorenzo had first asked her to do this, she'd pictured a sweet little old lady who'd light up at the sight of Lark, be so relieved her darling boy had found someone at last. Lark hadn't expected someone who hissed and glared.

She took out the picture of her and Justin she always brought with her if she was sleeping somewhere else—their engagement photo. His parents had paid for a photographer, and they'd gone to the Common. In the photo, Justin had picked her up, and their foreheads were resting against each other, both of them radiating joy.

We loved with a love that was more than love.

They really had. It was good to remember that.

It just seemed so long ago.

At 6:58 p.m., she and Lorenzo got out of a hired town car and walked into the Copley Plaza. Lark wore the dress and shoes he'd chosen, as well as a pair of diamond stud earrings Addie had given her as a maid of honor present. The adorable purse contained her phone, wallet and tissues, since she knew she'd get teary at the toasts. She'd texturized her hair, then spent half an hour securing it into an updo with no fewer than twenty-two bobby pins and half a can of spray so it would stay put. Mascara, blush, neutral lip gloss.

Lorenzo had looked at her as she emerged from her room at 6:29 p.m., simply nodded and opened the door so they could leave. He wore a tux (custom made, no doubt) and looked as icy and handsome as a Norwegian prince.

The other Santinis were gathered in the foyer, all looking beautiful and a lot more approachable. Sofia wore a pale blue Grecian-style gown, looking like a movie star with her curly black hair piled on her head. Izzy had on a short, bright green shift dress, and Anita was dressed in a floral blue and white print.

"Oh, my God, you look amazing!" Izzy said. "Turn around! Girl! Look at this low back! Fire, honey. Fire! Dante, help us out here, or Lark's gonna burn the place down."

Dante glanced her way, did a double take, then recovered. She felt her own cheeks grow hot.

"You look very handsome, Dante," she said, nodding at his blue suit.

"You clean up nice, too, Doc," he said. He gave her a quick smile and glanced away.

Noni was in a long dress (no wig, obviously), and Lorenzo immediately went to her side and bent over to say hello. There. He smiled. He *was* capable of it. Then he pushed her wheelchair into the St. James Room, the "intimate" space for only 150 people. The rest of them followed.

"I feel like I'm on the set of *Bridgerton*," Izzy said. "Wow."

Wow was right. The carved wooden ceiling was dazzling, and the giant chandelier glowed. On the tables sat lush flower arrangements of blush roses, creamy lisianthus and pink peonies with trailing English ivy. Huge windows overlooked the street, and all the guests were dressed to kill. Lark was suddenly glad she had on this particular outfit. She definitely didn't look poor and out of place, as Lorenzo had so inelegantly put it.

There were probably seventy-five people there, sipping cocktails, talking in clumps and clusters. Lots of laughter, lots of excitement, definitely good mojo. Sofia and Henry moved through the crowd, greeting their guests. Henry was his mother's only child—his dad had remarried and had one or two kids significantly younger, as Lark recalled. But Jocelyn had quite a few siblings, she learned, and there were lots of aunts and uncles on both sides.

"So nice to meet you," Lark said over and over. "I'm Lark Smith, Lorenzo's girlfriend."

"Lorenzo has a girlfriend?" was the standard response.

"It's still new," she said, feeling her cheeks flush with the lie.

Mom had had a point about dishonesty. But she was welcomed and kissed and complimented as her date stood by like a disdainful royal, watching and judging, his expression only thawing a bit when he looked at Sofia, clearly his favorite sibling, or spoke to Noni, who seemed sharper around him.

He really wanted to impress, Lark thought with a pang of sympathy. He wanted everyone to see *this* . . . his success, his generosity, his good taste. It was sad. She would've loved to see him laughing, flirting with some of the older women, as Dante and Silvio were, showing genuine warmth and affection. But he was not hers to fix, and he didn't think he needed fixing.

When they sat down, Silvio took the microphone and welcomed everyone, and Jocelyn said a few words, too, then Sofia and Henry said how glad they were to be here.

"Thanks to my wonderful big brother for throwing us this absolutely beautiful party," she said, her eyes shining with tears. "I'm so proud to be your sister, Lorenzo."

Lorenzo gave a courtly nod. Lark put her hand over his and gave it a squeeze. He *was* a generous brother, and Sofia's happiness was contagious. After a second, Lorenzo squeezed back. He didn't let go, either.

It was not a comfortable sensation. Lark suddenly felt like there was a spotlight on the two of them, on their joined hands. It felt weird and unnatural, like her hand wasn't her own, really. She tolerated it as long as she could, then subtly slid her hand free and took a sip of champagne.

She didn't like touching Dr. Satan. Robbie and Grandpop were going to be disappointed. Not the rom-com they were looking for.

Other than that one moment, Lorenzo more or less ignored her as the evening went on. Oh, he made sure she had a glass of champagne and pulled out a chair for her, but talking? No. But that's what she was here for, right? To be charming and not emotionally needy or too attached to her date. Maybe she should've taken Lorenzo up on his offer to pay her after all.

All her life, Lark had been used to a certain amount of attention. She was an identical twin, which came with instant celebrity. She knew she and Addie were pretty (possibly beautiful). All the Smiths were. But Addie had always been the center of attention when they were together, the life of the party, the organizer of the events. Lark had been better at hanging back to admire her twin (which she totally did), holding Harlow's hand or playing with Robbie and Winnie. Even with her closer friends, like Jordyn from elementary school, Luis from work, or with Joy, she liked being a sideliner, listening more than she spoke, encouraging their stories, their feelings. It was safe and comfortable, something she'd learned from the uterus on.

Maybe that was why Justin had made such an impact on her when they were five. He *saw* her. Not as the quiet twin. Just as herself. With him, and with his parents, there'd been room for her to shine, too, and the love she'd gotten from Justin had been as warm and steady as the sun.

The point was, she thought now, chatting about the wedding with Sofia's best friend from college, being a sideliner had always allowed Lark to see things.

And what she saw now was that Lorenzo was avoiding his family. He loved Sofia and honored Noni as the matriarch, both protective of and deferential to her. But otherwise, he kept a huge distance. It wasn't pride, she thought. It was . . . shame? He would glance at his parents, then quickly look away before they saw. He seemed irritated by Izzy, maybe because he felt she should've become a doctor, maybe because she lacked the slight air of worship

Sofia had for him. A tight smile for his mother, then back to Noni, who was drinking gin and frowning at the appetizers.

But he could barely look at Dante. Every time Dante was in his line of vision, Lorenzo's gaze bounced away. There was a universe of unspoken emotion lurking between the brothers. Dante, on the other hand, would look at Lorenzo steadily, without hostility but without a sliver of warmth, either.

"Hey," said Izzy, appearing at her side. "You doing okay?"

"Oh, sure," she said. "I don't get to play dress-up too often. How about you? Having a good time?"

"Absolutely."

"Do you have a special someone, Izzy?" she asked.

Izzy snorted. "No. Just broke up with a radiology tech after he wasted six months of my life. Why pretend you're interested in marriage when you're still on Tinder, huh? Why?"

Lark shuddered. "You're better off without him."

"I know. Still." She rolled her eyes. "Sofia's the only one of us who found the golden ticket so far." She smiled at her sister, who stood just a few feet away.

So Dante was single, too, then. She hadn't seen a date, but she was also trying not to pay attention to him, and also not to ignore him, and also not to blush if she did catch his eye, and also to feign interest in and chemistry with Lorenzo. And she'd thought organic chem had been hard.

"Did you just call my son the golden ticket, Isabella?" said Jocelyn, approaching with a glass of champagne in her hand. "Thank you, honey. He's a good boy, for sure."

"When do we get to meet his dad?" Izzy asked.

"Oh, he'll be at the wedding. He lives in Oregon with his second family and couldn't make it tonight. We talk every now and then. Amicable divorce and all that. He went back to his parents in China for a while after we divorced . . . Henry was fifteen or so . . . and we didn't talk much then. I think his second wife really brings out the best in him, though. She pushed him to reconnect with Henry. I really like her. Maybe she upped his game in the bedroom, too. He was terrible in the sack. Don't tell my son I said so. Sorry, am I oversharing?"

"You are," said Izzy, smiling at Lark. "And we love it."

"Any secrets on Lorenzo, Lark?" Jocelyn said. "He's a bit of a mystery in the family, isn't he?"

"Yeah, Lark. Any secrets?" Izzy raised an eyebrow.

Did she know?

Lorenzo was looking at her. Like a dog hearing his name, he was paying abrupt attention.

"You know," Lark said carefully, "I think he takes the role of firstborn son very seriously. Always feels like he has to be in charge, which makes him a great surgeon. But it's hard for him to relax. Once he does, though, he's great." A statement that might well be correct, Lark thought. Not that she had any first-hand knowledge of it.

"He is?" Isabella asked, looking at her brother. "Lorenzo, are you great when you relax? Because that's the rumor over here."

"Whatever Lark says must be true," he said somberly.

"Okay, then." Izzy smiled at him. "I look forward to you re-laxing."

See? Lark wanted to tell Lorenzo. *She likes you. You could be friends.*

During dinner, Lark sat between Lorenzo and Anita, and to his credit, Lorenzo spoke to her. "Is your dinner okay?" and "No, thank you" when she offered him bread. Otherwise, he spoke in Italian to his grandmother, with Silvio occasionally commenting.

"Sofia, Dante and I don't speak Italian," Izzy said in response to her unasked question. "We feel very inferior, right, Dante?" The two sat across from her.

"Absolutely," he said. "We're the Luddites of the family. Lorenzo got all the smarts."

"I resent that," Izzy said. "I mean, *you're* dumb, Dante, but I'm quite smart."

"You're not dumb, honey!" Anita said. She put her hand on her younger son's arm. "Do you have a single sister, Lark? Maybe you could fix him up." She beamed.

"I *do* have a single sister," Lark said, smiling back.

"Sign me up," Dante said. "I don't even need to meet her. If she's your sister, Lark, she must be great. Call the priest, Ma."

"And you said you have a single brother, so that takes care of me," Izzy said.

"I'm pretty sure he won't be single for long," Lark said. "He's in love with our big sister's best friend. You'll need to move fast."

"It would make holidays very simple, if three of my kids married three Smith kids," Anita said.

"Okay. I'll tell my parents," Lark said, laughing. "We could do a three-for-one wedding and save money."

"Are you and Lorenzo already talking marriage?" Anita asked, her eyes wide. Lorenzo gave Lark a knifelike look. "Because if the answer is yes, I approve! I'd be over the moon! I'd—"

"Easy, Ma," Dante said as Izzy laughed. His dark eyes were warm on Lark. "You have to be more careful," he explained. "She's been saying novenas for my brother to find a wife since he was fourteen."

"Sorry, Anita," Lark said. "It's way too early for anything like that just yet. I was kidding."

"Of course you were, sweetie. But if you weren't, that would be fine, too."

"Let me change the subject," Izzy said. "Lark, what do you like doing in your spare time?"

"Well, I'm a resident, so a lot of my time is spent researching things that come up at work," she said. "But I paint a little, since my mom's an artist. I ride my bike a lot, because we have the Cape Cod Rail Trail. Connery likes to come, too." She took her phone out and pulled up a picture of Connery sitting in her bike basket. "I should put him in modeling school. He's a natural."

"Like Toto in *The Wizard of Oz*," Anita said, smiling. "And, Lark, *you're* so pretty, you could be on the cover of a magazine. Seriously, you're tall enough to model."

"And yet she chose to use her brain instead of becoming a human coat hanger," Lorenzo said. "Shocking."

An awkward silence fell over the table. Dante stared at his brother, unsmiling.

Lark gave Lorenzo a hard look. "I'm pretty sure it was a compliment, Pooh Bear," Lark said, knowing the endearment would grate on him. "And thank you, Anita. My twin sister did some modeling, actually. It's not as simple as it seems. You need to know the market you're selling to, and understand photography and light. It can be really physical, too."

"Excuse me," Dante said, getting up from the table.

"Can we circle back to Pooh Bear?" Izzy asked.

"No," Lorenzo said.

Conversation wandered back to Sofia and Henry, but yes, Lark was sure now. Something big had gone down between the brothers. It wasn't just sibling rivalry.

"All finished here?" a waiter asked. "Oh, hey, Lark!"

"Hey!" It was . . . gosh, what was his name? "Lionel! How are you?"

"Great! I'd hug you, but . . ." He smiled and shrugged. She

and Lionel had been at BU together, lived on the same hall freshman year and stayed friends throughout school.

In other words, he'd known Justin.

"What's new with you?" she quickly asked.

"Oh, not much. I was a paralegal for a while—corporate tax law, so boring—then thought I'd become a chef. Got a job with this caterer to learn the ropes."

"Excellent!" She smiled hard, but she knew it was coming.

"Listen, I want to say how—"

"Oh, shoot! My phone!" Lark said, whipping it out of her purse. "It was so good to see you, Lionel. Message me sometime, okay? I'm on the Cape, but we should reconnect. Sorry! Bye!"

She put her phone against her ear as if she had heard it ring and zipped out of the room, the silk dress swishing against her legs, the air cool on her back. Her heart was thudding.

Things like this happened all the time. All the time. Just . . . not for a while.

There had been the friends who'd been there every step of the way for her and Justin—Jordyn and Mike, Justin's freshman year roommate. Luz, her study partner in calculus at BU. Family, of course. There had been the people who'd come to the funeral. The people who had sent donations to Dana-Farber in his name, or had sent touching cards or had called or emailed or texted. And then there were the people who had known but hadn't done squat.

Lionel was in that last group. She didn't want his condolences seven years too late. He could've sent a fucking card. A Facebook message. *Something.*

Being here, in *this* hotel, the nicest in Boston, was abruptly too much. After all, this was where she and Justin had first been together, the love story that had begun as children finally consummated when they were college students. She'd been determined not to make their places a shrine of sorrow, had been to this hotel at least five times since Justin's death, but . . . but . . .

He was getting to be so long ago. So long ago.

Tears burned in her eyes. What she wouldn't give right now for a glimpse of him, leaning in the corner, smiling at her, that thick dark hair, his navy blue eyes. But the memories of him in real life were being replaced by the movies of him, photos. His smell, his voice, the feeling of his hands, his laugh had been fading for years now, a sad, fragile mist succumbing to the harsh rays of every day that had passed since his death.

A wedding was taking place in another ballroom—the beautiful marbled lobby was packed with people in tuxedos and sparkling dresses, clearly waiting for the happy couple. Yep. There was the bride, beautiful dress, gorgeous hair. Lark pasted on a smile and slipped around people and smiled some more. The hotel lobby was huge, and once she cleared that crowd, she headed down the hall and found a little quiet area near the Dartmouth Street entrance.

An empty chair, some cool air and maybe she could fend off the storm of memories battering her. Turkey club sandwiches and root beer in bed. High tea with Heather. Her twenty-first birthday, when Justin had brought her here for her first legal drink. Brunch on graduation weekend, the Smiths and the Deans, talking about the future, that happy future filled with jobs and medical school, a wedding, children, a home filled with love.

Let's get married right now.

The memory of her own voice echoed in her head.

Get it together, Larkby. Addie's voice, always bringing her back. Her strongest tether to this life. Her twin's advice, imagined or real, was spot-on. She'd just sit a minute and take a few breaths and maybe text the Deans. She blotted her eyes with a tissue, grateful for the waterproof mascara, then took out her phone and sent Heather and Theo a quick message.

Thinking of you guys. Love you!

A second later, Heather answered. We love you, too, sweetheart! What are you up to tonight? Want to come over?

At a friend's engagement party in Boston. Very fancy and fun! She almost hit "send," then changed *engagement* to *birthday*. Izzy had taken a picture of her an hour or so ago so she could send it to Addie, and Lark now sent that same picture to the Deans. Check out my dress!

So! Damn! Beautiful! Have fun, darling! Love from Theo, too. 💜 💜 💜

They were *such* good people. So kind. They'd never begrudge her happiness. No. They wanted her to live a full life, find a new person to love, have children. They'd said so a dozen times or more.

Lark was the one who had a hard time picturing all that.

"Hey. You okay?"

Her head jerked up, and light seemed to flash through her veins. She felt her face flush. *Be cool*, she told herself. *Remember why you're here.* "Hi, Dante. Yeah, sure. Just needed a little quiet." His face was somber. "Are *you* okay?"

He sat in the chair next to her. "Yep. I imagine it's kind of a lot in there, all those people for you to meet."

"I'm having a *great* time."

"Liar." He winked, as he'd been taught to at the Hot Fireman School, no doubt. "I'm pretty sure I saw a tear or two just now."

Damn it. "Happy couples make me weepy."

"Same." God, he was adorable. "You sure, though?" His mischievous grin dropped a notch or two. "I have sisters. I know how to listen."

She felt her heart knot. *I lost my virginity in this hotel, Dante. With the boyfriend who became my fiancé who then died.* "I'm sure. How about you? I can't help noticing you and Lorenzo are . . . well, you're not super close, are you?"

He laughed a little, that nice ashy sound that made the pit of her stomach clench. "That pretty much sums it up."

"I have a brother and also know how to listen," she said, smiling as she echoed his words. "Do you want to talk about it?"

He slid her a look, and man, his eyes were so dark, they were almost black. Espresso brown. "I do not. Let's just say there was a girl."

"Oh! There was a *girl.* I see." She ventured a pat on his knee. "I'm happy to tell you there are more girls in the world, and I've seen about twenty checking you out tonight."

He laughed again and shook his head. "Are you as nice as you seem, Lark? Because if you are, you—" He stopped. "Sorry. Never mind."

"No, no, you can't do that. What were you going to say?" Because it suddenly seemed very important that he finish his sentence. Her heart banged against her sternum. God! This wasn't like her.

He looked at his hands. Were his biceps straining against the sleeves of his suit? Yes. That wasn't important (but my God, wow). Dante took a breath, then said, very carefully, "I'm guessing you're very good for my brother. I hope he's good for you, too." His voice was low and she *felt* it. Every cell in her body seemed to surge toward him.

"Who was the girl?" she asked.

He looked at her a long time. Then, just like that, whatever electricity flared between them was gone, turned off by some switch Dante had just flipped. The mood was normal again, and he was just the nice brother in a family she was getting to know.

The disappointment surprised her.

"She was a model," he said. "And that's all I'm gonna say about that. Coming back to the party, miss? Want a hot firefighter to escort you?"

Message received. *I'm just the flirty brother, nothing to see here.* "I do, yes," she said. "Can you find me one?"

He threw his head back and laughed. "Oh, she's a firecracker, all right. Come on, pretty in pink." He offered his hand, and she took it as she stood, and a current of heat ran straight down her arm.

"After you," he said, letting go of her hand and gesturing for her to go ahead of him. "And, uh . . . helluva dress, Lark."

She turned and looked at him over her shoulder. "Thank you for noticing, sir."

Yep. Dante Santini was going to be a problem. For one, Lark was supposed to be dating his brother. For two . . .

For two, she was terrified of ever being in love again.

TWELVE

LARK, MANY AND MANY A YEAR AGO

A few weeks after she'd chosen her wedding dress, Lark left her shift at Mass General and headed to Justin's for dinner. It was a thirty-minute walk, and she could cut through the Common. She was already mentally rehearsing the story she wanted to tell Justin—she had been bathing a man, rolled him on his side, his back to her, when eleven days' worth of poop had exploded out of him, onto the bedding, the bed, the floor, the far wall and Lark herself. The other CNA had been more experienced and knew to leap out of the way.

Lark had had to take a shower in which she scrubbed her skin five times with the hospital's sharp antiseptic soap. She went back to the patient's room later to see how he was doing, and the poor man had been so apologetic. Lark said it happened all the time (not really, but . . .). These stories were the gifts of being a CNA, and she knew Justin would appreciate it.

While Boston would inevitably get one more snowstorm, just to test the endurance of New Englanders, today was one of those teaser days in late March that, if you weren't careful, made you believe winter was over. The temperature was in the midfifties, the sky gently drifting into a darker shade of blue as the day came to a close. Birds sang from the trees, some of which were setting up to bloom in another few weeks, and the air smelled like garlic and, less noticeably, sewage, a hallmark of the fair city. Lark chose to focus on the garlic.

In the Common, early daffodils looked like scattered candy against the dull winter grass. Lark watched a young mother pushing her toddler in a tricked-out stroller. She and Justin wanted kids, after med school, of course. Addie, too, wanted kids and would probably be first. Maybe one of them would have twins. She hoped so. Pulling out her phone, she texted Addie to say she was thinking about her and couldn't wait to hear how tonight's "meet the parents" was going. Things between Addie and Nicole were getting serious, and while Nicole was kind of uptight, she had a good heart. Hopefully, Addie's love would loosen her up a bit.

When she got to Justin's, she punched in the code to the street entrance of the building and went up the stairs to his apartment. The door was locked, which was unusual, because he usually left it open when she was coming. No worries, she had a key, of course.

It was oddly quiet. She should've texted him, but they both agreed they didn't want to be *those people* who needed to communicate every hour or texted each other from twelve feet away.

"Honey?" she called. Did she have the right night? Yes, of course she did. They'd talked about what they'd cook when he'd called her on her break this morning.

She turned on a light. The bedroom door was closed. She went in, and there he was, under the covers, curtains drawn.

"Honey?" she said. "Are you okay?"

He stirred, glancing over his shoulder before letting his head drop back to the pillow. "I feel like shit," he said. "I left work at two."

"You should've texted me." She sat on the bed next to him and felt his forehead. It was warm, and sudden fear flashed through her. "You have a fever," she said, keeping her voice calm as she pushed back his thick black hair.

"I know. The flu or something. I have a wicked headache. A rash, too."

Her muscles gathered, the instinctive response to fear. "What kind of rash?" Her voice sounded almost normal.

"I don't know. Little red dots."

"Can I take a look?" she asked.

"I just need to sleep," he muttered, eyes closed.

"Show me and then I'll make you some soup." She turned on the light, and Justin squinted.

"Hi, by the way," he said with a tired, lopsided grin.

"Hi, babe." She tried to smile, too.

He tugged off his shirt and held out his arms. Tiny clusters of red dots. She pressed on one red clump, and it stayed red.

And because she'd been studying acute lymphocytic since the age of fourteen, she knew this was *not* a rash. It was petechiae, a sign of a low platelet count. And low platelets came from abnormal cancer cells in bone marrow.

She felt under his jaw with both hands, but he jerked back. "What are you doing?"

"Checking your lymph nodes."

"You're not a doctor yet, Lark." His tone was accusatory, but she heard the fear underneath.

"I know, honey, I know." She tried again, and this time, he let her. There was a raised lump, round and hard.

"Ow," he said.

Their eyes met.

She swallowed. "We need to call your doctor, honey."

And just like that, their world disintegrated. Tonight's plans, off. Work tomorrow, no. Driving down to New York City to see Jordyn Rae this weekend? Not gonna happen. They stared at each other, abruptly adrift in a dark ocean of fear.

"It's probably just a virus," he said, then cleared his throat.

"Right. You've . . . you've had viruses before. We'll just be extra neurotic, okay?"

He nodded. "Actually, I feel better now. Better than earlier."

"Good! Great! I'll make something really nutritious for dinner. You stay put, honey. Did you take any Motrin? Actually, how about some Tylenol?" Because Motrin wasn't good if you had low platelets. She got two tablets of Tylenol, a glass of water and the electronic thermometer. "One hundred point two," she said. "Hardly anything. Want to watch TV while I cook?"

"Sure!" Justin said, and his voice was overly cheerful.

"Call Dr. Kothari, okay?"

"I will."

They knew, though. As she chopped carrots and onions and garlic and ginger, added cilantro, sliced chicken, threw in some turmeric, she was aware that she was shaking. Her phone chimed with a text. Addie.

Everything okay?

That twin radar. She didn't want to answer, but that would make things worse. Yes! Staying at J's tonight. Love you.

They'd have to call his parents. Get in to see the doctor *tomorrow*. Spinal tap. Bone marrow biopsy. Lymph node biopsy. T-cell therapy. Stem cell therapy. Chemo. Bone marrow transplant. Radiation.

She stirred the soup, put in some brown rice and turned the

heat down to a simmer, then went to the couch and cuddled up next to Justin. "You look incredibly handsome today. That bed-head looks good on you."

He smiled, but not really. She understood. She turned his face to hers and kissed him. "I love you. I love you so much, Justin." Their whole history flickered through her heart. Kindergarten, birthday parties, movies, dinners, the first time they held hands, the Copley Square Hotel, Venice, yesterday when he'd gotten up early to make her scrambled eggs with cheddar cheese on English muffins, her favorite.

"I love you, too, little bird," he said, stroking her cheek. Then he smiled for real this time, and kissed her back.

"Whatever happens," she said, "we're in it together."

"Exactly. But I bet it's just the flu," he said. "Which I just gave you. Sorry."

"I'll take it." She'd happily take a flu, or Ebola, or give up a leg if it meant Justin had not relapsed.

Tonight, they'd be two people in love. One had a little virus. They'd eat chicken soup and watch something gripping on TV. They'd hold hands. They might even make love. She wouldn't cry, because this might be the last day she would be able to stop herself from crying.

Tomorrow, she knew, their lives would be very, very different. But tonight . . . they had tonight.

It was the worst possible news. Three days later, they sat in Dr. Kothari's office at Dana-Farber Cancer Institute—Heather and Theo, Justin and Lark—all of them white-faced as the doctor gave them the test results.

The leukemia had returned to his bone marrow and central nervous system. It would require immediate and aggressive chemo injected directly into his spinal canal and into a tiny catheter they'd place in his brain. Oral meds. Radiation therapy. And the most terrifying words of all . . . experimental treatment.

"I'm sorry it's not better news," Dr. Kothari said, "but I want you to know what we're up against." *We.* That was nice, Lark thought numbly. "When you've had ALL as a kid—and you had central nervous system involvement then, right?"

"Right," his mother said.

"Well, I'm afraid this recurrence means your prognosis is a rough one." He let that sit a minute, then said, "The median survival rate is six months."

There was a moment of silence. Then Heather vomited right onto the rug, and Theo burst into tears.

"That can't be right!" he sobbed. "There's got to be a mistake! He has a *ninety percent* survival rate!" He dropped to his knees and bent like a tree brought down by lightning. "You're wrong! You've got to be wrong."

Justin and Lark just sat, white and hard as marble statues, clenching each other's hands as their lives were eviscerated.

Six months? Six *months*?

Dr. Kothari handed over a box of tissues—the good kind, with lotion, because he knew the drill. He said he'd give them a moment, and left the office, and it was so odd, so surreal, Heather wailing, pulling on her hair as Theo tried to get her to stop. Justin said nothing. Lark said nothing.

"My baby, my baby," Heather said, and Justin got up and hugged her. The smell of vomit was strong. Lark didn't feel so good herself.

Dr. Kothari returned with a ginger ale, some crackers, Windex and paper towels. He gave the food to Heather, then very kindly cleaned up her vomit.

"I know this is incredibly hard news to hear and absorb," he said after he'd washed his hands. "Of course, there are some promising therapies out there, and we have a clinical trial going on right now that I'll get you into."

"Good! Great," said Theo. "So there's hope."

Dr. Kothari hesitated, then said, "Of course. No disease is the same, and we can't predict individual outcomes. Of course, we hope you'll respond well to the therapy. If you go that route, there's no time to waste, so we'll want to get you set up for chemo immediately."

Heather nodded vigorously. "Yes. You'll feel better when we're doing something about this, sweetheart."

Justin said nothing.

"Honey?" Lark whispered.

He glanced at her, almost surprised to see her, it seemed. Cleared his throat. "Yeah. A hundred percent. I wanna go for it. Throw everything at me. I have a lot to live for." His words sounded strange and wooden.

"You absolutely do," Heather choked. "You'll beat this!"

"You're young and strong, Justin," Theo said. "You'll get through this."

"Yeah," Justin said, sounding stronger. "You're right. I will. I beat it once, I'll beat it again."

"You're goddamn right," Theo said.

"Of course you will. Attitude has a huge impact on treatment, honey, and you're so healthy and young." Heather's voice broke on that last word.

Lark looked at Dr. Kothari. He returned her gaze, and in his dark brown eyes, she saw the truth, a terrifying black maw of fact. For a second, she thought she might faint.

Justin would die. Was, right now, dying, the end of his life now measured in months and weeks and days and hours, not years or decades. Of course, people beat the odds all the time . . . but in cases like Justin's, most people did not. Maybe that was why it was called *odds*. Because it would be odd if you did beat it. A fluke.

Then came all the words, because *there wasn't any time to waste*. Lark's job was to know what the words meant—she'd be going to med school, after all, right? B-cell phenotype, leukemic blast cells, immunophenotyping, high disease burden, flow cytometry, allogeneic hematopoietic stem cell transplantation, CVAD.

Median survival rate, six months.

How . . . how could that be possible? Justin ran eight miles every other day. They didn't eat red meat! They didn't smoke weed or cigarettes or do drugs or even drink that much! A bottle of wine could last *weeks* in their house. He had very little stress, loved his job, loved her. They even did a corny little gratitude meditation every morning. He was *healthy*, damn it.

Median survival rate, six months.

Six months wouldn't even get them to their wedding.

"Can I have a moment alone with Justin and Lark?" Dr. Kothari asked, and Lark gave a tiny nod. Theo and Heather left the room, arms around each other.

"You have very loving parents," Dr. Kothari said.

"I sure do," Justin said. "And the world's best fiancée."

"I think I hold that honor, actually." She smiled, or hoped she did, but she felt her cheek muscles quivering with the effort.

"We met in kindergarten." *So you better not fuck this up, Dr. Kothari. We are childhood sweethearts. That shit is sacred.* The swearing, even though she hadn't said it out loud, shocked her.

"I would be remiss if I didn't mention another option," Dr. Kothari said, again letting his words settle before continuing. "You could decide not to pursue any treatment, Justin. We'd focus on palliative care, keeping you comfortable, concentrate on quality, rather than quantity, of life."

Though Lark had tried not to work on the palliative care floor of the hospital, she'd done a shift or two when it couldn't be avoided. Some of the patients were there for simple pain relief during treatment for their illness. Some were there on hospice, which meant they'd been diagnosed with six months or less to live and had decided not to try to seek a cure for their disease . . . they were just there for comfort as their lives wound down.

"Are you saying Justin qualifies for hospice?" she asked, her voice a squeak.

"Absolutely not," Justin said sharply. "I'm fighting this. Leukemia can be cured. Right, Lark? Don't you agree?" There was terror underlying his words, and he needed her to agree. To believe.

She looked into those dark blue eyes. "Um . . . I—I obviously want you to live forever, honey. But you . . . I . . . I—I want you to be okay. To be . . . yourself."

"See? We're all on the same page."

What Lark wanted to say was that she didn't want him to writhe and scream out in pain, or have him endure the vomiting and diarrhea from chemo, the weight falling off him till he was skeletal . . . and then not make it. If there was a guarantee that this would cure him, different story. She'd put him through hell and back if he'd end up healthy.

Whole decades of her future shifted and slid and evaporated in front of her. Their three children—two girls and a boy. A lovely home on the Cape. The weddings of her siblings. Becoming Uncle Justin and Auntie Lark. Their tenth anniversary. Hosting dinner parties. Justin opening his own firm. Their twenty-fifth class reunion. Their kids' graduations. Becoming parents-in-law. Having grandchildren.

Life without Justin? The idea was obscene. Impossible. She'd loved him since she was *five*. Five years old. That saying—two halves of a whole? They actually were. No one, not even Addie, loved her as much as Justin did. He had been her first friend, the boy who was nice, who'd keep the mean kids from picking on her for being shy. When he'd gotten sick the first time, he had given her a purpose in life, a mission that transcended being a Smith kid or a twin or a simple adolescent girl. She'd been *needed*. And she needed him, too. Forever. Till death, when they were both old.

But the odds were not in their favor. They were, in fact, overwhelmingly stacked against them. She wanted him to be comfortable and happy, not spending the rest of his life—oh, God!—the *rest of his life* in and out of the hospital for tests and infusions and more tests and infections and side effect management. She didn't want him to die because fluid filled his lungs, drowning him in place, or because the chemo made him so weak that his beautiful, kind, thoughtful heart would no longer beat.

Please let this be a dream, she prayed. *Please let me wake up.*

Dr. Kothari had said something. She'd missed it. She was already screwing up.

"There's got to be better treatments out there than when I was a kid," Justin said.

"I've read about the monoclonal antibodies cocktail," Lark

said, surprising herself by pulling out that information. "That and radiation, it can be a game changer. Right?"

"She's so smart," Justin said. "Hasn't even started med school." He looked at her and smiled.

"Yes, of course, there's always reason to be hopeful," Dr. Kothari said. "Treatment can be pretty grueling, Justin, and hospice is—"

"No. Nope. We're going for it. It's the 2004 Pennant, game four, bottom of the ninth, and I'm the Red Sox, okay?" He smiled and squeezed Lark's hand.

"I'm sorry, I don't understand," Dr. Kothari said.

Lark forced a smile. "He means we're gonna win. Even when it seems like we're not." Yes. Yes. That was the attitude. Because if Justin thought he could beat this, how could she be the one to doubt him?

"Ah," said Dr. Kothari. "Baseball. Got it, and I will look that up, Justin. All right, then."

He told them where to go next, how to get their parking validated (seriously? Did that matter right now?) and shook both their hands.

Lark deliberately left her purse on the floor, so when they went into the waiting room, she said, "Shoot. Forgot my bag," and went back in and closed the door behind her. Dr. Kothari looked up.

"If he was your son," she said quietly, "what would you recommend?"

Dr. Kothari's eyes grew shiny. "We all die, Lark," he said quietly. "The last months of our lives can matter as much as all the months that came before."

She stared at him, then nodded and rejoined the Deans.

Justin's blood was drawn, an emergency CAT scan was done,

and the Deans took them out to lunch, getting a table far away from other diners. Justin's fever had passed quickly; he was ravenous and an oddly light mood settled over the three Deans.

"You're as strong as a Clydesdale," Heather said. "If you lined up a hundred people with this, you're the obvious choice to beat it."

"And you're getting *married*," Theo said. "If that's not something to live for, what is, right, Justin? You can't leave this beautiful girl!"

"I have no intention of it," he said, kissing her hand where the diamond ring glittered.

At the end of the meal, Heather said, "Okay, we all had a huge shock, but now we have a game plan. We'll get through this."

"Absolutely," Theo said.

They all hugged, long and hard, and finally parted ways.

Lark and Justin headed to the Common. "I'm in the mood for ice cream," he said.

"Same," she said, though she was lying. They got their cones—strawberry for her, chocolate chunk for him—and found a bench near the fountain.

"Let's get married right now," Lark said abruptly. "Today. We'll go to city hall. They're still open."

Justin blinked at her. "Um . . . no. Absolutely not. Why? You don't think I'll make it? Jesus, Lark. You have to believe in me." There was anger in his voice, rare and sharper because of it.

"I do believe in you," she said. "I do, honey. I just . . . I just want to be your wife through this."

He looked away. "You'll be my wife after. I'm going to live, Lark. This life is too beautiful to even think about anything else. I want the big fancy wedding and I want to see you in a white dress and have your whole family there, and all my midwestern cousins and our friends. It'll be all the better because I beat leukemia again. This is just a bump in the road."

She felt ice run down her spine. "We can do the big wedding later. I promise, I'd feel like I won the lotto if we got married right now. Hand to God, Justin. Please."

"No," he said firmly. "We're getting married in December. Wear white."

"Justin—"

"No!" Then he rolled his neck, sighed and kissed her hand. "I won't leave you, Lark. We'll get through this. Positive thinking only. I mean it."

She could've fought him on that. Later, she'd think she *should've* fought him. But for now, she knew he needed her faith. If he thought he could make it, she had to think that, too.

"Red Sox, 2004," she said, taking his hand and sliding her fingers between his. His face relaxed. "Obviously, I'm moving in with you," she said. "It's me, or your mother."

"It's you. It's always you. Always has been, always will be."

His words made her heart quadruple in size. Even now, even on this horrible day, he could make her feel like the only woman on the planet. God, she loved him.

Strangely enough, Lark didn't cry. For once, she didn't cry. It was as if her tear ducts had been removed. She called Addie that night, because Addie knew something was off and had been texting and calling. In as few words as possible, she told her sister the news, asked Addie to tell the rest of the family immediately. Then she set up a group text so she could update everyone simultaneously and said she appreciated their love and prayers and told them she and Justin were feeling really optimistic. And also, please communicate only through this group text or Addie, because she was going to be too busy to respond individually for the next few months.

The rest of the week was spent going to the hospital lab for radiology and more blood work, a detailed CAT scan, back to Dr. Kothari's office, over to another doctor's office, to the surgical center for a spinal tap. Oncologists from every specialty—radiation, surgical, medical, hematologic—all weighed in. Lark quit her job, apologizing that she couldn't give more notice.

Dana-Farber incorporated holistic treatments into its battle plans, so acupuncture, yoga, meditation, tai chi, strength training, music therapy were added to a strict calendar. Lark stocked the kitchen with organic food, tossed the cleaning products and bought nontoxic stuff instead. The smell of Windex made her sick to her stomach now, anyway, memories of Dr. Kothari cleaning up Heather's vomit so humbly.

When Justin was at work—because he was going to keep working, isolated, wearing a mask—she and Addie took the day off and cleaned his apartment with the new stuff, washed all the clothes, sheets and towels. As if that would slow the leukemia. But no, no, everything could help. She had to stay positive. Busy and positive.

"How are you?" Addie asked after four hours, and Lark just shook her head, blinking. Addie nodded, understanding that if the dam cracked, it would crumble. Lark's dam would hold, by God. She, champion weeper, would not cry. She wouldn't be scared. She'd believe Justin would beat this. Hell, yes, she would. He had before. He would again. Period.

She went with him to every appointment and kept a notebook, taking copious notes broken down by doctor, specialty, treatment, medications, side effects, the medications to combat the side effects. She ran his schedule, talked optimistically to his bosses, who said he could do as much or as little as he wanted, and messaged their friends. She filed claims with the insurance company, talked to the asshole administrators who denied this treatment or that medication, and won every time. The Deans were well off, but she'd be damned if the insurance company would get off the hook.

She planned their meals for the next two weeks to minimize the number of times she'd need to go grocery shopping. She talked to Heather and Theo a few times every day, had them over as much as possible and didn't go home to the Cape. There was no time for that.

Positive affirmations were written with a thick Sharpie pen and taped up everywhere, not the normal, smarmy stuff, but lines from movies they loved. From *Band of Brothers*, Justin's favorite book and TV show, *They hadn't come here to fear. They hadn't come to die. They had come to win.* From the *Avengers*, *I can do this all day*, spoken by Captain America. From *Lord of the Rings*, *I can't carry it, but I can carry you*, the words spoken by sweet Samwise Gamgee when Frodo collapses at Mount Doom. *At dawn, look to the east.* Helm's Deep had seemed to be an unwinnable battle, and yet, on the morning of the fifth day, in rode Gandalf on his beautiful white horse, and they won. They won, goddamn it.

After that initial tremor, she banished the idea that Justin would die. He was strong, and as he said, he'd beaten leukemia once. He could do it again. That six-month prognosis . . . that was for other people. Older people, people who were more frail or had other health issues or were simply less determined to live. Justin would not go meekly into that dark night, no way. He'd charge into the dawn, like Gandalf on Shadowfax.

Justin had surgery so they could implant a catheter in his brain to get the medicine to his central nervous system. To attack the leukemia in his spinal fluid, he had to lie in a fetal position while the doctors told him not to move and drove a needle into his spine. They dug out bone marrow from his hip, twisting the needle like a corkscrew as Justin tried not to scream (so much for the Xylocaine shots that were supposed to help). And because his bone marrow was also invaded by the leukemia, he needed oral chemo as well, which took away his sense of taste.

That was just in the first ten days.

When the team of doctors, PAs, nurse practitioners and nurses learned that Lark wanted to be a doctor (and had scored in the top 2 percent on the MCAT), they included her in the conversation and narrated the treatments and procedures, as if she were a colleague. They were so positive and upbeat—and so used to this—that it made it seem, for a little while, like this relapse wasn't such a big deal after all.

"It'll get worse before it gets better," said one nurse, and that became their refrain.

The chemo brought on a book of Job type of suffering. When Justin vomited until his throat bled, she sat on the edge of the tub, a cold cloth against his neck, clinging to that phrase like it was a rope tossed into a stormy sea. She wrapped that thought around her hand and clenched it so hard she couldn't feel anything else.

"It'll be worth it," Justin panted in between retching. "I'm sorry, Lark. But"—retch—"worse before better, right?"

"Absolutely, honey. You can do this all day." The Captain America quote always made him smile. "And don't forget, we first bonded over puking. It's all part of our sexy dance."

He laughed, then retched again.

Twenty-three days after Dr. Kothari gave them the news, Justin had lost thirty-eight pounds and most of his hair. He forbade her from shaving hers when she volunteered.

"I love your hair. Don't do that," he whispered, his lips cracked from dehydration and the toxicity of his medications.

He had sores in his throat that made swallowing a study in agony, and his bones ached constantly. He got devastating headaches from the chemo, and the steroids made him irritable. Finally, Dr. Kothari prescribed him Dilaudid, which made him loopy.

"I love Dilaudid," he said as they were lying in bed, watching the original *Iron Man*. "Let's serve it at the wedding." Their pinkies were linked, the most contact he could bear at the moment.

"Okay," she said. "It'll help Winnie loosen up. Grandpop would love it, I'm sure. Robbie's been giving him gummies for his back pain, and Grammy already has medical marijuana."

"But Dilaudid is next level. Can you see my mom stoned? That would be so fun. We have to get Mom stoned. Can you buy some gummies for her?" He was definitely a little high, but he was happy right now, and that was all that mattered.

"Sure," she said. "She and I can have a girls' night. Gummies and dancing, binge-eating potato chips . . ."

"You should. She would love that. She loves . . ." He was asleep before he finished the sentence. Hopefully, the Dilaudid would let him get a few consecutive hours of rest.

She watched Justin a lot when he was sleeping, studying his face for signs of improvement or decline. His face was gaunt now, and his eyebrows and lashes were sparse. Pretty soon, they'd be gone altogether. Something was going on with his teeth, too . . . they looked bigger and had a gray tinge. His skin had a yellow cast.

But he was still the boy she had loved since she was five. Still protective of her, still trying to hold the door for her, still asking about how *she* was holding up. "I'm sorry to put you through this, little bird," he'd whispered just last night. "I wish we were roller-blading along the Chuck instead. I wish you didn't have to do so much for me, honey."

"I *love* doing so much for you," she said. "Your turn will come when I'm in med school and weepy and exhausted. Or when I'm hugely pregnant and can't see my feet."

"I can't wait for that, little bird. I can't wait."

How many times does your kindergarten crush end up your husband? How many times does the nice boy who first kissed you at age fourteen turn out to be the only person you'll *ever* kiss? They were meant to be. They were Larstin, adored by everyone, held up as truth of the fairy tale.

The universe could not let them down.

THIRTEEN

LARK

After the party, Lark and Lorenzo had gone back to his apartment.

"I hope you sleep well," Lorenzo said. "Feel free to help yourself to breakfast. I'll be at the hospital early."

"Okay," she said. Scintillating conversation. But she did admire his success as a surgeon. Sunday mornings meant nothing when you were Lorenzo Santini. He would be off saving a life. Bringing hope. Being a rock star.

The bed in the guest room was wicked comfy, that was for sure, and Lark slept like the dead until seven thirty. When she went into the kitchen, there was a note on the island.

Thank you for attending last night. You looked very nice. Will be in touch.

"Wow," she said. "A compliment!" Not the tingle-inducing type his brother had given her, but hey.

Well, she had to get back, since she was working in the ER this afternoon. Rather than sully Lorenzo's kitchen by making breakfast, she figured she'd stop at Dunks on the way out. His coffee machine resembled a jet engine, and God help her if she messed up the settings. She packed, checked the gorgeous bathroom to be sure she had everything, then lugged her suitcase and dress bag the two blocks to her car.

It wasn't there.

"Are you kidding me?" she said to no one. She'd been towed. Apparently, her perfectly legal spot had become illegal overnight. Or the car had been stolen. She tapped her phone—*How to tell if my car has been towed in Boston*—pulled up the site, entered her license plate, and sure as shit, it had been towed. For street cleaning.

"Thanks for the notice!" Lark said, exasperated. Only in Boston.

Another few taps, and she saw that her car was currently at the impound lot a few miles from here. She called the number. "Our offices are closed and our operators are unavailable," said the recorded message.

Lark sighed. None of her siblings would be able to make it off-Cape to get her; the traffic was awful on Sundays in the summer. She'd have to take a Lyft. Another few taps on the phone and she winced. More than five hundred bucks, since it was a beautiful summer day with a lot of people heading Capeward.

But the Santinis would be going back to the Cape, of course! She could get a ride with them, then deal with her car tomorrow. Or ask Lorenzo to do it.

She texted Izzy. Any chance of catching a ride down to the Cape with you guys? My car was towed.

A second later, the answer came. Oh no! We're already at the bridge and it took forever to get here. Hang on a sec.

Lark sat on the curb, draping her dress bag over her suitcase. It was already eight thirty, and she had really hoped to get home, see her nieces and eat before heading into the hospital for the evening shift, which started at three thirty. Her phone dinged.

Help is on the way! Just texted Dante, and he
can drive you. Here's his number.

Wincing at the hard tingle of electricity that sentence caused,
Lark wrote back, Thanks, I'll take it from here. So much fun last night! See
you soon. Xoxox

Then she texted Dante's number. No need to come get me. I can
grab a Lyft back, but thanks.

Her phone rang. "Hey," Dante said. "I'm three blocks away.
I'll take you home. I was headed down to the Cape anyway."

"Is that actually true?" she asked.

He laughed. "No, but I don't have to work tomorrow, so I can
spend the night with my folks and win some brownie points."

She glanced at her watch. He was her best bet of getting back
at a reasonable time. "Okay. Thank you so much, Dante."

Five minutes later, she was sitting in the cab of Dante's
pickup. "I really, really appreciate this," she said.

"You've already said that. It's not a big deal." He flashed her
a smile, then pulled away from the curb.

As she sat in the passenger seat, that dark, electrical current
in her bones intensified. It was . . . disturbing. And inexplicable.

Once, when she was about fourteen, she babysat for a family
in Truro. Very sweet little boys, lovely house, chocolate chip cookies on the counter for her. The dad—Allan—drove her home at
the end of the night. The whole way, she'd had a similar feeling . . .
an intense and indefinable discomfort for no apparent reason.

Allan dropped her off at her house, thanked her and drove
away. Two months later, he'd left his wife for an eighteen-year-old
girl. Had she had a premonition that Allan was a creeper? Was
that what it had been?

"How old was your last girlfriend?" she blurted.

He glanced at her. "Why?"

"No reason."

"Uh . . . thirty-one? Thirty-two?" Dante replied, changing lanes.

Okay, so not that. Another time, she'd refused a ride home from a party when she was in college. The driver had seemed sober, but had crashed. Blood alcohol level almost twice the legal limit.

"You didn't have too much to drink last night, did you?"

"That's quite a topic change." He gave her a curious look. "I had two beers and a couple of sips of champagne. Why? Is my driving making you nervous?"

You're *making me nervous*. "No. Just checking."

"Guess that's the doctor in you. But don't forget, I drive for a living. Big shiny trucks."

She smiled a little, and the darkly electric sensation subsided. She risked another glance. Dante wore a T-shirt and jeans, and his hair was thick and rumpled. She'd seen him somewhere, she knew it. That wasn't a stretch . . . Boston, despite its boom in the past generation, was still a small town, and she'd gone to school there for eight years, after all. Firefighters were out and about all the time.

Oh. Wait. "Are you in a firefighter calendar, by any chance?"

He laughed. "Mr. October, last year. I was holding a gray kitten."

That was it. Jordyn had sent her that calendar for Christmas, as a joke, and yes, Lark had looked through it appreciatively, then put it in recycling.

"Mr. October," she murmured. "I knew I'd seen you before."

He glanced at her but didn't comment.

Traffic was bad enough that they didn't talk until they were in Plymouth. "My grandparents live here," Lark said. "My aunt, too."

"Oh, yeah? You guys close?"

"Well . . . not really," she said. "We see them a few times a year, but they're kind of disinterested in us. My other grandparents are great, though. Grammy died a few years ago, but my grandfather is still around. He works at the bookstore with my sister, and he's the best."

"Nice."

Lark hesitated. "Are you close with your grandparents? Other than Noni, I mean?"

"Well, we see Noni all the time," he said. "But as you can tell, Lorenzo's her favorite."

"He said he grew up with her."

"He did. Our other grandparents live in New Hampshire. Mom's folks. They're more normal." A grin flashed and was gone.

"Lorenzo told me about how she kind of raised him," she said.

"Yeah. He went to this school for supersmart kids, and that was kind of the end of that."

"Of what?" she asked.

Dante shrugged. "Of him being one of us. He never really fit in once he left. He became almost like an only child, and that school didn't help. I mean, it was a great education and all. But it made him feel pretty superior to the rest of us."

"St. George's, right?"

"That's the one. *Where excellence is expected and rewarded.* That was their motto."

"Pretty heavy burden for a seven-year-old," she said.

"He was meant for that school," Dante said. "He was speaking in full sentences on his first birthday. Mom and Dad had his

IQ tested when he was five, and it was like a hundred and eighty or something. Way past genius level. So he fit right in, let me tell you. Became their king by the end of the first year." He glanced at her, amused. "Can you imagine?"

"I can, actually. How old were you when he went?"

"Three."

Her heart squeezed at the thought of two little boys being separated. "You must've missed him."

Another glance from his dark chocolate eyes. "Cried myself to sleep for a month, according to Mom."

Remembering her conversation with Lorenzo about that time in his life—and also her promise not to talk about it—Lark said, "Bet he missed you, too."

Dante laughed. "You'd be wrong. Lorenzo was always too good for the rest of us. Thought he deserved everything. And everyone."

"Everyone?" she asked.

Dante shrugged, not looking at her. "I mean, he definitely got Noni. Sofia pretty much worships him. Mom and Dad are in awe of him, a little dazzled with everything he's done. It's Izzy and me who want to smack him." He gave her a quick smile. "You might feel the same way the longer you date him."

She laughed a little. "There have been moments. Let's change the subject. Do you like being a firefighter?"

"Of course I do. Best job in the world."

"The shiny trucks and universal adoration?"

"You nailed it."

"How often do you save kittens and babies?" she asked.

"Oh, daily, of course," he said, grinning at her with that Firefighter Wink. "We deal with a lot of car accidents, medical calls and automatic alarms, too. But Boston has a lot of fires. Last month we pulled eleven people out of a burning building. Five kids in the mix. Two dogs, too."

"Oh, my gosh, yes! I saw that on NECN. I *knew* I recognized you. They played that story for days." Massachusetts worshiped their firefighters.

"It was a good call. No one got hurt."

"Okay, answer me this," Lark said as they inched across the Sagamore Bridge. "How did you avoid a Cape accent? Even a Boston accent. All four of you sound like you're from Connecticut or something."

"How dare you," he said, tossing her another million-dollar grin that made her bones melt a little. It also made her realize how seldom Lorenzo smiled. "Mom's mom, my other grandma, is British. She beat it out of us. Every time we dropped an R, out came the cane."

"Well, that explains it," Lark said.

"The British part is true, anyway. I can sound like a Southie when I need to."

"Prove it," she said. Her face flushed. This might be flirting. She was fairly sure it was.

A car cut them off at the rotary. "Nice fuckin' move, ya moron!" Dante yelled, smiling as he leaned on the horn. "Stop gropin' your cousin and keep your hands on the wheel!" He looked over at her. "How was that?"

"Wow," she laughed. "I take it back. For a second there, it was like I was at Whitey's."

"You've been to Whitey's? Best dive bar in the world. You really *are* perfect."

Don't read into that, she told herself, reading into it. (He thought she was perfect!) "I went to BU, then Tufts. Of course I went to Whitey's. How about you? When did you move to Boston?"

"Right after high school. I wasn't really the college type. Worked in construction for three years before I got hired."

"And how is it you're still single, Dante?" she asked. "I mean, a cute firefighter, saving dogs and children, a nice family, the name Dante . . ."

Yes. She was flirting.

He tilted his head a little. "Don't know how much of this you already know, between Lorenzo and my sisters. And my mother. She's been trying to marry me off ever since I was seventeen."

"Did you ever come close? To getting married, I mean?"

"Yep."

Nothing more. Just *yep*.

"Does this involve the girl you mentioned last night?"

He didn't look at her this time. "It does."

Her phone buzzed. It was Rena, the ER unit secretary. Sched-uling error. No need to come in tonight. See you tomorrow.

"Oh. I just got canceled. Shoot, Dante, I'm sorry. You didn't have to drive me after all."

"Want to go back so we can take care of your car?"

"No, that's fine. We're in Barnstable already, and look at the traffic going off-Cape." It was bumper to bumper.

"You got it," he said. "Wellfleet it is."

"You can stay for lunch, if you want. My landlady will adore you, and her house is amazing."

He didn't answer for a second. "Sure. Thanks. I haven't been out that way in a long time."

"So back to your almost marriage," she prompted. "Actually, we don't have to talk about that. I'm sorry."

"No, no, it's fine. She was the model."

"Oh, I see." Hence his leaving when they were talking about Addie's brief stint in the fashion world.

"Lorenzo thought she was shallow. Turned out he was right. She dumped me for someone else."

"Did you love her?" she asked.

"I did." He glanced at her, then back at the road. Just then, his phone rang, and rather than have it on the truck's speakers, he switched it to private. "Sorry. Gotta take this. It's work."

His end of the conversation informed her there was an issue with a grievance filed about a lieutenant, and Dante was part of the group who was handling it. She turned to look out at the familiar landscape of Route 6—oak trees and scrubby pitch pines, the sky overhead turning more and more gray. Good. They needed rain. The traffic had thinned, and they cruised along.

She dumped me for someone else. Ouch. So Dante Santini had had his heart broken. She wondered how long ago that had been.

After about half an hour, Dante hung up. "Sorry about that," he said. "Work politics, irritating coworkers, all that. I'm on a committee, and you know how that goes."

"No problem. I guess even the best jobs have their moments."

"How about you? You like your job, Lark?"

She hesitated. "Yeah, I do. I'm kind of on hiatus, though. I really want to work in oncology, not emergency medicine."

"Hm."

She looked at him, a little curious at his lack of a follow-up question.

His gaze was fixed firmly ahead.

Suddenly, that dark, unpleasant electrical buzz wrapped her entire body and amped up. Her eyes widened, and she couldn't breathe.

That profile. His hands on the wheel, the tattoo. He had been younger, obviously, but it was definitely . . .

Her throat slammed shut, all breathing cut off. She tried to suck in a breath and failed.

"Lark?" he asked, glancing at her sharply. "You okay?"

"It was you," she managed, her voice choked. "Oh, my God, it was you."

FOURTEEN

LARK, SEVEN YEARS AGO

Twelve weeks after Justin was diagnosed with his relapse, things were looking really, really good. It was practically miraculous.

Yes, he'd lost a lot of weight, dropping from 165 pounds to a low of 126, less than Lark. But he'd gained back 11 pounds, and in the past two weeks, he seemed to have adjusted to the regimen. He was tired, but not comatose, and he wanted to talk when he was awake, or have her read to him, or watch TV. He'd lost muscle mass, but he was simply weak, not "neurologically challenged," meaning he didn't list to one side, fall, show any facial drooping or slur his words. In other words, the cancer hadn't gone to his brain.

While his blood pressure was low, he wasn't fainting. His lungs were clear (Lark had picked up some diagnostic skills wicked fast), and his pulse was steady. He had to wear a mask anytime he was in public, and so did Lark and his parents. Addie, too, when she came to see them. She was the only Smith who was allowed to visit, and she'd been a champ, bringing delicious vegan treats from Clarke's Cakes & Cookies, picking up organic vegetables, making soup, which was the one thing Justin had been able to keep down from weeks two to eight. Addie would then flop in the chair and *not* ask about Justin's symptoms, instead complaining about regular life, their siblings, Nicole's irritating brother. She bragged a little about the trip to Ecuador she and Nicole were planning, first-class tickets, a spa resort in the rainforest . . . being herself, in other words. She was Lark's portal to normalcy, a glimpse of the future when Justin would be past this.

Nine of the twelve weeks had been sheer and utter hell. A few times, Lark thought he'd die, he was so sick—a headache so bad he lost his vision for two terrifying hours, violent shivering during his infusions. One particularly horrible night, when diarrhea caught him in bed, he'd cried because of the indignity. She'd gone a little Captain America herself and *carried* him to the bathroom to clean him up. As she was kneeling in front of him, he vomited into her hair. She'd managed to get him into the tub and rinsed him off (and her own hair), and even though the water was gentle and warm, he cried out in pain.

That was the *normal* stuff. The "don't be surprised if" side effects. Then there were the complications. He'd been hospitalized once for pneumonia, once when his heart rate went up to 180 because he was so dehydrated from vomiting and diarrhea.

Then, miraculously, he turned a corner at the end of week nine. He woke up and didn't have a headache. Ate a pancake and a half for breakfast. Kept it down. Wanted to take a walk around the block. The next day, he didn't need Lark to help him get out of bed. He took a shower by himself. He opened his laptop and looked at a project he was still included on, out of the kindness of his manager. By the third day, his inimitable sweetness returned, and he was once again not just a cluster of symptoms, but Justin. Day by day, his appetite increased, his strength grew and his attitude went from grim determination to a sense of wonder. He was getting better. He was doing it, just as he'd said he would.

At his twelve-week checkup, Justin's T cells, blasts, red blood cells and leukocyte count were all moving in the right direction. Dr. Kothari seemed almost surprised. "This is excellent news," he said, raising his eyebrows as he looked at his computer screen. "You're doing so well, Justin."

"Of course he is," Heather said. "Honestly, the power of positive thinking is amazing."

"He's a fighter," Theo said, his eyes shining with tears of pride.

Lark squeezed his hand, and Justin smiled at her. "Told you," he said.

"I love when you're right," she said, and for the first time in a long time, she felt like she could see beyond his treatment.

"When is the wedding?" Dr. Kothari asked.

"December tenth," Heather said. "Justin refused to call it off. Just six months to go." She beamed at Lark. "They are a remarkable couple."

"We'll invite you," Lark said. "It'll be on Cape Cod."

"I would be honored, and not to blow my own horn, but I am a wonderful dancer," Dr. Kothari said with a smile. "Of course, we still have to be careful about infections. But I'm very pleased with what we're seeing."

"Thank you for helping me, Dr. Kothari. For believing in me," he said, his voice rich with that sweet earnestness, and there he was, the old Justin.

Leaving his office today was nothing like it had been the first time. Today, they were still deployed in this terrible war, but they were nearly done. They were Easy Company in the 101st Airborne, and Germany was just about to surrender. Almost home. Almost done. Remission was around the corner. Justin was *on the right track*, and Dr. Kothari was optimistic.

Theo and Heather swung by the Laughing Monk Cafe for takeout and met them back at Justin's. For the first time in twelve weeks, Heather brought up the wedding and asked where they might want to honeymoon.

"Somewhere warm," Justin said. "Right on the beach. Lark in a bikini, and finally, some alcohol. That's what heaven is, right there." They all laughed. Lark could picture it—white sand, long sunsets, gentle walks . . . and sex. Lots of sex, because she missed it. They hadn't had any since early in the treatment, and it had been terrified, desperate sex.

And then, she thought, a baby. Forget waiting. Maybe get pregnant on the honeymoon, because how sweet would that be? Heather would be delirious with joy. Lark smiled at her, picturing her bursting into tears when they told her and Theo. Her own mom would be delighted, too, and oh, gosh, Grammy and Grandpop! How thrilled they'd be.

"How's your family?" Theo asked. "Your gram doing okay?"

Lark nodded. "She is, yes. Two cancer warriors in the family." Grammy was done with her much milder treatment for breast cancer and was back to reading obsessively and taking walks with Winnie every evening.

While they hadn't wanted to risk exposing Justin to anyone who might have the slightest cold, Grandpop, who still worked in Boston two days a week, had met Lark at the Common a few times, and though she had to wear a mask, it was so good to see him. Harlow had sent books and care packages, funny T-shirts and chocolate. Mom and Dad had come to town once a week, even if Lark couldn't see them, leaving packages in the building's foyer—beautiful white rocks from the beach and one of Mom's ocean paintings to hang over their couch, blueberry bread she'd baked from scratch, a loving letter from Dad.

Lark's eyes filled with tears. Her family had been there for them, even if they hadn't been allowed to actually be physically present.

"You must miss going home," Heather said, squeezing her hand.

Lark glanced at Justin, who was demolishing his pad Thai. "Nah," she said. "This is home now."

He put down his chopsticks. "Babe, you should go down for the weekend. I'm doing great. You heard the doctor. Your family would love to see you, and I know you miss them."

She felt her heart tug. She missed Harlow's calm, kind presence; Winnie's dry sense of humor; Robbie's pranks and irreverence. Justin was right. She wanted to see them, have dinner in Mom and Dad's big disorganized kitchen, sleep in the room she'd shared with Addie, curl up in the bookstore, eat a cheeseburger at the Ice House. God, she missed cheeseburgers!

"We'll stay with Justin," Theo said. "He's right, sweetheart. You've been incredible, and you deserve a break."

"I don't need one," she said, twisting her beautiful engagement ring. "Really. Don't tell Justin, but I'm kind of developing feelings for him, you know?"

They laughed, but all three of the Deans were insistent. It was the third week of June, and the Cape sure was beautiful at this time of year. Mom's wild, rambling garden would be bursting; Wellfleet's Main Street would be all spiffed up and bedecked with window boxes and flowerpots; and soft breezes would grace the evenings, bringing the smell of ocean and good food.

Heather was clicking on her phone. "I just booked you a facial and massage at Shui Spa in P-town for this weekend," she said. "Ooh, how about a mineral bath afterward? There."

"That's so sweet of you, but—"

"Nope. It's done." Heather took Lark's hand. "You have to take care of yourself, too, honey. You look tired. God knows, this has been hard on you, too."

She *was* tired, and she'd lost a couple of pounds with the stress of Justin's sickness.

"Go, little bird," Justin said. "Fly home to the Cape and come back to me, clean and sweet-smelling."

She threw a napkin at him. "I'm clean now, thank you."

"Admit it," he said, grinning. "You're codependent. Don't start liking this arrangement, future Mrs. Dean. I'm on the road to recovery. You'll have to find a new hobby."

He looked so happy, so much healthier, his cheeks pink, eyes gleaming . . . almost vigorous. "Okay," she said. "I'll do it. Unless anything changes, but sure. Thank you, guys. I am pretty homesick."

It was Monday. She'd leave on Thursday morning and come back on Saturday to avoid the bridge traffic that started each May.

On Wednesday night, Justin cooked dinner for the first time in months. He lit candles and poured them each a glass of wine.

"Larkby Christina Smith, I love you," he said. "I've loved you with all I am since I was five years old, and every day, I love you more."

Her eyes filled with tears. "I love you, too," she whispered.

He kissed her then, smoothing away her tears with his thumbs. His lips had healed from their cracks, and though his mouth tasted a little strange from all the medications, and while he was still so thin, he was hers. Her Justin. The love of her life.

Dinner could wait. They went to the bedroom, hand in hand, and undressed each other, so gently. It was almost like their first time, and it had been so long. Their kisses were almost shy. Lark thought she might break under the weight of love and gratitude. This was how they were. This was their love in physical form, deep and eternal and pure. Soft sighs, the hum of desire, gentle hands. When they came together, tears slipped out of Lark's eyes, the happiest, most grateful kind.

They were still them. The leukemia hadn't stolen that. As long as they had this, they had everything.

Being back home was wonderful. The weather was sparkling, and the sky was that special shade of Cape Cod blue, so bright and hopeful, as if nothing bad could possibly happen. On Thursday night, the whole family went to the Ice House, where she got a giant cheeseburger with bacon. Beth, the owner, brought out two bottles of prosecco and comped their desserts. Lark and Addie sat next to each other, Nicole on Addie's other side. Harlow sat on Lark's left, her arm around Lark's shoulders. Grandpop was in fine form, making them all laugh, and Mom and Dad held hands and smiled at their offspring. Grammy's cheeks were pink, Winnie seemed more relaxed and bickered amiably with Robbie.

Afterward, Lark FaceTimed Justin from the bottom bunk of her room. "How are you, sweetie?" she asked. "Surviving without me?"

"I'm great," he said. "Mom and Dad cooked enough for a football team, and then we watched *Iron Man*."

"Without me?" she said. "How dare you, sir!"

He laughed, then coughed, just once. "Listen, babe, I'm gonna do some work. I'll talk to you tomorrow, okay?"

"Is that cough new?" she asked, immediately on alert.

"Nope. I just had ice cream, and you know how cold food makes me cough sometimes."

That was true. Long before the leukemia had returned, Justin coughed after ice cream. Vagal nerve irritation. "What flavor?"

"Coconut."

"You cheated on me with Iron Man *and* coconut ice cream? Justin! It's like an orgy there!"

He laughed. "It was vegan, so settle down. How about you? What did you have for supper?"

"I can't tell you. I want you to respect me."

He laughed. "You ate meat, didn't you?"

She nodded. "Babe, it was so good. A cheeseburger from the Ice House. With bacon."

"I'm so jealous." His smile was so warm, his dark blue eyes so beautiful. "I love you."

"I love you more," she said. "Talk to you tomorrow."

"Have fun at the spa, honey. You deserve it." He smiled and ended the call.

After three hours of fragrant bliss at the Shui Spa on Friday, Lark floated to the dressing room, took off the fluffy robe and pulled on her clothes. She sniffed her arm and smiled, remembering Justin's quip about returning sweet-smelling. She checked her phone, and the smile froze.

Nine texts, five missed calls. Just then, someone knocked loudly, then cracked the door. "Miss Smith, there's an emergency call for you at the front desk, I'm so sorry. Please follow me."

Lark followed him to the desk, mouth open, then swallowed, and took the phone. "Hello?"

"It's Theo, honey. Come right now. They think it's fungal pneumonia."

Fungal pneumonia. The floor dropped away.

Fungal pneumonia. That one seemingly harmless cough last night hadn't been from ice cream. It had been from a fungus growing in Justin's lungs. She should have known. Should have told him to go to the hospital. She should have *sensed* something.

"I'm on . . ." Terror cut off her voice, and she had to force herself to speak. "I'm on my way. Can I talk to him?"

"They're intubating now."

No. "Tell him I love him." Her voice was taut and strange.

"Drive fast, Lark. Safe, but fast." Theo's voice choked off, and then the call ended.

She ran to the car.

Fungal pneumonia was the single greatest fear they'd had these past twelve weeks. Spores could burgeon in the lungs, and Justin's already too-active white blood cells would swarm to fight them, which would then prevent enough oxygen from being in his bloodstream. What was the treatment? Antifungals, antibiotics . . . but they weren't always effective . . . or fast enough.

He had coughed Wednesday, too. Yes. They'd laughed in bed after making love, and he'd laughed so hard he choked a little. That happened, of course, it was even normal, but . . .

The fungus had already been in his lungs then. She hadn't picked up on it. Oh, God. When they'd said goodbye yesterday morning, he'd rubbed his chest. Just an idle motion, but pleuritic chest pain was a sign!

She'd missed it.

She tore out onto Bradford Street. Blew through the stop sign, did fifty in a thirty-mile-an-hour zone, was yelled at by a bicyclist, passed her, then squealed onto Route 6. It would be an hour to the bridge, best-case scenario, another hour and fifteen to Dana-Farber. Without traffic, but there was *always* traffic.

Goddamn it! She'd be lucky to get there in three hours, and she'd be hitting Boston at prime rush hour on a Friday.

Shit, shit, shit.

"I love you, Justin. Please, honey, I need you." She was speaking out loud, she realized, flying past the other cars. If a cop flashed his lights, could she get a police escort to Boston? *Get the fuck out of my way*, she thought viciously, illegally passing an SUV. Could she get away with seventy miles an hour? How about seventy-five? The slowdown in Eastham at all their damn traffic lights. The rotary.

She was passing the sign for Harwich when Addie's number appeared on her phone. She hit the "accept" button.

"Justin's at Dana-Farber," Lark said without preamble. "Fungal infection. I'm on my way there. He's intubated."

"Oh no. Oh, shit, Larkby. Okay. Um . . . we'll be right behind you," Addie said. "Why don't you pull over, and I'll pick you up? You probably shouldn't be driving."

"No. I'm past Harwich already."

"Okay. All right, we're on our way, honey. Hang in there."

"They won't let you in the hospital," she said. "He's too high risk."

"That's okay. We'll be close by. I love you." Her sister's voice shook.

Lark swallowed against the jagged piece of metal that seemed lodged in her throat. "Addie, don't let anyone call me. I need to concentrate."

She hung up. Route 6 was a one-lane highway at this point with stupid yellow metal poles so you couldn't pass. The person in front of her was doing fifty-five. That was only five miles above the speed limit. Was this or was this not Massachusetts? No one did the speed limit! She pushed the button for the hazard lights and leaned on her horn, bringing her car inches from his bumper.

"It's a fucking emergency," she screamed. "Get out of the way!"

He pulled over. She passed, and soon after the road widened to be two lanes. Lark stomped on the gas and flew west, tailgating, passing, nearly sideswiping a landscaping truck. Her hands were sweaty on the wheel.

"Hey, Siri, call Heather." Her voice was thin and tight with fear.

"Calling Heather," said the phone. Heather picked up right away.

"How is he?" Lark asked.

"It's not good," Heather said through her tears. "He said he started coughing last night but thought it was allergies. After breakfast, he took his temperature, and it was one hundred and one, Lark." The desperation in her voice made Lark grip the wheel even harder. "His white count dropped to four eighty. They're waiting on the culture, but they started antifungals already." There was a pause. "I'm scared," she said, and her voice was just a whisper. "Where are you?"

"Coming up on Mashpee."

"Oh, honey, hurry."

"Is he . . . conscious?"

"They sedated him for the ventilator, but his sats are still low. Seventy-nine right now."

Do not cry. You're driving. Stay calm or you'll kill someone. Or yourself. "Love you, Heather. All of you."

"Be careful, Lark. Just . . . just get here as soon as you can."

She heard Heather sob before the call ended, and that scared her more than anything. Not once—until now—had the Deans wavered in their granite optimism that Justin would beat this.

There was construction at the bridge, and along the canal, and onto Route 3. Ten miles north, though, and the highway opened up. It was hotter on the mainland, and she put the AC on high, pushing the car to eighty-six miles per hour. Thank God she'd filled up her tank yesterday. Then, just as soon as she started to make good time, there was a sea of taillights. A traffic sign informed drivers that there was a disabled vehicle in Kingston. She called Heather again.

"His fever's up to one hundred and four," Heather said without saying hello. "Lark . . . they told us it's grave. The x-ray . . . his lungs are inflamed, and they said . . . something about lesions and nodules."

Oh, Jesus. Please, God. Please help him. Lark took a slow, shaky breath in. "He's young. He's healthy." Of course he wasn't healthy. He had *leukemia.* "Is he . . . scared?"

There was nothing but silence, and Lark knew Heather was crying. "He knows it's bad," she whispered.

"Tell him I'm on my way, and I love him so, so much."

"I will, honey. Drive safely."

She was *not* driving safely. She was driving like the Masshole she was, weaving in and out, speeding up, then slamming on the brakes. She was driving as if the man she loved was dying . . . because he was.

If he could pull out of this, she'd give anything. Anything. Forget med school. She'd be a stay-at-home wife and worship him and make him so happy every single day, he'd be the happiest man in the history of the world. She'd have their kids and they'd look just like him, please, God, and Heather and Theo would be the best grandparents, and if he wanted to stay in Boston, that was fine, she loved Boston, they could live wherever he wanted, Sweden, Ethiopia, Antarctica, *anywhere*, as long as he pulled through. She would give him foot rubs every night and never argue with him, because really, they never argued now, and every day would be so wonderful and filled with gratitude and all that shit.

"You can do this, Justin. You've got this. You're not going anywhere. You promised you wouldn't leave me." Her stomach clenched with terror.

When Route 3 turned into 93, there was more traffic. She was probably twenty-five miles away, and yet she was in stop-and-go traffic in fucking Hingham. She gripped the wheel so hard her hands went numb. When the traffic breathed again, she floored it.

Her phone rang. Heather. "He wants to talk to you."

"Is he better?" she asked, hope like a flash fire.

"No. Here."

"Lark." His voice was so thin, she could barely hear him. She shut off the air conditioner.

"I'm here. I'm here. I love you. I love you so much. Fight this, honey. You've done it before."

"I'm sorry." His words were just breath now.

"No, you're not! You're not because you've got this, Justin! You're the most amazing person I've ever met. You have nothing to be sorry for!"

"Love . . . you."

"I love you, too. I'm coming, honey. Please, Justin, hang on. Fight, baby. You have to fight."

There was silence. "Justin?" she whispered.

"It's Theo," came his father's voice. "Are you almost here?"

"Quincy," she said, her voice breaking.

"Anything you can do to get here, Lark, do it. He needs you here."

"I'm trying." She pushed "end" and called 911.

"Nine one one, what's your emergency?" said the dispatcher.

"My fiancé is in critical condition at Dana-Farber and I need to get there and I'm stuck in traffic on 93 in Quincy."

She heard typing. "Ma'am? How can we help?"

"Can I get a police escort? Please? I have to get there. He's . . . he doesn't have long." Don't let that be true. Let that just be her pulling out all the stops.

More typing. "Stay on the line, ma'am."

Please help me. Please help me. Please. Please.

The dispatcher came back on. "Ma'am, the police in the area are unavailable. There's a—"

"Help me!" she screamed. "Help me get there before he dies!"

"Ma'am, I'm so sorry. We can't do anything at this—"

Lark hung up. Ahead of her, brake lights glowed like the gates of hell. Fine. She'd get off the highway. There was an exit, just past National Grid. She shoved her way in front of the car in the center lane, ignoring the horn blasts and curses, then did it again to get into the line of cars for the exit, which was just as packed. "Come on, come on, come on," she sobbed. "Hurry!"

She turned on Freeport Street, heading northwest toward the hospital. If Boston had been like other, normal cities, she wouldn't have to deal with all these one-way streets, but no, it had to be a tangled mass of yarn. Once she hit Hancock Street, though, it should be easier. Still, the traffic was barely moving. She could stay on Hancock or take Pleasant.

But they weren't moving now. At *all*. Why? She was so close! She laid on the horn and then . . . then she saw the smoke. And lights. Fire trucks and police cars had their lights flashing and were directing traffic to do a U-turn. But a U-turn was impossible, because now traffic was backed up on both sides of the street. No one was moving an inch.

She was four miles away from Justin, give or take. Four miles. She could run it if she had to.

Lark turned off the car, grabbed her bag, flung open the door and ran toward the first responders. Cops were milling about, doing whatever cops did at fires, being useless, really, when they could've given her an escort. Firefighters tromped around, dragging hoses and talking into radios. A ladder was extended toward the smoke. So many trucks, so many people, so much noise, not to mention all the bystanders filming on their stupid phones.

"Please!" she yelled at a cop. She grabbed his arm, which he immediately pulled away. "Please help me! I have to get to the hospital!" She was shaking head to foot, and God, it was hot. Her shirt was stuck to her with sweat.

"Are you hurt, ma'am?" He looked her up and down. "Or are you lookin' for a fix?"

"No! My fiancé is sick and—"

"Yeah, we can't help you, lady." The cop had a thick Dorchester accent. "Take a look around, okay? The Asian mahket's on fiyah. Get back in your cah."

"Fuck you," she spat, then ran to a firefighter. They were nicer, anyway. No one ever protested about firefighter brutality, did they? "Please help me," she blurted, then dropped to her knees as her legs gave out. "Please help me." She grabbed on to his leg and looked up at him. His helmet read *District Commander*. "My fiancé has leukemia, and he's at Dana-Farber, and he's . . . he's dying. Help me! Help me! Please!" She grabbed on to her own hair, and she didn't recognize her own voice, it was so hoarse and terrified. "Please! Please help me." Sobs of anguish and despair ripped out of her, and the pain made her fold over.

There was a hand on her back. "Okay, dahlin', we can do that. Take it easy, now. We got you." He pulled her to her feet.

"Hey, you," he called to someone. "Over here. The lady needs a ride to Dana-Fahbah. Take my cah, lights and sirens."

"Yes, sir." He wore turnout gear and took Lark by the arm. She stumbled, and he slid his arm around her, There was something wrong with her legs. "Right this way, miss," he said, practically carrying her.

There was an SUV with *Boston Fire* written on the side, and he opened the door for her, lifted her in, then went to the driver's side, slid off his jacket and got in. The vehicle made some bleeps and whoops, and then they were moving, past the other trucks, taking a right, then a left.

Lark was shaking so hard she wondered if she was having a convulsion. She was gasping, unable to catch her breath. The tears that had been dammed for the past twelve weeks burst forth, and her nose was running. *Please. Please. Please.* She might have been talking out loud.

"Try to take a deep breath and hold it, miss," said the firefighter, but she barely heard him. "We're almost there."

With shaking hands, she texted Heather. Almost there. Minutes.

The firefighter put a hand on her shoulder and gave it a squeeze.

Another left, a few more blocks, and even in this car with its flashing lights and blips and bleats, it was taking so long.

Finally, they were here.

The firefighter pulled to the curb. "I hope everything—"

She flung open the door before the vehicle even stopped, and ran, her purse flopping at her hip. In the lobby she looked around, frantic. She should've asked what room he was in. Which floor. She started to text Heather again, then saw Theo.

He was slumped against the wall next to the elevators, sitting on the floor. "Theo!" she said, running toward him. "What . . ."

Theo looked up, his face gray and twenty years older.

"I'm so sorry, Lark," he said, his voice faint. "He died ten minutes ago. He tried to hold out till you got here, but he . . . he just couldn't."

Justin's room was dark and quiet. Heather fell into Lark's arms, and the three of them stood in an agonized little circle, sobbing. Lark didn't want to look at Justin. She didn't want to turn her head and see the truth of him not being alive. If she didn't look, it wouldn't start, this impossible, apocalyptically bleak world where she would be forced to live without him.

But she did look, of course. She had to. She pulled back from the Deans and went to his bedside.

The nurses and CNAs had done their sad, kind job, and the tubes and needles were gone, the monitor black and silent. It was simply Justin, lying in the hospital bed.

He looked so still. His skin was not the right color . . . it was all one shade somewhere between taupe and gray. He looked smaller. But he didn't look dead, either, not yet. Just . . . just not quite alive. Yesterday on FaceTime, he'd been so vital. From the Latin, *vita*, which meant "life." His eyes had been alert, his grin adorable.

How could this be him now? Maybe there'd been a mistake, and this was someone else. Someone who looked a lot like him, but Justin . . . he was down the hall, responding well.

Stupid thought.

He'd had this fungus in him for at least three days, she thought. The cough. The rubbing of the chest. Even so, it had moved horribly fast, preying on his devastated immune system.

Now his skin was growing whiter while she looked at him, the blood in his body, no longer being pumped, succumbing to gravity. Hypostasis. The way he lay on the bed was different . . . he had sunk into it. His cheekbones looked more prominent. Muscle flaccidity.

Even when he was in horrible pain, he had looked better than he did now, because he'd been *alive* then. He'd been living. She'd take him screaming and shitting himself over this.

Quickly, before he was completely dead (what a ridiculous thought), without thinking to ask Heather and Theo, she climbed in next to him and put her head on his shoulder, her hand over his heart. Nothing. No rise and fall, no thump. His chest felt hard and bony, but he was still warm. Wasn't that what everyone said? *He was still warm. He looked like he was sleeping. You wouldn't know he was dead.*

Heather and Theo said something about giving her a few moments and left, and then it was just the two of them. Someone had turned off the light, and even the color of the air seemed gray and sad. Probably the smoke from that fire was hanging over the city, turning the previously beautiful day into dusk. It would be appropriate—nature acknowledging that the world could not be as bright without Justin.

Lark's throat was too tight to speak. Her stomach felt like she'd been kicked, and her chest . . . it actually felt like there were shards of thick, jagged glass being shoved into her heart.

"I'm sorry," she finally whispered. "I'm so sorry."

She shouldn't have gone to the Cape. She should've known that his chest was hurting, that the cough wasn't from ice cream. She shouldn't have gotten a facial. He wouldn't even know how sweet-smelling she was. She should've taken the service road in

Dennis or gone down 6A. She should've taken 495 instead of 3. She should've kicked that cop in the balls and rammed the fire trucks blocking her.

Oh, Justin. She gripped him hard, sliding one arm underneath him, pulling him to her, and he offered no resistance and no help. She let go, horrified. That wasn't how it felt to hug him. That was *obscene*, this lack of reciprocity, this nothingness. She put him back as he was and once again rested her head on his shoulder, sobbing, shaking, her tears soaking into the sheet that covered him. She reached up to stroke his head, his still-bald head. He would have hated this to be the last image she had of him, but the bastard had left her no choice, had he? He smelled like hospital, and that was also a profanity. She buried her nose in his armpit, and there, that was his smell, and the shards of glass in her heart grew barbs and twisted.

This would be the last time she'd smell him. Twenty-one years of love, over. How would she survive? She didn't know life without Justin. She barely had memory before him. *No, thanks*, she wanted to tell God or the universe. *I'll pass.* Her hands gripped the sheets as wave after wave of anguish crashed over her, drowning her.

Ten minutes. All she'd needed was ten minutes, and at least the last thing he would've seen was her face, the love in her eyes. He wouldn't have died wondering where she was. If she'd been in Wellfleet, even, that would've been enough, but no, she'd had to go to the stupid spa, somehow thinking she deserved a break. So wrenchingly selfish. If she'd gotten off in Quincy and gone the back way. If that 911 dispatcher had had an ounce of sympathy.

She was dimly aware that she would have to get out of this bed. The Deans would want to come back in. But Lark didn't want to move. If she just lay here, the rest of her life could wait,

unknown and unlived. She stayed where she was, tears streaming, sobs shaking her body, aware that she was in shock but not
caring, exhausted from the adrenaline that had been raging
through her bloodstream the past four hours.

Finally, she raised herself up and looked at Justin's face. This
was the last time she'd lay at his side, ever. His lashes were gone,
and his eyebrows mere fuzz, and she'd never see the dark blue of
his eyes again, would she? She wouldn't marry him. Ever. She
wasn't a fiancée anymore. She wasn't sure what she was now.

We grew up together, Larkby. Let's grow old together, too.

Guess I'm shit outta luck on that front, she thought. She'd never
tease him again. He'd never tease her.

She got out of the bed. It was the hardest thing she'd ever
done, because in that move, their story, their beautiful, pure,
happy story was over.

FIFTEEN

LARK

"You're hyperventilating," Dante said, putting a hand on her knee. "Knock it off, or I'm gonna have to pull over, okay?" His voice was calm. "We're almost at your house, right? Hang in there."

Her breath was shuddering in and out at an alarming rate, it was true. Was this what they meant by "triggered"? Her feet felt weird and tingly, and her teeth were chattering.

"What's your address?" he asked.

"Four . . . four eighty f-five Chequessett Neck Road," she said.

At the light, he tapped it into his phone, as talking was not her current strong suit. She tried to slow her breathing, but it was easier to just let her head fall back against the headrest and panic. She could smell the smoke from that day, hear the crackle and roar of the fire. The feeling of Dante Santini putting his arm around her so she didn't fall, him lifting her into the battalion chief's SUV. His hand on her shoulder. She heard her own anguish, coming out as keening sobs.

Dante pulled into her driveway. She tried to open the door, but her arms were rubbery, so she waited while Dante came around to help her.

"Easy does it," he said, holding her upper arm.

"This way," she whispered, listing up the path toward her little guesthouse, glad for his steadying hand. Otherwise, she wasn't sure her legs would hold her.

"Key?" he asked.

She handed him her bag, and he opened it, found her keys and chose the right one, then opened the door and steered her to the couch. Her legs did give out then, and she flopped against the back.

The blips and beeps from the vehicle. The siren. Sickly sweat making her shirt and jeans stick to her skin. There was a high-pitched staccato sound, here or in her memory, she wasn't sure.

"Looks like your dog wants to see you," Dante said.

Oh. Right. That sound was Connery barking. A second later, the dog jumped on her lap, whining, his little paws pushing against her lap. She petted him vacantly, but her arms felt weak and loose. She'd run as fast as she could from the fire chief's car to the hospital door, but every step had been in slow motion, her legs unpredictable and weak, Theo, gray faced, waiting for her by the elevator. The rasping sound of her own breath in the here and now.

"Here's some water," Dante said. He pressed a glass into her hand. "Go on. Drink."

She chugged the entire glass. Looked around. Inhaled deeply, exhaled on a sob. Another big inhale, a shuddering exhale.

"Nice and slow, nice and slow. Breathing, when done correctly, is really good for you." He smiled at her. "You're safe. You're home. You're okay."

Those were good thoughts.

He went into her bathroom and came back with a wet face-cloth. "Put this on your forehead," he said.

She did as he instructed—it was cold—and closed her eyes.

You're safe. You're home. You're okay. Connery snuggled against her hip. The painful buzzing feeling in her feet and hands slowly subsided, and her breath slowed incrementally.

Seven years was a long time. She'd had seven years since that horrible day. A lot of hours. She was safe. She was home. She was okay.

She reached up and pressed the cooling facecloth against her eyes, then set it on the coffee table and looked at Dante.

"It was you," she said.

"Yeah." His beautiful brown eyes were sad. "Sorry for the bad memories. I was hoping you wouldn't connect the dots."

"You knew? You recognized me?"

"Yep. The second I saw you." He took her hand, and his was so nice and warm. "And since you were Lorenzo's girlfriend, I did the math." He looked down. "I'm really sorry for your loss, Lark."

"Thanks," she whispered. She inhaled slowly, calm now, then shook her head. "I knew I'd met you before. I just . . . didn't want to place you, I guess."

"Did you get there in time?" he asked, and his voice was so soft and deep.

Her throat closed. "No," she whispered. "But thank you for trying."

His hand tightened on hers, and he sat back against the couch, his shoulder against hers. "Well, that really sucks," he said, and she sputtered on a surprised laugh.

"It really does," she said. Then she started to cry. Not the ugly, heaving sobs from seven years ago, not the panicked gasping in the car . . . just sad, normal crying. "I was ten minutes too late."

Dante pulled the throw blanket from the back of the couch, tucked it around her, then took her in his arms and let her cry, her head against his chest.

He didn't feel like Justin. Didn't smell the same way. But it felt nice all the same.

You're safe. You're home. You're okay. Her hand curled in his T-shirt, and she knew he wouldn't take it the wrong way. All these years later, and still the tears could come so fast and hard. As they should have. Justin deserved nothing less.

When she was done, she straightened up, got off the couch and blew her nose. Washed her face. Poured herself some more water, found a beer in the back of the fridge and offered it to him.

"Thanks," he said.

"Need a glass?" she asked, and he gave her a mock scowl before twisting off the cap and taking a pull.

"What's your dog's name again?" he asked.

"Connery. I share him with my landlady."

"He's wicked cute." Connery wormed onto Dante's lap and licked his chin, and Dante laughed.

Lark took a photo off the wall, went back to the couch and handed it to Dante.

"Justin Dean. We met in kindergarten."

"Wow. That's really sweet."

"It was. He was." She sat down next to him again, grabbed another tissue and wiped her leaky eyes. Connery stood against her chest and tried to lick her face. "Thanks, puppy. You're a good boy."

"You look happy," Dante said, studying the picture. It had been taken in Venice, the day they got engaged. The gondolier had taken probably a hundred photos of them. He'd hugged them both goodbye.

"We definitely were." She gave Dante a watery smile.

"So tell me about him," he said, and she did. Oh, she did.

Once she started talking, she couldn't stop. Their fateful kindergarten bonding. The science fair project about photosynthesis when they were eight. Fourth-grade gym class, where the gym teacher had them hold on to the edge of a parachute, raise their arms and then slide underneath it as the fabric billowed and floated above them. She and Justin lay next to each other, and it seemed like they were the only ones in the room. How Joey Weiner had chased her at recess, trapped her against a tree and was trying to kiss her in fifth grade, and Justin had shoved him away.

She got out her photo albums, kept meticulously since grammar school, and showed him pictures of her, her family, Justin, Heather and Theo. She couldn't seem to stop talking. He didn't seem to mind.

"How are his parents doing?" Dante asked.

"Well . . . they're still here on the Cape. I see them a lot. But he was their only child." Her voice turned into a whisper on those last couple of words.

"So tough. I don't know how people handle it, losing a kid. Worst thing ever."

"It really is."

"And who's this? Miss Trunchbull?" he asked, pointing to a picture of her mom's mother.

"That's my grandmother."

"Oh, shit," he said. "Sorry. I meant to say, 'Who's this beautiful older lady?'"

She laughed. "No, it's okay. She's kind of . . . sour. When Justin died, she told me I was too young to get married, anyway. That was it. Nothing else."

"Wow. Did you punch her?"

"I wanted to. Also, how do you know who Miss Trunch-bull is?"

"I'm not illiterate, Dr. Smith, no matter what my brother may have told you." He paused. "Also, Izzy came to a Halloween party dressed as her last year."

"Please tell me you were Matilda."

"I admit nothing, but Izzy might have pictures."

She laughed again. "Hey, are you hungry? I should make you lunch, or gosh, dinner, I guess. Dante, I'm so sorry. I've taken up your whole day."

"You hear me complaining? Sitting here on the Outer Cape with a pretty girl? I'm doing just fine. But yeah, I'm also starving."

"Let me make you a sandwich." She got up, opened the fridge and sighed. "Let me take you out for dinner. Or no! Hang on." She sent a quick text to Joy, asking if she could use her kitchen and cook dinner for a friend.

Of course! Make yourself at home. Your mom
and I are at Mahoney's. Just sat down.

"Even better," she said, smiling at Dante. "I'll cook you din-ner at Joy's. She's my landlady, and she's out right now, but I know she'd love to meet you. My mom's staying with her for a little while, so you might meet her, too."

"The more the better. Older women love me."

"I bet they do. My mom just kind of appeared here a couple weeks ago. I mean, she knew Joy, but all of a sudden, she's living with her, and I'm not sure my father's okay with it. I guess he has projects to work on, but I can't ever remember them being apart."

It was like something had been . . . dislodged, because Lark could not stop talking. She brought him over to Joy's house and opened the fridge. Steaks (which she'd replace, of course), salad fixings, a nice loaf of French bread in the pantry.

"Will this be okay?" she asked.

"It's fantastic," he said. "Let me help. You want me to man the grill or make the salad?"

"Salad, please."

It wasn't awkward. It wasn't weird. She didn't feel like she was betraying Justin, or that Dante shouldn't be here. It felt . . . natural. Like she was with a friend. And yes, he was a good-looking guy, and she'd blubbered all over him, and yes, she could admit that she felt a little something for him.

But knowing he'd been with her on the worst day of her life, and he'd been kind, and he'd done his best to help her . . . well, right now, she almost loved him. The man definitely deserved a steak.

They were washing the dishes when the door opened, and Connery began his crazed song of love. Mom and Joy were laughing as they came in.

"Hello, hello!" Joy called.

"Oh! Your friend is male," Mom said. "I didn't expect that. Hi, I'm Ellie Smith, Lark's mother." She offered her hand, and Dante took it, and oh, holy heck. She had failed to mention just who Dante was. She should've warned them.

"And I'm Joy Deveaux, Lark's friend and landlady," Joy said, tilting her head. "You are a beautiful human!"

"Takes one to know one," he said, taking her hand with a cheeky grin. "Very nice to meet you, ma'am."

"Don't you dare call me ma'am. I'm Joy."

"This is Dante Santini," Lark said. "Lorenzo's brother. You know. My boyfriend?"

"Is that right? Lorenzo's *brother*. Well, it's lovely to meet you," Mom said. She smiled at Lark and winked, and Lark relaxed. "Are you a doctor, too, Dante? I love your name, by the way."

"I'll tell my mom," he said. "And no, I'm not a doctor. I'm one of Boston's bravest."

"Bravest what?" asked Joy.

"He's a firefighter," Lark said.

"Oh, my heart," Joy murmured, fluttering her false eyelashes.

"I get that a lot," he said, grinning. "Makes up for the crap hours and smoke inhalation. But I'm afraid I have to be on my way. Lark, let me know if you need help figuring out your car situation, okay? And thanks for dinner. Joy, thank you for letting us eat here. This is a beautiful house."

"Oh, please come back anytime," Joy said. "Really. I mean it. Anytime."

"Mrs. Smith, great meeting you. I can see why Lark is so pretty."

"And he's an excellent flirt, too," Mom said. "We like you, Dante."

"Glad to hear it," he said, flashing another killer smile. "Lark promised I could marry one of her sisters, so we'll be family soon."

"I'll walk you out," Lark said. "Back in a flash, ladies."

It was fully dark now, and the fireflies were twinkling over the beach plums. The shell driveway crunched under their feet, and the salty, comforting smell of low tide hung in the air.

"Thank you for the ride, Dante. I . . . I'm sorry I took up your whole day."

"Weirdly enough, this has been one of the best days in a long time," he said. "For me, anyway, if not for you. No apology necessary."

They looked at each other for a minute, and though she'd talked so much today, there was a lot more she wanted to say. "Thank you, Dante," she whispered. "For that day, and for this day, too."

She was the one who kissed him. Without thinking, without knowing she was about to do it, she was suddenly standing on her tiptoes, her hands on his warm, strong shoulders, her lips against his.

A fleeting kiss, almost platonic. Almost. He looked at her a long second, face unreadable, and she remembered that as far as Dante knew, she was his brother's girlfriend.

"Sorry," she whispered. "I . . . um . . . yeah. Sorry."

He cleared his throat. "No, I . . . yeah, it's been an emotional day for you. Don't worry about it. I . . . I'll see you soon, I guess."

"Yes! I'm sure you . . . yeah! Drive safely, okay?" Her face was burning, and she was glad for the dark.

"Good night," he said, and he got into his truck and backed out onto the street. She waved as he drove off, then stood there a second, her head swimming.

She'd *kissed* him. And though the kiss had lasted less than two seconds, the impression was that it had been . . . amazing.

Except that she probably had just made him wonder what kind of person she was, kissing her boyfriend's brother. *Not cool, Lark. Not classy.*

But it had been amazing just the same. With a sigh, she headed back into Joy's.

"I love him," Joy said. "Come on in, your mom and I are too full to go to bed. Ellie, didn't we love him?"

"We loved him," Mom confirmed. "Too bad you're fake dating his brother."

"My thoughts exactly," Joy said. "Can you ditch the doctor and just swap in the firefighter?"

"Uh . . . no, not really," Lark said.

Connery leaped up, barking, and ran to the door.

"Hello?" came Addie's voice. "Can I come in? Calm down, doggy." She appeared in the living room. "I *knew* you were having a party without me," she said. "Hi, Mommy. Hi, Joy." She sat next to Lark. "What's up with you? You're flushed."

"Oh. Um . . . the heat?"

"I'll say," Joy said, and she and Mom sputtered in laughter.

"I'm glad you two are getting along," Addie said. "And one of these days, you'll tell us what exactly you're doing here, Mom, since you and Dad are usually welded together."

"I'm staying with Joy because your father has some messes to clean up, and I'm tired of watching," Mom said. "Ask your twin how she spent her day."

"Tell me, twin."

"Oh! I, um . . . well, I went to Sofia's engagement party last night." Addie looked confused. "The sister of my fake boyfriend?"

"Right, right."

"And I stayed at his place afterward."

Addie gasped. "You did not!"

"In the guest room. He barely speaks to me. Trust me, there's nothing rom-commy about him. And then my car got towed, and his brother gave me a ride home."

"And she cooked him dinner here," Joy said. "The extremely good-looking firefighter brother."

"And we met him," Mom added.

"Cool," Addie said. She looked at Lark. "Oh. Oh! Really?"

"No, no," Lark said, feeling her cheeks burn again. "He's just super nice. And we actually met once before, turns out. He was at a fire in Boston way back when, and he . . . gave me directions."

"And you like him." It was not a question. Addie didn't need to ask questions.

"He's very nice. Cute. He's sweet. A good guy." She clammed up before she sounded more idiotic than she already did.

"Got it," Addie said, lifting an eyebrow. "Does anyone want to hear about my day, and how cute Imogen was at her little pal's birthday party?"

"Do we have to?" Joy said at the same time Mom said, "Of course!"

And so Addie gave her a little grace period, and she listened to the tales of her niece sharing pre-chewed bites of carrot with the other three-year-olds.

But while Lark smiled in the right places during Addie's adorable and disgusting story, Imogen's antics didn't blot out the image of Dante looking at her the second before she kissed him.

She had the impression the kiss was not unwelcome.

SIXTEEN

JOY

While having Ellie stay with her was a delight—a girlfriend! She'd never had a girlfriend!—Joy was becoming a little more aware that she . . . well . . . that she didn't do very much.

"What are your hobbies?" Ellie asked the second week.

"Well, I love makeup," Joy said honestly. "I could do you anytime. You have beautiful bone structure."

"Um . . . maybe. I generally don't wear makeup. I get that you don't need to work, Joy, but what do you love to do? How do you fill your days?"

"I like to keep up with the news," she lied, knowing TMZ and E! didn't count. "I . . . I like to shop." She did buy a lot of things; even the Amazon guy was a little judgy, sighing as he backed out of her driveway almost every day. Damn it. She didn't do much of anything. Hours and hours spent online, looking at . . . stuff. Wondering about getting more plastic surgery. Getting specialized facials at Artisan Skin Care in Orleans. Planning her own funeral.

"So you never really had a career? Or a calling?"

"No," she said. "Not really. My brother was kind of the center of my life."

"Huh. Well. How about volunteering?"

"It's just that most volunteering involves children, and I hate children."

Ellie laughed. "Points for honesty. Did you like your painting lesson the other day? Because I'd be thrilled to keep that up."

"I did like it," Joy said, trying to sound enthusiastic. "Sure."

"So . . . not really. That's okay. It's not for everyone."

"I liked the wine and laughing part."

"So you just kind of shop and . . ." Ellie's voice trailed off, and Joy felt a flash of regret. This was where her previous friendships always broke down. When other women realized there wasn't much to her. Ellie had been very interested in hearing about her childhood, and very sympathetic . . . no, enraged! . . . at hearing how her parents had either ignored or belittled her and Paulie. But to a woman like Ellie, who'd had a passion early on in life, who was a wife, who had five children, who ran a business and made beautiful paintings, Joy would be boring. Of course she would be.

"I go to a lot of open houses," she said. "Maybe I'm interested in real estate. And I . . . I like to plan my funeral."

"What?" Ellie's eyes widened.

"Oh. Don't you?"

"No," Ellie said. "That's a . . . a hobby?"

"Um, sort of? I mean, I'm alone in the world, so I need to take care of the details myself."

"But as a *hobby*, Joy?"

"Just to see which funeral homes offer what," she mumbled. Yes, she'd been to at least five funeral homes in the past year. Yes, it gave her some pleasure to make sure she'd get a beautiful casket and urn. Yes, it was comforting, sometimes, to imagine herself dead, if only to be with Paulie again. And sure, she could see how someone like Ellie Smith would never have those types of thoughts at all.

"Have you ever seen a therapist?" Ellie asked.

"I just never found anything I loved," Joy said. "The makeup artist stuff was kind of fun, but to be honest, my specialty was getting married. And the thing I loved most was being with my brother." She grimaced. "I'm probably a little addicted to plastic surgery. There's not much to me, Ellie."

"Oh, nonsense," Ellie retorted. "You're incredibly bighearted, for one. You're so interested in other people. And I get the impression that you're very empathetic."

"What does that mean?" Joy asked.

"You feel the feelings around you. I bet if Lark is sad, you're sad. Or if your brother was upset, I bet you were upset."

Joy's mouth fell open. "That's true!"

"As for the husbands, you were just looking for a place to belong. I get it. Listen, I'd love to keep talking, but I want to get some painting in today. That's *my* therapy. All my fury at Gerald, splattered on the canvas. I can't tell you how good it feels to not be working on a sunset."

"Rage-painting," Joy said, nodding.

"See? Empathy. I'll see you tonight, okay? My turn to cook."

The conversation left a niggling feeling in Joy's brain. She *should* be doing something. Funeral planning as a hobby did sound weird. She just wanted to make sure her ashes and Paulie's would be buried together, or scattered together. Just together somehow. He'd been her person.

When you lost a spouse, you were a widow, and everyone knew to offer condolences and ask how you were doing and offered to fix you up when enough time had passed. If you lost a child, well, there were people who'd check in on you for the rest of your life, understanding that you were damaged goods from then on out. At least, Joy assumed you would be.

But when you lost your person, and that person was your sibling, you didn't get the same respect. Paulie had been Joy's person. The first one she'd call. Her favorite friend to do things with, whether it was gossip or see a movie or eat. She had nobody now. Her mother still walked the earth, but she didn't count. And until recently, Joy had never had a female friend. Lark was such a sweetheart, but she was decades younger than Joy.

But Ellie . . . Ellie *was* becoming her friend. When they'd first met the day Lark moved in, Ellie had cocked a curious eyebrow at her. Joy saw a woman with paint-stained clothes, a trim figure and a face untouched by Botox or filler. One of those irritating earth mother types, she'd thought, certain that Ellie was drawing her own negative conclusions about Joy. And yet here they were. Ellie was going through a rough patch with her marriage, and Joy was *empathetic*. Ellie was full of energy and life, even while she was figuring stuff out with Gerald (who'd always seemed a little pompous to Joy).

But for the past few weeks, the two women had talked and laughed and shared and bonded.

Suddenly, Joy wanted to do a little better. Be a little more. She could be the type who'd take lessons here and there, try new things, have more in her day than the internet and her own upkeep. She was . . . what was that word? When you had energy but weren't sure what to do with it? *Restless*, that was it.

"Come on, Connery, we're going for a ride," she announced. The dog tore circles around her, yelping with delight.

Route 6 didn't have any traffic heading west today, so she breezed down to Orleans. She'd take 6A, maybe, to kill more time. Maybe she'd start antiquing. That was a big deal on Cape

Cod. She could learn to love antiques and fix them up and sell them. Except she didn't know how. But she could learn! Or maybe she could learn to sew. There was a fabric store in Orleans. She could make her own clothes. Become a designer. Or she could go to Rock Harbor and see if she liked deep-sea fishing. Actually, not that one. She hated fish, and the idea of hauling one out of the water, touching its cold skin, already had her dry heaving a little.

Okay, what else? She did love open houses, that little glimpse into someone else's life. Yes! She could become a real estate agent. But she knew from selling the town house and buying this place that there was a lot of paperwork involved. Legal stuff, very boring. So not that, either. Oh, what was that career called, where people brought in furniture and throw pillows and made an empty house look sophisticated and full of promise? So it would sell quickly? She could do that! She *was* good at buying stuff, that was for sure, and life with Paulie and Abdul had upped her awareness of quality furniture.

"You want to be a whatchamacallit, Connery, baby?" she asked. He grinned up at her, his brown eyes twinkling. Paulie would have loved her fur-baby.

She was checking her right eyelash in the visor mirror when a sign on the left caught her eye. With a screech of tires, she took a hard left into a wide driveway flanked by gates, causing Connery to skitter on the seat.

"Sorry, baby, sorry!" she said, reaching over to steady him.

A white and blue carved sign with gold letters announced BAYVIEW SENIOR LIVING COMMUNITY. Below that, a smaller sign read MODEL HOME TOURS AVAILABLE DAILY.

Basically, an open house, plus a chance to see the staging. *There* was the word. *Staging.* She'd check it out.

A senior living community, huh? Her mother lived in crappy little senior housing development (trailer park) in Florida and hated everything about it, but that was her calling card, wasn't it? Joy could tell this place was nice. Expensive landscaping, brick sidewalks, gray-shingled buildings with white trim and window boxes. Very Cape Cod, very tasteful.

She found a parking space, clipped on Connery's leash and went into the main building.

"Welcome to Bayview," said an attractive woman behind the counter. "Can I help you?"

"I was just passing by," Joy said. "I have a home in Wellfleet, but maybe I wanted to check this place out. You know."

"Of course!" said the woman. "Let me get Vicki for you. And hello, handsome! What's your name?"

"Connery. Like Sean," Joy said. The girl looked blank, and Joy sighed. Kids today.

A moment later, a woman about Joy's age came out of an office. She was dressed to kill—beige suit that looked amazing against her brown skin, but which would've made Joy look washed out. She had close-cropped gray curls, tortoiseshell glasses, high heels . . . supersophisticated.

"I'm Vicki Simpson, the manager here," she said.

"Joy Deveaux. And this is Connery."

"Hello, Connery! I'd be more than happy to show you around. Our sales director is off today, but we're thrilled you're here. Are you looking for yourself or someone else?" They walked down the hall, Connery practically skipping alongside them.

"Possibly my mother," Joy said, though she'd stab herself in the face before bringing her mother within a thousand miles of her. "She's quite senile." If only that were true. Mama had turned meaner in her old age and loved nothing more than to bring up

Joy's failings as a daughter, starting from when Joy was around three and didn't fit into an Easter dress Mama had made. Another unpleasant topic was how wonderful Daddy had been. Joy would say, "Was it wonderful when he broke your arm?" or "Like that Christmas when he knocked out two of your teeth?" and Mama would hang up on her. It was proof of life, at least.

Bayview was swanky, that was for sure. There was a media room with plush recliners and a big screen, a game room, art room, music room. A dining hall that was quite attractive, overlooking the golf course. A library with a big fireplace.

"As you can see, our residents really enjoy the space," Vicki said. It seemed true . . . everyone who saw them smiled, and one guy winked at Joy. His wife glared at her, as if Joy was the one at fault. *Lady, please*, she thought. *I could do a lot better than your husband.*

They went into the model home. Yep. Staged. There was a rather ugly modern light fixture over the dining table, a navy blue couch in the living room, big candles in the fireplace. Some boring-looking books on the built-in shelves. Meh. She could definitely add a little flair. For some reason, there was a bowl of real lemons on the marble counter. At least a dozen.

"Don't those rot?" Joy asked.

"Oh, um . . . I imagine someone comes in and takes care of that. Have you thought about your own housing plans?" Vicki asked.

"I live on Chequessett Neck Road in Wellfleet," she said, having learned that the address usually got some admiration.

"Very nice," Vicki said. "And you'll be able to stay there as you get older?"

"Mm-hmm." She had no plans to get that much older. If the day came when she couldn't make herself a gin and tonic and shop on the internet, she'd just swim out to the horizon or, more likely, toss back some sleeping pills with a vodka chaser. She looked down the hallway to a set of doors. "What's down there?"

"That's our Memory Care Unit," Vicki said. "Alzheimer's, dementia, folks who need closer supervision. Maybe that would be appropriate for your mother?"

Hell would be appropriate for her mother, but Joy said, "Possibly."

This section was equally posh, but the residents were neither coming nor going. Many were in wheelchairs, and Joy's immediate impression was . . . well . . . not to be too self-involved, but holy crap! She was *young* compared to these folks!

"Hello, beautiful lady," said one little old man. "Would you like to date me?"

"Oh! No, but thanks," Joy said. "I'm flattered."

"Bob here is our resident flirt," Vicki said. She closed the hallway door behind her. "You can see we have excellent security measures so no one wanders off," she added in a lower voice. "Bob, how are you today?"

"I'm sad and bored," he said. "Can I go home? Or would this beautiful lady like to date me?"

"A dog!" said one woman. "Is this my dog? Can I keep this dog?"

Over my dead body, Joy thought. "This is Connery."

Connery put his gentle paws against the woman, who started to cry with happiness. "I love you," she said. "Thank you! I can't believe you're here!"

"Florence loves animals," Vicki said.

Connery moved to the next patient and nuzzled his leg, and the gentleman automatically reached down to pet him. Another resident came out of his room, moving slowly with his walker, to see Connery.

Vicki smiled and sighed simultaneously. "Sorry, we just lost an activities director and we haven't filled the position yet. There's not usually so many folks just . . . hanging around. We pride ourselves on keeping our residents engaged and active."

"What kind of activities are there?" Joy asked as one woman opened her mouth wide, exposing a complete lack of teeth. Seriously, what kind of things could they do? Eat soft food? Nap? Cry?

"We have music therapy, art and movies. There's a master gardener who teaches about houseplants and window box herb growing."

"Where are my shoes?" one woman bellowed. She only had a few wisps left for hair. "You stole my shoes! I know you did! You! Black lady! You took my shoes."

Vicki ignored her. "We also have certified therapy animals come in once a month. And once we find a new activities director, I'm sure that person will come up with some new ideas, too."

Activities, huh? It didn't look like some of these people could do much more than sleep and . . . well . . . die, Joy thought.

"You have beautiful hair," Bob said. "I could look at hair like yours all day."

"Thanks, hon," she said. "I pay a lot for it."

"You're a beautiful lady. Would you like to date me?" he asked.

"I'm all set, thanks," she said.

"Give me back my shoes!" the balding woman bellowed.

"Betty, I don't have them," Vicki said calmly. "You're wearing shoes."

"These are not mine," Betty said. "These are not my shoes!"

"Did you check your closet?" Joy asked. "I bet they're in there." She remembered going to see Nonna in a nursing home . . . people parked in hallways, tied to their wheelchairs, or wandering in johnnies through the halls like extras in a horror movie. This place was quite nice. Money could buy a lot of comfort, that was for sure. As always, she felt a rush of gratitude for Abe. Best ex-husband she'd ever had.

"Anyway, would you like to see the restaurant? That's another dining option," Vicki said.

"That activities director job . . . what are the requirements?" Joy asked.

"Really, it's about personality," Vicki said. "A person who's fun, tolerant, comfortable with the community, creative . . ."

"How about me?" Joy asked. "Can I apply?"

An hour later, Joy was a part-time assistant activities director at Bayview Senior Living Community, Memory Care Unit, as long as she passed a background check, which she would. She'd make forty cents above minimum wage, had a flexible schedule and wasn't sure what the heck she'd signed up for.

Aside from doing makeup for Paulie, she hadn't had a job since she worked at O'Dell's Auto Parts when she was first married to Frankie. She wasn't sure she'd last very long, but you know what? She had a *job*. She had somewhere to go every day where people would be waiting for her.

She couldn't wait to tell Ellie and Lark.

SEVENTEEN

ELLIE

Let me know when you'll be out of the house.
I need to get some things.

Such was the nature of her communications with Gerald these days. No frills. Ellie had been living with Joy for weeks now, and she had to say, she didn't miss Gerald. Nope. The man who'd talked about her in such a skewed way? The man who'd been flirting with and confiding in another woman, sharing secrets about their life, intimating that he was a poor, neglected husband while his work-obsessed wife just glided through life?

She didn't miss that asshat at all.

She did, however, miss the old Gerald. The pre-iPad Gerald. His humor, his thoughtfulness, his devotion, his friendship, his style of fatherhood and grandparenting. She missed their ridiculously good sex life, though the thought of that right now made her queasy. Had he ever fantasized about Camille Dupont when they were making love? If so, she'd castrate him.

She hadn't told anyone but Joy and her sister. She and Grace had met for lunch in Falmouth, and Grace had been so kind and sympathetic. But there'd been a note of gratification in Grace's voice and expression, as if she'd been waiting for this moment, when Ellie and Gerald were proven to be plain old married people, not the golden couple. An expectation finally realized. Grace's husband was horrible, and now, finally, Ellie's husband was, too.

Grace had been putting up with Larry and his infidelity for decades. Oh, she never had any solid proof, she always said, and she didn't want any. To know would force her hand, and Grace didn't want to start over. Didn't want to "air their dirty laundry," as Mom would say. He was a good provider. They had their rhythm, their marital flow. "Larry's distracted lately," Grace had said six or eight times in the past thirty-some-odd years. That was her code for what was clearly cheating behavior. But Grace stayed, neither she nor Larry quite miserable enough for divorce.

"I don't think you should've moved out," Grace had said over lunch. "Your odds of divorce just skyrocketed. It's pretty hostile, Els. An act of war."

"I *am* at war," Ellie said. "I'm defending *me*. I'm Ukraine, just sitting there, minding my own business, and he's Putin, deciding to launch a strike against our marriage. You're damn right, I'm hostile."

"But what's your endgame?" Grace had asked. "Don't you want to patch things up and stay married?"

"I don't know. I really don't."

"Then what will you *do*, Ellie?" Grace was more upset with her ambiguity than with Gerald's little sidepiece.

But Joy . . . Joy seemed to understand. "You really just want to time travel back to before he started messaging that slut," she said as she sipped a margarita, petting Connery, who was splayed in her lap, belly exposed for rubbing. "To right before he took that first step, so you could see what he was thinking."

"Yes. And I could behead him right then and there. Use his life insurance."

Joy laughed. "Here's to beheading."

Today, Ellie was at Long Pond Arts, currently locked in her office, once again chafing with energy and simmering rage, which had replaced the stunned hurt and fear she'd felt initially. She'd been letting Meeko earn his keep, honestly not caring how well the gallery did this summer. She had bigger problems. She went there to check in, to paint, to do a lap around the rooms, maybe eat lunch in the courtyard. Otherwise, she'd been driving a lot. Riding her bike. Sitting on a beach, staring at the water. But she missed home. She wasn't sure what exactly she needed there, but she wanted to see her house, minus Gerald.

Her phone dinged. How much longer are we going to not talk, honey? Can we see a marriage counselor?

Not ready for that. When will you be out of the house so I can stop by?

I'm working at urgent care in Orleans. You could go now. I'll be back at 7:30 or so.

Oh, so *now* he was able to work? Yes, she had instructed him to do just that, but it was irritating that a meltdown had been required to get his head out of his ass and see that she was worried about money.

She grabbed her bag, told Meeko she was leaving and walked out into the bright July sunshine. Said hello, nodded, smiled to tourists and locals alike.

"Ellie!" cried Jane, who worked at Preservation Hall. "Where have you been? We were hoping you'd do one of your wonderful classes this summer."

"I'm afraid I can't this year, Jane. Good seeing you, though."

She kept walking, not breaking from her fast, hard stride. Well, well, well. She'd said no. Good for her. Winnie, her toughest child, would be proud of her. Tough in the good sense . . . not battered by insecurity or fear, just a straightforward badass.

She'd been avoiding the kids, texting them rather than calling, because they knew something was off. She saw Lark in passing, and often. That young man she'd had with her the other night, the firefighter, felt like a huge shift in her daughter's life, but Ellie knew better than to comment on it. She'd gone to Addie's the other day to see the girls, and Addie had sniffed around like a bloodhound until Ellie told her to stop. Harlow was giving her space in a most annoying and sensitive way, and Robbie didn't seem to care too much, though he sent her a nice photo of a two-masted schooner. Thought you might like this, Ma. That was it, but still. Sweet (and unusual) of him to think of her.

She turned onto her street. In a town where each house was prettier than the next, the Smith household was a bit of an eyesore. Sort of a nothing style, the kind the 1970s had been famous for. Not a Cape, not a Colonial, not a bungalow, not modern . . . just a rather uninspired house they'd only been able to afford because it had needed so much work. New roof, new septic, a sump pump in the basement. They'd had plans to do more renovations— the beautifying kind—but they'd never gotten around to it.

She immediately saw that the lawn mower was out of the driveway. Gerald would have to get a sticker for that. Likewise, the rotted portion of the fence had been removed, and there was some new wood lying on the ground. The branch in the backyard had been cut up and stacked for firewood.

So what? He'd managed to finish a few things. Atonement chores, like Robbie when he was a little boy. He'd get in trouble for a bad report card or for ruining something of Winnie's or for sneaking out, and suddenly his room would be clean. Fixing the fence did not erase the fact that her husband had been deceitful.

She went inside. The house was tidy and still, and the smell of home made her chest ache. Their aging cat, Buster, had died in his sleep over the winter, and suddenly, she missed him horribly, his creaky little meows and bony back. Tears flooded her eyes. Sweet little Buster.

Home. The family room, with its rather ugly, squat fireplace and cheerfully crowded bookcases, the kitchen with its cheap Corian countertops and mismatched chairs. The electric stove they'd always meant to replace with gas. The mudroom, which had once burst with coats and boots and backpacks, now a place for old newspapers and, when she was living there, whatever had to go back and forth to the gallery. To the left was the half bath, with its blue toilet and blue sink. She'd let the girls paint it when they were in middle school—coral, for some reason. It hadn't looked good then, and it didn't look good now. She'd asked Gerald to paint it at least three times in the past few years, and he said he would, and nothing ever happened. She stopped asking, because what was the point? She figured she'd do it someday when Gerald went away for a weekend. Which he never did, not without her.

Husbands seemed to become toddlers after a decade or so of marriage. You had to direct them, arrange playdates for them, be their friend, entertain them. *Do you think you can paint the bathroom this weekend? No? You don't want to? Okay, then. Why don't you call Matt and see if he wants to shoot some pool at the Governor Bradford? No? Don't you think that would be fun, honey? Please? You want* me *to play with you? Oh. Okay.*

That was the truth. The other truth was that Gerald was her best friend, the person she most admired, the only one who really knew her, every insecurity, every bad moment, and loved her anyway. Her biggest fan, and the one who broke her heart. Because make no mistake . . . her heart was cracked right in half, a jagged, ugly break that she wasn't sure would ever heal.

She went upstairs. As the eldest, Harlow had always had her own room. Addie and Lark had shared another until college, and Winnie and Robbie had been roomies until Harlow left for college, when Robbie was, gosh . . . eight? . . . at which point, Winnie got Harlow's room. It seemed so long ago, all those kids under the same roof, like a happy dream whose details were fading.

And here was the primary bedroom. Their bed was under a skylight, which had fogged with age and poor installation. A giant bureau, since they lacked a closet. Pictures of the kids and grands and the two of them on the walls.

Their bed. Tears filled her eyes and spilled over. They still fell asleep touching, after all these years, just a foot or a hand, maybe. Whenever she had a bad dream, she'd reach out for his solid shoulder, which had grown hairier and rougher over the years. He had always made her feel safe. *Everything will work out.* That was his motto. Was that true now? Would they work things out?

"Hello? Gerald? Are you home, son?"

Her father-in-law, famed for stopping by without checking first.

"Hi, Robert," she called. "I'll be down in a second."

She went into the bathroom and blew her nose, splashed some water on her face, then headed downstairs. "Hi. How are you, Robert?"

"Elsbeth! How wonderful to see you!" He was nattily dressed, as always—linen trousers, a crisp white shirt, a vest. He opened his arms for a hug, and she gave him one. Robert was everything her own father was not—kindhearted, well read, thoughtful, sociable. Only Gerald had an edge where his father was concerned.

"Can I make you something to eat?" she asked.

"I just came from the Ice House," he said, "where I had the biggest salad of my life, Ellie! There were hard-boiled eggs in it, and bacon, and cheese, and it was *wonderful*. But I could use something cold to drink, if it's not too much trouble."

"No trouble at all," she said. She opened the fridge, then glanced at her watch. Four thirty. "Want a gin and tonic?"

"Oh! How *deliciously* indulgent! Yes, please. I feel like a naughty schoolboy, having a cocktail with a pretty lady, and before five at that." She smiled and poured them both a healthy slosh of gin, added ice and poured the tonic on top.

"I don't see any limes, I'm afraid."

"We will have to soldier on without them, in that case. Thank you, my dear. Is my son around?"

"He's taking a shift at the urgent care center in Orleans," she said. "He'll be back about seven thirty. Is everything okay?" She sat across from him at the table.

"That's what I was going to ask him, as a matter of fact," he said. "But I think I'm quite lucky to find you here instead, because *you* are the one I'm worried about, dear Ellie."

"Oh." She took a sip of the drink—the tonic was flat. "Um, thanks."

"You're still not living here?"

"No. I'm staying with Joy."

"A *lovely* woman! So interesting and colorful, and those eyelashes! She's like an exotic bird, don't you think?"

Ellie laughed. "That's a good description."

Robert sipped his drink, his gentle blue eyes kind. "Ellie, if it's none of my business, please say so, but do I need to have a strongly worded conversation with my boy?"

There were those tears again. "He's a senior citizen, Robert. I'm afraid he's past the age of parental lectures."

"Nonsense. If one's parents are alive, a lecture is always an option." He looked at the table and traced a knot in the wood. "I'm under the impression he's been careless with you, Ellie. Am I wrong?"

Should she be talking to her father-in-law about this? Why not? It wasn't like her own parents would offer anything valuable. Robert had been a rock for two-thirds of Ellie's life. She should be allowed to talk to him. "No, you're not wrong. And 'careless' is the perfect word."

"Irredeemably careless?" he asked, wrinkles deepening as he frowned.

"I don't know." A tear slipped out, and she dashed it away. "Robert, how did you and Louisa do it? Sixty-seven years of happiness seems impossible."

"Well, my dear, of *course* we had our difficult times. I worked in Boston five days a week, don't forget. She was essentially a single mother."

Yes, it was Gerald's chief complaint about his father. Robert had only become a devoted family man after Harlow was born, a far better grandfather than he'd been as a dad. "I remember," she said.

"And this was in the day when infidelity and flirtations were very much part of the landscape."

She blinked. "Did you . . . never mind. I withdraw the question."

"No, I never did," Robert said. "But there were many times

when she and I were unhappy with each other. I wanted to raise Gerald in the city, and she insisted on staying here, and so we were a family divided. I called every night and came home every Friday afternoon, but it was challenging. There were months at a time when things were strained. We always found our way back to each other, though."

Ellie nodded.

"No marriage is perfect," he said. "But you and Gerald have made yours close to that. Until now, it seems?"

She swallowed. "Let's just say his attention . . . wandered. Nothing actually happened. Just a lot of secret conversations and a lunch or two. Then he ended it."

"What an *idiot*," Robert said. "What do they call that these days? An emotional dalliance?"

"Yeah, pretty much."

"Well, he's a fool." Robert's face looked strange, since he rarely was anything but happy or struck by wonder.

"Thanks, Robert."

"Is he taking the appropriate steps to come crawling back to you?"

She laughed, surprising herself. "Yes, I guess he is. I just . . . don't know if I want him back."

Robert shook his head. "Love is so fragile," he said. "It cracks a thousand times throughout the years. But what I've found, Ellie, is that if you glue it back together, it gets stronger. More durable if less shiny, shall we say. And you and Gerald have had a very shiny marriage."

She nodded. "Yep. That's true."

He reached over the table and took both her hands in his. "I'm on your side," he said. "People say not to take sides, and to that, I say, ridiculous! There's right and there's wrong. I'm on the side of right. Whatever you choose to do, Elsbeth, your old father-in-law loves and admires you."

She gave a wet laugh. "This is why the kids worship you, Robert. We're all so lucky to have you."

"I'm not sure my son will agree, once I take him to the woodshed. I'm generally against corporal punishment, but at the moment, I could be swayed." He squeezed her hands, then let them go. "I must head out, my dear. Frances and I have a date. We're learning about astronomy! I've always wanted to recognize the constellations, but with these old eyes, time is running out!"

That was the magic of Robert Josiah Smith. Ninety-one years old, and the happiest, most optimistic person she knew. Ellie had always felt she was a happy person, too. She was tired of feeling this way . . . hurt, angry, sad. Time to take action.

After Robert left, she went back upstairs, grabbed a few more clothes from the bureau, washed the glasses and, after thinking about it for five minutes, wrote Gerald a note.

Let's set a date and discuss next steps.

Her marriage wasn't bulletproof, she thought, and it had taken a direct hit. It was in critical condition, but it wasn't dead yet.

EIGHTEEN

LARK

In addition to reading case studies on new oncology treatments, listening to oncology podcasts, and taking online classes in oncology, Lark was getting a lot from being a hospice volunteer.

Her last client had been a sweet old man who smiled when she came into the room and enjoyed holding her hand. She had read to him—*Odd Thomas* by Dean Koontz—and while he'd been nonverbal, he'd smiled in places at the unique way the title character spoke. He had died after three weeks—cerebral vascular disease. His lovely wife had written Lark a note afterward, thanking her for cheering him up. Lark would keep that forever, she knew.

She'd also visited with a Mrs. Kaye, whose profile said she enjoyed listening to Dean Martin songs. Lark had pulled some up on her phone, and the old lady had smiled at the sound of the crooner's voice, though she didn't open her eyes. She died the next day, and though they'd only had that one visit, Lark felt a pang.

Lark wasn't allowed to act as a physician in the program. She was just a person, not allowed to administer meds, adjust the patient, even give a drink of water. Her job was simply to be present, and it was strangely difficult not to be able to help in some way—to bathe the patient, or transfer them from bed to chair, or help them in the bathroom. Her job was to talk if they wanted to talk, ask the family members how they were doing. To listen. Not to fix.

She'd just come off the night shift in the ER and was washing up in the locker room when she got another request from Darlene, the head of the hospice volunteers.

Lark liked the night shift (so far, anyway). She had the advantage of being single with no kids, so she could go home and fall into bed afterward. Generally, the patients who came in at night were more of the true emergency types—cuts, falls, seizures, accidents. There were also more patients suffering substance abuse, whether it was alcohol or heroin or anything in between. The "my foot hurts" type of patient was less likely to show up at 3:00 a.m. than 3:00 p.m.

Lark liked the camaraderie when the department slowed down for a collective breath, as it seemed to at least once per night. Last night had been a good shift—two heart attacks, stabilized and sent upstairs; an obstructed bowel, sent upstairs; a baby with a stomach virus, given IV hydration and heading home. The loser of a fight had required three stitches in her chin; the winner required a cast on her hand, since she'd broken four bones delivering the punch. A very bloody woman had cut her head on the corner of a cabinet—she looked like Carrie on prom night—but had required only two staples. Three frequent fliers had overdosed, been rescued in the field, brought in, observed and sent out to use another day, unfortunately, having rejected the offer of counseling. The opioid crisis had its claws deep in Cape Cod.

But that was life in the ER. Lark was getting used to it. Every shift, someone was made better. That was something. It was good to be busy. She was sleeping better than when she'd been an on-cology resident. That was notable, too.

She was washing up when Darlene's text came in. A patient's husband had asked for coverage this morning so he could do a few errands. An hour, ninety minutes tops. Lark hesitated, then offered to go. It was on her way home, after all.

Great, Darlene texted. Sending you the info now.

Nancy Doane, a fifty-six-year-old woman with end-stage stomach can-cer. Married, three grown children, the youngest about to graduate college. She has a four-month-old granddaughter, her first grandchild. Family is very close and involved. Nurse thinks days, not weeks.

Shit. For a minute, Lark thought about rescinding the offer. She could just call Darlene and say she couldn't make it. She was tired and deserved a long nap. Fear of what she'd see at the pa-tient's house made her knees feel weak.

But if Lark wanted to be an oncologist, she was going to have to make friends with death, as Dr. Hanks had said.

She said goodbye to Mara, who had worked the night shift with her, and hello to the oncoming shift, then drove to Dennis, where the patient lived.

Lark got out, took a breath of the damp air, and went in the house.

"Hi," she said when a man about her father's age answered the door. "I'm Lark, the hospice volunteer."

"Oh, fantastic," he said. "Andrew Doane. Can you stay with my wife while I run to the drugstore? I have to get a prescription refill and thought I'd grab some groceries, too."

"Of course," Lark said. Her hands were shaking.

"Let me introduce you." He led her down a hallway lined with family photos—the family at the beach, babies, weddings, someone with missing teeth, a boy with a baseball mitt, a couple in front of the Eiffel Tower. The images flashed past, and then they were in a bedroom, where a skeletally thin woman lay on a hospital bed.

"Babe, this is Lark, from hospice. She's gonna stay with you while I do a quick errand, okay?"

The woman turned to face Lark. She had a few tufts of hair left, no eyebrows, and her eyes rolled a little—morphine, Lark guessed.

"Hi," she breathed. "I'm Nancy." She smiled, and her teeth looked enormous and yellow, thanks to the chemo.

"Lark," she said. "Great to meet you." Her gaze bounced around the room. More pictures of children. A small statue of a dog. A jewelry box on the bureau, a necklace hanging from the corner of the mirror.

"I'll be back in an hour, ninety minutes tops, okay?" her husband said. "Love you."

"Love you more. Wait." She took a slow breath, eyes closed. "Can you . . . go to the . . . beach and get me . . . a white stone?" She probably had lung metastases, Lark thought. God.

The husband hesitated.

"Alone time," Nancy breathed, and she smiled, though her eyes were closed.

"You'll have plenty of alone time soon enough, don't you think?" he said, trying for a joke. But his voice caught.

"Breathe the . . . air for me. Come back smelling . . . like the . . . ocean." Breathing was definitely labored. If Lark had her stethoscope, she knew she'd hear all sorts of horrors.

"Okay, honey," said the husband, his voice thick. He kissed her hand and rested his forehead on her lap for a second. His wife touched his hair with a thin hand, and Lark had to look away.

"Okay." He stood to leave. "Whatever you want. Thanks, um . . . what was your name again?"

"Lark. Oh, does she have everything she needs? I'm not allowed to give her any food or drink."

"Right there," he said, nodding at a water bottle with a straw on the night table. There were at least ten prescription bottles there as well, in addition to tissues, wipes, a lollipop. "I'll be back soon. Love you, honey."

"Love you," Nancy whispered back.

When the front door closed, Lark sat in the chair next to the bed. Nancy seemed to be asleep. Someone had painted her nails recently. Bright pink. Very cheerful.

"Is there anything I can do for you, Nancy?" Lark whispered.

No answer but for her labored breathing. Lark's heart shook, but she took Nancy's fragile hand in her own. "You're safe," she whispered. "You're home. You're okay." Dante's words. Just the thought of him made her feel a little braver.

"Thanks," Nancy breathed. She opened her eyes, looked at Lark's T-shirt, which read *Sorry I'm late. I saw a dog*, and smiled. "I'm more of . . . a cat . . . person."

On cue, a striped cat jumped up on the bed and started purring. "Who's this handsome beast?" Lark asked.

"Oscar. My . . . buddy." Her other hand found the cat and stroked his fur. "I'm pretty close," she said. "I can . . . feel it. I was thinking . . ." She paused for breath. "Now . . . would be good."

"Good for . . ." Lark's toes clenched, and her heart rate kicked into A-fib. *This is not about you. Or Justin. Be here. Be present.*

"Dying." Her voice was so weak. "I don't want them . . . to see me go." Tears leaked out of her eyes. "The kids . . . were here last . . . night. Baby, too." Her breath was rattling now. "Don't want . . . to say goodbye again. I can't."

"I hear you," Lark whispered. It was one of Dr. Unger's lines, just to let the patient know that whatever the reason they were here, he was listening. "That white stone is more for him, then." Her voice shook, but not too badly.

"Exactly." Nancy opened her eyes again and looked at Lark. "I'm tired," she whispered. "I don't want . . . to die. But this . . . isn't living."

"I understand." Her eyes burned, but she'd be damned if she'd let a single tear fall. "I get it."

"Talk . . . to me. About anything."

"Um, sure. Sure. Well, it's kind of humid out, and um, I guess . . . rain maybe later." Oh, God. What would she want to hear about? What had Justin wanted to hear? "I can feel how much love is in this house, Nancy," she said. "All the family pictures. Three kids, thirty years married, your file says?"

Nancy, eyes closed, gave a faint smile, a half nod. "Thirty . . . two."

"How lucky," Lark said. "A little granddaughter, too."

"Wanted to see her. Stayed alive . . . to meet her."

The tears did spill at that statement, but Lark's voice was steady. "You did, Nancy. You did that. Your daughter will always have those memories of you and your granddaughter." *Fight*, she wanted to say. *Fight. Give them another day, another week.* Maybe there'd be an experimental—but no. Nancy was *dying.* Right now. Her hospice training had told her this happened quite often. People chose to die alone, to protect their loved ones from having to see it.

Had Justin done that? Did he die on purpose before she could get there?

No time for him right now. Nancy's breathing was irregular and jerky. And she wouldn't die alone. Lark was here.

She'd been around a lot of dying people. But she'd been there to try to save them. To cure them. To give them a little more time. There was always something more that could be done to prolong life.

She'd never been there just to bear witness.

This was a different animal. Hospice was about making the best of the last part of your life. The end was not in question. And Lark's job, right now, was to help this very last part be . . . be something more than just a tragedy. To be, perhaps, something a little bit beautiful.

"What was it like, when you held your granddaughter for the first time?" she asked. Tears spilled out of her eyes, but her voice was steady. The cat remained firmly against Nancy's side, still purring. "Did you smell her head? I bet her skin was so soft. Those sweet little hands, grabbing on to your finger."

Nancy made a humming sound of affirmation.

On impulse, Lark let go of Nancy's hand. "Hang on one second." She dashed from the room into the hallway. There. Six or seven people, plus a baby. Andrew looked the same, more or less, and Nancy was smiling, a scarf on her head. The baby was a newborn, just a little pink burrito with a pink cap on.

She ran back into the room, sat back down and held the picture. "Open your eyes, Nancy," she said. "Look at all this love. You made that happen. You did this."

Nancy did open her eyes. She smiled again, and then her eyes drifted closed. Lark set the picture next to her and took her hand in both of hers.

"I'm here, Nancy. You're not alone." A rattling breath. "You're safe. You're home. You're not alone. It'll be okay."

Another noisy breath. A pause. A breath. A longer pause.

Another breath did not come.

Lark counted to thirty. Put her free hand on Nancy's chest and felt nothing except bone. For a few minutes, she just sat there, tears streaming silently out of her eyes.

"Great job, Nancy," she whispered. "Well done. You can rest now."

Then she let go of Nancy's hand, gently, gently put it on top of the photo. She stroked Oscar the cat.

"Good boy," she whispered.

Then she called her supervisor, who said she'd send out the bereavement counselor.

When Andrew got home, Lark met him at the door.

"I'm so sorry," she said.

"Ah, shit," he said, his face crumpling. He went into the bedroom, and Lark waited. A few minutes later, he came out, his face streaked with tears.

"I'm sorry," Lark said again, and he hugged her.

"Thanks for being here with her. I should've known she'd sneak out if she had the chance."

"It was really peaceful," Lark said.

"You brought her the picture. That was . . . that was so kind. My kids will be glad to know that."

"Oscar was with her, too."

"Oh, yeah? That's . . . that's nice." He wiped his eyes. "You think you're ready for this, but you're really not, are you?"

"I don't think anyone could be," she said.

He nodded, sighing. "I guess I should call the kids."

"Do you want me to straighten up the room?" she asked.

He nodded, patted her shoulder and pulled out his phone as he went into the living room.

Lark went back into the bedroom, tilted the hospital bed back and adjusted Nancy so she was a little straighter. Brushed her hair and wiped off her face with a warm, damp facecloth. Neatened the covers, found a bag in the corner and put all her medications in there. No need for the trappings of sickness. Nancy wasn't sick anymore.

In the end, all medicine, all interventions fail. Lark knew that. And now she'd seen it up close, borne witness to it, had watched as death came in and quietly, kindly took Nancy away.

"Thank you," she said, putting her hand on Nancy's. "Thank you for the privilege."

NINETEEN

ELLIE

There. You're gorgeous! Gerald will spit blood when he sees you." Joy stepped back and squinted approvingly.

Ellie smiled. "Definitely what I'm going for. Thanks, Joy." She studied herself in the mirror. She looked quite . . . lovely. Herself, but a little younger, maybe. "The last time I wore makeup was to Addie and Nicole's wedding." Would Gerald notice? She hadn't seen him in three weeks, but tonight, they were meeting at the Wicked Oyster for dinner. Not on a date. For a conversation.

"My pleasure! You can raid my stash whenever you want. I'm doing a makeup session tomorrow at work for my activity."

"Really?" Ellie asked.

"Mm-hmm. Just because you're senile doesn't mean you can't look your best," Joy said, and Ellie sputtered. "Maybe I shouldn't say 'senile,'" Joy amended. "Just because you're at death's door doesn't mean you have to look that way. Better?"

"No." Ellie laughed. "What about the men?"

"Men wear makeup, too."

"True, true. So you like work?" Joy had been practically levitating the other day when she told Ellie about her job.

"Oh, I love it!" she said. "I feel so *useful*. We did chair dancing today. Joyful Movement, I'm calling it. Get it? Because of my name? I basically blast a playlist and they sit there and move whatever parts they still can. Florence fell dead asleep, and Bob almost toppled over, but at least he can still stand on his own. They practically rioted when 'Uptown Funk' came on."

"That's the best song."

"Don't I know it."

Ellie's phone rang. Unknown caller, but a 508 area code. "Hello?"

"Hello, is this Elsbeth Smith?"

"Yes."

"Hi! This is Anita Santini, Lorenzo's mom."

Ellie looked at Joy, then hit "speaker." "Hi, Lorenzo's mom. How are you? Is everything okay?"

"Oh, gosh, you sure are a mother, aren't you? Isn't that always our first question? Everything's great! I was just saying to my husband that we Santinis should meet the Smiths. Our kids have been dating for two months and we haven't even gotten together yet. Are you free this weekend, by any chance?"

Oh, dear. "Um . . . you know, I think I am, personally," she said, unable to lie. "Not sure about anyone else, though. Have you run this past, um, the kids?" She pulled a face at Joy.

Anita laughed. "Not yet. I figured we moms are really the ones in charge. I haven't thought this through too much, but Lorenzo said he was off, which doesn't happen that often, let me tell you, and Lark told Izzy she had Saturday free—Izzy's my youngest—and anyway, whoever's around could get together. I just feel like it's time, don't you?"

"You know, I . . . um . . ."

"Hello?" said Joy, leaning down to speak directly into the phone, her generous cleavage forcing Ellie to lean back. "Hi, this is Joy, Lark's landlady and Ellie's friend. I'd say I'm Lark's other mother, but Ellie here would smack me."

"Joy!" Anita cooed. "We've heard such lovely things about you."

"Really? Thanks! Hey, why don't you come to my house? I have a place on the water, and it's huge. I've been dying to have a party. My brother and I used to host get-togethers all the time, and I've really missed that since he passed away."

Shit. Ellie shook her head and made a slashing motion across her throat. Joy took the phone and turned away, smiling.

"That's so generous, Joy. Silvio and I have been saying we want to come down to Wellfleet. It's such a pretty town."

"Joy," Ellie whispered. "Not a good idea."

"Then consider it done! However many Santinis can come should plan on Saturday at, oh, one o'clock? I'll have Ellie here rally her kids, and we'll have a wonderful time!"

"Lovely! Thank you so much, Joy!"

Ellie threw up her hands.

"I can't wait to meet you all," Joy said, beaming at the phone. "I'll grab your number from Ellie's phone, and we can talk tomorrow, how's that?"

"Perfect! Looking forward to it."

Joy clicked off and handed the phone back to Ellie. "A party! How fun!"

"Did you forget Lark's not actually dating this guy?" Ellie asked. "Now we'll all have to pretend they're a couple."

"I know, but the *brother*, right? Tell me you picked up on some chemistry there. The air was throbbing with, oh, gosh, what's that word that means horniness?"

"Pheromones. The brother thinks they're dating, too, Joy."

"Oh. Right." Joy put her hands on her hips. "Well, we can figure it out. Anyway, you should go, or you'll be late. Should I wait up?"

"I . . . it's your house, Joy." She took a breath. You know what? This party was Lark's problem. She'd warned her daughter not to be dishonest, and now the chickens were coming home to roost. "Thanks, Joy. For the makeup and . . . well, for being a wonderful friend." She hugged the other woman. "Wish me luck."

Because yes, she was about to meet her husband. Possibly her soon-to-be ex-husband. Who would now be invited to Joy's house this weekend where they, like Lark and Lorenzo, would have to pretend to be a happy couple.

What goes around, comes around.

Gerald stood up when he saw her. Wisely, he'd commandeered the most private table in the place—in the corner of the smaller dining area. Most patrons had chosen to sit out back, since it was a warm night.

"Hey," he breathed. "Wow. You look . . . beautiful."

"Thanks," she said, taking her seat before he could hold it for her.

He did *not* look beautiful, and she was immediately gratified. He looked exhausted. Bags under his eyes, a little patch of gray stubble he'd missed shaving, a slightly musty smell around him. The smell of home, she realized. His hair seemed to have more gray in it.

"Chardonnay, please," she said when the server came over to take their drink. Ah, it was Brianna, who'd gone to school with Robbie. "Hello, honey."

"Mrs. Smith! Mr. Smith! How are you? Gosh, you guys look exactly the same. How's Robbie?"

"He's just fine," Ellie said. "I'll tell him you said hello. Can we order now, sweetheart? We have to discuss some family plans and need a little privacy, if that's okay."

"Of course!"

"I'll have the risotto with scallops," she said.

Gerald took the hint, glanced at the menu. "Want to split the calamari?" he asked. They usually shared an appetizer, but this was not a regular date.

"I'm all set," she said, handing the menu back to Brianna.

"I'll have the same thing she's having, then," Gerald said. "Thanks, Brianna."

"You bet." She walked off, and they looked at each other.

"How have you been?" Gerald asked. She could feel the nervousness rising off him.

"Good," she said, keeping her tone neutral. "Joy's house is beautiful, and we're becoming really close."

"Great. Good. That's . . . that's great. And the gallery?"

"I don't know, actually," she said. "Meeko is running it this summer. I check in, do some painting, whatever. I'm on sabbatical. You know. Since I haven't had a vacation in ever, really."

"You deserve it. Definitely. I'm . . . well . . . God, this is awkward, isn't it?"

"I wonder why." She narrowed her eyes at him, letting him know she wasn't here for pleasantries. Brianna came back with their drinks, and Ellie sipped hers, not looking away from her husband. "Heard from Camille lately?" she asked.

"No! Not since January, Ellie. I deleted my Facebook account."

"Are you expecting a trophy for that?"

He took a slow breath. "Look, honey, I will apologize for the rest of my life, if that's what you need. Whatever it takes, I'll do."

"And yet I have no way of trusting you anymore. How will I *know* you'll do what it takes? You lied to me, you were sneaking around—"

"I met her once for lunch. It was one sneak."

Her stomach burned with fury. "You were sneaking around every time you took out your little iPad, hiding in the attic to DM her and tell her about your tepid marriage and bitchy wife. Meanwhile, you said *nothing* to me. You didn't tell *me* our marriage was so lackluster, Gerald. We've never gone for more than a few weeks without sex, and that was usually because I'd just pushed a baby out. So that part is a bit confusing."

"You're right," he said. "I lied to her. I wanted her to think I was more available than I was."

"So you lied to me, and you lied to her. What a catch you are."

He swallowed, glancing around in misery. "I'm sorry."

"That fixes absolutely nothing," she snapped. "This unhappiness of yours . . . this loneliness, this busy wife who ignored you . . . you made all that up because you wanted to reconnect with a high school crush? You risked our *marriage* for something that insignificant? You'd break up our family for that?" She was leaning forward, hissing like a snake, and forced herself to sit back up. They knew far too many people in this town.

Brianna brought their dinners, told them to enjoy and left again.

Gerald didn't say anything.

"Speak," she growled. "Explain yourself."

He took a long, slow breath. "Okay. Okay. Ellie, I've obviously been thinking a lot about how this happened, and why. All

I can tell you is how I was feeling last year. How I was *feeling*, not how you were making me feel or anything like that. I'm not that stupid. I know this is all my fault."

"Go on." She stabbed at her risotto.

"So . . . I'd hurt my back, remember? Lifting that guy off the floor at the hospital?"

"Yes, I remember." Gerald hurting his back meant he was in agony, unable to move without breaking into a sweat, his face reddening, breath coming in short gasps. It happened every couple of years, despite the exercises he did, despite the physical therapy he'd had. And when his back was out, it meant she had to do everything for a solid two weeks, from grocery shopping to helping him shower. She never minded, not until right now. Sickness and health, good times and bad. Forsaking all others, goddamn it.

"And that was pretty much that, career-wise. I mean, I'd been cutting back my hours, but all of a sudden, it was decided for me. That part of my life was over, just like that. It surprised me, how much I missed it."

"And yet, here you are, picking up shifts again."

"Because you wanted me to. Because you needed me to."

"So now you're husband of the year?"

"No. I'm just saying, I'm trying to make things right with us. You asked me to, and I am."

"Anyway. Hurting your back made you have an affair?"

He started to contradict her and then, wisely, did not. He took a bite of his meal, chewed, swallowed. "I felt like an old man," he said. "You know? Once upon a time, I could do anything, and now I had to lie on the couch with ice and Motrin."

"Sounds like a vacation to me."

"And I'm married to the most capable, talented, energetic—"

"Ew. Stop."

"No," he said, putting down his fork and leaning forward. "No, Ellie. You are. You are those things. Look at you. You're sixty-three years old, and you've never done more than you have in the past five years. You run the gallery, you're a grandmother . . . I mean, the way you connected with Matthew was so beautiful and instantaneous, and Esme and Imogen worship you. Our kids are in awe of you. You paint *and* run a business. You're a success in every way measurable. I think you're right up there with Grace Henry and Winslow Homer, and you just get better every year."

She took a bite of the risotto and said nothing.

"And I'm lying on the couch with ice and Motrin, and I can't even fix the fucking fence. Or paint that butt-ugly bathroom, or do half a dozen things I've been wanting to do. I have to pace myself, like an old man, or I'll end up back on the couch."

"Why didn't you say your back was the reason you didn't do those things? You always acted like you were just about to do them as soon as you finished something more important."

"Yeah, well, I'm not incredibly proud of it." He took another long, slow inhale. "I didn't want you to know. Stupid male pride, wanting my woman to think I'm still big and strong and capable."

She had always loved when he called her his woman. Against her will, the words caused a tingle in her veins.

"So, last September," he went on, "I had a forced retirement, and you . . . you were just hitting your stride. You sold every painting last summer. It was amazing."

"Let's not forget the summer of Mathilda, Gerald. I've had to dumb down my work ever since."

"You say that, but your stuff is still gorgeous. I . . . I was jealous. And a little . . . ashamed. I know you went back to work because I could never earn quite enough. We both know that."

"I was always going to paint again, Gerald."

"I know. But you started up earlier than you wanted to. In that moment, that year, I needed you to. I never said it out loud, but we both knew it. We were scraping by, and you stepped up. Fast-forward twenty years, and yeah, you have the business and your art, and you have an employee and the baby artists who think you're a goddess, and I . . . I didn't have anything like that. I didn't know how to tell you that I was so proud of you and so jealous at the same time."

She let that sit for a minute. It felt . . . authentic. "You could've tried, Gerald. You owed that to me. And you could have done something to expand your own life. Taken a class, started a new hobby, spent more time with the kids or your dad. Instead, you go to Facebook and start flirting with an old classmate." Her anger rose again. "Did that fix your ego? Because the guy on Facebook chatting with Camille Dupont sounded utterly pathetic. 'My wife is so busy! I'm so boring.'" And you're not. You never were."

"Thanks," he said.

"It's not a compliment. It's a fact." She speared another scallop. "Back to Facebook. What made you start talking to a woman who's completely devoid of morals and makes a pass at a married man?"

He winced. "Yeah. Well, I didn't know I'd . . . connect with her. I was literally flat on my back, watching *The Crown* on my iPad, feeling like a loser. Figured I'd see who was around, which people might be out there I'd like to get to know again. I didn't seek her out. I'd forgotten about her, to be honest."

"Until you remembered her."

He nodded, shame painting his features a dull red. "Yeah."

"And then you were young again? A new man? Full of potential and excitement? I mean, Gerald, we watched so many other couples fall apart. Remember when Brad Fairchild left Lillie, and you were so disgusted with him? So embarrassed for him? Then you do the same thing!"

"No, Ellie, I didn't do the same thing. I let myself be entertained. I never would have cheated on you. It was a flirtation. I never did more than kiss her on the cheek that one time we met. It was . . . fun."

"I guess I'm not fun, then."

Gerald sat back, his face hardening a little. "You know what, honey? At the time, no. You were working. You were painting these beautiful canvases and running the gallery and hiring Meeko and mentoring the baby artists and teaching classes, and then, at the end of the day, I'd cook us dinner, and we'd have an hour, two hours, together, then go to bed."

"I think that's called *marriage*, Gerald," she spat.

"I know. I know. I just felt . . . lonely, Ellie." His voice broke. "The kids were gone, the summer was over, our grandson went back to California, my career was done, my body's falling apart, and you didn't see any of that. I know I'm completely at fault here, but that's where my head was."

"Damned if I do, damned if I don't," she said. "I'm amazing for doing what I do, and I'm blamed for the same damn thing. You told her you wanted to be an APRN, and that's *bullshit*, Gerald. *I* wanted you to do that. Do you know how it felt for me to read that? I've been jealous of *you*, because *you* got to semi-retire, then fully retire, and have the time to do all the things we'd put off for so long. *I* had to keep working, and while I was doing that, you reached out to someone else! You broke my heart, Gerald."

She was crying now, and she put her hand up to her face so no one else could see.

She felt his hand on her arm. "I know," he whispered. "I know. And I'm so, so sorry, honey."

They stayed that way for a few minutes until she stopped with the tears. She hated crying. Hated it. She wiped her eyes, took a deep breath and finished her wine. Was this what their talk was supposed to accomplish? Was all this honesty actual progress? It felt more like doom.

They sat in silence a few minutes. At least she could still eat. No misery starvation for her, no sir. Joy's trashy food, crap she'd avoided for decades, was delicious. Those cupcakes with the peel-off frosting? Fantastic. Bugles? Salty deliciousness. She'd probably gained ten pounds over the past few weeks.

"My father reamed me another orifice, by the way," Gerald said. "Can't wait till the kids find out and do the same. I'll be Swiss cheese by the time they're done."

"Your father is a near-perfect human," she said.

Gerald nodded. "Can't disagree there."

"Will you ever forgive him for being so . . . absentee when you were growing up?" There. Steer the conversation to other waters, because there was no point in staying in their storm-tossed waves.

He tilted his head, those blue eyes still so damn gorgeous. He had a little Paul Hollywood going on there, that salt-and-pepper hair, those husky-bright eyes. Unfair. "It always seemed like everyone got the best part of him, and Mom and I were left with the crumbs until I was an adult. That's what I never wanted to do to you, Ellie. I never wanted you to feel second to my career."

"I never wanted you to feel that way, either," she said. "I was really, really careful for that not to be our way. We both were."

"And it worked."

"Until it didn't, apparently."

"I made a big mistake, Ellie. It was impulsive and stupid, and it will never happen again. Please forgive me." He reached over and cupped her cheek, his eyes so full of concern. "Please let me make this up to you."

"Not yet," she said. "I'm not over it."

"Don't leave me," he whispered. "We can fix this. Please."

"We'll see. I want to, Gerald. But I don't know if I can. I'm not the most forgiving person in the world."

To her surprise, he laughed. "I know. It's one of my favorite things about you. Grudge holding."

"What grudges? I don't hold grudges."

"What about Larry?"

"I don't have a grudge against my brother-in-law. I've always hated him. He's never given me reason to stop."

He smiled. "How about the little girl who used to bully Winnie? Pushed her off the slide? And her mother told you to stop having kids because you were driving up town taxes."

"Oh, God. Lorraine Brandowski and her little demon, Oakley. The kids called her Poison Oakley. Winnie needed three stitches. You're right. I wouldn't pee on them if they were on fire."

Gerald chuckled. That history of theirs. That long, rich, wonderful history.

"What if you get bored again?" she whispered, tears rushing back into her eyes. "What if you're lonely again? How can I believe you, Gerald, when you were thinking of another woman for four months?"

His brows drew together, and his blue eyes were so . . . shit. They were so sincere. So beautiful. "Faith?" he said. "I hope you'll think we're worth a second chance. I really, really hope you'll think that, Ellie. You're the love of my life. You *are* my life."

The words hit her straight in the heart. "You were on a roll there, but no Hallmark card stuff, okay?"

He quashed a smile, knowing her through and through.

"I'm gonna stay with Joy for the time being," she said. "I haven't forgiven you yet. You've done damage. It doesn't just evaporate because you're sorry."

"I understand. And I miss you."

She missed him, too. More than she wanted to. "By the way," she said, "Joy is hosting a party this weekend with the fake boyfriend's family."

"Oh, are they still doing that?"

"Yes. You'll come, and if the kids ask you, tell them you're still working on the house stuff." She stood up. "Thanks for dinner."

"I love you, Ellie."

She grabbed her purse. "I love you, too. That's the problem." Then she turned and walked out of the restaurant into the breezy night.

TWENTY

LARK

Somehow, without Lark's knowledge or consent, Joy was throwing a party for all the Santinis and all the Smiths. Even Henry's mother was going to come. With her falcon.

Lark was still trying to wrap her head around it. But here it was, Saturday, and the caterers were already dropping off giant foil tins of food.

"I'm so happy!" Joy cooed. "You know, Paulie was always the one who organized things when we lived in New York, but I'm really enjoying myself."

"Great," Lark said. "That's . . . yeah."

"Will the handsome firefighter be coming? Dante?"

"I don't know," Lark said. She'd worked six shifts in five days, gone to Boston for a lecture from an oncologist at the Mayo Clinic and driven back the same night and spent four hours with a hospice patient. She'd only found out about the picnic via an all-caps text from Lorenzo Thursday night.

WHY IS YOUR FAMILY HOSTING A PARTY
FOR MY FAMILY? RESPOND IMMEDIATELY.

The thought of seeing Dante again was both distressing and (she couldn't lie) exhilarating. He was so stinking funny and gorgeous and kind, and a great brother. He loved his family. His arms were like something sculpted by Michelangelo, and his lips . . .

Yeah. Her brain was essentially in a blender at the moment.

But the party was happening, as evidenced by all this food. Mac and cheese, pulled-pork sandwiches, salads, deviled eggs, a complete New England clambake, shucked-on-the-spot Wellfleet oysters.

"Whose idea was this again?" she asked.

"Anita's. This is what you get for being deceptive, honey," Mom said, patting her shoulder.

"Thanks, Mom. That helps." She rubbed her tired eyes.

"Everyone knows to pretend, not to worry. We won't blow your cover." Mom took a tray of food and went downstairs to the covered deck, where the buffet would be.

"I ordered an ice-cream truck, too," Joy said. "I thought that would be fun."

"Joy . . ." Lark sighed internally. She couldn't fault Joy, whose heart was as big as New England. "This is amazing. You really went all out."

Her friend's face was bright with happiness, which reminded Lark that she hadn't shot that face up with anything in the recent past. Not that she'd mention it. Joy looked prettier for it.

"You're welcome, sweetie! I love entertaining. I've been so sad, I kind of forgot."

Lark's heart melted a little more. "In that case, I'm really glad we're doing this. I'll pay you back somehow."

"Nonsense! This is my groove! Oh, did I tell you? Your mom's going to do a painting class at Bayview, isn't that great?

Who knows? Maybe one of those old geezers is a Vincent Picasso in the making. Grab those bottles of wine and bring them downstairs, okay? Your dad is bringing ice."

She obeyed, and for the next hour, ran trays, set out napkins, picked and arranged flowers, dumped ice over bottles of wine and cans of beer. Connery ran around her, excited by all the activity.

"Stick with me, Connery," she said. "You're my ally today. And don't get eaten by the falcon, okay?"

It really was a perfect day for a picnic. Not a cloud to be seen, low humidity, enough of a breeze so that the hot sun wouldn't drive anyone inside. And yes, Joy's house was perfect for a party. The two huge decks; expansive lawn; vast, cool interior and views of the sparkling ocean. The girls would have a blast running up and down the wooden boardwalk. The shed contained all sorts of beachy accessories—kayaks, beach chairs, inflatables. Dad was down on the sand now, setting up a volleyball net.

And here came everyone. Addie, Nicole and the girls. Harlow; her boyfriend, Grady; his daughter, Luna; and Rosie, Harlow's best friend, who was visiting for a couple of weeks. Robbie was with them, having been crushing on Rosie since he was, oh, ten years old. Harlow's dog, Ollie, was here, too, and immediately began romping and tussling with Connery in case there wasn't enough chaos. Winnie, stone-faced, had driven Frances and Grandpop, who was wearing a blue seersucker suit and panama hat.

Lark could always sneak off to her little guesthouse to hide.

But no. The Santinis came right on their heels, piling out of a huge SUV like it was a clown car. Dante wasn't with them, she noted. She was relieved and disappointed at the same time. Mostly relieved, she told herself. They poured into the yard, the house, onto the deck, and Lark greeted and kissed and hugged and stuck bottles of wine in the appropriate places, took a cake from Anita, showed Izzy where to park Noni.

"Where's the alcohol?" Izzy asked. "I've been in the car with the Crypt Keeper for almost an hour here."

"Lorenzo! Honey, there you are!" Anita cried.

"He came in his Maserati and wouldn't even let me ride shotgun," Izzy muttered.

"Hello," Lorenzo said, accepting a hug from his mother. He looked sullen and gorgeous, like an ad for a very expensive cologne.

"That's him?" Nicole said. "I can see why she's with him. That's a Patek Philippe watch."

"Tone it down, Nicole," Winnie said.

"Hello," Lorenzo said to Lark, his voice grim.

"Hi," she said. "I . . . yeah." Since they were being watched, she stood on her tiptoes and kissed his cheek. He didn't visibly recoil, so points for that. "Sorry," she whispered. "I had nothing to do with this."

"And yet here we are."

"I'm simply a tenant." She turned to her family, who stood on one side of the large kitchen. "Mom, Dad, meet Anita and Silvio Santini. This is Lorenzo, my . . . boyfriend, and this is Noni, Silvio's mom. This is Isabella, who's a nurse—Izzy, my dad is also a nurse, I'm sure you two can swap horror stories—and this is Sofia, the bride, and her handsome fiancé, Henry Chang, and his mom, Jocelyn."

A chorus of hellos rose up.

Lark took a deep breath. "Santinis, meet my parents, Gerald and Elsbeth—"

"Call me Ellie, please," Mom said.

"Our wonderful hostess, Joy Deveaux, my landlady and friend. There's Grandpop, his girlfriend, Frances—"

"Hello, hello!" Grandpop said.

"And these are my siblings, in birth order. Harlow; her best friend, Rosie; her partner, Grady; and his adorable little girl, Luna."

"I'm five," Luna said.

"Five is awesome," Izzy said.

Lark smiled and continued. "This is Addison, my twin, obviously, and her wife, Nicole, and their gorgeous daughters, Esme and Imogen. That's my sister Winnie, and that's my brother, Robbie, and did I leave anyone out?"

Everyone seemed to speak at once. Lorenzo gave her a dark look, then took the handles of his grandmother's wheelchair and pushed her into the dining room, away from the din of conversation. Lark followed, and Winnie drifted in as well.

"Hi," Winnie said. "I'm Lark's youngest sister. Nice to meet you, Mrs. Santini."

Noni raised her head—she'd gotten a new wig—and eyed Winnie. "You," Noni said in her whispery voice. "I no like you. Your face, it's not nice."

"Okay," Winnie said, straightening up. "Well, based on that, I no like you, either, ma'am."

"Excuse me," Lorenzo said, his voice like a knife. "She's an old lady."

"Yeah. Rude, too," Winnie said, unimpressed.

"How about some respect?" he said.

"I called her ma'am," Winnie retorted, and Lark smothered a laugh.

"Mom," Silvio said, coming in with an apologetic expression, "let me take you onto the deck. Are you cold? Let's get you in the sunshine. Excuse me, kids." He removed Noni, to Lark's relief. She was never sure Noni wasn't about to shiv her.

Winnie and Lorenzo eyed each other. "So you're the asshole doctor?" Winnie asked.

"Winnie," Lark sighed.

"I am," Lorenzo said.

Winnie glanced around. "Let me just say that intimidating my sister into pretending to date you is a shitty thing to do," she said in a low voice. "I told her to file charges against you."

"I didn't *intimidate* her. This is a completely voluntary situation," Lorenzo said. "I resent the implication."

"Hey, walk that back, Winona," came Robbie's voice. He appeared in the doorway, holding Rosie's hand. "Hi, I'm the brother, in case you missed it. Love this whole situation. Totally romantic. I've seen this movie, in like, eight different versions."

Lorenzo gave Lark a pitying look.

"Hi," said Rosie. "I'm Harlow's friend, Rosie Wolfe."

"Also my girlfriend," Robbie said.

"It's almost true," Rosie said. "We are close to finalizing negotiations."

"Wait, what?" Izzy entered, holding a drink. "Lark, I was promised a husband, and now I learn your brother is already with someone? Hi, I'm Isabella Santini. Just kidding. Very nice to meet you, even if we won't be husband and wife soon. Sorry, and your name again?" She smiled at Rosie.

"Rosie. I'm not related to anyone here. I just pretend to be."

Izzy laughed, but Lark was already exhausted. Why did she have so many siblings? Why did Lorenzo?

Lorenzo took her by the arm and towed her to the butler's pantry. "This is ridiculous."

"I know," she said as he closed the door to the small room.

"Lying is exhausting. Can't we just tell everyone we're not to-gether?"

"No."

"Your grandmother is more likely to bite me than give us her blessing, and anyway, no one has to tell her. It's not like we'll be staying together." Dating his brother, though . . .

"Lower your voice, for one. For two, don't be fooled. My grandmother wants what's best for me, and because of some out-dated European notions of family, she thinks a wife is that thing."

"For one, wives are not things, and for two, I'm not your wife! I'm your fake girlfriend."

"I'm well aware, Lark! Believe me, I wouldn't marry you with a gun to my head, not if it meant having to deal with your family."

"Are you yelling at my sister *and* insulting my family?" Ad-dison had just opened the door and stepped in, ignoring bound-aries like a good twin. "Also, there's a Santini coming up the stairs from the yard, so stop yelling."

"She yelled first," Lorenzo said.

"I don't care," Addie said. "Also, Lark never yells. She's per-fect in every way."

Lorenzo heaved a sigh, looked at Lark and walked back into the melee.

"Charming, isn't he?" Lark said.

"You okay?" Addie asked.

"No. Not at all. I was ambushed by this."

"He really is gorgeous," Addie said. She peered out the win-dow. "What's that on Grandpop's arm? Is that a falcon?"

A nap. Definitely a nap. Or a kidnapping, if she could get someone to pop her into the trunk of a car and drive off some-where.

An hour later, though, Lark found herself standing alone on the shaded patio, looking out over Joy's lawn. Tiger lilies and black-eyed susans bobbed on the breeze; the hydrangeas were an electric shade of blue; the kids were flying kites on the beach with Robbie, Rosie, Harlow and Grady. In the yard and on the deck, people had separated into little clumps of conversation. None of Lark's family had outed the fake relationship, though at this point, it would've been a relief if they did. An oysterman was shucking at the raw bar Joy had set up, and the food was fantastic. Aside from herself and Lorenzo (and Noni), everyone seemed to be having a great time.

Especially Joy. Lark smiled, watching her. She hadn't seen her this animated . . . well, ever.

"You."

"Jesus!" Lark practically leaped out of her skin. It was Noni, like a ninja in her wheelchair. "Sorry. Hi, Noni," she said. Apparently Noni could get around on her own, a fact previously undisclosed to Lark. "Can I get you anything?"

"You love my grandson?" she asked.

Which one? Lark thought, then cringed. "He's very . . . special."

"He alone mosta his life. He need somebody."

"Yes. I agree."

"I die soon."

She knew? Lorenzo made it seem like she was in the dark about that. "How are you handling that? Would you like to talk a little?"

The old lady shrugged. "We all die." She glanced up at Lark. "I no like Lorenzo alone, working, no life, no love. He need kids. Happy times."

Okay, then. So she did have human emotions. "I'm sure he'll have them," Lark said. It was possible.

"You gonna be good to him?"

"Sure. Of course. You don't have to worry about him, Noni. He's . . . he's well loved." By someone, surely.

Noni narrowed her eyes. "Eh. Whadda you know? Go find my son."

"You got it." Like a prisoner who'd just been pardoned, Lark leaped off to find Silvio and told him where his mother was lurking. Grabbed a pork sandwich and ate it, accepted a glass of wine from Addie.

"Larkby," her sister said, "when this summer is done, how about if we have a twin weekend, just us? Spa, food, wine, more food, fun. We both need it."

"I'm in," she said. It was a nice thought, but honestly, if she got back into Oncology, she'd be way too busy for that. And she would get back in. She'd sent Dr. Hanks a report of what she was doing, from the studying, the classes, podcasts and papers, the hospice work, and he'd emailed back, saying she was on the right path.

So good for her.

"Oh, Jocelyn's waving to me," Addie said. "She said the girls could feed the falcon, and I want to get some pictures for Instagram. See you later." She shoved her wineglass into Lark's hand and dashed down to the beach, where Jocelyn was indeed showing Otto off to the little ones. (Lark had tucked Connery into the guesthouse, just in case.) Grady and Harlow were holding hands, watching, and Robbie and Rosie were notably not in sight, probably making out somewhere. Dad was talking to Grandpop and Silvio, and Mom was coming out with more food.

"Hello, Lark. There you are!"

Lark froze, then turned. Heather and Theo Dean stood in front of her.

"Hi!" she said. "Um . . . how are you?"

"I *told* you she forgot, hon," Theo said, giving her a hug. "Whale watching today? Dinner at the Red Inn afterward?"

Her heart dropped like a stone. "Oh no, I did forget," she said. "I'm so sorry. I . . . I've worked an awful lot this week, and then Joy threw this picnic, and I . . . I'm so embarrassed."

"Honey, it's just us," Heather said, kissing her cheek. "Don't apologize. It happens. Do you want to skip it, then? We can do it another time."

"Lark, do you have a key to the shed? Henry and I thought we'd take a kayak out, and Joy said . . . Oh, sorry! I didn't mean to interrupt."

It was Sofia and Henry. Lark felt a little dizzy.

"Hi. I'm Heather, and this is my husband, Theo," said Heather. "We're friends of the family."

"I'm Sofia Santini, and this is my fiancé, Henry Chang. I'm Lorenzo's sister."

"Nice to meet you," Henry said.

"And who's Lorenzo?" Theo asked as they shook hands.

Sofia glanced at Lark. "Lark's boyfriend," she said with a smile.

For a second, both Deans froze. Lark tried to say something and failed. Her heart rolled in rapid, sickening thuds. Heather looked like Lark had just stabbed her, and Theo's eyes were too wide.

"Theo! Heather! So nice to see you!" It was Mom, charging to the rescue. Hopefully to the rescue, anyway.

"We apparently . . . um . . . we mixed up dates," Heather said, recovering a little. "We didn't mean to interrupt your party."

"No, no, not at all," Mom said.

"We'll find the key ourselves," Henry said, apparently sensing the tremor in the force.

Lark swallowed. "Under the flowerpot to the left of the door," she said.

That left her standing there on the upper deck with her mother and the Deans.

"You have a *boyfriend*," Heather said. "That's wonderful, Lark." But the bleakness in her voice belied the words.

"Is he here? Can we meet him?" Theo asked. His face looked a little gray.

"I'm not dating anyone," Lark blurted. "It's a long story. I didn't tell you because . . . it's not a . . ." She looked at her mother.

"Tell you what," Mom said briskly. "There's a little Shakespearean comedy going on here right now. It's not what it seems, in other words. Lark is doing a colleague a favor, being his date for a wedding this summer. Why don't we have dinner or drinks sometime? I'd love to come by your house. It's been ages." She gave Lark a pointed look, then steered Heather and Theo back into the house, her voice getting fainter. "How's your summer been? Are you going back and forth to Boston, or . . ."

Mom would be getting a huge birthday present this year. Huge. Very expensive.

You know what? This would be a great chance to sneak into her house, check on Connery and breathe into a paper bag. She slipped through Joy's, went out the side door and ran up the path to her place. No one called out her name or saw her, thank the adorable seven-pound Christ child, as Dr. Unger was fond of saying.

Her little house was quiet and neat, an oasis of calm compared to the barbarian hordes of family at Joy's. Connery danced up to her, little tail wagging, and she scooped him up, then sat down on the couch. This shit was getting out of hand, just as Mom had predicted. Lesson? Mothers are always right. Noni wasn't exactly yearning for Lorenzo to be with her, and Lorenzo's promised introduction to the Dana-Farber team was probably not going to be necessary. Accepting his proposal had been a decision made in fear and a hurry. Again, Mom had been right. Lark could get back into Oncology on her own. If she even wanted to.

She reached out for the picture of her and Justin—the same one she'd shown Dante—and stared at it. Had she always wanted to be a doctor, or had his sickness pushed her there? Would she have chosen oncology without a boyfriend who'd had leukemia? Would she have made it her life's mission if not for his death?

"I miss you," she said.

Connery, thinking she was talking about him, nuzzled her arm as if to say, *No need, I'm right here.*

But the truth was, she hadn't been missing Justin as much. Once, it had seemed as if her arms had been amputated, she'd been so unsure of how to live without him. Even after the shock of his loss had faded, there had been so many days when breathing seemed foreign and complicated, when she sat in a dark room for hours, unseeing, baffled as to how her heart kept beating. Days when tears were always close, and the idea of the rest of her life felt like a lead-filled body bag she had to drag behind her.

That wasn't true anymore. She *was* living without him. She'd become a doctor. She had friends and colleagues. She was a volunteer. A sister and sister-in-law. An aunt. She'd met the Santinis. She was even enjoying work.

She had a crush. It wasn't a question any longer.

So life had gone on, just as predicted. And she'd been healing, even without realizing it.

With a sigh, she put the picture back. She had to get back

to this excruciating party. She could use a fresh shirt, though, since hers was damp with sweat. She went into her bedroom and froze.

Dante was asleep on her bed. Fully clothed in faded jeans and Boston Fire T-shirt, one arm over his head. Sofia had said he'd had a long night at a fire and probably wouldn't be coming. Sofia had been wrong.

Lark sat down next to him—it was her bed, after all—and took a long look at him, possibly for the first time, since all those other times were fraught with that dark electrical feeling, or more recently, her panic attack, or just embarrassment because of said crush. Now she studied the details—his long legs; lean waist; broad, solid chest rising slightly with breath. His arms were things of rock-solid beauty, the bottom of his tattoo peeking out from under the sleeve of his shirt. The Bible verse he'd gotten for his mom. Damn.

His jaw was lean, lips full. There was a bump on his nose, possibly from a break. Long, dark lashes, strong brows, a small burn on his forehead, then all that thick, wavy brown hair, tawny streaks from the sun.

God, she liked him. She liked everything about him.

Suddenly, he jolted awake and shot into a seated position. "You okay?" he asked.

"Yes," she said, smiling, because who woke up like that?

"Good." He looked at her a long second, his eyes turning as warm and inviting as maple syrup.

Then he kissed her.

A soft, warm kiss that was very clearly *not* a mistake. His lips were full and smooth, and his hand went to the back of her head, and Lark leaned into that kiss, everything in her softening and answering. She let out a little sigh, her hand going to his chest, and he was so warm and solid. His heart thudded against her palm.

It felt so good, so new and strange . . . and it also felt like home.

He pulled back, his hand still at the back of her head. "I know you're with my brother," he said, and his voice was a little rough, "and I shouldn't have done that. But I felt like I might regret it the rest of my life if I didn't."

His words sank into her, hot and warm and heavy.

The banging on the door made Lark leap back, scrambling to her feet.

"It's me, so relax," came Addie's voice. She poked her head in the bedroom door. "Hi. I'm her identical twin in case you're blind. It's toast time, apparently, and Mrs. Santini the Younger is wondering where you are, Larkby."

"Okay," Lark said. She glanced at Dante. "Um, this is the brother."

"The brother who's up to no good, I see," Addie said. "Nice to meet you."

"Dante Santini. Hi."

"Oh, my God. That name is even better than your brother's. If I weren't gay . . . anyway, give Lark thirty seconds so it doesn't seem like you two were making out in here."

Dante grinned. "Nice to meet you, Addison."

"I'm very confused, Larkby," Addie whispered as she towed Lark down to Joy's. "I thought you were fake dating the other one."

"I am," Lark whispered. "I'm just . . . kind of falling for that one."

"Were those the Deans I saw?"

"Yes. A very exciting day for me." She grimaced and squeezed Addie's hand.

Addie laughed. "Oh, honey. I haven't seen you this alive in way too long." She shoved Lark through the door.

"There you are!" Joy said. "We're doing toasts!"

"Do we have to?" Robbie muttered.

Harlow smacked his head.

Lark made her way around the living room to where Lorenzo was standing. "Where have you been?" he hissed.

"Shush," she whispered, forcing a grin. Were her cheeks red? They felt very red. "Your mother's about to say something."

"I've had to deal with your unruly—"

She elbowed him in the ribs, hard, which did the trick.

"I just wanted to take a minute and thank you, Joy," Anita said. "What an amazing feast you put together for us!"

"Hear, hear," said Grandpop. "Joy, you are a wonder!"

"And thank you to all the Smiths," Anita said. "We already feel like family."

"For God's sake," Lorenzo muttered.

"We have one happy couple who'll be getting married in just a few weeks," Anita said, beaming at Sofia and Henry, then turning to Lark and Lorenzo.

"Shit," Lorenzo muttered.

"Here it comes," Winnie said, rolling her eyes.

"And who knows? Maybe we'll have another happy couple to toast soon, too! Oh, Dante, sweetie! So glad you made it."

"Hi, everyone," he said. "I'm the brother."

"No, *I'm* the brother," Robbie said.

"I'm the heroic firefighter brother," Dante corrected.

"Shit. You got me beat there. But I'm the irresistibly adorable—"

"Will you two shut up?" Winnie snapped.

"*Thank* you," Lorenzo said.

"To happy couples," Lark said, raising her glass. "Mom and Dad, Anita and Silvio, Grandpop and Frances, Addie and Nicole, Harlow and Grady, Sofia and Henry, maybe Rosie and Robbie. Cheers!"

Before Anita or any other Santini could add her and Lorenzo to the list, she chugged her drink. "Now, who wants to play cornhole?"

An eternity later, Lark lay in bed, her head spinning from too much sun, wine, family, friction, fright and pheromones.

Dante Santini had kissed her.

She had to break up with his brother. Fast.

TWENTY-ONE

LARK

Hello! What brings you to the ER today?" Lark asked one Mr. Darren Holmes, age forty-eight. He was a red-faced man with a beer belly, a Red Sox Nation T-shirt and a Boston cap on his head.

"My head aches," he said, giving her a cursory scan. "Are you old enough to be a doctor?"

"I'm twelve, but I'm very advanced for my age," she said with a smile. "Just kidding. I'm thirty-three. Tell me about your headache. When did it start?"

"Four days ago."

"Has it been constant, or does it come and go?"

"Pretty constant," he said with a slight shrug.

"Did you take anything for the pain? Tylenol, Motrin, aspirin, weed, narcotics?"

"Nope. I had a couple beers the first night, but it didn't help."

She quashed a smile. "I see. Do you get headaches often?"

"Not really."

"Any visual changes?" she asked.

"No." He scratched an ear.

"I'm gonna shine this light in your eyes, so just look at my finger and follow it, okay?" Lark clicked on the light and had him track her finger. Pupils equal, round, reactive to light. "Can you tell me, where is the pain specifically?"

"My head," he said, as if that cleared things up.

"Front, back, left side, right side . . ." she coaxed.

"Kind of right here," he said, pointing to the top of his head, slightly to the left.

"Let's have a look. Would you take off your cap, please?"

"Sure." He did, and a huge flap of scalp flopped over from the top of his head almost to the tip of his ear.

"Yikes!" she yelped. "Okay! Wow! You have . . . a very large laceration there." It was *inches* of scalp. Inches, just hanging there.

"Yeah. I hit myself with a crowbar. I figured the hat would help it heal." He reached up to touch the wound.

"Don't touch!" she commanded.

His hand went back to his side. "It didn't work, huh?"

"No, it did not. You said this happened four days ago?"

"Yeah. Friday."

"Did you lose consciousness?" she asked.

"Like, faint?"

"Black out, fall to the ground, see stars, anything like that."

"No. But, man, that thing bled like a motherfucker."

"I bet." Dr. Unger would love this. "I'm just gonna have you lie back, okay, and get my supervisor in to take a look." She adjusted his bed so he was more prone. "No, nope, don't put that hat back on." The inside of it was crusted with blood. Mr. Red Sox Nation was not the brightest star in the sky, was he? Then again, he might have suffered a brain injury.

She went into the hall. "Dr. Unger? I think you might want to see this."

"Oh, goody. I'm tired of heatstroke and UTIs. What've you got?" said Howard.

"Patient presented with vague headache, left upper anterior."

That was all she said, not wanting to ruin the surprise. She opened the door, and Howard said, "Hello, young man, I understand you have a—well, tie me down and spank me with a fish! That is a *lot* of scalp, sir! How did this happen?"

Red Sox Nation had been busting up some concrete, raised the crowbar a little high and dropped it.

"He thought the baseball cap would jump-start the healing," Lark said.

Howard looked at her, his eyes dancing. These were the calls that made work fun. Cocktail party stories. Lark had started to dictate them into a phone (no names, of course).

"And what would you recommend, Dr. Smith?" he asked.

"Well, I'd get an x-ray to rule out a fracture. No LOC on the scene, the patient reports. If the x-ray is clear, I'd irrigate and suture it closed, since it's fairly deep. Prophylactic antibiotics, since it's been four days."

"Sounds good to me," Dr. Unger said. "Mr. Holmes. Mind if we bring in a couple other people for this exciting teachable moment?"

"Sure!" said the patient. "Can I see my cut?"

"You bet," Howard said. "We'll grab a mirror."

Lark was the belle of the ER for the rest of the shift. "You're buying beers tonight," Luis said, because yes, they were all going out, once they finished documenting and updating the incoming shift.

They were a merry bunch as they went into the London Brewing Company, which was next door to the Naked Oyster.

That one was a bit too pricey for a bunch of residents, so beer it was. After this, Lark was driving to meet Lorenzo in Chatham, as he'd ordered when she'd requested an audience. She suspected her rapport with the staff at the Naked Oyster irritated him.

"How's Satan?" Luis asked, reading her mind.

"Oh. Well . . . I'm not sure it's going to last." She felt herself blushing, still sorry for lying to these nice people.

"Time of death, happy hour," Danny said, grinning.

"I can't believe you've lasted this long, to be honest," Lalita said.

"You Americans," Mara said. "Let your parents find someone for you. Your Western fairy-tale Tinder bullshit is not working." She held up her left hand, which sported a very sparkly diamond. "Aashish and I fell in love about three minutes after we met."

"Show-off," Miriam said, bumping her shoulder against Mara's. "Can your parents find someone for me? Look at poor Lark here. Don't make me walk that path, dating a wretched man in a desperate attempt to find someone."

Lark felt a pang of loyalty for Lorenzo. "That's not completely accurate. Dr. Sa—Lorenzo's not as bad as he seems."

"What a stirring and passionate defense," Luis said.

"Okay," she said, laughing. "It's weird, I get that. But you know how it is, guys. A patient comes in with, I don't know, gas, and we all sigh and think, 'Is this really an emergency?' But then you find out that they lost their mom and haven't cried yet, and they're just looking for someone to talk to, and that gas is really heartache."

"Are you drunk already?" Danny asked.

"So Lorenzo Santini is to love as a gassy patient is to the ER," Lalita said. "That tracks."

"Well, he *is* a genius," Howard said. "I once saw him save a patient who—listen up, this is a great story. A guy came in. He'd been working outside, tripped, fell, and stabbed himself in the chest with the screwdriver he was holding."

"Phillips or flathead?" Danny asked.

"Excellent question. Phillips. I bet the flathead would've killed him. Anyway, he gets in his car, steers with one hand while pressing a roll of toilet paper against his chest with the other."

"He drove?" Lalita asked.

"Yep. He lived in Yarmouth, figured he'd bleed out if he waited for the ambulance."

"He wasn't wrong," Mara said.

"Exactly. So he drives himself here. Triage nurse can't believe what she's seeing—this yellow-handled screwdriver sticking out of his chest, a guy completely soaked in his own blood, trying to stanch the wound with Charmin. She pages Surgery, super stat, the patient collapses in front of her, we all run out, get him on a gurney and into the ER. He's soggy with blood, I'm afraid to take out the screwdriver because he'll bleed out for sure. He already is, right? I'm thinking there's just too much damage to save him. We intubate, but by now we're standing in a veritable lake of blood."

Lark was transfixed. They all were, leaning forward, beers forgotten.

Howard continued, well aware of his storytelling prowess. "Blood pressure is almost nonexistent, pulse is fluttering, and I think, 'Sorry, pal, you've lost at least half your blood because this is what happens when you stab yourself in the heart.'" He leaned back and took a sip of beer. "Enter Santini. Says one word. 'Scalpel.' We give the man a scalpel, and he does an anterior thoracotomy right then and there. Spreads the ribs, reaches in and grabs the patient's beating heart. He's holding the guy's heart *in his hand*, and somehow puts pressure on it enough to slow the bleeding. And that's how they wheeled him into surgery—Santini elbow deep inside the guy's chest. Nine-hour operation, ten units of blood. And by the grace of the thumb-sucking, brown-eyed baby Jesus and Lorenzo Santini, the guy made a full recovery."

"Wicked pissah," Danny said.

"Wow," Lalita said.

"So he's an asshole, sure, but he *gets* to be an asshole," Howard said. "Another round, my ducklings?"

"I'm actually meeting the legend himself," Lark said, "so I have to go."

"Good luck. Tell him we admire and fear him," Mara said. "And if his people skills improved, he'd be the head of a worldwide cult in two days, tops."

Lark paid for the round of drinks, waved to her friends and walked to her car, wishing she could stay a little longer. This was something she hadn't had in Oncology. In her year of residency there, she'd never felt . . . celebratory. If a patient responded well to treatment, obviously that was fantastic. They had the bell to ring for the last session of chemo.

But there always lurked the fear that the cancer would come back. There was no high fiving, no muffled laughter. Yesterday, Howard had done a needle aspiration on a tonsillar abscess and had been so pleased with the amount of pus he'd gotten, he'd trotted up and down the ER, showing everyone his prize before discarding the tube. They'd reset a dislocated hip last week, and when the patient had come out of sedation, she'd said, "Oh, my God, I feel *incredible!*" and kissed Danny on the lips.

Obviously, there were the tragedies, too. But most times, they weren't right there in front of her, day after day. Send them up or send them out, that was the motto. By and large, she finished each shift knowing she'd helped someone feel better, whether it was through medication or knowledge or, in a lot of cases, just by being kind. The golden retriever effect.

The sun was setting as she pulled into the Chatham house driveway next to Lorenzo's "look at me" Maserati. The sky was a gentle lavender and pink here on the ocean side, and the air was soft. It sure was a beautiful home. She rang the bell.

"You didn't change." Lorenzo stood in front of her, looking at her scrubs.

"Hi," she said. "Great observation."

"Unsanitary." He stepped aside to let her in.

"Nice to see you, too, Satan. Thank you for letting me and my germs desecrate your perfect house. Did you make us dinner?"

"No. I ate already."

"Well, make me a sandwich, if you have bread in the house, that is. I'm starving."

His blue eyes narrowed slightly. "I don't remember you as being so . . . brazen," he said.

"It's your influence," she said, sitting at the kitchen table. "You're very direct and don't care if anyone likes you. I'm learning from you."

"I'm honored. Will a grilled cheese suffice? I don't eat cold cuts."

"A grilled cheese would be lovely. With mustard and tomato, please."

As he assembled her sandwich and stood at the stove, watching it cook, Lark had to admit he was right. She *was* a little different these days. Once, being the nicest, most helpful, kindest person anyone had ever met had been Lark's life mission. Maybe it was because this particular good deed—being Dr. Satan's date this summer—hadn't had the desired effect on Noni. Maybe it was the ER, where patients didn't always like you—you didn't give them the drugs they wanted, or you contradicted what Google had told them. They thought you were too young to be diagnosing them and wanted a "real" doctor, or this was their fourth time here for the same problem, and that was your fault somehow.

Her skin was thickening. It beat the pulsating, open-wound feeling she'd had these past seven years.

"Here," he said, setting the plate down in front of her.

He'd cut the sandwich in half, and she took a bite. Oh, that was good. She bet the cheddar was top-drawer stuff, and the bread was sourdough.

He got her a glass of water, one for himself, and sat down across from her.

"Thank you," she said. "This is fantastic."

"So why did we need to meet, Lark? I'm very busy."

"Right, right," she said, taking another bite. "Um . . . this is a little awkward, but I'll just say it. I have a crush on your brother."

His head jerked back a little. "Dante?"

"Do you have another brother?" Another bite of sandwich. She could eat four of these, she was sure.

"But Dante? Seriously?"

She swallowed. "Yes, Lorenzo. He's handsome and funny and good-hearted."

"But he's a firefighter."

"Exactly. People love firefighters. Straight women especially love firefighters."

He looked pissy. "I assumed that after talking to one, you'd change your mind."

"Wrong again."

Lorenzo pushed back his chair and folded his arms. "How did this crush develop?" he asked.

"Does it matter?" she asked, her mouth full. Sadly, that was the last bite. She'd ask for another, but she already knew the answer.

"Yes."

"Well, we actually met a long time ago. I didn't recognize him right away, but he . . . he did me a favor a few years ago in the course of his work."

Lorenzo didn't ask for more details, and she didn't offer any.

"He also drove me back from Sofia's engagement party when my car got towed. I texted you about that, by the way. My brother had to drive me into Boston so I could get it back from car jail. It would've been nice if you'd helped me."

"Why would I spend half a day at a tow lot when I'm a world-class surgeon with a very full schedule? Why, Dr. Smith?"

"For one, it only took half an hour, and two, I was towed because I came into town to be your date. Anyway, back to your handsome, lovely, helpful brother . . . he's very . . . nice."

Lorenzo cocked his head to one side, not looking at her. "Has he made a play for you?"

Her cheeks grew hot. *She'd* made the first play, hadn't she? After he'd spent the afternoon being generally wonderful, holding her and letting her cry all over him. But that hadn't been much of a kiss.

At the picnic, though . . . different story.

"He kissed you, then?" Lorenzo asked.

Oh, he absolutely *kissed me, Satan.* Her mouth made a few squeaky noises before forming words. "Well, I . . . yeah. It was not . . . unwelcome." She tapped her finger against the side of the glass.

"I see." He drank some water, expression neutral. "Let me give you a little information that might put that in context. My brother was dating a woman a little while back. A model named Brie, like the cheese."

"I know. He told me."

"Anyway, the minute I met her—"

"He's told me this story, by the way."

Lorenzo gave her an irritated look. "Please curb the interruptions and work on your listening skills, Dr. Smith. I doubt he's told you all of it. As I was saying, the minute I met this Brie person, I could tell Dante was in trouble. He didn't see her for her true self. She was . . . ambitious."

"Oh no, an ambitious woman, how dreadful, did the world stop spinning?" She *brazenly* scratched her nose with her middle finger.

"Ambitious in that she wanted to marry him."

"I think we humans call that love."

"Oh, she didn't love him. It was obvious."

She was curious against her will. Not her business, and yet impossible not to want to hear more. "How so?"

"Well, at first, she hung herself all over him, and Dante, the poor idiot, gobbled it up. But it was for show. It made us all very uncomfortable, especially my grandmother, who doesn't approve of public displays of affection."

"So I've learned. At Joy's picnic, she told me I'd spoil my niece by kissing her."

"Anyway," he said pointedly. "I took Dante aside, explained my concerns—"

"What did you say?" Lark asked. She was kind of enjoying interrupting him, since it so clearly irked him.

"I said exactly what I thought. I didn't like her and thought she was fake and shallow. He told me to get over it, because he was planning to propose." Lorenzo huffed. "She *was* very attractive, I'll give him that. A swimsuit model."

The little flash of jealousy surprised Lark. When was the last time she'd done a sit-up, after all? Tenth grade? "Go on."

"I knew she'd do wrong by him. She was greedy, and a woman like that would not have been satisfied as a firefighter's wife."

"God, you are so arrogant."

"Dr. Smith, give me some credit. She looked at this house with dollar signs in her eyes. I think she assumed there was family money, since my parents' home is also quite nice. Because I bought it for them."

"Yes, you've told me at least seven times. So what happened?"

Lorenzo shifted slightly, and his gaze went to just over her head. He didn't answer the question.

"What happened, Lorenzo?"

"The second time we met, she made it very clear to me she would trade up. Ditch my brother, take up with me."

Lark sat back in her seat. "Oh." Dante had said she'd left him for someone else. He hadn't said that person was his brother.

"Yes," Lorenzo said. "So I told him about it, and he broke up with her, but he blames me for the situation."

"How long ago was that?"

"Two years. Which was a shame, because . . ." He stood up and brought her plate to the sink, then leaned against the counter, the kitchen island between them.

"Because why?" she asked when he didn't pick up the thought.

He shrugged. "We'd been getting a little closer. I took him to a Red Sox game. Box seats, right over the dugout. He invited me to his housewarming party. Little things, but I thought that since we're adults now, even though it took him much longer to get there, obviously—"

"You have such a way of insulting people, Lorenzo," she interrupted. There was that *brazen* thing again. "Even when you try to say something nice, it comes out as damning. You should work on that. Just say the nice thing, then shut your mouth."

He held out his hands, palms up. "You asked for this story."

"And what is the point of it? To show your superiority to your brother because his girlfriend was a money-grubbing social climber?"

"Yes. No, I mean. My point, is, he probably kissed you to get back at me."

She rolled her eyes. "You just did it again."

"What?"

"You implied that Dante would kiss me only to get back at you. I'm not hideous, Lorenzo. A lot of people think I'm very nice, in fact, and fairly attractive." Not Lorenzo, though. Her looks didn't affect him one bit. It was a little refreshing.

"You *are* attractive," he said. "That's the reason I first approached you. You being very nice is more of a weakness, wanting people to like you—"

"Okay, fuck off. There. That needed to be said. Listen. I don't want to pretend to be your girlfriend anymore, Lorenzo. Okay? I'm tired of it."

"Can't you just wait till my grandmother dies?"

"I have a feeling she's going to live forever."

"She's not. She stopped eating. Just thickened liquids for the past few days. She needs oxygen now." For the first time this evening, Lorenzo looked . . . human. A little sad. Her dopey heart softened.

"I'm sorry to hear that."

"It's not unexpected."

"I'm still sorry." She sat back in her chair. "How do you think you'll be after she dies?"

He didn't answer right away. Then he looked at her, and his eyes might have been a little shiny. "I don't know. Fine, I'm sure. But she took care of me all those years. She was the only one who didn't look at me like . . . like a zoo animal. I know I'm smarter than everyone else"—no ego there, no sir—"but she also treated me like a kid. And she's the only one who noticed that I was . . ."

"That you were what, Lorenzo?" she asked.

He looked away. "Lonely."

"Lonely," she echoed.

"You can tell I don't exactly fit in with my family. I have colleagues, not friends. I don't know that I've ever really had a friend. I've talked more with you than with just about anyone this year." He folded his arms across his chest. "So of course I'll miss her. She's the only one who treats me like a regular person. An exceptional person, but a person just the same."

She had to smother a smile. "I think your family loves you more than you see, Lorenzo. You're very guarded around them. Maybe if you weren't so . . . clenched and trying to show off all the time, it would be easier."

He gave a nod. "Well. The situation with Brie didn't help. Anyway. Are we done here?"

"What about our arrangement? Can we end it?"

"Why? So you can date my brother? I just told you he's only interested in you to get back at me."

She sighed. Loudly and pointedly.

Lorenzo looked at the floor. "Can't you just stick it out till Sofia's wedding? It's three weeks away. I'd rather not have to deal with anything else right now."

He looked . . . tired. Well, he would be tired. He *did* have a full schedule, and he *was* a world-renowned surgeon. He might not be the easiest person, but he did a lot of good, she had to give him that. "I'll think about it, how's that? Great talk. Seriously. You're doing well in becoming a human." She couldn't help a weird rush of fondness and tousled his hair as she walked past.

"Dr. Smith?"

She turned. "Yes?"

"I appreciate that you . . . that you're trying. And also that you wouldn't do this for money. It speaks well of you."

She smiled. "Good job, Dr. Santini. And thank you for noticing."

With that, she left.

TWENTY-TWO

JOY

Joyful Movement had become the most popular class at Bayview. Previous activities directors had chosen golden oldies for the playlist, but Joy hated that. Why be reminded of a youth that was fifty or sixty years ago when all these dead singers were at their peak? She'd kept a few classics, but filled in most spaces with Britney, Rihanna, Eminem, Bruno Mars, Cardi B and Justin Timberlake (though she'd had to replace a song or two when Evelyn started singing "Put your filthy hands all over me" in the hallways). Aretha always got everyone jazzed. "Get those arms up over your head, Florence," Joy yelled. "R-E-S-P-E-C-T, find out what it means to *you*! Atta boy, Hugh! Okay, boxing moves here, sock it to me, sock it to me, sock it to me, sock it to me, that's right!"

The residents loved it. One guy, Gary, came to every class, even though he wasn't in the Memory Care Unit. He always made meaningful eye contact when "I'm a Slave 4 U" came on, but Joy ignored him.

Her makeup class had gone over well, though she wouldn't try false eyelashes again, since three clients had had glue incidents, one requiring a nurse to get her eyelid unstuck. Lesson learned. Another day, she'd blown up balloons and had them play slow-motion volleyball. There were upscale field trips for the higher-functioning residents of Bayview—museums, art fairs, fishing—but Joy let the other directors head those up. She stayed in Memory Care, but more and more, the regular residents were migrating to her sessions. She liked finding things no other activities director had done yet. For example, today's class.

"A lot of you might have some muscle memory with this," she said from her table in the crafts room. "You fold the paper in half, then open it up so you have a nice crease. Put the filter on the end, then sprinkle, oh, let's say, a quarter teaspoon right in there. Make sure it's ground up. You don't want big chunks in there. Even it out and then just roll, lick the paper so it will stick, like so. Then tamp it down and twist the end, and voilà! You have a joint."

"So easy," said Etsie, who was in her late eighties and sharp as a tack. Another person from the regular unit who'd been dropping in on her classes.

"You just have to buy your own weed," Joy said. "I'm a lot of things, but a drug dealer isn't one of them." Everyone laughed. The class was full today.

"Excuse me!" came a voice. Oh. It was Meredith, the sour-faced daughter of Etsie. "Are you actually teaching my mother to roll a joint?"

"Marijuana is legal here, and yes," Joy said.

"It was more of a refresher," Etsie said.

"You can't do that!"

"Why?" Joy asked.

"Because she's . . ." Meredith lowered her voice to a harsh whisper. "Impaired."

"Oh, for God's sake, Meredith," Etsie said. "I am not, and if you keep this up, I'm changing my will. If I need a little toke to relax and help with my knee pain, I can do that."

"Just not inside," Joy reminded her. "We are a nonsmoking facility. Now, obviously, gummies are easier on the lungs. Edibles take a little longer to relax you, and I recommend starting off with a half if you haven't tried it before."

"Oh, come on. We were all alive in the summer of love," said Ward, who was crushing on Etsie. "We know what grass is. But I do appreciate the class. Never did have to roll my own."

"Every dispensary carries pre-rolls, too," Joy said.

"Think we can get the Bayview bus to take us to one?" asked Gertrude.

"I can ask," Joy said. "Okay. Who wants to play Cards Against Humanity?"

"I can't believe they were making us play bingo when this game was out there," Etsie said. "I laughed so hard last time, I wet myself."

"It happens to the best of us," Joy said. "Meredith? Want to stay?"

Meredith did not. Oh, well.

As Joy drove home that night, she was aware of an unfamiliar feeling sitting in her chest. What was the word? Kind of like satisfied or after you had a good meal . . .

Fulfillment. Yes. She hadn't been shopping in days. Not even online, and for her, that was a record. Her last chemical peel had been months ago, and while she knew she could ask Lark for a Botox session, she always seemed to forget these days.

She didn't dread being home anymore. She loved home now, loved having Ellie there, though that wasn't guaranteed to go on forever. But for now, she and Ellie took turns cooking. Joy! Cooking food!

"If you can read, you can cook," Ellie had said. "It doesn't have to be fancy, but I'm not eating takeout every other night. Too much salt."

Sometimes Lark came over, too, though her hours didn't give her much time. She was also doing some volunteer work with dying people, something Joy was going to start, too, as part of her job. But whenever Lark did come, the three of them had so much fun. At least once a week, another one of Ellie's daughters would join them, too, "just to hang out with you and Mom." It was wonderful, like a sorority, Joy imagined. Like having nieces.

"I think you and Lark saved me," she said that evening as she and Ellie were eating arugula salad with beets and pecans (not Joy's favorite dinner—too healthy—but there was macaroni and cheese in the fridge for later). "I've been so lost, and then I got Lark, and then you, Ellie, and now I have a job I love! I can hardly believe it."

They were sitting on chaise longues on the deck, Joy in a silk caftan with matching wrap, Ellie in jeans and a T-shirt that read *Blackbeard's Bait and Tackle*. They couldn't be more different, Joy thought.

Ellie took a sip of rosé and said, "I don't know about that. I think you saved yourself. You started by being kind and generous and giving Lark an affordable place to live, and let me tell you, there's not much out here. Then you gave me a place to stay at the worst moment of my life. And now you're brightening up the lives of the residents at Bayview. I think what you're seeing is that you're happiest when you're helping someone else." She glanced at Joy and smiled. "What do you think about that?"

Joy blinked. "I . . . I never thought I had much to offer."

"Well, you were wrong. Think about it. When you married Abdul, you were doing it for Paulie and him, so they could be together. You said that was a happy time. And not just because of the money, Joy. Because you helped them be together. This is a happy time because you're sharing your home with two people who needed it. You're the one who's saving people."

Joy's throat tightened. "I never thought of it that way."

"Well, get thinking of it that way, missy."

"I will." She pushed some leaves around on her plate. "How are *you* doing, Ellie? What's on your mind lately about Gerald?"

She sighed. "Mostly, I feel sad, you know? I trusted him a thousand percent up until this. I'll never get to do that again. I can forgive him, I think, because he did end it. It wasn't like he stopped because he was caught. But we'll never be the same."

"Do you have to be? It's like a chip in the windshield, but the windshield hasn't shattered. It still works."

"You're right." She stared out at the ocean, the sky darkening bit by bit. "I can't stay here forever."

"Well, you could." Joy finished her wine and poured a little more. "Can I ask you something?"

"Sure."

"What's it like, being married to someone who really loves you? Someone you love just as much?" Because with three and a half husbands, Joy had never experienced that. Frankie had loved her, but it wasn't mutual. Carl had used her, George had abused her and Abdul . . . well, he had used her, too, even if she signed up for it.

Ellie stared at the horizon. "Oh, it's . . . it's home," she said with a little shrug. "You feel so safe and accepted and adored. Even if you just let out a huge burp or haven't showered in three days. You look into each other's eyes and you just . . . click into place. You can relax completely and know that just by waking up, you made someone's day."

"That sounds nice," Joy said wistfully.

"It is. It's so nice. And I do miss it. And him." She looked at Joy. "Did you know that being here is the closest thing to a vacation I've ever had? Being somewhere different, somewhere lovely . . . Gerald and I never got to do that. Too many kids, too little time, not enough money. It's been so restful, even though I came here when I was angry and upset and sad." She reached over and squeezed Joy's forearm. "Thank you, Joy. You're a wonderful friend."

"Stay as long as you want," Joy said. "You're a great friend, too. The best friend I've ever had, other than my brother."

They sat there, sipping wine, watching the sun sink into the ocean. The orange and purple clouds lit up, deepened in color, then faded, and still they sat. Two middle-aged women, sitting on a deck, living in the moment. And this moment was perfect.

I want you to marry me, Joy," Gary said the next day, cornering her in the library.

They'd finished a rousing hour of karaoke, and Joy was now unpacking a box of books, adding some spicier stuff to the boring old classics they currently had. She'd spent the morning at Open Book, getting recommendations from Destiny, who was always good for a chat (and had an enviable wardrobe). "Make me the happiest man alive."

"Oh, gosh. That's very sweet, Gary, but no."

"Joy. You were meant to be married. I'm a rich man! Make me happy in my final days." He smiled at her cleavage.

"I'm pretty flush myself, Gary. I don't need your money."

"That makes sense. I mean, you look very well maintained. But don't you want companionship?"

"I have companionship."

"Of the male variety?"

"No, you have a point there. But would my life really be better if I married you?" she asked.

"You'd have a husband, so of course!" He laughed.

"And?"

His face fell a little. "Romance?"

That sure had been lacking in her life. Frankie had brought her flowers from time to time. Left her notes and stuff like that. Otherwise, her relationships had been about sex (except for Abdul, of course).

"What does romance actually look like?" she asked.

"Oh. Well, I'd, uh, tell you how special you are," Gary said. "Give you little gifts and flowers. We could take a cruise and hold hands."

"You're not really selling it, Gary. I can buy my own gifts and flowers. And book a cruise with my friends."

"What about . . . intimacy?" he asked, raising a sparse eyebrow.

"I have a vibrator."

"I'm better than a vibrator, I hope."

She looked at him, amused. Bald, a big nose, small eyes, significant gut, hair springing out of his ears like Spanish moss. Men and their confidence.

She was never going to have what Ellie had described. Maybe, if she'd stayed with Frankie, she could've felt that sense of home and safety. She'd been too young to appreciate his love back then, too fixated on her outer self and being anyone but who she was. It was time for her to find love, sure. Find love for her own damn self.

"Thanks just the same, but I'll pass. I bet you could find

someone else, though. Someone you've known longer than a few weeks." She patted Gary on the shoulder and walked down the hall.

Once upon a time, Joy Deveaux needed a man to feel worthwhile, to give her an escape, to fill her life, whether it was a husband or, yes, even her brother. Someone to undo the damage wrought by her father, another man.

She was sixty-seven. Yep, there it was, her actual age, first time she'd let herself acknowledge it in years. For the first time ever, she wanted to be independent, not just waiting for someone or something to fix her.

It was quite a . . . oh, gosh, what was the word? When you thought of something you'd never thought of before? A *revelation*, that was it! Quite a revelation indeed.

TWENTY-THREE

LARK

When her shift ended that day at three thirty, Lark quickly finished her notes, got into her car and drove to Boston. Mass General was offering a grand rounds lecture on new tools that measured residual disease in acute leukemia. If tools like that had been around seven years ago, it was possible that Justin's leukemia could've been caught earlier. He would have had a better chance at . . .

No. Best not to go there. It didn't serve any purpose.

She'd texted Heather and Theo after Joy's party, doing her best to explain that she was being a date—not romantic, of course!—for a surgeon she knew. No girlfriend situation there.

Heather's response was short and polite. Your mom said as much, but if there was a boyfriend, it would be okay, honey. We don't expect you to be single forever.

That made her feel worse, somehow. She'd responded by suggesting a date for the missed whale watch (not that she had time for one) and asking Heather what she wanted to do for her birthday in September. In the past, they'd gotten pedicures and had lunch . . . and gone to the cemetery.

Traffic was not as wretched as usual, and Lark made it to Boston in plenty of time, parked her car in a garage, since she couldn't trust street parking anymore. She even had enough time to stop at a Roxy's food truck for a grilled cheese, then ate it as she walked through the Common toward Mass General. Families were out in force, little kids running and shrieking, people walking their dogs, sitting on blankets, eating, laughing. A Boston Fire engine went by, sirens blaring, and she flushed abruptly. Chances were low that Dante was on that one, but it was possible, of course.

It had been two nights since she'd sat in Lorenzo's kitchen. No communication from any other Santini, though, aside from a text from Izzy about possibly going to a movie sometime before the wedding. That would be nice.

She found herself at a bench she and Justin had frequented in their college days here. They'd brought the Yorkshire Breakfast Hamper to the Common quite often. She sat down and finished her sandwich, feeling a slight melancholy.

She missed Justin. She missed his lovely, gentle smell—pencils and pine needles and rain. She missed his loud laugh, his inky black hair, his eyes crinkling as he looked at her. She missed his weight on top of her; his soft, wonderful lips; the way he called her *little bird* with such love.

But she was also forgetting him.

Seven years. Seven *years*. Every day was a step away from their life together. That would never change. She would only get further and further from him. She would never marry him, and oh, God, how she had wanted to be his wife. How she had wanted ordinary days with him. She wasn't even his widow. She was just someone who used to be a fiancée.

Someone who used to be.

It wasn't enough anymore. He was gone, and she . . . she wanted more. Until this summer, she hadn't been able to picture what that looked like. But pretending to be Lorenzo's girlfriend had given her a glimpse of the kind of future she'd never been able to picture. Someone's partner. A sister-in-law. Daughter-in-law. Lorenzo was handsome as anything, but her ovaries hadn't so much as twitched, given his personality.

Dante . . . different story. That kiss had made her weak and soft and reminded her that she was a healthy, heterosexual female in prime breeding years. That kiss—both kisses—had made her remember what it felt like to want someone. To feel connected again. The flame that had burned so strong for Justin had finally flickered.

It would be devastating if Lorenzo was right, and Dante had kissed her in some kind of revenge move.

There was one way to find out. But she'd come here for that lecture, so she got up and walked to the hall. For the next hour, she listened to developments in cancer detection tools, taking notes, paying close attention, pulling out her phone to google a few terms she hadn't heard before.

"We will end cancer in our lifetime," the guest doctor said at the end. "And you sitting here . . . you'll be part of that. It will be the greatest medical breakthrough in human history."

Everyone clapped, and Lark's throat felt tight. That had been the goal since Lark was an adolescent. Treat cancer. Stop cancer. Cure cancer. Eradicate cancer. God, she hoped the doctor's words would be true. But whether or not she'd be part of it . . . that was flickering, too.

Then she went outside, took a few breaths of the muggy night air, and texted Dante.

> Hi, it's Lark. Are you in Boston? I was
> wondering if I could talk to you.

Almost immediately, the three dots began waving.

I'm home. You okay?

There was that question again. The immediate concern for her. Yep. Can I pop over?

Of course.

His address appeared on the screen. Her phone said it would take her twenty minutes to get there.

In fact, it took eighteen. His house was rather ordinary, a gray two-family with blue shutters. He greeted her at the door.

"Hey," he said. His hair was damp, and he smelled like . . . heaven. His feet were bare. Apparently, he'd just showered. Possibly because she was coming.

"Hi," she said. "Sorry to just appear like this."

"No, it's great. Come on in."

She followed him into a surprisingly lovely living room—fireplace with built-in shelves encasing it, paneled ceiling, big iron radiators. It was sparsely furnished with a couch, a recliner and a coffee table, a big TV on the wall. To the left was an empty dining room. An arched entryway led to the kitchen.

"Want something to drink?"

"Sure."

"Water, beer, coffee? I might have a Coke somewhere."

"Water's good. Thanks, Dante."

He left the room, and she went to the fireplace. On the mantel and bookshelves were pictures of his family, and that . . . that got to her. Little Izzy, Dante and Sofia, first day of school, maybe, all of them with backpacks and lunch boxes, the girls looking very proud, Dante pulling a face. His parents dressed up for a function. An older couple she assumed to be Anita's parents. The four kids, maybe ten years ago, Dante skinnier, Sofia gorgeous, Izzy in a miniskirt, Lorenzo looking stiff and irritable. A black and white dog chewing on something blue.

"This is a beautiful home," she said as he came back in.

"Thanks," he said, not looking at her. "It was built in the twenties. Great craftsmanship back then, you know? It was kind of a pit when I bought it, which is how I could afford it. It's coming together bit by bit, though."

"Are you doing it yourself?"

"My dad helps a little, but yeah." He ran a hand through his hair . . . a good hand. A big, masculine hand. His tattoo peeked out from under his white T-shirt.

She sat on the couch and set her bag beside her. From upstairs, she could hear a kid laughing, a parent's voice, more laughter, then the pounding of feet. It made her smile.

"Those are the Grishams," Dante said, sitting in the chair. "Two kids. They love to run. A lot." He smiled, his eyes crinkling. "I should've put in more insulation."

"It's a good sound."

"Yeah, I think so, too." He took a sip of water, looking at her. "So what brings you to Quincy, Lark?"

She felt herself blush. "I was in Boston for an oncology lecture, and I thought . . . I wanted to . . . you know. Ask you something." Her face grew hot.

"Fire away."

She could feel her heartbeat in her throat and wrists. "I was talking to Lorenzo the other day. And he told me . . . um . . . well, he told me about Brie, and I was wondering if . . . you know. If that had anything to do with, um, you kissing me." Her face blazed.

"Why would Brie have anything to . . . oh." He sat back and ran a hand over his face. "Okay, just for the record, you did kiss me first."

She closed her eyes, grimacing. "I know. I'm sorry."

"I'm not," he said easily. "And secondly, no. I wouldn't do that. I'm not a shitty person."

"No, of course not. It was just . . ."

"What did he tell you?"

Lark squeezed her pinkie finger. "That he . . . never mind. Maybe you guys should talk."

"No, maybe *you* should talk, Lark. That was the reason you came here, right? What did he say about Brie?"

She took a breath. "That she made a play for him. That he suspected she wasn't . . . well, good enough for you."

"And did he tell you how he . . . proved that?"

A sense of dread came over her. "No."

Dante sat back in his seat. "You should ask your boyfriend for the entire story, Lark."

"Can you just tell me instead?" she asked. She wished Connery were here. He would definitely lighten the mood.

"I'm not sure you want to know."

"I do."

He stared at his hands, clasped loosely together in front of him. "Yeah, okay. You probably *should* know, since you're dating him."

Lark pressed her lips together at the untruth but didn't say anything.

"So . . . Brie was—is—very pretty. Lively. Always up for a

good time. I loved her, and I wanted to marry her because I'm a dumb fireman who thought that was enough. I brought her home to meet the family, it's all going great, she likes my sisters, brought wine for my parents. Then Lorenzo pulls up in his asshole car, casually mentions how he bought Mom and Dad their house, practically shows her his tax return. Fine. That's what he does. We all know him. But for some reason, he doesn't like her. Tells me she's gonna break my heart. That she was materialistic and . . . not nice."

He stopped for a second and looked out the window, then took a drink of water. "Not what I wanted to hear, obviously. So I told him to mind his own business, whatever. But he was right. Because Brie *was* a materialistic person without a strong moral compass, and Lorenzo proved this by sleeping with her."

Lark didn't move. Her eyes, though, suddenly felt very, very wide. "Say again?"

"Yeah. Brought me her panties as proof and said something like, 'She's not very loyal, is she? Sorry to be right.'"

Horribly, it sounded exactly like him. "Oh, Dante."

"Yeah. I mean, it was a very convincing presentation, so kudos to him for that. I broke up with her—she didn't seem to mind—and she went to Lorenzo, who completely blew her off. Then she told me she wanted to get back together. Much to her surprise, I declined the offer. The end."

"Oh, my God. I'm so sorry."

Dante was quiet for a second. "The thing is, Lark . . . he really did think he was doing me a favor. And that I would need something . . . big . . . to see her for who she was. I'm not telling you he's a horrible person. Just that he has a very bad way of . . . relating to people."

"You're defending him?" she asked.

"No. Not really. I mean, I don't want to trash-talk my own brother. He's not . . . well, he got you, so what do I know? Maybe he's great and I just can't see it."

"I'm not really dating him," she blurted. "I'm just . . . a prop, sort of. A companion for the wedding and family stuff. We've never even kissed."

He looked confused for a second. Then he tilted his head, and his eyes got a little hard and flat. "You're not dating him? My whole family thinks . . . are you serious?"

"I felt really bad about lying to your family," she whispered.

"Yeah. You should."

She bit her lip. "He wanted your grandmother to think he had somebody. To be honest, Dante, I think he's lonely."

"And whose fault it that?"

"His. As you said. He has a bad way of relating to people. His head is so far up his ass he can't see how much you all love him."

Dante looked at her a long second. "Well, that's one take on it. Jesus. You've been lying this whole time?"

She set her water glass down on the table. "Dante, I . . . I said I'd do it because your grandmother was on hospice. It seemed like her dying wish was for Lorenzo to have someone who loved him. So I said yes. And also because Lorenzo is a little pathetic, you know? He wants so much for you all to be impressed by him and believe he's got his life together. He thought having me around would . . . distract from the truth, maybe. That he's gifted, sure, but has no idea how to connect with people."

"What's in it for you? I mean, I find it hard to believe you'd just do this out of the goodness of your heart. It's a pretty big ruse, and we met you, what? In May? So three *months* of this, just because?"

"Um . . . well, he had some contacts in the field I want to

work in. I never planned on being in emergency medicine forever."

"Right. You still want to be an oncologist." Emotions flickered through his eyes.

"But . . . well. Never mind." It didn't seem right to dump her uncertainties on him.

Dante didn't say anything for a minute, then stood up. "Well. Nice seeing you, Lark."

"Are you . . . are you mad at me?"

He threw up his hands. "Yes! You just told me you've been lying to my family for the past couple of months. I'm not happy."

"But you understand, right?"

"Not really, no."

"I was trying to do something nice, Dante. That's all. I got kicked out of my residency. I panicked, and Lorenzo gave me a possible way back in. He went to med school with the head of Dana-Farber. So I said yes, because I thought it would make Noni happy and also because all I was ever supposed to do was become an oncologist."

"Because of your guy. Justin."

"Yes. Exactly. And now, I don't even know if I want that. But I'm not dating your brother. Not at all. And I . . . I'm starting to . . . I like you, Dante. A lot." Her knees ached with nerves, and her heart was thudding against her ribs.

He sighed, then ran a hand through his dark hair. "I'm not really sure what to do with that. But for now, I think you should go." His voice was gentle, and it made it that much worse.

With that, he walked her out, waited till she was in her car, then closed the door and turned off the porch light.

TWENTY-FOUR

ELLIE

Gerald had thrown out his back. This news came via Winnie, who reported that she'd swung by the house and found her father lying on the floor, sweating in agony.

"I'll be right there," Ellie said.

She was at the studio, painting more of her rage work. That wasn't really an appropriate name for it anymore. Her mood had gentled over bit by bit from when she'd first started. She had her moments, but these days, she was enjoying doing something different. Would she stop being a landscape artist? Probably not, but there was no law that said she couldn't just mess around with paints. Rage had gotten her to that realization, and she would honor that.

The gallery was doing oddly well without her. Maybe *because* she wasn't present, who knew? Meeko had stepped up his game, and maybe it was his youth, his good looks or his accent, but it would be a strong season.

And, Ellie admitted, some of her anxiety had doubtlessly seeped into the gallery atmosphere. Maybe her desire to make a sale had hinted at desperation. She'd been like a mother hovering over her child at the playground, stopping him from making friends because she wanted so much for him to make friends.

She had thought a lot about what Gerald had said . . . his jealousy over her work, whether it was the time it took, the creativity, the mental space, whatever. Had she neglected him? No. She hadn't. But had she noticed his blues when retirement came so fast for him, when Robbie left home? "Last time I'll move out, Dad, I promise!" their son had said. She could've taken more care, listened a little more attentively, looked a little more deeply.

Was it her fault that his attention wandered? Hell, no. A person was the only one responsible for their actions, and no one could force someone else to behave any kind of way. But she had seen what she wanted to see—her wonderful husband, their enviable marriage—and hadn't wanted to know anything else. She could own that, at least. He hadn't started talking to that trashy Camille Dupont for no reason. It hadn't been a good reason, and he should have come to Ellie with his worries, but he hadn't. Maybe she just hadn't given him the space. Maybe she hadn't wanted to know he was no longer middle-aged . . . that he was a senior citizen now. Maybe she didn't feel like she had the time or patience to deal with him being anything but the best version of himself.

That wasn't fair. He'd put up with her flaws and irritations, insecurities and frustrations all these years. She owed him the same.

"See you tomorrow," she called to Meeko, who was talking to a couple in front of one of her cranberry bog paintings. Huh. She hadn't realized he'd hung it. *Good for you, Meeko*, she thought.

The lawn mower had been in the driveway so long it was still strange to have it gone. The grass had been cut recently, and the flower beds had been weeded, a job she knew her husband hated.

She went inside the house.

"Hi, Mom," Winnie said, kissing her on the cheek. "I got Dad to the couch, but I have to run. A baby shower in Orleans."

"Hope it goes well, honey. Thanks for helping your father."

"You bet." Winnie was her favorite. Well, all the kids had their moments, but right now, she really appreciated Winnie's matter-of-fact ways and dearth of questions.

There was Gerald, lying awkwardly on the couch. "You didn't need to come," he said. "But hi. Thank you."

"What happened?" she asked.

He'd been at the urgent care center, helped a rather large man sit up on the examination table, and that was it. Felt the pop, the shredding pain in his lower back, and had walked in baby steps to his car. He thought lying on the floor might help—it sometimes did—but not today.

"Did you take a muscle relaxant?" she asked.

"Not yet. They're upstairs." His forehead was damp with sweat, and his face was flushed—a blood pressure spike because of the pain.

"Let's get you into bed," she said.

"I'm fine here," he said. "It's okay."

She put her hands on her hips. "No, it's not. Come on. Arm around me."

She bent to help him, and as he stood, leaning heavily against her, she had the thought that this was where she belonged. That no one could do what she could do in this moment, knowing exactly how to support him, what he'd need, how he liked the pillows.

They went up the stairs, slowly, Gerald gripping the railing hard. He was breathing through his teeth when she got him into their bedroom and helped him recline.

"Jesus," he hissed, taking a slow breath.

She got a pillow for under his knees, ran down the stairs for an ice pack. The countertops were clean, and a new clock hung in place of the one that had stopped working back when Robbie was in high school. She went back to Gerald and tucked the ice pack underneath him. Then she found the bottle of Baclofen tucked up on the high shelf in their medicine cabinet, though it had been years since they'd needed to stow prescription drugs away from the kids. A throwback to another era. She filled a glass with water, brought it to him and handed him the pill.

"Thanks, Ellie. I appreciate it."

"You're welcome."

He swallowed the pill and lay back. "I'll be good from here. I'm sorry Winnie called you, but I'm also glad she did."

She sat next to him, wanting to smooth his hair back. She could do that. He was her husband, after all. So she did, and the feeling of his coarse, silvery hair under her palm made her eyes fill.

He reached up and caught her hand, pressed it against his lips and then tucked it over his heart. "I miss you," he whispered.

"I bet you do," she said with a little smile. "I see you've done a bunch of projects around here."

"I did. I'm trying to lure you back by fixing the place up."

She laughed and wiped her eyes. "I think we should just sell it."

His face went gray. "Why? Are you divorcing me? Oh, Ellie, please . . ."

"No! No. I was just kidding." She paused. "Actually, why *are* we living in a four-bedroom house, Gerald? We *should* sell it. We should downsize."

"We?"

She cocked her head and looked at him. She thought of Joy, who had never loved any of her husbands, who didn't get to have *this*. No, Gerald wasn't perfect. She wasn't, either. Thirty-eight years of doing their best for each other, though . . . that counted for a lot.

"Yes. We. We've had thirty-eight fantastic years together. You wavered. I wasn't paying attention, you were going through some stuff, and you wavered. But you realized you messed up, and you ended it. I'm not ditching four decades because of that."

"Really?" His blue eyes were bright with tears.

"Yeah. I'm over it. I forgive you. I'll never be okay with what happened, but I don't have to drag it alongside me for the rest of my life."

"God, I love you," he said, and he put his hand over his eyes, because he was crying. "Thank you, Ellie. Thank you."

"We'll be okay," she said.

Because, of course, they would be.

TWENTY-FIVE

LARK

There'd been a shooting in Mashpee. Two teenagers, one hit in the leg, the other in the stomach. Gunshot wounds were the worst kind of injury . . . foolish, preventable and often catastrophic. The fact that both kids were expected to live was a miracle. Howard had put her on as lead doctor for the leg shot. The bullet had gone completely through, and it seemed like the kid's femoral artery had been nicked on its way through, because the paramedic-applied dressing was soaked with blood. The other teenager needed exploratory surgery of his abdomen.

Lark had done well. The adrenaline had pumped through her, and she'd kept mentally repeating steps and warnings, making sure she ticked every box as the team flew through the necessary steps. Airway, breathing, circulation . . . the pulse in his foot had been faint, so she'd had Luis start a large-bore IV. Compression, bandage, tourniquet. X-ray to see if the femur was shattered. Type and cross for transfusion—better safe than sorry. She checked him for other injuries, because sometimes a patient could feel only one at a time. She ordered prophylactic antibiotics and fluids.

It was both terrifying and thrilling to be in charge, needing to think of all possible medical scenarios—was he going into shock? How were his vitals? What secondary damage had been done inside his leg? Irrigate the wound now, or leave that for the OR?

Mara was lead on the other shooter, and Howard had gone between the two patients, ready to suggest or confirm a step if they missed anything. They hadn't. Still, when the patient was transported, Lark felt limp with relief as she sat at the computer station, dictating her notes for the vascular surgeon. And then she moved on to the next patient, a kid who had a rash. The shift was over before she knew it.

Instead of listening to an oncology podcast on the ride home, she just rolled down the car windows and stuck her hand out, letting the wind push against her fingers, gradually letting go of the controlled chaos of her job.

Connery was waiting on her steps, and she scooped him up as she went inside.

"Who's my little buddy?" she asked.

He licked her face eagerly, and she smiled, then set him down. She was starving . . . alas, she hadn't been to the grocery store in ages. She went to the fridge and opened it. Oh! That was a nice surprise. Someone—Addie—had filled it. Four or five kinds of cheese, wine, clementines, salad fixings, olives, some stuffed bread from Wellfleet Marketplace.

She called her sister, missing her horribly all of a sudden. She hadn't seen Addie in a few days, and then it had been just a quick visit to see the girls for smooches and bedtime stories.

"You're welcome," Addie said by way of answering.

"I love all the cheese," Lark said.

"It's like I know you."

Lark laughed. "It's like you do."

"How are things, Larkby? And I'm not talking about the ER. I'm talking about the hot brother you were kissing."

The stab of loss—even just the loss of potential—was sharp and fast. She hadn't heard from Dante since she'd stopped by his place, and she didn't blame him.

"Yeah, that," she said. "It's on hold or dead. Kind of complicated. I think I botched it." Even with Addie, it was hard to talk about.

"Dead? The first guy you've liked since you were five? It can't be dead, honey."

It was the endearment that made her throat tighten. "Well, it's not exactly alive."

"Good thing you're a doctor, then," Addie said. "Resuscitate immediately."

There was a crash and a scream in the background. Two screams, so both nieces.

"Everyone okay?" Lark asked.

"Probably," Addie said. "Nicole is with them. We're looking for another au pair. They keep quitting."

"I'll babysit my next free night, how's that?"

"That would be amazing. You know how Nicole is. If she doesn't get attention, she gets bitchy."

"Sounds like a twin of mine," Lark said.

"Bite me," Addie laughed. "I should go. Love you."

"Love you, too," Lark said. "Thanks again, Addie."

She ended the call, still gazing on the bounty of her refrigerator. All that food. Connery was curled into his cinnamon bun pose on the couch, ready for snuggling. She left the fridge, went over to the couch and looked at the wall behind it. There were . . . let's see . . . five framed pictures featuring Justin . . . the two of them with his parents, with Addie, in Venice, at the beach.

But today, those pictures reminded her of Dante. The innate kindness and gentle curiosity as she'd shown him the photo albums, how he'd listened as she told him the story behind the pictures. How he'd simply tucked her against him as she cried for a man he'd never met.

Her stomach growled.

"Connery?" she asked, still staring at her engagement picture. She had crow's-feet now that hadn't been there back then. Her face had been a little rounder, her cheeks pink with love. "Want to go for a ride?"

Fifteen minutes later, she pulled into the cemetery, the Yorkshire Breakfast Hamper in one hand, Connery's leash in the other. She spread out a blanket, sat down next to Justin's headstone and opened the picnic basket.

"Justin, you'll be happy to know the Yorkshire Breakfast Hamper is being put to good use," she said, taking out a block of cheese and slicing a piece off. She handed it to Connery, who ate it delicately, and then sliced off another piece for herself. The sun had set an hour ago, but daylight took its time fading at this time of year, reluctant to give over the sky to darkness. A night bird trilled nearby, and Lark could hear the gentle rush of passing cars on Route 6. Connery tilted his little head but otherwise seemed content to snuggle and mooch. He didn't like the olives, though. More for her.

"So, Justin," she said. "I met someone. I think I'm . . . I think I'm in love."

Only the night bird answered.

It would be so nice if he'd send her a sign, letting her know he was okay, that there was indeed an afterlife—she thought there was, but who really knew? A sign that he watched over her and his parents, that he was happy, that they'd be together again someday in some form. But in all these years, the only dreams she'd had about him involved her coming into a room only to catch a glimpse of him leaving it. Yes, she saw cardinals, and butterflies, and feathers, and dimes. Didn't everyone?

She was tired of being tragic. Tired of trying not to be so . . . pitiable. Tired of loving someone who'd been gone so long. Tired, she now realized, of building a career based on a tragedy. It had never been her destiny to be an oncologist. It had been her penance, assigned by herself. She wanted to be kissed again, to be loved, to have a person waiting for her. She wanted children. And, she knew, Justin would want that for her. Heather and Theo already did. She was the only one holding herself back.

We loved with a love that was more than love. But what happened to the guy who had loved Annabel Lee? He'd gone to her tomb by the sounding sea and lay down with her . . . which, creepily enough, was what Lark was doing right now.

There had to be more for her. All she had to do was say yes.

The lid of the Yorkshire Breakfast Hamper banged shut, and she bolted upright. Connery barked twice and whined.

The wind. Except there was no wind tonight.

"Justin? Is that you?" she whispered. Goose bumps rose on her arms. There was no answer. Just the little night bird, trilling again. It seemed to wait for an answer "Justin? I . . ." He knew she loved him. Never once had that been a question. "I'll always be glad we were together, honey."

Because it was true. Despite the ending, the fear, the sorrow, those had been beautiful, happy years. Tears flooded her eyes, but they were different this time. These tears were warm and lush and full of tenderness and gratitude for the boy, the man, who had loved her so well.

They had loved with a love that was more than love, yes. It

had been special and magical, pure and authentic. And it was over. It had been for years now, for the sole reason that life was horribly cruel sometimes. Invasive fungal pneumonia spores had found Justin's lungs, and he had died.

Not because she, who hadn't even been a medical student at the time, had failed to diagnose him before he showed signs of infection. He hadn't died because of traffic, or because she'd gone home that weekend. Justin had died because he'd been devastatingly sick. And she had mourned him enough. She would always love him, but she wasn't going to spend any more of her life based on what hadn't been. Some of the happiest years of her life, absolutely. But there were more ahead of her. Not just okay years. Happy, joyful, wonderful years.

That sepulchre, tomb-lying version of herself . . . she was leaving that here tonight. With Justin's blessing, she decided. She'd asked for a sign, and she'd gotten one.

Picnic baskets didn't bang shut for no reason.

Fly, little bird, she imagined him saying. *Get the hell off my grave and live your life.*

TWENTY-SIX

LARK

They were fighting before they even got in the car. *Her* car. His stupid Maserati was broken.

"I'm not going to my sister's rehearsal dinner in a *Honda*," Lorenzo snapped, sitting in the front seat of his Italian status symbol.

"Then you shouldn't have bought such a precious and delicate car. Get in. You hate being late."

She'd worked overnight, managed to catch a few hours of sleep this morning and could've sworn she'd just seen a red pickup truck going in the opposite direction as she turned onto Lorenzo's road in Chatham.

She hadn't spoken to Dante since she'd seen him in Quincy. She hadn't spoken to Lorenzo, either . . . just acknowledged his text ordering her when and where to show up. Izzy and she hadn't been able to find time for a movie, and it was just as well. The Santinis were not hers to keep. But it was wedding weekend, and this morning, Sofia had sent Lark a text saying she couldn't wait to see her tonight. So Lark supposed she was still Lorenzo's girlfriend in the eyes of his family.

Except for Dante, of course.

"Lorenzo! Stop being so classist and get in the damn car," she said, leaning on the horn.

He tried starting the Maserati one more time, glared at her, then got out and put his suitcase and tuxedo bag in the back before slumping into the passenger seat like a sulky teenager.

The rehearsal was tonight at St. Cecilia's in Boston, followed by dinner at Venezia, a restaurant overlooking the water. Tomorrow, the wedding started at 4:00 p.m. at the church, followed by a reception at the Boston Public Library. It was sure to be a gorgeous affair, and Lark hoped it would be all Sofia and Henry wanted.

After that . . . well, Lark wasn't sure if she'd ever see a Santini again.

"How's Noni?" she asked, pulling out of his driveway.

"Winding down. A month, tops. She'll have an aide with her today in case she gets tired. Tomorrow, too."

She glanced at him, thought about putting a hand on his knee, decided against it. "I'm sorry. That must be hard."

He shrugged and looked out the window. Message received.

"Was that Dante's truck I saw on my way here?" she asked, unable to stop herself.

"Yes."

"More, please."

"Yes, it was Dante's truck you saw."

She sighed. Loudly.

Lorenzo caved. "We had a small family dinner last night. Just the four of us and our parents, and he came to see me today before heading to Boston."

She waited for more. More didn't come. "What did he want to talk about?"

"Nothing I'm willing to discuss right now," he said.

"Really?" She turned onto the on-ramp and waited for a gap in the traffic. Route 6 was only two lanes here—eastbound and westbound—separated by irritating little yellow poles. It took a solid minute before she could sneak into the line of traffic. "It's going to be a long drive if you're not speaking to me."

"I think it'll be a very pleasant drive, not speaking to you."

She couldn't help a smile. He was a rude pain in the ass, but he was very consistent.

"Hey, I love the dresses you picked out for me."

In her suitcase were two gorgeous dresses, matching shoes, matching handbags. For tonight, a Naeem Khan off-the-shoulder dress with a big bow on the shoulder. For the wedding, a navy blue Jason Wu crisscross gown. Fabulous shoes, and a Judith Leiber handbag shaped like a butterfly. "If this doctor thing doesn't work out, you could always be a personal shopper."

"The doctor thing has clearly worked out for me," he said, no trace of humor in his voice. "You, however . . ."

"Rude."

Then she slammed on the brakes, her arm instinctively going out to shield Lorenzo as they swerved off the road and onto the grass, barely missing the bumper of the Miata immediately in front of them.

There was a massive pileup. Two, three . . . five, seven or more cars askew in front of them with a box truck at the end, preventing her from seeing farther up the highway. She heard the screech of brakes and a car horn. Someone pulled up right behind her. Behind them, traffic was stopping.

Lark put on her hazard lights and looked at Lorenzo. "You okay?"

He looked stunned, eyes wide, mouth open. "That was close."

She grabbed her phone from the cup holder and dialed 911.

"Big accident on Route 6 westbound, in Harwich after the on-ramp from 124. Injuries unknown, but assume mass casualty. I'm an ER physician, and I'm with a surgeon. Yes. Okay. We're assessing right now." She looked at Lorenzo and got out of the car. "Go time, Dr. Santini." Her arms and legs vibrated as adrenaline flowed into her veins.

Traffic on the eastbound side was stopped, since a pickup had swerved into that lane. The air smelled like antifreeze and rubber. A horn was blaring up ahead. From the back of her car, Lark grabbed her bag, glad to be neurotically overprepared. Alcohol wipes, gauze, gloves, Steri-Strips. The last time she'd needed anything medical was when the falcon ate the pigeon off Noni's head. Seemed like a century ago.

"Stay in your cars!" she yelled. "I'm an ER doctor. I'll come to you!" They'd had a case last month of a guy who'd been hit because he'd been standing on the side of the road, changing his tire.

The car in front of them wasn't damaged. After that, no such luck. The next car had rear-ended the SUV in front of it. The hood was badly dented, and the airbags had deployed. Lark peered in the passenger window. Female, forties, two wide-eyed kids in booster seats in the back. "I'm an ER doctor. Are you okay?"

"We're . . . we're fine," said the driver. "Just shaken. Kids, you're okay, right?"

"We hit that car," said the older one.

"Does anything hurt?" Lark asked.

"My tooth came out last night," said the younger kid, showing her. "It was a little sore."

"I think we're good," said the mom.

"Great. Stay in the vehicle. EMS is on their way." Several people were attempting to get out of their cars. "Stay in your cars," she shouted again. "If you're hurt, wave to me. I'm an ER doctor."

A hand came out of a window, and she ran to that car. Damage to front and back, the bumper hanging.

"Where are you hurt?" she asked.

"My leg," the driver said. Male, sixties. "I think it's broken."

Lark looked down, gripping his wrist without thinking. Pulse steady and strong. Yep, his shin was crooked, and there was a nasty cut halfway up. It wasn't bleeding heavily, though. "Stay put for now. EMS is en route."

"What should I do?" Lorenzo asked. She'd almost forgotten he was here.

"Stick with me. EMS can triage everyone."

"How will they get here?" He had a point, since traffic had stopped in both directions now. She wasn't sure what the answer was.

"Just see if there's anyone critical," she said.

In the next car, everyone seemed fine. Glass from a broken window had cut the driver over the eye, and blood trickled down his face.

"Clean that up," she told Lorenzo, shoving her bag at him.

The next driver had a broken wrist and was white-faced with pain. "Try not to move it," Lark told her. "We'll get you fixed up really soon."

Then Lark jolted to a stop. Two cars ahead was a red pickup truck with a Boston Fire insignia, turned almost sideways in the single lane. The windshield was shattered.

In a blur, Lorenzo ran past her. "Dante!" he yelled. "Dante!" He yanked open the passenger door. "There's no one in here. Where is he?" He looked at the eastbound lane. "Dante!" His voice was thick with fear.

Lark forced herself to keep going. She couldn't start screaming his name—Lorenzo had that covered, and she had a job to do. If Dante was part of that job, she would know that very soon.

"Help us!" said a woman in the next car, a two-seater with more damage to the rear of the car than the front. Two females, twenties, one on her phone.

It was amazing how the human brain could think of so many things at once. Dante's body might be in the road. He might've been thrown from the car. The ambulances and fire trucks should be coming any minute. Thank God for seat belts, or these women would be dead. "You okay?" she asked the women.

"She's on with 911," said the passenger. "My stomach hurts."

Lark reached in and palpated it gently. The woman winced.

"You stay here and don't move a muscle," Lark said. "There's a chance you've hurt your spleen or liver. It's probably just a bruise from the seat belt, but do not move, you understand?" She looked at the driver. "If she loses color or starts to faint, come get me immediately. And tell the dispatcher to alert Hyannis ER for mass casualties."

The driver repeated Lark's words, her voice tight with fear.

Lark went to the next car. "I'm fine, keep going," said the driver. "I'm fine."

Lorenzo stood next to Dante's truck, his face was white. "My brother . . ." he said, and his voice was small and scared.

"There he is," she said before her brain fully processed the sight. Dante was doing exactly what she was doing, going from car to car, checking. Her heart surged with relief and gratitude.

He did a double take when he saw them and ran over. "Lark! We got a bad one. Everyone else can wait." He had a cut next to his eye, and there was blood on his left hand.

"You okay?" she said, her voice shaking.

He gave her a crooked smile. "I'm good."

"Jesus, Dante," Lorenzo said. "I thought you were . . ." His voice choked off.

"You're needed up there, big brother," he said. "You even more, Lark. I'll be right there. I've got some tools in the back of my truck. Go."

Lark ran. A few people were standing on the side of the road, most on their phones. An older woman was lying on the grass, her husband fanning her with a magazine. "She's just hot," he called. "We're okay."

The highway was clear in front of the box truck, which had a completely deflated front tire, apparently the cause of the accident. Rammed into and just under the back of it, though, was an SUV. The entire front of the vehicle was crumpled, the windshield smashed, the engine shoved onto the driver's lap. He had a face full of blood, and his jaw was clearly broken or dislocated. Legs were probably trapped under all that engine.

Not good. But he was conscious . . . for the moment, anyway.

"I'm a doctor," she said. His eyes were wild, hands flailing. She grabbed them. "I need you to stay calm. We're gonna take good care of you."

Airway, breathing, circulation. He coughed, and blood and a couple of teeth came out of his mouth. She tried to open his door to get closer to him. It didn't budge. She reached inside his broken window and tried to open it that way. Nope. Chest contusion, probable broken ribs, probable broken legs, possible internal bleeding, definite facial trauma, possible spinal damage. She felt the pulse in his neck. Strong and steady, if fast.

He made a gurgling sound.

"What have we got?" Lorenzo was standing right behind her.

"We're gonna lose his airway," she said, her voice calm. "Find a water bottle with a straw, a razor blade or a box cutter." She'd have to add those items to her bag, or better yet, just buy one of those paramedic bags.

"I've got a box cutter in here." Dante was back, a heavy canvas tool bag in one hand, a crowbar in the other.

"Good," she said. Her heart rate was probably over a hundred, and adrenaline was flooding through her. "There are alcohol wipes and latex gloves in my bag. I've got rawhide shoelaces in there, too, in case we need to tourniquet his legs." A person could bleed to death from a broken femur, and his legs had to be badly broken underneath the snarl of wreckage that had once been his vehicle. "Find me that straw, Lorenzo."

"Got it."

"Tell me what to do, Doc," Dante said.

She looked into his dark eyes, suddenly feeling a lot better. "Always good to have a firefighter around," she said. "Get that door off."

The man made another choking noise. "Hang in there, buddy," he said, putting the crowbar against the bent door frame. "She's a doctor, and so's my brother. We're gonna get you out and fix you up." He glanced at Lark. "We'll need a helicopter for this guy. Anyone else?"

"Possible spleen or liver damage in the orange Subaru. Nothing else that seems life-threatening."

"Can I help?" asked a middle-aged woman with short gray hair.

"Yes," Lark said. "Call 911 and tell them we need a chopper, and then tie some cloth—a shirt or towel—to the orange Subaru and the gray Audi. The blue Tesla, too. That way, EMS will know who needs help first. If you can find some blankets or beach towels, we'll be using the side of the road for triage."

"On it." The woman nodded and went off.

Dante was doing his best, but it was like trying to open a can with a spoon. She wished she could stabilize the driver's neck, but they'd have to wait for EMS for a brace. She went to the other side of the cab. Not much room, given the damage to the car. Could she squeeze in there and do an emergency tracheotomy if he stopped breathing? She doubted Lorenzo would fit.

She boosted herself up and wriggled through the window, wincing as the bits of glass dug into her stomach. She made it through and knelt on the sliver of seat that wasn't obscured by the mangled engine.

"Hang in there, sir," she said. "Breathe with me, okay? Nice and calm, in and out. You're doing great."

He wasn't. His breath was thick with blood and teeth, and there was possible soft tissue damage in his throat. His face was swollen, the lower part of it misaligned. She gently felt his neck for an obvious deformity, tenderness or swelling. Negative. No apparent head trauma, no bleeding from the scalp.

"You're gonna be fine. Not what you had planned for today, but we've got this." Her voice was calm and friendly, same as Howard Unger's always was no matter what the situation.

The man gave another gurgle. It sounded thicker this time. The metal of the door screeched and gave a little, but not enough.

Lorenzo was back. "Got the water bottle."

"Cut off four inches of the straw and sterilize it," she said. "Dante, no pressure, but we're losing his airway here."

With a massive tug, he bent the door frame back, all the muscles in his arms straining. There was the bottom of his tattoo, the prayer. They'd need it today. The sun was hot. She was thirsty.

Words from the other drivers and passengers floated to her—*unfuckingbelievable, man, it's okay, we're safe, be brave, my dad is gonna be so mad.*

The driver's eyes were rolling, a sign that he was losing consciousness. "Stay with me, sir," she said. "Hey! Look at me, okay? I'm Lark, did I tell you that? Like the little bird." The memory of Justin calling her that flashed through her mind. *Help us out here, Justin. We need everything we can get.* "You're gonna have a great story about this." His eyes rolled again. "Sir! Sir? Stay awake, buddy. Look at me."

He was unconscious. Make friends with death, Dr. Hanks had said.

Fuck that. She was an emergency room doctor. She was fighting back.

"He's not breathing," Lark said. "Lorenzo, hand me the box cutter."

Then there was an unholy screech, and the door popped open.

"Is he stuck?" she asked. "Can we get him out?"

"I think so." Dante bent and, somewhat miraculously, freed the guy's legs. Lark held on to his head, Lorenzo slid his arms under the man's back, and they eased him out of the car and onto the pavement. Both his lower legs were definitely broken, lying crookedly on the pavement.

"Want me to rig up a splint?" Dante asked.

"What's the ETA on EMS?" she asked.

"Four minutes."

"His legs can wait, then."

"Got it," said Dante. "I'll go check on the others."

The man's face was a gory mess. His nose was smashed almost flat, and she could see his knocked-out teeth and blood in the back of his throat.

"Jesus Christ," said someone. He was filming.

"Back the fuck off," Lorenzo barked. Lark didn't bother to check whether the idiot obeyed.

The man was choking to death. "Sweeping his mouth," she said. It didn't help. "Alcohol wipe," she said, sticking out her hand. Lorenzo handed the little packet to her, and she tore it open with her teeth, then swabbed the man's neck. She felt his Adam's apple, then massaged just below it with her forefinger. "Right here," she said, pulling the skin back.

Lorenzo double-checked the location, took the box cutter and made a half-inch slice in the man's throat. "Holy crap!" someone yelped. Lark pulled the skin apart, revealing the crico-thyroid cartilage, a yellowish, rubbery membrane. Lorenzo sliced that as well—the box cutter was doing a great job—then took the section of straw from his shirt pocket and worked it into the man's trachea.

"Now what?" he asked.

"Switch with me," she said.

He obeyed without protest, and she leaned over the man, hand on his chest, and blew into the straw. His chest rose. She did it again, then pulled back and waited.

His chest rose again. "He's breathing," she said. Yes. Another breath. His eyes fluttered, and Lark glanced at Lorenzo. "Great job."

He let out a breath. "You too, Dr. Smith. You too."

Then the paramedics were there with their backboards and radios, and Lark was talking in the code of emergency services, briefing them, sending them to the other cars, checking the woman with the possible spleen injury, the older lady lying on the side of the road who was not just hot but possibly having a heart attack, the man with the broken leg. She heard the reassuring sound of a helicopter and helped pack up the broken-faced man. He grabbed her hand as they loaded him in.

"You're gonna be okay," she said, and she believed it.

Nine people were taken to the ER. Lark caught a ride with the second ambulance, and the instant it stopped, she ran straight to Howard. "Can I help?" she asked.

"The newly born legend arrives," he said. "Absolutely. Get some scrubs on and join us."

The other injured people were brought in and triaged. Broken bones, back pain, bruises, panic attack, sore shoulder, mild concussion. The woman with the bruised spleen and the man with the broken leg were admitted, as was the lady who'd been lying on the side of the road.

Lark didn't know what time it was when Howard finally came over to her.

"Helluva job, Lark. I heard you were quite a boss out there."

She blew out a breath. "I was terrified."

"Of course you were. Did you have your moment?"

She knew exactly what he meant, and abruptly, she felt the sting of tears in her eyes. Tears of pride this time. "I did. I was a real doctor out there."

"Hell, yes, you were." He smiled. "We'll be sorry to lose you. Dr. Hanks emailed me. You're back in Oncology."

"Really?" she said. "Oh. Wow. Um . . ."

"Go on," he said fondly. "Make my day."

"Can I stay here instead?"

"Ha!" Howard fist pumped. "I knew it! I knew I'd lure you over to the dark side. Attagirl. Sure, call him Monday. Now get out of here. Go have fun. Don't you have a wedding this weekend? I think your guy is out there in the waiting room."

She looked at her phone. Holy guacamole, it was only five

o'clock. She had nineteen messages. She didn't read them all, but . . .

Addie: You! Are! Amazing!

Harlow: Honey! I'm so proud of you!

Winnie: Great job, Lark. Grace under pressure.

Robbie: Fucking badass.

Grandpop: WE HEARD EVERYYTHING AND AREE VERY PROUD OF YU DEAR LARK!

Mom: Are you okay? We're so proud of you, but you must be drained! Call when you get a chance. Love you so much!!!

Heather: Theo and I are so proud. 🖤

Joy: You're famous, Lark! It's all over the news!

And it was. As she went into the waiting room, she could hear the story on NECN, the singsong voice of newscasters. "Tonight, motorists in a *devastating* crash on Route 6 in Harwich today were *luckier* than most. Two *brothers*, one a Boston *firefighter*, the other a world-renowned *surgeon*, just *happened* to be on the scene. Lorenzo Santini, MD, his brother Dante of Boston Fire, as well as an emergency room *physician* were heading to a family wedding in Boston. The following footage might be *disturbing* to some viewers . . ."

"Hey."

It wasn't Lorenzo.

Dante stood up from the chair he'd been sitting in, all brawn and Boston Fire T-shirt. He had a darkening bruise under the eye that had sustained a cut, and it did not hurt his appeal one bit.

"Dante! You okay?"

"Yeah. Are you? That was pretty impressive today."

"I don't think I'll sleep for a week." She glanced around. "Is Lorenzo doing a press conference or something?"

Dante's smile deepened. "Nah. He did one at the scene, then took a car to Boston. Didn't want to miss the rehearsal. Or the adulation."

"Shouldn't you be there, too?"

He smiled. "Someone had to wait for you. I drove your car, since my truck is totaled."

"Are you hurt, Dante? Did you get checked out?"

"Yeah, a nurse looked me over. I've got this shiner, and I'll be a little stiff tomorrow."

She swallowed. He was okay. The delayed terror at the sight of his truck and the reality of him standing right in front of her made her throat tighten and her knees grow weak.

"So listen, Lark," he said, a smile in his voice. "I had a little talk with Lorenzo this morning. Told him I had a thing for his girl. Figured I'd let him keep his pride and not tell him that I knew this was all fake."

"Oh." Her heart was thudding and her cheeks were on fire. "What did he say?"

"He said you weren't his type."

She laughed. "He's not mine, either."

"Excellent news. So." He took her hands, and his were big

and calloused and warm. "Will you be my date for my sister's wedding?"

She nodded.

"You sure?"

"Yes."

"Absolutely sure? I don't want you to feel like you have to say—"

She kissed him. Oh, she kissed him right there in the waiting room, and he pulled her against his solid frame, and she didn't care if people were watching or filming. There was only him, his mouth smiling as he kissed her back.

It was good to be alive. Alive, and with a future that shimmered with hope.

———————————————————

TEN MONTHS LATER

Lark and Dante, take a minute to look at all the people who are here today to offer their love and support to you," the minister said.

Dante squeezed her hands, and they did look, and yes, all that love, all that hope, that joy, echoed back at them.

The little church by the sea was packed. Addison was maid of honor, of course. Lorenzo was best man. The two brothers had come a long way. Imogen and Esme and Luna Byrne, now Lark's niece, thanks to Grady and Harlow having gotten married, looked adorable in their pastel flower girl dresses. Mom and Dad sat in the front row, holding hands, next to Silvio and Anita, wiping away happy tears.

Two sets of parents, seven siblings, their spouses and partners, three nieces and two nephews—Matthew, up from Georgetown, and William, Sofia and Henry's three-week-old son. Anita's parents, and Grandpop and Frances. Joy, of course, with a corsage to mark her special role in Lark's life. Mom's parents, and Aunt Grace, minus Uncle Larry—they were getting a divorce (no real surprise there). Dante's aunts and uncles and a dozen or so cousins.

Noni *wasn't* here. At Sofia and Henry's wedding, Lark and

Dante hadn't wanted to overshadow the happy couple. Interestingly, only Noni (and Lorenzo, of course) seemed to notice their new arrangement. Noni had said only, "Eh. I never like you for my Lorenzo. He can do better. You, kid"—she looked at Dante with her good eye—"you can have her."

"We'll call that her blessing," Dante whispered, squeezing her hand under the table as Lark tried not to laugh. The rest of the wedding had been utterly beautiful . . . and Lorenzo didn't once mention paying for it.

Ten days later, Noni passed away in her sleep.

Heather and Theo Dean sat in the middle of the wedding guests, beaming at Lark, and she let her eyes rest on them for a few seconds. They would always love her like the daughter they never had, and that was a gift.

Now Dante, standing in front of her at the altar, their hands joined, would become what Justin never did—her husband. Lark looked back at Dante, saw the smile on his face and the love in his eyes, and felt her heart swell with pure and simple joy.

The minister smiled and continued. *In sickness and in health. In good times and in bad. Until death do you part.*

Those words no longer filled Lark with a sense of foreboding. Life was unpredictable, and yes, her almost husband was a firefighter. Something awful might happen to him. She knew the risks. She saw them every day at work.

The key, she had learned, was to live in the here and now. Not the back then or the what-if, but right now. Not to worry about the shadows or the times of sorrow and darkness. They would come, of course. No one was immune. The trick was to carry hope and determination like a torch into the dark times. The way Justin had in his last few months. The way she would now.

The trick, Lark now knew, was to look on the bright side.

ACKNOWLEDGMENTS

Thanks to Brian McGuire, MD, who let me shadow him in the ER for one of the most interesting and fun days of my *life*. Thank you, Brian! It was truly an honor to see a doctor who cares so much about his patients and gets so much done.

In the fall of 2022, I became a hospice volunteer through my local hospital. It was not my intention to include hospice in this book, but sure enough, it showed up. While I took liberties with Lark's involvement in the program, the training for hospice is a lengthy commitment of time and spirit. I am very grateful to the people at Middlesex Hospice, especially Diane Santostefano and Susan Daniels, for guiding us volunteers along in this remarkably kind and compassionate program.

To the team at Berkley, my heartfelt thanks yet again for shepherding this book to fruition. From Editorial to Marketing, Publicity, Art, and Sales, to the support staff who so tirelessly and cheerfully move things forward, there are dozens of people whose fingerprints are all over this book. Thank you.

Thanks to my agent, Christina Hogrebe! Seriously, Christina, thank you. Lark's middle name didn't come out of nowhere. Meg Ruley, you have my deepest gratitude for the additional wisdom and guidance. To the entire team at Jane Rotrosen Agency, thanks for the absolutely stellar care you've taken with my career.

To my wonderful friends in the writing world—Joss Dey, Jennifer Iszkiewicz, Sonali Dev, Jamie Beck, Barbara O'Neal, KJ Micciche, Alison Hammer, Kwana Jackson, Robyn Carr and Susan Elizabeth Phillips—I am so grateful to be among such smart, hardworking, talented people. Love and appreciate you all, especially in the hardest moments.

To Hilary Higgins Murray, my sister and best friend; to my mom; to Jackie Decker, my other sister; and the sisters of my heart (you know who you are), thank you for being there and being fun and smart and kind. How lucky I am to be surrounded by such wonderful, strong, intelligent women.

To my lovely family—Terence, Flannery, Declan, Mike and the little Peeper. You are what I am most proud of and most grateful for in this life, and the next, and the one after that, too.

Look on the Bright Side

Kristan Higgins

Discussion Questions

1. Lark knows she's a weeper, even jokes about it. Do you think her emotional interactions with patients infringe on her ability to treat them? How would you feel if your doctor got teary-eyed or cried with you? How do her emotions make her a better or worse doctor?

2. Lorenzo clearly has a difficult relationship with his family—and people in general. Do you know anyone like him? Do you think his abrasiveness has more to do with his upbringing, or was that just the way he was born?

3. How do Lorenzo and Lark help each other beyond their arrangement? What do they learn from each other? Did you expect them to end up together?

4. After seven years, Lark finally feels attracted to someone again. Why Dante? What qualities does he have that affect Lark? Did you suspect that Dante had met Lark before?

5. Beauty is becoming an increasingly controversial topic now that social media has put photoshopped images of beautiful

people at our fingertips. Do you relate to Joy's obsession with beauty? Why do you think her brother supported her in changing her exterior self? Do you judge her for placing so much importance on her physical appearance?

6. Many marriages change after retirement. Gerald explains how after his retirement he felt increasingly invisible and inconsequential in the face of Ellie's continued success. Do you sympathize with him? At one point, Ellie says she's damned if she does, damned if she doesn't. Did you relate to her feelings?

7. Gerald and Ellie are known by everyone for having a "perfect" marriage. Do you think they do? What's good and what's bad about it? What kind of pressure might come from being seen this way by their kids, friends and acquaintances?

8. Do you think Gerald's emotional affair is forgivable? Is Ellie justified in her anger and sense of betrayal? How would you react if you found your partner had been having a similar interaction with someone?

9. Joy and Ellie form an unlikely friendship. Joy has essentially been a kept woman all her adult life, and Ellie has had to work and raise a family at the same time. How do those differences help each woman see herself? Why do you think their friendship works?

10. Lark's attempt to get to Justin's side is one of the most wrenching parts of the book, and something she can't forgive herself for. Later, when she's with Nancy, she wonders if Justin purposefully dies before she can get there. Do you think that

could be true? Have you ever heard of a situation when a dying person's final breath seems to happen at the one moment when they're alone?

11. Lark thinks being an oncologist is her life's purpose, so her switch to emergency medicine makes her feel like a failure. Ellie, too, has had a role in life—the perfect wife—which is suddenly taken from her. Joy says she's always felt that she was a costar in her brother's life, and without him, she feels lost. Did you ever feel that you were meant to be one thing, then became another, either in your professional or personal life? Did that swerve happen to you, or did you make a choice to go another route? How do those swerves help the women in the book grow and change? How did your swerve change you?

Kristan Higgins is the *New York Times, USA Today,* and *Publishers Weekly* bestselling author of more than twenty novels, which have been translated into more than two dozen languages and have sold millions of copies worldwide. The happy mother of two snarky and well-adjusted adults lives in Connecticut with her heroic firefighter husband, cuddly dog, and indifferent cat.

VISIT KRISTAN HIGGINS ONLINE

KristanHiggins.com
 KristanHigginsBooks
 Kristan_Higgins
 Kristan.Higgins

Ready to find
your next great read?

Let us help.

Visit prh.com/nextread